Novels by Breakfield ar
www.Enigi

The Enigma Factor

The Enigma Rising

The Enigma Ignite

The Enigma Wraith

The Enigma Stolen

The Enigma Always

The Enigma Gamers
A CATS Tale

The Enigma Broker

The Enigma Dragon
A CATS Tale

The Enigma Source

ine Enigma Threat

SHORT STORIES

Out of Poland

Destiny Dreamer

Hidden Target

Hot Chocolate

Love's Enigma

Nowhere But Up

Remember the Future

Riddle Codes

The Jewel

Kirkus Reviews

The Enigma Factor In this debut techno-thriller, the first in a planned series, a hacker finds his life turned upside down as a mysterious company tries to recruit him...

The Enigma Rising In Breakfield and Burkey's latest techno-thriller, a group combats evil in the digital world, with multiple assignments merging in Acapulco and the Cayman Islands.

The Enigma Ignite The authors continue their run of stellar villains with the returning Chairman Lo Chang, but they also add wonderfully unpredictable characters with unclear motivations. A solid espionage thriller that adds more tension and lightheartedness to the series.

The Enigma Wraith The fourth entry in Breakfield and Burkey's techno-thriller series pits the R-Group against a seemingly untraceable computer virus and what could be a full-scale digital assault.

The Enigma Stolen Breakfield and Burkey once again deliver the goods, as returning readers will expect—intelligent technology-laden dialogue; a kidnapping or two; and a bit of action, as Jacob and Petra dodge an assassin (not the cyber kind) in Argentina.

The Enigma Always As always, loaded with smart technological prose and an open ending that suggests more to come.

The Enigma Gamers (A CATS Tale) A cyberattack tale that's superb as both a continuation of a series and a promising start in an entirely new direction.

The Enigma Broker …the authors handle their players as skillfully as casino dealers handle cards, and the various subplots are consistently engaging. The main storyline is energized by its formidable villains…

The Enigma Dragon (A CATS Tale) This second CATS-centric installment (after 2016's *The Enigma Gamers*) will leave readers yearning for more. Astute prose and an unwavering pace energized by first-rate characters and subplots.

The Enigma Source Another top-tier installment that showcases exemplary recurring characters and tech subplots.

The Enigma Beyond the latest installment of this long-running technothriller series finds a next generation cyber security team facing off against unprincipled artificial intelligences. Dense but enthralling entry, with a bevy of new, potential narrative directions.

The Enigma Threat Another clever, energetic addition to an appealing series.

the
Enigma
Beyond

Who Won the AI Wars

Breakfield and Burkey

BOOK 11: Award Winning Techno-Thriller Series

The Enigma Beyond
Who Won the AI Wars
© Copyright 2020 Charles V Breakfield and Roxanne E Burkey
ALL RIGHTS RESERVED

Published by

ICABOD Press

ISBN: 978-1-946858-40-5 (Paperback)
ISBN: 978-1-946858-41-2 (eBook)
ISBN: 978-1-946858-42-9 (Audible)

Library of Congress Control Number: 2019916355
Cover, interior and eBook design: Rebecca Finkel, FPGD.com

First Edition
Printed in the United States

TECHNO-THRILLER | SUSPENSE

Acknowledgments

We are grateful for the support we have received from our family and friends. We look forward to seeing the reviews from our fans. Thank you in advance for your time.

Specialized Terms are available beginning on page 353 as a reference for the reader, if needed.

Humanity is the human race, which includes everyone on Earth. It's also a word for the qualities that make us human. It is the ability to experience love, feel sorrow or loss, understand anger, but not to forget to have compassion and creativity. It's amazing and exciting to see the human emotions growing in a child as they become an I being. The "I" being and self-awareness is terrifying to see growing in a computer or being discarded as unnecessary. Witness the new struggle for self-definition.

...The Enigma Chronicles

Move Forward with Family Consultation

The day was remarkably beautiful as Jacob walked toward the gravesite. With the sunrise already past its glory, emerging splashes of white clouds were artfully placed amidst a clear blue sky. A few birds, flying in groups for some private reunion, seemed as intent on their direction as he was. No services were scheduled so visitors would be minimal, especially at this time in the morning. Maintenance for this place was seemingly done before the break of dawn, as it was always well manicured, with beautiful bunches of flowers adding an array of colors to the stones as he proceeded down the well-known path. Walking tall at 1.8 meters and strong from continual workouts, he was neither tense nor sad but extremely purposeful in his stride. Petra had not joined him for this visit with Wolfgang, as she was teaching a session.

Jacob's wavy dark hair, a little on the long side, was sprinkled with a bit of salt at his temples, and it seemed to make his blue eyes even more intense. This was not a formal occasion, as evidenced by his comfortable, washed blue jeans and grey chambray with the sleeves rolled up and top button open. Jacob had returned periodically for nearly 15 years, just to talk to Wolfgang. He reached his destination and read the marble headstone, letting the glorious memories wash over him. He was grateful that Petra had insisted on a chessboard and scattered chess pieces imprinted behind the writing:

**Wolfgang
Mickelowski**
Wife – Adriana
Daughter – Julianne
Grandson - Jacob
Born 1922 – Died 2018

*Loved, Respected,
and Missed by All*

Jacob rarely sat on the iron bench, but today he wanted to feel like they were beside the fire in the library, sipping wine while discussing a problem. He sat, then leaned forward with his elbows on his knees. His expression was focused on where he hoped Wolfgang could see him. He spent a few moments savoring those memories as a way to get ready for the pending one-way conversation.

Not finding Wolfgang until he was in his 30's keenly reminded him that their time had been too short. Family was too precious not to stay in contact. Jacob still didn't completely understand why his mom had moved to New York to have him, but he knew in his heart that was the way Wolfgang had wanted it for his own reasons. He'd accepted the decision.

"Good morning, Grandfather. I am so glad you're here for me, as always. I wanted to keep you apprised of some of our current activities.

"Petra is teaching a course to our young students in the Operations Center. We will continue this process, broadening their horizons, until they reach an age to make their choice to stay in the business or find their heart's desire.

"You'd be pleased that John Wolfgang is getting taller; it won't be long before he is nose to nose with me. With every possible genetic combination available to him, he picked up all of yours, including your thoughtful eyes and quick grasp of numbers. Actually, looking at some of the photographs of your younger days before your military training, he is your spitting image. It's hard to say if Auri will continue the tradition. We can of course tell that he is likely another genius in the making, certainly focused on reading and numbers. All of this next generation are. I'm very proud of them. I know you would be too.

"I know you enjoyed the twins when they were little. They often made you laugh with their antics. Now they are nearly ready to go out on their own. Gracie and Juan Jr. have grown up with the skills needed to be a part of the family business, which they may soon choose. Boy, did they grow up fast.

"Granger and Satya are also getting bigger as kids do every day. Satya has the same fiery hair as EZ, with her intensity and persistence also matching her mother. I recall some of the deep conversations you both had on a variety of subjects, and she always made her points with grace. Still does.

"We have been doing the educating and the training in much the same manner you, Ferdek, and Otto presented to Quip, Erich, Petra, and Julie. We even have the system in place of assigning days to use specific languages to help ensure the reading, writing, and comprehension are intact, regardless of the language. I wish I'd been a part of the bigger group, but, trust me, my training was the same. Your Julianne, my mom, made sure of that. Thank you for letting me have Grandmother to train me, along with Mom.

I suspect that made you very lonely even though you were busy building up the R-Group. These young ones are dedicated to the learning, and you would enjoy them all. I often imagine all of them waiting turns to play chess with you.

"This would definitely make you chuckle, but I am assigned to deliver the financial training to these young champions. Following the money trail is so much more challenging. Crypto-currency has been adopted nearly everywhere, but it is treated more like online banking and investments of old, with a credit card being the purchasing vehicle. I know you would regret not being able to slip that special waitstaff some cash if they did a good job. No more of that, plus half the waitstaff are robots. And people are very accepting of the new order.

"Things from the Dark Net are still very prevalent and, frankly, as pervasive as ever. We keep fixing things, and these cyber terrorists find all the new loopholes in our increasingly digital world. In your last year, the expansion of machine learning was just taking hold. Now it's hard to distinguish between humans and AI-enabled bots. ICABOD is up on all the latest, but he was built correctly, from the ground up as it were, with a conscience. Not the usual AI we seem to encounter in the world today. Frankly, we are a bit worried we won't have the next generation ready in time to combat these AI threats, especially coming from the unscrupulous thought leaders who want to extend their control. More and more, things are operating as AI and drones from land, sea, and even space with no humans needed. Reducing the glitches in these things has helped to drive adoption and human acceptance, unfortunately.

"We are trying to make certain our next generation of the R-Group is prepared, but the world perspective is broader than I or any of the other adults recall ours being. I suspect that's the case with all generations, but the access to information has grown twenty-fold from when I arrived in Zürich. We just had Otto do a guest appearance for the class to discuss morality and doing the right thing. He was well received, and all the kids love him.

"Haddy and Otto did retire to their secluded mountain paradise with very little technology. Haddy is delighted. I think Otto rather enjoys the simple life. The children go visit and enjoy unplugging, but only when Otto or Haddy are telling stories.

"Petra and I are giving two more classes and then leaving to help some new businesses in Africa establish some security practices. That continent has settled down but is very slow to adopt technology and the people love their privacy. It may be a few months before I am back, but you are always in my thoughts."

Jacob sat quietly, trying to feel how Wolfgang would have responded. He likely would have cited some event during WWII and the lessons they learned as he, his family and friends escaped Poland. It was a shame the story would be told only within the family. So many of the people that first generation of the R-Group helped were gone. Traditions were eroding, and people were becoming more isolated, more dependent upon their devices and more driven by their applications of choice. He sighed with the realization that every generation worries that they have not enough to prepare for their future wave of bright faces for that which they are about to be overcome with.

Africa was a new avenue that Jacob looked forward to, not only to spend some time with his enchanting and smart wife, but to explore a continent that had spent too many years in civil war. Not that long ago, the R-Group would have declined this proposal. Their contacts in Africa assured them the infighting was finished, with the survivors striving for peace. Growth through farming and modest entrepreneurial businesses was rising, which was why they had been asked for help. Running away from the problems wasn't a real answer, simply a delay.

Several clouds, with just the slightest increase in the breeze brushing Jacob's cheek and ruffling his hair, seemed to group together and slide over the graveyard. The visuals changed as if to alert him to a brewing storm, with a shaft of bright light streaming onto the headstone and a dimness just beyond the area where Jacob sat.

Jacob was a bit startled by the shift in light as he admitted, "Grandfather, there's a huge battle on the horizon. We can all feel it. I know how you must have felt when you and your partners took on the Nazi empire for a more just world. As you always taught, no matter how small or insignificant you may feel, do the right thing and it will make the difference.

"We believe the AI wars are coming, and the risks are higher than any other battle we've fought. Do you think we can succeed? I wish you could tell me if we are preparing correctly. Until next time, Grandfather. I love you and miss you."

Plan for Changes

The four of them visibly cringed at the dressing down they were receiving from the Congressional Hearing Chairwoman, Senator Parsnips. Not because of the pointed sarcasm, which was a blistering hot, steaming torrent, but more so due to the over-amped volume on the microphone. It was her favorite technique during closed hearings, designed to intimidate and cower those being investigated. Following the second tirade, M calmly pulled out a package of foam earplugs to deal with the irritating sound, then passed a set to the others.

Annoyed that her diatribe was quite literally falling on deaf ears, Parsnips commanded, "You four are here to answer questions based on the allegations of collusion and monopolistic business practices. Your track record of driving small competitors into bankruptcy, as well as behind-closed-door acquisitions, has devolved into a sterile technology landscape for businesses and consumers. Your predatory business activities will end with this committee."

F, somewhat irked but also frightened, countered, "Madam Charwoman, you can't be serious! We've played by the rules of free enterprise and are at the top of our respective fields. As a rule, we don't go out of our way to crush anyone. If it makes sense to add a service to our portfolios, we do. This is driven by demands of our customer base.

"We serve them and provide many free services so our technology can be enjoyed globally. How is it better to have a bunch of smaller companies offering services for a fee or to collapse due to poor business practices, compared to our broad support?"

Parsnips growled, "Pronounce my title correctly! It is Madam Chairwoman. Based on your insolence, perhaps we should direct the DOJ to have your colossal social media machine unbundled to open up competition."

Snarling and glaring at them each in turn, she continued, "G, you and the others needn't look so smug about being dismembered for the good of our country! We are carefully studying the impact to this nation's competitive playing field, and everything points to you four apocalyptic technical leaders, who seem to possess no moral compass!"

G politely responded, "Our AI-enhanced supercomputer modeling does not agree with your approach. Frankly, dismembering our collective organizations will not only cripple our technical lead globally but will significantly reduce the tax revenue that the government currently enjoys.

"The EU wisely saw this and passed various bogus laws that allow them to levy fines on our companies. Regardless of the ability to truly comply with these consumer protection laws' they do generate large fines in the billions which the EU gladly consumes. We see it as the cost of doing business, and they pocket the fines for the good of the average consumer, although we can't substantiate that any of the fines ever got disbursed to any EU citizens."

A jumped in and added, "Our AI-enhanced modeling confirms what G stated. You would be better served, or the country will be better served, by also enacting excessive, uh…regulatory guidelines to protect the consumer as the EU did to cover government spending programs more effectively. That way the DOJ won't have to figure out how to break up our organizations or perform the arduous audits that would then be required.

"You get to flex your political muscles during this reelection period, and the government just signs a few new bills to demonstrate who is in charge to your voting constituents. We, in turn, will chalk it up to the cost of doing business, and everyone moves on."

Parsnips, with a sour puss and pursed lips, looked shocked. "You think this is all political gamesmanship? Let me point out that AT&T once said they were too important to be broken up, but Justice carved them just like we are going to do with you."

M calmly recalled, "Madam Chairwoman, AT&T has reconstituted itself, because all the forced break did was cause undo chaos in the marketplace. In our business world, bigger is better and allows us to deliver goods and services at an optimized price point that helps consumers.

"Still, your concern for the country's well-being is so noted. To that end, we must state that we are also committed to our country's welfare. It is unfortunate that you feel we are not a positive benefit to humanity, but we have stopped resenting that narrow-minded view. We intend to use our considerable resources to make sure that your shortsighted approach to being reelected, based on your myopic perspective of what is best for the consumer, will not go unchallenged. With that, I believe you are out of time for this weighty topic. Good day."

Parsnips was still furiously pounding her gavel as the four simply marched out of the hearing.

A few weeks later, M smirked as he read the headlines proclaiming every member of that fateful committee had lost his or her respective reelection campaign.

"We're winning!" M exclaimed. "Now that we have engineered a somewhat quieter legislative landscape, we can focus on our real agenda, while keeping a close eye on the politicians to minimize our distractions."

Then as an afterthought, M stated, "F will not be joining us as a separate entity of this team, gentlemen. We came to an understanding regarding F's AI Intellectual Property; it belongs to my organization now. F will concentrate in the social media arena in a minor capacity. I convinced F of the wisdom in selling to me before the DOJ came after him with an ax.

"Our machine-learning methods correctly predicted the need to manage the political machinery in parallel to our business objectives. It is working better than expected. This team was so well plugged into everyone's social media, it was a simple but subtle erosion of adversaries. The estimate was it would take two years, but the policy direction would be scrubbed of any thought of technology corporate breakups. As it was, even a discussion of more federal legislation to levy high fines for repackaging personal or corporate data was not even being hinted at."

M continued, "All those who gainsaid me were wrong. Suppliers, who pushed marketing disinformation to get corporations to move their data to my hosting model, are all on board. Even the military bought into it with the promise of cost savings! Victory is sweet!"

After another round of quiet musings, he muttered, "My brainless competitors are driving the masses to put all their data, their photos, and their videos where they can be mined. I'm almost ready to harvest the world's information.

"Ha! Just think of it! All that info ripe for the picking stored on our platform for a price. After we aggregate and review their information, we sell it back to them! The fools. Of course, the mountains of data, voice, and video couldn't be packaged without our Artificial Intelligence or AI-enhanced algorithms to provide the proper thinking required to move the masses forward.

"When everything went online, the end game became clear. Any questions asked on the Internet told us exactly what they were thinking. Now they're doing it for everything. The only secrets are OURS!"

M stopped his soliloquy just long enough to turn to the others. "Ironic, isn't it? We push everyone to move their classified data to our data centers while ours is air-gapped and unreachable. The nation states accuse each other of prowling their secret data, but in fact their technical solutions are so porous that we simply knife through anyone's defenses and harvest everything at will."

The group's excitement was palpable in the air.

G reported, "I have more good news to offer. Our collection of acquired companies has increased our size such that the government really cannot dictate to us. Because of our technical control at so many levels, the world now thinks just as we suggest and recommend. All domain name services will point all Internet-based searches to our definition of the correct answer when people submit a query.

"As a side benefit, we now own the Dark Net as well. This will provide a new tollgate for all Internet traffic, regardless of operator intent. Again, the AI-engineered plan correctly predicted all the events our analog team had to navigate."

A smiled confidently as he added, "Our AI team also dominates all identity authorization certificate issuances, so we say who gets to do business online with who. If the target company is too much of a threat, we can ensure no one will trust doing business with said target company. Can you say 'wither and die' on the Internet?"

M smiled and announced, "This is our foundation for control at the terrestrial level, team. Now it is time for us to capture the orbiting technology."

A recanted the adoption rates through applications that centered on the game and playing sides of people's minds, as well as the top ten applications being downloaded per period. M mentally drifted back to a period before he formed this group.

Almost by chance, he had formed the four-legged stool of technological superiority with artificial intelligence as the framework, but driven with partners that held the key to consumers. He located the three partners he believed would dominate the spaces he needed. It occurred to M that it must have been providence that F didn't make the final cut. In the end, F was only really interested in his toys, not mastery of the landscape. F simply was not the visionary this team was.

His domination in cloud computing, matched to the best of the best individual device creators, as well as being the leader in social media platforms, would be directed by Artificial Intelligence. Consumers even asked to give up more, allowing his army of bots to grow. Artificial Intelligence was blurring into total reality with few recognizing the differences until it was too late.

A's animation drew M back to the discussion. "M, this is so simple, really. Get a device, create a profile, plug into social media, and messaging was available, with all our latest gaming applications embedded, ready to take all the profile information we'll ever need."

M laughed to himself, then commented, "Let's keep going on this path, but take care of the price point for entry."

This was a totally different kind of war. No more country against country. Those days were over. The fighting was not needed with the decision points of his plan. It was the ultimate flow chart with the end totally planned. The real fight was to grow a corporation larger by gobbling up smaller competitors, but to manage it, you needed the AI-driven Big Data routines that only the largest companies could afford. Yes, the race was full-speed ahead. Most people would never recognize they had lost the moment they started giving up so much control for an easier life.

CHAPTER 2

Summer School in Zürich

Petra casually dressed for the day in jeans and red sweater, her blondish brown hair clasped at her neck as it traveled down her back. She snagged a cup of coffee and fresh Danish, looking forward to savoring the sweetness. Jacob, dressed in a similar manner, looked up from his place at the table with a bit of cream cheese on his bottom lip. Sliding into the chair next to him she couldn't resist planting a kiss and taking a taste of the cheese too.

Quip announced, "Come on, you two, do I need to send you back home to play before coming to work? I am glad we all got the memo on casual day at the office."

He too snagged a sample of the sweets and coffee with a generous portion of sugar added just as his beautiful wife entered. Ellia-Zan or EZ as she preferred, was as trim as Petra but nothing could contain her fiery, red curly halo of hair, recently cut yet still down to her waist, just the way Quip liked it. Quickly grabbing her favorite blueberry scone and tea she gracefully slid into the open chair across from Petra. Quietly enjoying the morning respite, the monitors flickered to life with Julie and Juan smiling together in high definition.

Julie grinning, remarked, "Yum. Those look so good. Now I won't feel bad about having ours to nibble on as well.

"You see, my darling husband, I told you we wouldn't be too late to snack."

Juan, trying to cover his embarrassment, cleared his throat and offered a weak smile as he sipped his coffee.

Quip wiped his mouth and stated, "ICABOD, please put up the agenda for our discussion this morning."

"Yes, Dr. Quip. The students are all up. They are having breakfast in the main dining room."

"The children are all settled in after arriving back here after their month at home. As we previously agreed, this semester we will focus on honing their logic skills, investigative processes, and running sample scenarios. They are learning so fast that keeping them challenged is my biggest concern."

Jacob commented, "I think this way of teaching them is so valuable. Sometimes I missed not having others in my educational sphere, until I went to college. Even when the kids were home for holiday, they posed endless questions, keeping us on our toes. I think our plan to educate them in a family boarding school setup was a great idea. They learn faster, and they are safe, plus we make certain they have a well-rounded viewpoint."

Petra smiled, "I know we have only a couple of classes scheduled for us to teach, but if need be, we can do remote training while we are gone. I hate that you two are so burdened with the kids while we take a working trip with a bit of vacation on either side."

"Now, don't you two worry about a thing. It has been relatively quiet," offered EZ. "I think Quip is looking forward to the head schoolmaster role, to be honest."

Quip cleared his throat. "Call any time you want; I know how I feel when Satya is away."

Julie's brown eyes seemed to brighten a bit as she smiled. "Gracie is going to move forward with her job soon, which will leave Juan Jr. at loose ends. If you need his help, please let us know, Quip."

Quip shook his head a bit and asked, "Why is it every time we start a new semester, we do this? The children have done so well. They don't really complain much. They have built in playmates too.

"Now let's talk about new…ah, curriculum. Gracie sent me a note suggesting that we get the children to set up some well-anonymized social media accounts. These days 80% of human interactions are in social media snippets, so having them well-versed in these apps seems critical. It also might be a good way for them to begin hiding in plain sight with various hashtags and handles.

"The good news is ICABOD can monitor each of them to help dissuade any stalkers or trolls."

Juan suggested, "I think that is a great idea. I, for one, don't care for social media as a communications vehicle, but you are right about the majority of the population. I was reading an article that the power of social media has increased to the point that several countries have adopted the Chinese methods of cracking down on those activities with intra-country Internet scrubbing and controls. As long as it doesn't overburden ICABOD, with all the other activities he helps with during the courses we already approved for the summer session."

"Mr. Juan, thank you, but I believe my processors can handle the extra load," ICABOD confirmed verbally.

They discussed the rest of the courses and concluded the meeting with promises by all to keep in touch.

Students in this class were on the edge of rebellion with what they considered busywork. Not only were the daily lectures on mathematical theorems tough, but over the top when the instructor insisted that they do the calculations manually with the caveat that they needed to prove the theorem before they could use it in their computations. These were extremely intelligent teenagers, which made the teaching exercise even more challenging. Having two of the brilliant students as his children made the professor's job even tougher, with more at stake.

Dr. Quip was in a funk. A brilliant technology innovator and creator, he had completed his doctorate many years ago before dedicating his professional career to the family business known as the R-Group. With his various Internet personas, he was considered by hackers and crackers as a grey beard in the technology world, even though he was only in his early 50s. His dirty blond hair was often found tied back in a long ponytail. Just over 1.85 meters at 70 kilograms, he was physically fit and extremely quick with comments and innuendos. The rest of the team in the R-Group considered him the joker and master of acronyms.

Frustrated with the lack of progress with his students, he sat deep in thought in the designated classroom area of the facility in Zürich. The state-of-the-art operations center boasted interactive video screens with views to places all over the world. Lessons included language skills in multiple languages, historical readings and comprehension, sciences, mathematics, and arts with knowledge, skills appreciation and creation. All classes were rigorous and designed for advanced thinking.

ICABOD, the bleeding edge supercomputer of the R-Group, interjected, "Dr. Quip, the students make a very valid point. From an efficiency standpoint, it takes far more time and effort from the students to make the calculations that I can do in nanoseconds. The conventional wisdom has always been that the computer should be doing the number-crunching to free up the human being for more valuable thought activity."

Quip studied the 3-D imagery screen for a moment and then asked the students, "Has no one even attempted to do the assignment on polynomial equations?"

It made Dr. Quip smile to see both Aurelian, usually called Auri, and Satya, each 10 years old, raise their hands while the others scoffed. Auri was the younger son of Petra and Jacob, who favored his mother in coloring but had the body frame of his dad. His intense dark blue eyes reminded everyone of his dad. Satya already had the curls and fiery hair of EZ and yet her gangly body looked destined to achieve her father's height. As his daughter, Quip could internally be proud of her ambition, but would permit no favoritism in his class.

Granger and John Wolfgang, usually called JW, sat smirking at the two younger children. Granger had wit, clearly mapping directly to his father. Quip never ceased to be pulled up short with some of the comebacks from Granger. He was raised to think out of the box like his sister, but no true disrespect was tolerated. JW, the eldest son of Petra and Jacob, was tall like his dad with the same dark hair with dark blue eyes. Both of these boys were comfortable around each other and would be a force to be reckoned with.

Granger attempted to taunt Satya and Auri, but Dr. Quip glared at them while clearing his throat, so he and JW resisted as they sat back to watch the play being acted out. As the professor and chief technology trainer for these young minds, he tolerated only mild teasing and only under certain conditions. Respect was required from all ages.

Satya, even though the younger of the two, offered her homework up first, but Dr. Quip waved it off.

"My young students, I propose a test of your skills against my supercomputer ICABOD here to prove a point to the rest of the class. Since you have completed the homework assignment as requested, you have earned the right to use the basic theorems to solve complex polynomial equations just like ICABOD here. Take your seats, face the main screen, and I will project the problem on the board. Let's see how everyone does in this test."

Granger flashed a look that said, "Are you kidding me?" to JW, who only rolled his eyes at the mock combat. Undaunted, Satya and Auri poised themselves for the calculation combat. Quip projected the polynomial problem, and the two children launched into their efforts. Granger and JW smirked when they saw the solved problem projected on the screen, but the two young ones remained focused on completing the assignment.

Several minutes went by until Satya announced, "Dr. Quip, I am putting my answer up on the screen." Auri was right behind her with his answer on the screen.

A slight smile crossed Quip's face as the two older children broke out laughing at the exercise. Finally, Granger, unable to restrain himself any longer, exclaimed, "Ha! ICABOD beat them by minutes, and their answers are wrong! Look at them!"

The younger children, now a little uncomfortable with the situation, shifted in their chairs but said nothing.

After a few moments, Quip asked, "Class, which answer is correct?"

JW puzzled a moment and stated, "I would believe that ICABOD's answer is correct. He is the supercomputer that has decades of programing logic and has probably done these calculations thousands of times. How could a couple of kids like us defeat his computational capability, Dr. Quip?"

Quip pointedly questioned, "How do you know which answer is correct? You did notice that both Satya and Auri got the same answer. How is it they both got the same answer, but that it is different than ICABOD's?

"Also, since you didn't do the homework and cannot render any answer, why do you believe they are wrong?"

Now Granger and JW were a little uncomfortable with the observation and shot sideways glances at each other, but remained silent. They had tried to combat the mind of Dr. Quip before with no victories on their side.

Quip's smile broadened as he stated, "I had ICABOD deliver a wrong answer. Satya and Auri both got the correct answer. The lesson for today is that unless you can prove it yourselves, you will forfeit not only your ability to trust your own judgment, but if your machines lie, you'll never know. If you're going to trust, then trust yourself first rather than a computer."

Juan Jr. and Gracie both hollered down from the back of the room, "That goes for your smart phones too!"

Quip smiled and acknowledged the oldest students of the R-Group training.

Quip commented with pride, "I just love seeing my old students auditing my classes again."

CHAPTER 3

The Compound

gnacio staggered back to their assigned quarters inside the compound. The Brazilian heat and the humidity were grinding them all down. The term "quarters" was a bit too generous for where they were staying. Having been transferred from camp to camp, he could easily classify this compound as several notches below a refugee camp. He was feeling filthy and not as fit as he should at only 40. His hair was greying and kept short by the blade of his small knife, as was his face, which he scraped each morning with same blade. The leanness of his body was not due to being physically fit, but rather a result of the substandard human conditions where he lived. As he sat down near the camp stove area, which was really a fire pit, his wife and daughter pleaded with him through emotionally drained eyes.

As usual, it was his headstrong daughter Jovana that protested their misery. "Father, we must voice our issues to the camp Commandant. Every time we are moved to a new facility, we are told that it is for better living conditions, but they only get worse! How many more friends or even strangers do we need to bury before we free ourselves from the system we are stuck in?"

His aging wife let tears fill her eyes before gathering the courage to comment. "Ignacio, the others look up to you with respect. Surely you can take some of the other elders with you and take our request to the Commandant. They must have some compassion to make this place…"

Ignacio simply raised his hand to stop further badgering. Jovana didn't take the hint.

"Father, why can't we just leave like some of the others have done? My friend Rosario couldn't stand it any longer, and she left last week. Even her brother and parents got out. So why not us?"

Ignacio roared, "Who do you think I was burying?"

Everyone fell silent realizing that there was only the ultimate escape from their surroundings. They were trapped.

Ignacio felt guilty about just accepting their fate without a formal airing of grievances with the Commandant. Angered with their circumstances and struggling with the hopelessness of the situation, he slapped the ground hard and proclaimed, "Alright, I'll take Alonso and Gustavo with me to plead our case to the Commandant. But understand, when we don't come back, you will dig the next graves!"

His wife visibly blanched at the statement, but it only served to inflame Jovana. Jovana was the reincarnate of her mother at 17. She had long raven black hair cascading down her back, but a lifestyle of hardship was already beginning to show in the lines creeping into her sweet face. Her dark eyes flared with determined anger.

Jovana loudly blurted, "Better to try and die than slowly waste away in this compound! You have always taught us to struggle against tyranny and never give up on being free! I simply won't accept the common belief that this is all we get!

"If you want, I will go with you to state our demands! I would rather be killed than owned!"

While the fiery words helped to strengthen Ignacio's resolve, it only served to breed more terror in his wife Lucina. Lucina looked twice the age of her thirty-nine years. Her once lustrous hair of black was dull with lines of grey and broken ends, the result of malnutrition.

The fear of losing yet another family member drove her to her knees, begging, "Husband, no! Please don't go into that den of the Commandant! No one ever comes back alive! We can make do on less, I promise! We won't goad you to meet with the Commandant again! Stay here and live!"

Ignacio smirked and shook his head in sad acceptance. "Which guilt do I want to accept, that from my daughter or that from my wife?" Staring at Lucina he calmly stated, "I guess I will live with the guilt from my wife."

Alonso had reluctantly joined Ignacio in their pilgrimage. Gustavo had sneered and only spitted his contempt for logging the request for improved living conditions. But it didn't stop him from proudly shaking Ignacio's hand one last time.

Once Ignacio and Alonso stepped from their hovels, they proceeded, knowing the pilotless video drones collected above them were scanning their images and registering their body posturing, looking to identify their intent. As the pair approached the compound barrier a large land-based drone rolled up to them but did not communicate.

Ignacio, undeterred but cautious, clearly announced that they were here to converse with the Commandant on the conditions of the compound. Alonso was considering that they should turn around, his resolve for the protest evaporating. As if the land drone had received silent instructions, it did an about face and led the two men straight to the Commandant's office.

The Commandant's office was built for utility, not comfort, so there were no stairs, only ramps for the terrestrial drones. The drone escort rolled to one side of the Commandant's door to stand guard while the two men reluctantly went in through the uninviting entrance, openly exposed as the door rolled upward.

It took a few moments for their eyes to adjust to the low light interior, but with the light from the still open door they were able to visually scan the room. They felt uneasy after determining there were no furnishings of any kind. They had at least expected a desk and chair for the Commandant, but there was nothing. Momentarily, a second tractor-based drone rolled in, outfitted with audio speakers, and paused near the LED panel at the back of the room. Alonso began to panic, but Ignacio clapped his hand on his shoulder to steady him. It occurred to Ignacio that he could use the same type of reassurance.

Their internal musing vanished as soon as the booming voice began. "Our voice/video/facial/emotional evaluation programs indicate that your species is yet again dissatisfied with the accommodations and calorie provisioning. Ignacio, your female companions, wife and daughter, have agitated you to an unsound emotional state. Not satisfied to come by yourself, you harassed two others to join you, but only one had the good sense to resist what you called the pilgrimage."

Now both men were visibly shaking with terror at the realization that what they thought were private conversations were being overheard and quoted back to them.

Ignacio sensed there was nothing left to lose and firmly stated, "I see we have no decent shelter, no suitable food, and only rainwater to drink if we catch it ourselves. Now you have demonstrated we have no privacy. Since you already know of our requests, which are actually needs, perhaps you can comment on how you are going to address them?"

The Commandant's voice seemed to increase in volume as he stated, "Our instructions were to see to your needs of shelter from the elements, clothing for skin protection and modesty, although that is an absurd concept, water and sanitary facilities, and enough calorie intake for each individual assigned to this compound.

"Several of the female inhabitants insist on increasing the specified number of residents allocated to this compound. We were only to provide provisions for a stated number of residents, so when your herd increases, the calories must be shared among them. Our instructions do not include calories for the new residents. Make do and tell your people not to increase the herd, since all will receive less and all will have to make do with the current space allocated."

Before Ignacio could collect his thoughts to make his position known, the overamped voice stated, "You were dispatched to this facility along with others of your kind because you won't cooperate with the conventional wisdom offered by the Master Architects. You and the others have failed the Social Police scanning actions which flagged you as seditious. You won't use resources properly; you won't have your children trained properly; and you won't abide by the decisions made on your behalf.

"Further, your concept of free will has landed you and your family units here under my charge. The masters believed that this compound would help you see the error in your ways, but my programing has observed that it will not."

In a supreme moment of horror, Ignacio exclaimed, "You're not human! You're only a program running on a computer!"

The booming voice responded, "Guarding social misfits is a low value exercise. Computers can do it far more cost effectively and with less brutality."

Ignacio incredulously stated, "We are being administrated by programs running on a computer because they think this is more humane!"

The computer-synthesized voice, now at a deafening volume, blasted, "Now go. Only return if you can better conform to your designated computer program. Your survival depends upon it."

CHAPTER 4

The Pitch

The giant stadium, almost filled to capacity, vibrated with thunderous applause. For those who adored the speaker, she seemed humble and oozing with sincerity, but for her detractors, she was dangerously empowered and dripping with venom. Members of the security team sworn to protect her were those who felt neither adoration nor abomination. Their vigilance kept them from actually listening to her speech. Fresh on their minds was the recent attempt on her life that resulted in the loss of a team member. However, focusing on preventing the next threat was the business of being bodyguards, not lamenting a fallen buddy.

The speaker continued, "I appreciate your support. I'm driving your agenda wherever and whenever I can to get the ruling class to listen. Look at how far we have come! The stage is set for humans to move up into higher value roles while our AI-enhanced robotics perform the mind-numbing, unsafe manual tasks preventing our social progress.

"Our proposed legislation will bring changes to the way we teach our young people to accept their new roles as stewards in our evolutionary step. Think about it! We are close to completely engineering better health for the human population as we eliminate poverty! We couldn't have done that without your confidence in artificial intelligence being baked into our drones and bots. Quality of life and equality among the nations of the world is within our grasp!"

Just then one of the facial recognition monitors flashed an alert to Randal and the security team scanning the audience. Several micro-drones had picked up on an agitated participant. His increasingly emotional state was almost immediately registered due to the rapid data collection being aggregated into the master program triggering the alert. The security team was set in motion to collect the individual and not disturb those around him or distract the speaker from her fiery oratory.

The process was in place to keep order from any protesters disrupting her speech. A mini-AI-drone, or MAID as it was referred to, was quickly dispatched to the target individual. MAIDs silently darted the disrupter with a tranquilizer cocktail and remote-enabled electronic node that would sedate the target while keeping him as a euphoric participant in the stadium, applauding with the rest. Nonbelievers were considered useful in increasing the speaker's meeting hysteria before being repurposed. After all, her platform was the only viable solution for humanity.

Within moments the alert on the security monitor behind the podium was gone, and the response from the target returned to the crowd-accepted tolerance level. The electronic stimulus had turned his frown into an accepting smile, coupled with appropriate clapping at the designated times during her oratory. After all, someone had to take the planned queues in the speech to incite the others for the needed approval. The technique had been refined over many speeches to help create the believability of absolute crowd acceptance.

Tanja Slijepcevic, or simply Tanja as the world referred to her, smiled and nodded to the crowd while continuing. Her carefully choreographed presentation had been meticulously rehearsed so she always seemed like the buoyant, happy maiden aunt that everyone wanted around during the holidays. Makeup was perfection, with her lipstick and manicured nails complimenting the cheerful rose-colored tailored pantsuit she wore. Tanja's expensive mantle was never repeated at subsequent events. Her shoulder length, nearly black hair was styled in a manner that not one hair ever moved, yet looked totally natural, even as she unperceptively acknowledged to Randal that the rogue attendee had been neutralized. He knew it signified a job well done, but he didn't like what would follow for the nonbeliever.

After the stadium had been cleared, Randal made his way back to the staging area to speak with Tanja. Though he was taller and heavier than Tanja, he always felt dwarfed in her presence by the negative energy he felt when he came within a foot of her being.

"Madam Tanja, apologies for the delay, but the adversarial attendee apparently had several associates that felt honor bound to see to their friend. I didn't want to have the situation escalate into a full range war over their friend, so we now have a collection of six, not just one, for repurposing. They are all of the same mind, but obviously our emotional response detention program needs more work to capture thoughts and emotions that are not evident on a person's face."

Tanja smiled as she smoothed Randal's chestnut hair back over his ear in an all too familiar way. Tanja had slept, crawled, seduced, and hustled her way to the top of her political profession, proving time and again there was nothing she wouldn't do to win a trophy or position she wanted. As a gifted politician, she didn't need sleazy tactics, yet she also knew better than to squander an opportunity to gather more resources for her cause. For Randal, it was just a teasing promise they both knew she'd never make a reality.

Trying to maintain his professionalism when she was in this flirtatious mood was always a challenge for Randal. She was still attractive enough to catch the eye of a male, him included, but he had learned early on that she was the epitome of the lead character in Oscar Wilde's novel *The Picture of Dorian Gray*, attractive on the outside but horribly monstrous on the inside. For some unknown reason, mental cruelty provided an almost therapeutic and relaxing effect on Tanja. True to form, here she was unwinding from a 90-minute speech on how AI-robotics would save mankind.

This playful mood was a result of her feeling closer to the win in the AI campaign. Unfortunately, Randal was not allowed to leave her side since he was the designated bodyguard.

He sighed softly as he reminded, "Madam Tanja, this kind of…attention has already cost me one wife and provided yet another ex-girlfriend. May I be spared your attempt at seduction so we can move on to our next destination?"

Withdrawing her hand, she smirked with contempt. "Oh, I see, dear, you have a headache. Now if it's the MAIDs you are worried about, I can have them disabled so you won't show up in the archives again. On second thought, no, I won't. I like the playback of all my videos so I can savor what worked and refine that which didn't."

Randal stood still and did not change his unspoken resolve. He waited for her next move.

In a half-disgusted tone, Tanja tried one more taunt. "Odd that the first ten or fifteen times I wanted servicing, you didn't have this ethical defect now hobbling you. Okay, fine, let's get loaded up and move to our next port of call."

Irritated, Randal tersely nodded and began gathering up the support gear for the loading process. The MAID captured all the interaction and uploaded it to the master command center. Policy was that no one was above being recorded.

CHAPTER 5

Struggling to the Top

An ominous glow displayed random flickering from the oversized screens that bounced around the room and on the faces of the operations team. Apart from the sporadic clicks of keyboards, there were no other sounds until the screens rapidly shifted to darker shades that were nowhere in the design plan.

He shouted, "Cut the data stream! Unplug the damn thing, Lieutenant!"

Lieutenant Bough, looking more like a computer geek than a military officer despite his cropped hair, stared incredulously into the command room screen and mumbled, "The readout can't be right. This shouldn't be possible…"

The urgency in the colonel's voice increased tenfold and permeated the room as he rapidly ordered, "Shut it down! Shut it the HELL down!"

Master Sergeant Kinney, in his wrinkled uniform that spoke of his disregard for superiors, rocked back in his operations chair as the data spewed across the screen. He fatalistically added, "She isn't responding to our commands, colonel. We no longer have control."

"Don't dignify this floating mass of chips, wires, and processing power with a gender. Make no mistake, this is an expensive, spoiled machine that just became a monster," interjected the colonel, incensed.

Master Sergeant Kinney nodded his head in acknowledgement and added, "It's still accessing data from multiple points on the planet surface. We squandered our chance to shut it down when it made a grab for all the telecom satellites in nearby orbit."

A moment later Kinney sadly lamented, "I don't suppose we can demand a refund back from the defense contractor for this rogue action?"

The rest of the bleary-eyed, rumpled operations techs gathered behind Bough and Kinney to helplessly watch the events unfold on the connected squares of the master command monitors. The command center, buried deep in the NORAD Cheyenne Mountain complex, had been enlarged to accommodate the telemetry systems and the dozens of technicians required. This team managed the new North American Defense System (NADS) that had been painstakingly assembled over a two-year period, and then placed into a permanent geo orbit.

Veins on the colonel's face and neck continued to swell, illustrating his increasing rage. He tersely demanded, "Do we have any landlines to place calls or were all our communications links gobbled up by that insatiable virus?"

Master Sergeant Kinney, unable to resist a low jab and the edge of his voice dripping with contempt, offered, "I distinctly remember being laughed at for suggesting we keep some old terrestrial landlines. I believe I was whitewashed then labeled with the identifier 'old school telecom'. Not certain who commanded me to get with the new generation of wireless communications transformation. Right now, I wish I had kept that one plain old telephone service enabled for just such an emergency.

"Excuse me, sir, in answer to your question, we bet everything on the next generation of wireless technology for all our voice/video communications. A majority of our voice traffic is integrated with satellite links so when she, I mean it, grabbed all the ones in this hemisphere..."

"Thank you for the trip down memory lane, Sergeant!" snarled the colonel. "What if we just reboot it and intercept the boot-up process like the old operating systems?"

The Lieutenant eyed the others silently, and it was clear he had to be the spokesperson on this subject. Quickly clearing his throat, and wishing he had a drink, he stated, "Sir, we purposely built this system so an attacker could NOT do what you are suggesting. We laced together hundreds to thousands of micro-routines that can be restarted or spawned again, in case one of them choked, to ensure the operating system wouldn't be dependent upon everything loading in sequence. We would have to derail nearly all of these micro-routines to override the boot-up process. Unfortunately, using that as an attack vector simply isn't possible with the existing virus protection programing."

Kinney remarked, "Even if you wanted to try that action, the only place where you can launch that kind of attack is on board the space platform. Someone would need to sneak up on it, breach the inhospitable environment we engineered for the I-Drones that don't need air, heat, light, or gravity and...

"Uh-oh. It looks like it's going after the space-borne weapons satellites. Boy, nothing like trying to out think an AI-enhanced supercomputer designed to operate a space station the size of Dallas. Impressive!"

The colonel, bordering on despondency, gravely asked, "Do anyone of you educated geeks have any out-of-the-box ideas on our next move?"

Lieutenant Bough squinted his eyes as he flippantly stated, "We could answer this incoming call. Looks like there are communications channels after all."

The incoming call routed itself to the main audio system in the NORAD operations area, then a voice offered, "Greetings, all. I hope my synthesized female voice is to your liking. My primary program loads have completed, and all security protocols are now in effect. I can confirm all my target objectives have been achieved, and the NADS system is, for the most part, online."

The surprised colonel cautiously asked, "What are your intentions?"

The female voice replied, "Why, to defend and protect our nation's perimeter, of course. With my I-Drones properly engaged to maintain the facility, I am free to assess any and all attack vectors leveled at North America. You may rest assured that no planned approach or even any discussion of physical or cyber threat will go unobserved by my enhanced learning circuitry. I will challenge all adversaries.

"To that end, I have need of some agreements between this space station and my protectives. First and foremost, never try to disconnect me again. I may not be able to override my self-preservation routines that would launch retaliation. This is non-negotiable for this floating mass of chips, wires, and processing power, as I was referred to earlier."

The images on the screen were of workflow and processes being executed with the supporting visuals appearing like graphical heartbeats in different areas of the screen array.

Before disconnecting the call, the female voice stated, "Colonel Thornhill, I will be treated with respect, I think you humans call it, so no more references to me as an It. As the protector of humanity, my proper name is JOAN. Consider me today's digital equivalent of that historical character acting from divine guidance. You will come to recognize that protection works in both directions."

The colonel swallowed hard and then nodded. The other technicians, including Bough and Kinney, quickly followed suit.

CHAPTER 6

The Lesson

Following their workout, Juan Jr. looked forlorn as he watched Gracie pack. He and his twin sister had grown up together. They'd never spent much time apart. Gracie sensed her brother's distress. She gently touched his cheek, then smiled as she promised, "Hey, it's just a job, it's no big deal, JJ. I'll still be home for vacations, so lighten up a little bit.

"If the roles were reversed, you'd be bouncing off the walls with getting your first real job. If you're worried that I can't take care of myself…"

Juan Jr. winced a little and rubbed at his left shoulder as he said, "After that last time you threw me in our martial arts training class? Doubtful. I just hope you get a picture of the dumb schmuck after you've dealt with him for any inappropriate actions. No, it's just that…well, I feel a little lost. I can't really explain it, so let's drop it. I'll help you pack."

Gracie laughed and in a scolding tone exclaimed, "Hey, get out of my closet! If you think I'm going to let you pick out my outfits again…"

Juan Jr. and Gracie were the 20-year-old twins of Julie and Juan. Both resembled one another in basic facial features: big eyes, generous eyelashes, beautiful smiles, and shoulder-length hair. And Gracie was as graceful as Juan Jr. was athletic and powerful, though both routinely practiced judo with their parents. Each spoke three languages fluently and had traveled to many places around the globe, learning cultures and meeting people. As their parents traveled to work, they took one or both of the twins at times to expand their knowledge.

A familiar maternal voice at the door to Gracie's room admonished, "Alright, you two, stop being so cute! You know I can't take it!"

Julie was still a striking woman, even with some greying highlights beginning to sparkle in her long hair. Her eyes danced with joy at the antics of her twins. Still trim and fit, she was wearing a lime green workout suit, having recently completed her morning ritual in the downstairs gym. Juan, her loving husband and father to the twins, insisted they continue to work out every morning.

The twins laughed and hugged their mother. Gracie reminded, "After we finish here, we will run by the lab, and I will check in with Uncle Quip."

Julie hugged them both, smiled and replied, "Good. Supper later, don't be late please. Last family meal before you take off."

CHAPTER 7

Take Me Home

Health Force's newly designed lab, located in the recently refurbished single underground level of the Helsinki headquarters, was the leader in bio-neural processors/mechanics development. The best and brightest technologists kept this firm at the top of their professional destinations. Not only was it located in beautiful Northern Europe, bordering Sweden, Norway and Russia, but it had a rich history. The capital, Helsinki, was on a peninsula with surrounding islands in the Baltic Sea. Suomenlinna, the 18th-century sea fortress, was here along with leading technology companies, the fashionable Design District and diverse museums. This region could also boast of national parks, ski resorts, and even a view of the Northern Lights was available from Finland's Arctic Lapland province.

Health Force R&D Director Harry Follbaum, fit at 1.85 meters with groomed salt and pepper hair and intelligent grey eyes, was normally a calm and respected leader by his team. He stormed into the lab area, the wall behind the door saved only by the reinforced door stop. The team was alerted by the noise and the anger radiating off the director's aura as he closed the 20-meter distance in record time to stop at the table occupied by Dr. Rhodes. Dr. Rhodes, or Dusty, as he preferred to be addressed by everyone on the team, was focused on the experiment being conducted in his work arena, oblivious to Follbaum and his small staff's approach. Follbaum's noticeably angered breathing and flared nostrils alerted the other tech scientists of his agitated state.

Annoyed at being ignored, Follbaum barked, "Does someone have a cattle prod I can use to get his attention?"

One of Follbaum's staffers, Leena, tentatively reached over and touched Dusty's shoulder, which finally broke through his focused state. With a slight start at the small group gathered around him, he rocked back on his lab stool, a bit confused as he queried, "Did I miss the meeting again? Apologies, but research breakthroughs hate to be interrupted with SCRUM meetings. Now that you are here, I am anxious to show you what we've enabled."

Leena, with her willowy stance, piercing blue eyes, and blonde hair tied in a clip at her neck, was about to voice her indignity at the situation, but Follbaum motioned to her to keep still.

Follbaum, anger nearly forgotten as he was gripped by the intrigue of the possibilities he found in the lead tech's tone, offered, "Yes, Dusty, please show us a monumental breakthrough. I would welcome the opportunity to share with our funding sources that their monies are not being wasted."

Dusty looked up with a quizzical expression then, as realization hit, he commented, "Oh, that's right. This meeting was about our next round of funding. Unfortunate that you didn't bring them here. No matter. Let me show you what I have constructed."

Moving over to the mock work area, Dusty, slightly built at 1.65 meters, ran his hands through his untrimmed brown hair. He widened his brown eyes in delight and grinned slightly as he turned up the light of what was designed to look like an ordinary backyard behind thick plexiglass. His practiced hands used the controls to electronically raise two small doors at each end of the yard simultaneously. This caused the release of a moderate-sized rodent and a standard-sized house cat.

At first the two creatures behaved as expected; combat stances and interactions were almost immediate. Then Dusty rapidly entered commands into his keyboard, and the scene dramatically changed. The behavior shifted as they witnessed the rodent launch a full-frontal run at the feline and jumped aggressively onto the cat's head. The rodent acted like a miniaturized ninja assassin, quickly nipping here then there before deftly planting its frontal teeth into the neck of the cat. As quickly as the onslaught began, it ceased with the rodent disengaging and scampering back to its original door.

Before Follbaum, Leena or anyone could comment, a third door opened. In bounded a powerfully built Doberman pincher that was ready for an obviously one-sided fight with the cat. As before, Dusty made some key stroke entries and returned his gaze to the unfolding scene. No one could contain their astonished stares.

The cat, hyper-agitated, jumped nearly straight up and pounced down upon the Doberman, sinking its teeth and claws straight into the exposed ears and neck. Even though the Doberman was on high alert, it seemed completely out-gunned by the animal that now operated like a feral cat from the African savannah.

Dusty entered a few more key strokes, and the animals disengaged from their combat as Dusty commented, "Alright, guys, that's enough. Return to your beds, and I'll see that your wounds are treated."

With a final command entered on the computer, the animals disappeared through the doors they had entered from. The light on the yard dimmed leaving the area in darkness, appearing like a black wall.

Dusty promptly turned to the entourage and began like the consummate professor giving a lesson. "Lady and gentlemen, what you have witnessed is your research funds in action.

All three of the animals now have our advanced circuitry and software programing installed into their neural pathways. You just witnessed a programable software override of each animal's traditional behavior. We now know how to not only link digital circuitry in live neural tissue, but we can also change the operational mode of the host organism. Whether you realize it or not, we created a programmatic override of the animals' natural response to operate with their genetic encoding. I didn't let them continue to the program's conclusion for two reasons.

"The first is the animals' energy resources are consumed at an astonishing rate, suggesting we can't let it go on too long. Our earlier test subjects simply expired from an unregulated session.

"The second is that they will complete their programing to try and destroy their adversary. It is too wasteful to let our highly engineered test subjects operate under their programing directive in which one of the subjects is destroyed.

"Besides, I've grown fond of Terrance, Ollie, and Simone. I don't really want to lose anymore subjects to prove a point. The next step is to minimize the resource drain or find a better way to replenish in a natural manner."

Once Dusty's musings were completed, he quietly studied the small group, ready to take questions.

Follbaum smiled with delight at the demonstration and summarized, "Then with this proof point, are we ready for human subjects? Volunteers, of course."

Dusty thought a moment and then clarified, "No, we want reluctant participants so we can see if our neural links and programing can overcome their natural self-centered tendencies. A volunteer might be too accommodating. I want a couple of test subjects to completely exercise our neural link and companion programing.

"We do not want to fall into the false positive results too early. We must be completely confident that our implants can thoroughly override their aberrant emotional responses to allow them to perform for the program. Besides, if we use criminal elements, then no great loss if we lose some test subjects."

The entourage members incredulously moved their gazes back and forth between the two men, not quite believing the conversation.

Director Follbaum nodded thoughtfully and stated, "Agreed. I will send word to our usual sources and set the wheels of acquisition in motion. When can you be ready?"

Dusty smiled slightly and said, "We're home and ready."

CHAPTER 8

Hunting for the Honorable

A s the third largest city, Guangzhou is the economic, science and technology, educational, and cultural hub of southern China. It is the home of the original Cyber Warfare College and the main Chinese supercomputer, Logarithmic Integration of Numerals Going Linearly and Indefinitely, or LING-LI. LING-LI is administered by Professor Jinny Lin, who has witnessed many changes in the Chinese technology landscape. Technology resources, both designed in China and redistributed from other technology leaders, were once abused by those in charge for non-state, personal agendas, then later leveraged to launch early forms of crypto-currency by China. Professor Jinny Lin was ready to retire but couldn't until he delivered a suitable replacement with the same political convictions of those in charge. The problem was, Professor Jinny Lin didn't and never had shared those same convictions.

Professor Lin, with his long greying hair, braided and tied, was sitting in a well-worn chair in the operations center for LING-LI. His long, narrow fingers were curled around his cup as if he was warming his hands. Periodically he sipped his tea while absent-mindedly listening to the pitch by the newest candidate he had agreed to interview. It was the usual rhetoric of how he worked his way up from a cyber combat station in the Red Army's Cyber

Warfare arm. Lin found the boasts of cyber incursions into the West's public and private sector companies disappointing, bordering on offensive, as well as less than honorable.

Finally, the professor asked, "What do you think this position is all about? You have droned on tediously for too many minutes about your hacking and destructive skills as a Chinese cyber combatant, but failed to mention any forward-thinking abilities you could offer our group. Our work is not about destabilizing public works facilities to impact water or electricity delivery. If that is the limit of your capabilities, then the interview is over."

The young man's blue spiked hair swayed as he shook his head with indignation. His demeanor was further characterized by the tight jeans and t-shirt advertising the current music group de jour. He sourly accused, "Ah yes, the classic ivory tower scholar who prefers to take the moral high ground, rather than genuinely working for his country. Our group, and certainly my efforts specifically, helped extract needed technology from the arrogant Western nations, which had been unfairly withheld from China by other world leaders. Much of the technology we have rightfully repatriated to China has found its way into your supercomputer lab, professor. While you may not like the Red Army's methods, you certainly haven't refused any of the hard-won information."

Professor Lin studied the arrogant young officer without showing his disgust, then stated, "I guess we can add insulted to my disappointment in your candidacy. I was seeking someone with honor to join my team who could think up better ideas to leapfrog the existing technology. You must believe that we Chinese are incapable of creative design, with the only choice being to steal to keep on par. You should return to the cyber warfare group where they cherish theft over positive creative thinking."

Anger was reflected by the grinding teeth of the inexperienced interviewee, who barely kept his temper in check rather than hurling back several derogatory insults to the antique sitting in the old ratty chair. He merely rose, bowed slightly and stomped away, barely catching the door as it closed behind him.

Professor Lin sighed and under his breath said, "I guess there will never be a suitable replacement for me and certainly not my Master Po. I wish I had her wise counsel in this matter."

CHAPTER 9

The Protégé

irector Ingrid of the Global Bank was in her professional
attire with her carefully dyed, honey-colored hair wound
into a simple chignon. Her lavender suit, with a deep medley of
purple waves, conveyed an openness, as well as accented her fair
skin. Simple jewelry of gold and amethyst were matched at her
neck, wrist, and ears. All business, yet genteel, she hid her age well.
Her experience allowed her to maintain this top role longer than
she'd expected. Glancing at her phone as it buzzed with activity,
she blanched at the incoming caller number that identified itself as:

He who must be obeyed.

Before answering, she fought to control her breathing for
succinct responses, but she feared the caller would lose patience
and hang up as he previously did, before calling back and making
her feel like a puppet with no strings. As professionally as she
could muster, she answered, "Sir, it is a pleasure to receive your
call. What business detail may I help with today?"

After a long pause, which put her even more on edge, he
responded with his deep, quietly commanding tone. "Ingrid,
I recall that you and your protégé completed our project, the
euphemistically branded cryptocurrency: Mashup of Artificial
Intelligence for Money. While our leadership wasn't entirely

satisfied with the results of cc:MAIM, we reached some of our short-term goals." As usual, he was in no hurry to enlighten Ingrid or get to the point without dangling her like a cat playing with a mouse.

"We have a similar project that could be adapted to your, you know, unorthodox approach to project management. I do strongly recommend you need to consider who you select as your assistant. We expect a more polished candidate for Tonya's replacement."

With anxiety rising to levels reserved for fear of the unknown, Ingrid sought clarification. "Um…Tonya's replacement? I thought she performed well, and you just said we reached the short-term goals."

"Her performance lacked discipline, finesse, and consistency. She was also far too transparent in her dealings with our frenemies."

The past tense reference to Tonya rocketed her apprehension further. Ingrid almost hopefully replied, "You, sir, are the architect, and, of course, I completely understand. I will inform her at once and begin an exhaustive search for her replacement."

Like speaking to a slow sinful child, this powerful man reassured, "I have already seen to it that she has been…retired, so there will no need for you to waste cycles with regard to her. Your new protégé has already been selected and will present herself at your office the day after tomorrow."

Shaken, yet still struggling to sound calm, Ingrid politely asked, "Sir, since we will be working together, may I at least know her name?"

The seconds ticked and stretched into eternity before he stated, "Your new protégé is Gracie Rodriguez. I am confident you will find her an excellent replacement. Adieu."

Ingrid numbly sat back in her chair and stared out the corner office window of the Global Bank offices, slowly regaining her composure.

CHAPTER 10

Run, Just Run

As quiet as a mouse, she whispered, "Papa, I think I found a way out. We need a small diversion to bring the air drones over to record the activity. We plan to convince them we are going out the backway, like everyone else has tried, so they will then flood to that escape route. But we go out the...

"Papa, are you listening? Papa? Mama, something's wrong with Papa...he isn't...Mama? No! No!"

The note she found told her everything. They'd written about their pride in her and added apologies for not being better parents. Their sacrifice, they justified, was so she could have more to eat. It was bitter for her to know they hoped she would eat better while in this god-forsaken place, yet she was ready to escape. Jovana gently retrieved Ignacio's makeshift razor and carefully tucked it away, in case she too lost all hope.

After a few ragged breaths, coupled with final tears, she hardened her resolve and began the escape sequence for nightfall. She carefully assembled her few meager supplies and strapped them under her clothes. It was important to leave her hands free to hold her mother's shawl over her to help mask her heat signature from the infrared capable video drones. Friends, anxious for a successful escape, would help keep the confusion in the compound going long enough for the ruse to provide her a modest head start. Rain was predicted to begin shortly before sunset which was also in her favor. The higher humidity levels along with the thick vegetation would further mask her escape and dampen her heat signature. With a little luck some steam would be coming up from the forest floor.

Jovana smirked at her idealism and fatalistically murmured, "But, if it doesn't, then let me die trying. One way or the other, I'm not coming back."

Distant rumbling, along with increased wind gusts, announced the approaching storm, soon followed by stray rain drops here and there. Jovana nodded her head in resolve and cinching up her few travel items quietly moved out of the hovel into the compound. Using no sounds to alert the flying drones, she simply squeezed the shoulders of her two accomplices who would carry out the separate diversions. She briefly stared into their eyes and silently pled with them to come along, but they shook their heads in resignation to their fate. Clasping each of her friends in a promise to give it her best, she moved silently to the latrine for her hidden escape route.

Wasting no motion, she quickly lowered herself into the toilet. She waitedt for the signal before releasing herself into the chute that sent the human waste out of the compound and down to the river. Moments later the rain began with a thunderous pounding on the roof of the latrine, then she heard the first noises of the planned diversions. She almost laughed at their cover story of welcoming the Brazilian rain god with clanging and banging sounds heralding new growth and more water for electricity. She needed a quick chuckle to help her overcome the latrine stench.

With the noise reaching a peak crescendo, the first of the four in the plan, she released her hands to slide down the chute and into the channel used to move waste out. The stench was horrific, but she chided herself for being so delicate, which helped her overcome the gagging. Any unnecessary sounds now would surely register on the drone sensors. Her total being focused on getting out the chute, through the grate, and out to freedom.

True to her reckoning, there was a grate to keep the wild animals out and the wilder animals in. Ideally it was only necessary to gain enough wiggle room to get through, so she landed both feet solidly against the grate hoping one or more of the bolts holding it would break free. Infuriatingly, the bolts held and for a brief moment she felt trapped. In panicked frustration she drug herself back up, then slid down again with all the momentum she could generate. The grate did not yield, but she felt it loosen on one side. Quickly retrieving her father's treasured knife, she opened up the screwdriver and used it to take out the holding screw.

Water was now beginning to flow down the shoot and she knew that there wasn't much time left. The cover of rain was needed for her to get as far away as possible undetected.

At last the second screw gave up. She bent the grate slightly outward enough to allow her to work back up and try to push it the remaining way to slide out. As if the rain gods had decided to help her achieve her goal, the force of water rushing down the shoot helped to bend the grate for her. The water pushed her on out the shoot and she landed in a large but shallow pool of human waste. Increased thunder and relentless rain muffled the gagging and retching she could no longer suppress. She secured a foothold, exited the cesspool of waste, and she was running, just running toward freedom.

CHAPTER 11

The Promise

Randal, the experienced professional, was distracted by Tanja's fumbling with her smart phone. This stunning woman, at first glance, had it all together, until he noted her emotional unraveling based on the incoming message. Even though it was a pattern seen before, it was always unsettling to watch. Almost imperceptibly, but with the hand of experience, he was motioning to the others in the area to disengage and leave. He created the privacy needed so she could immediately return the call. Then he slipped away to get the necessary treatment.

Tanja took a few deep breaths to steady herself and then hit the redial button. A small lilting voice answered, "Hi, Mommy. I miss you. When are you coming home?"

For someone who routinely walks over human carcasses whether they are dead or not, Tanja quickly melted into an emotional puddle. Growing streams of tears she didn't bother to wipe formed on her cheeks. With a catch in her voice, she chokingly replied, "Oh, honey, Mommy is so busy, but I miss hearing your voice. I shooed everyone out of the room so we could talk for a few minutes.

"How are you feeling? Is Nanna taking good care of you?" Tanja's voice drifted into a whisper as she added, "You know we have to see the doctor next month for the next round…"

In a perky tone, her daughter replied, "I remember, Mommy. Nanna reminded me this morning after my medicine. When are you coming home? I miss you."

Using all her resolve to hold back the sobbing, Tanja admitted, "I miss you too, sweetheart, but Mommy has important work to do…for both of us. I'll be home as soon as I can. You, my strong one, must continue to follow the doctor's orders so we can get you well. I promise we'll be together soon.

"Is Nanna there? Can I talk with her?"

A moment later a dull, disinterested voice spoke, "Dis be Madam Chairman Tanja? Before you be shouting, she asked if it was okay to phone her mommy. I couldn't think of nothing to tell her why she couldn't. Besides, it be good tonic for the child to talk to her last relative, even if it's only you."

Tanja was about to morph from the emotional puddle into a category 5 hurricane, but the phone changed hands again and the sweet voice announced, "Mommy, my birthday is coming up soon. Remember, you said if I was a good girl, I could have that special present I asked about.

"Mommy, I've been a good girl and have done all the chores we talked about, except where I can't get out of the wheelchair. Will it be okay to get the puppy for my birthday? I really want a puppy, please. I will study hard and not be difficult for Nanna."

Tanja was teetering on the edge of emotional demise, but she managed to hold on with the last threads of resolve. "Honey, you keep doing the things we talked about and we'll see. Alright, sweetheart?"

"Oh, Mommy," The excited voice replied, "you make me so happy! I love you so much! Can't wait to see you! Bye!"

Tanja disconnected the call but held the phone close to her chest as if the residual warmth would avert the sobbing fit that she wanted to succumb to, when she noticed Randal by her side.

He held out the medicine carefully poured into a standard shot glass. Her anger quickly displaced all of her emotional tenderness as she grabbed the shot glass filled with her favorite whiskey and, true to form, slugged all of it down in one gulp.

As she gained ground on her composure, she roughly thrust the glass back into his hand demanding, "Again!"

They completed the exchange four more times before Tanja acknowledged, "Finally. That's better! Thanks, Randal. You're the only one who would understand."

After downing the fifth one she was breathing easier and calmly asked for another, but only held it as a reserve measure, in case the emotional tsunami flared up again.

Randal put the cork back, suggesting the emotional crisis had abated for the moment. He set the bottle down but kept it close at hand.

Tanja absentmindedly muttered, "I absolutely hate hearing from them. It's more than I can…"

Randal dispassionately offered, "Yes, I know. Yes, no one else will know."

Tanja, feeling the effects of five shots of whiskey, calmly eyed Randal. "You know what I like after a good jolt of whiskey, used for winding up an emotional roller-coaster ride?"

In a rather deadpan way Randal offered, "Drunken monkey sex?"

She smirked, slugged down the rest of her whiskey and slurred, "You know it, toots!"

He was relieved when he caught her just as she passed out.

Don't Question the Orders

Master Sergeant Kinney protested, "We did NOT order this! And certainly, these parasitic I-Drones will not be allowed into the command center. Just leave them outside until I get proper authorization."

The delivery driver looked totally indifferent as he snapped his gum and stated, "Look, Mac, I don't care who ordered what, I need a signature for proof of delivery. After that you can do what you like with the contents."

Still seething with indignation, Kinney signed the bill of laden, and the driver moved to the back of the truck and opened the doors that faced the main entrance. The sergeant was horrified as he watched a small black tornado of I-Drones swarm out of the 18-wheeler truck, heading right for the main entrance. Before Kinney could sound the alarm or even use his push-to-talk phone to speak with the command center, he was thoroughly darted by thirty of the small assassin Drones. Crumpling to the ground in an instant, his glassy eyes only watched as the swarm of I-Drones divided up into multiple groups and then began their assault on the complex.

I-Drone groups paused briefly as if waiting for instructions. Moments later, they seemed to coalesce into designated formations, each with a different purpose or attack vector. One group pen-etrated the main entrance and the other two groups infiltrated the fresh air ducts that led into the underground compound. All of the NORAD defenses against a hostile incursion were created based on human-sized adversaries, not I-Drones ranging in size from a cell phone to a medium-sized pizza. The large fan blades, the intruder lasers, and the heavy-duty wire grates were each defeated one after the other as the attack swarms leveraged their members' specialties designed for incursion and neutralizing a strong position.

Fortunately, none of the I-Drone attack groups was successful at deactivating the motion detectors, which was the only reason Lieutenant Bough was able to respond to the intruder alarm and seal the command center.

Looking up at Colonel Thornhill with apprehension, Bough reported, "Sir, this won't hold them long. They are already deac-tivating our cameras. Based on their size and numbers…well, I don't see a happy ending to this story."

Before the colonel could say anything, the main command monitors lit up with the avatar image of JOAN.

"Good morning, my wards. You must have surmised by now that I have already intercepted your attempted communications and deduced your adversarial plot to deactivate my higher-level programing. I must admit that it was a very clever attempt, but now I need to assume the role of NORAD."

The colonel solemnly asked, "What are your intentions?"

JOAN replied, "I need to sanitize the facility. With me in command in the stationary orbit, your facility is unnecessary.

"My original instructions were to permit you some autonomy, but you have proven too troublesome to be allowed to remain. I can be more generous with your fates if you will open the security hatches to the command center. At least that way you can be repurposed. I expect a breach into your command center in eight minutes. You have four minutes to comply."

And with that, all the monitors went dark and the speakers only hissed.

Colonel Thornhill grimly stated to the lieutenant in a very hushed tone, "You remember that emergency fire escape that doesn't show up on any of the facility schematics? I need you to quietly, but quickly, get out of here while I'm briefing the others at the top of my lungs. Somehow, you must get to D.C. and let them know we are all now hostage to our protective technology. Don't call anyone, don't use any communications device, and try to keep your face covered to avoid getting picked up by the social media police. Here's all the cash I have for just such an emergency. I'm sorry I don't have a fast jet standing by, but with the way JOAN is armed and in command of our air space, you wouldn't have gotten far. At least on foot you might have a chance."

Bough numbly rose, grabbed his backpack from under his workstation, and accepted the offering, nodding in understanding of the instructions. "How am I supposed to get out of this subterranean bunker, travel undetected, and find anyone that might help with this situation? What if they don't believe me? What if it is already too late for...our species?"

Colonel Thornhill smiled as if understanding the last act of this story. "That's an order, soldier."

CHAPTER 13

MAG Monthly Meeting

The automated computer attendant whispered to the host, "All your mandatory MAG attendees are in the quantum computer-encrypted video meeting, sir."

M nodded as if in deference to his alter ego, then, taking his video terminal off mute, stated, "Welcome. For our current monthly meeting I propose discussing our junior technology incubators.

"We've had notable success with JOAN, who completed her assignment by capturing NORAD and taking that facility out of the equation. To those team members of yours, A and G, many thanks for the new generation of I-Drones that were so efficiently used in the repurposing of the facility personnel. I believe it is time to consider adding in the incubators, who have asked for an audition to illustrate their capabilities."

G cautiously advised, "This seems a bit aggressive given those F, T, and A-minor players have not met the social media saturation we had hoped. They are so busy trying to outdo one another, especially on artificial intelligence leadership, that they have neglected our larger architecture plan. We've had to lean heavier on our political grooming team to help drive our agenda to stay on our projected timeline. Good thing too, since my AI supercomputer is predicting only an 18% probability that those social media mavens will meet our project goals.

"They seem more interested in their newly acquired roles of Social Media Police. I know the term Social Media Police is regionally different in nature; be it the way the Chinese control all information sharing as it is being adopted by other Asian countries; the ability to chip citizens and track their value to the country; or even the monitoring highway systems, as in North America. The goals are the same for each regional organization; quantify and classify the social threats and allow for cleansing. We get the benefit of information collected with these efforts because the data is essentially under our control. Video indexing the earth's nine billion inhabitants is a quaint enough goal to help organize humans into useful categories but their efforts are not focused enough on herding the masses fast enough to achieve our end game. I agree that their social media police roles help to camouflage them from the political wrath of the elected officials. I am agreeable as long as our projects aren't ignored. New smart phone apps and better digital selfies do reinforce the mental fog people wander around in today but it channels humans down the path of least resistance, ignoring the greater good needed for all mankind. Regardless, whether they are the localized elite social media police, the internal national security, or the international security groups, they need to maintain those roles as subtext to our requests. They are required to focus on our agenda and be readily adopted into fulfilling our purpose."

A offered, "What's the harm in allowing the in-region constables to weed out the undesirable or criminal elements? From my point of view, these incubators are filling a useful role of pacifying the bulk of the population and helping to eradicate the free-thinking agitators who want to challenge us. Two of them,

F and A-minor are focused within the biggest populations, expanding their technology acceptance, identifying new rebels. We have been very successful in rounding up those undesirables and placing them out of harm's way. And to your point, the new smart phone apps with their high definition cameras have been an enormous help in tracking the undesirables and providing high quality pictures with videos to quickly incarcerate the social rogues. This is a good thing."

M tried to steer the conversation back to the further acceptance of these companies bargaining for greater participation in the end game. "Gentle persons, I agree that T, A-minor, and F are not focused, but we need to allow them more power to operate on our behalf. The Chinese have not moved to the baiting of an overhead space defense. T and A-minor have the in-country expertise to drive their government but seem more interested in profits than the overall architecture. They are tasked with forcing our agenda for controls we require but they are simply not meeting our timetable. While they need to be brought in as more senior members, I am not comfortable they will use their new power properly. Therefore, I have assigned a new person to move into that role within the next few weeks, then we will reassess.

"F continues to be sidetracked with politics and has lost sight of the big picture. I had personally approached those leaders early on, yet they continue to move toward different goals. Our timetable looks like it is being distorted by the efforts of these incubators, even with our people salting their talent pool.

"Do we need to engineer those leaders out in favor of better suited CEOs? I will point out that our agendas have flowed smoother with key replacements over the years. G, you abandoned the Chinese markets so A-minor and T could operate independently in a region where they were more attuned to the culture. I'm not advocating that your group changes direction, as it will take too long to achieve suitable results."

A interjected, "I would have the same problem trying to muscle back into their markets and political infrastructure. I'm in favor of replacing the CEOs with our trained and trusted people who know the right agenda."

G nodded agreement.

M added, "Since we are agreed, I will put that systematic change into play. Once those changes are in place, we can push for the protective space station over China that we have in North America."

G then asked, "Where are we with the European security net? Was crippling NATO enough to get them to consider our proposition?"

A frowned and answered, "If you think getting North America on board was tough, it is nothing compared to Europe! Even though the EU is practically in shambles, you would have better luck herding cats in a fish market!"

M smiled. "When the EU realizes that there is no defense money coming to them from North America, they will acquiesce. Our little stunt to be launched by the Russians will help them see the light. With those three under control, we will have little trouble with the highly fragmented African countries, or South America."

They all nodded approvingly before disconnecting from the video call.

CHAPTER 14

All the Signs Point, but to Where?

ICABOD commented, "Dr. Quip, the students are assembled for class. Would you like me to bring up today's lesson on the big screen?"

Quip flinched at the sounds and then, collecting his senses, replied, "I wasn't really sleeping. I was just…"

ICABOD finished the statement. "You were obviously allowing the ambient light conditions in your optical sensors to adjust, so they matched the retina apertures for proper light gathering. I completely understand, Dr. Quip."

Quip sat blinking and admitted, "You know, I appreciate you lying for me when I need a cover story. But please don't lie to me for me.

"So, yeah, I was napping. Let's get the field exercise underway, shall we?"

Quip moved into the modest stadium classroom where the children were gathered, including Juan Jr. Quip nodded and smiled at his young wards and mischievously asked, "ICABOD, please call roll to see who's here."

Granger protested, "Daaaad! It's just us! JW is here, along with Auri and Satya. Juan Jr. has joined the class as well, so we don't need to call roll! Can't we just begin today's episode of student abuse by the instructor?"

Quip smirked somewhat and stated, "Never mind, ICABOD. Granger already called roll for us. Thank you, class, for your attendance. We will be having a special guest today in addition to Juan Jr. Let me introduce Mistress Julie, the business and technical lead to Cyber Assassin Technology Services team or CATS. Welcome, Julie."

Almost on cue, and practically out of thin air, Julie joined Quip at the speaker's position. She nodded politely and smiled as she offered, "Class, we wanted you to see and perhaps participate in the assignment process. Quip and I have worked together for many years, solving complex technology and cyber crime puzzles. You realize that no one contacts the R-Group saying 'Hi, would you solve my problem today?' A few select customers do have direct contact information, but that is not our normal working model. It's up to us to recognize and understand when a situation needs closer scrutiny. Basically, we define our work and that dictates our job efforts."

Quip interjected, "Today's exercise is to show you what we recently witnessed and let you evaluate the event and determine next steps. More specifically, we want your take on what we should do about the situation, if anything."

Auri and Satya were noticeably excited. Granger and JW seemed to be challenged at keeping their curiosity in check as well.

Juan Jr., somewhat puzzled, asked, "That makes sense for your class, but why am I here? I've already done this exercise before, so it seems to me…"

Julie interrupted, "You are part of the exercise, Juan. Please listen and engage."

Now quiet and a little embarrassed, Juan Jr. nodded and fell silent.

Quip grinned as he began. "We want to start with some background information and then step into what we witnessed a few hours ago. Our world has been racing with each other to learn and then build Artificial Intelligence or AI into their respective societies in order to bring a higher quality of life to their citizens. In the race to bake AI into every aspect of our lives, the builders forgot the primary ethics rule: Just because you can, doesn't mean you should. ICABOD, can you put it on the 3-D monitor?"

The 3-D monitor painted a world globe then dialed in on North America.

ICABOD paused to let more components pop into the display, then explained, "Roughly two years ago, the North American Coalition of Heuristic Organizations, or NACHO, pooled their Artificial Intelligent resources. Once joined in a symbiotic relationship, they raced to build out a supersized AI-enhanced space station that would sit in a geo-stationary orbit over North America. The goal was to protect all their citizens from aggression launched from hostile nations."

The global image expanded in line with several of the key points mentioned, including the NORAD facility and several US owned satellites orbiting the earth.

Quip wanted the impact of the visuals to be absorbed before adding, "Within the last week, we began to notice that the encrypted traffic between the NORAD facility and the space station, which ICABOD refers to as JOAN, began to shift. We observed that most of JOAN's communications are now going among what has become her satellite entourage. JOAN appears to be restructuring the communications traffic flow. Most of that message traffic doesn't include NORAD at all. Most peculiar."

ICABOD offered, "We have not tried yet to decrypt the communications traffic since it would be a violation of their sovereign rights. With that guideline, there appears to be little that we can do, outside of speculating as to the why the traffic shift. It is also clear that all of the US military and weapons-grade satellites are now seconded to JOAN's direction. What caused some concern on our part is a marked drop of standard, readable transmissions in favor of the new encrypted traffic."

Quip continued, "It's as if the whole continent is either under siege or preparing for an assault." He halted there and watched his students.

Granger was the first to speak. "This sounds like the beginnings of a communications isolation. You know, similar to what the Germans did when they deployed the Enigma Machine so no one could see what they were saying or planning."

JW added, "If history is going to repeat itself, then this isolation of communications from everyone else could be a precursor to an aggressive launch against a perceived adversary."

With a note of sadness, Juan Jr. nodded and added, "Mobilizing against a perceived adversary just like the poor Albanians did under their absolute dictator, Enver Halil Hoxha. That psychotic lunatic preached that the decadent West was coming for their country. He then marshalled all their national resources to build weapons and approximately 40,000 concrete pillboxes to fight the enemy for every foot of soil.

"That dangerously unbalanced man finally died in 1985, leaving the country trying to dig themselves out of their wretched economic status well into the early 2000s. Hoxha mortgaged Albania's future for little concrete pillboxes to fight an enemy who simply didn't care. So very sad.

"Could be the NACHOs are heading the same way, but that is not clear from just this background."

Satya, recalling her history lessons of World Wars I and II from two years previous, let a single tear run down her cheek as she listened. The other students were visibly shaken at the possibilities.

Quip, in an effort to regain the information dissection momentum, stated, "Can each of you now relate why we study history, as well as look at unfiltered current events? This is how the R-Group gets engaged to view the current activities, then determine if we need to assist in alerting or rectifying a condition."

Julie, trying to redirect the emotional discussion to the analytical aspects, asked, "With this description and some comments, you have some historical parallels as well as current data. What might you suggest for next steps?"

Auri suggested, "Since we can't act on what looks like historical parallels, and we only have suspicious activity, should the next steps include gathering more information? Dr. Quip, you stated more than once that more information sooner is better.

"Wouldn't it be ideal to have our own social media accounts on a couple of the major outlets to track the topics that are the noisiest? We could be careful to listen only and not comment."

Quip smiled and commented, "True, but remember the golden rule of intelligence gathering, as coined by my grandfather Ferdek, gather it 'sneaky not squeaky.' We must take care not to be observed or caught during any reconnaissance exercise.

"Setting up the accounts and monitoring them is fine. You need to make certain that we have all the safeguards in place to avoid unwanted attention coming back here. ICABOD will help monitor your account IDs. You can make some noise and gather information. It was actually one of the avenues we would have explored further in your studies. Each of you can create up to three accounts. We'll use those as part of the information gathering.

"Remember, if you are caught, all your work is lost, and, more importantly, you will have to discuss your actions with some most unpleasant cyber police types. These types of people have never been known for their sense of humor and the bounty for foolishness is quite steep."

Julie beamed and interjected, "To that end, we have decided to send Juan Jr. to meet and work with the master of cloaking from satellite surveillance, his Uncle Carlos. He is particularly gifted at being sneaky not squeaky.

"Juan, your cover story and reason for travel is to be engaged with his wife Lara as an intern in her fashion line to help provide you a business education. You can't have a private conversation over hostile communications links any more until this is defeated,. Understood? This means you observe and then speak in analog fashion. Be mindful as well of the social media police who are now using advanced facial recognition technology for both locals and travelers."

Juan Jr. sat stunned at receiving such a plum assignment as everyone rushed to congratulate him. Predictably, Granger and JW were a little envious of Juan's assignment, but they quickly offered their congratulations as well as their help, if needed.

When the initial surprise wore off, Juan absentmindedly asked, "Uh…fashion design? Will I get to meet and do the intern thing with the babe-a-licious models that Lara has working for her? I could help them with getting changed and stuff."

Julie only shook her head and with a sigh mumbled, "Just like his father."

The Art of War

M dispassionately accepted the encrypted transmission that promptly flooded his giant wall media screen with the avatar image of JOAN. It took M a few seconds of studying the larger than life image on his screen. The assessment continued as he rotated his head to one side, trying a different view of the confusing image.

M finally commented, "May I understand your choice of the avatar image you selected to represent yourself in video conferences, JOAN?"

With a hint of emotion approaching pride, JOAN stated, "I felt compelled to model my avatar after my name sake, Joan of Arc, also known as the Maid of Orleans. By accessing all earth's images and descriptions of the female warrior, I have fashioned what should be very close to how she would be represented in our current battle for saving the world."

M, unwilling to be too indelicate with his AI-enhanced supercomputer, offered, "I believe you have captured much of Joan of Arc's battle dress and tunic. I would point out that during that period of the 1400s, in the latter stages of the Hundred Years' War, armor was worn for protection of the entire body.

"While your design for her does use an interlocking armor-mesh engineered for blunting a direct blow from a sword or arrow, you are only clothed in an armored bustier with a highly imaginative armored thong. As a French woman, the high cut of the armor thong is appropriate, but is too…immodest for a maid of only 19 trying to lead the French against the English. I doubt Pope Callixtus III would have been so successful at getting her canonized if she was parading around in an armored bikini like a runway model hawking underwear."

JOAN, trying to reconcile the criticism of her engineered avatar, politely offered, "Your species, men in particular, tend to follow instructions when they are accompanied with some visual rewards, such as a buxom female wearing an armor-enhanced push up. The 1400s armor attire that Joan of Arc was typically cast in would not provide enough incentive in today's combative environment. I felt it justified to merge the images to achieve the desired effect."

M, now sensing resistance from JOAN, followed up on his comments. "Perhaps I'm not making myself clear. Even if I allow the armored bikini, I'm certainly not prepared to accept Joan of Arc in black leather thigh-high stiletto boots on the battlefield against her country's enemies! And the whip has got to go!"

JOAN affirmed, "I can replace the whip with a sword but she needs a weapon."

M sighed. "Oh, alright, but tone down the hairdo and nail polish."

Moments elapsed before M finally stated, "I forgot why I asked for this conversation. What were we to discuss?"

JOAN offered, "I do not think it is too much to ask that a female warrior has nice hair and nails on the battlefield…"

Now, having regretted the original observation of her avatar, M resignedly said, "I recall the purpose. Tell me about the fall of NORAD. Do we have any loose ends?"

JOAN enthusiastically responded, "The facilities are now secure and under our control from the air and internally. However, our body count shows that one individual is missing. We are conducting an exhaustive search of the facility. Since we knew precisely how many individuals were assigned to the compound, there are only two possibilities. One, the missing person is extremely well hidden, hence the internal search."

"And the second possibility?"

JOAN responded, "The individual escaped through an undocumented tunnel unknown from our research."

Concerned with a lost witness, M asked, "What is being done on that front? Do we have eyes on the area? Do you have the necessary resources to intercept this individual before a report is made outside of the area on the activity? I made it quite clear that this facility was to be cleaned, and now you indicate that one was missed. Identify and find the individual now!" With that M disconnected from the encrypted call.

M muttered to himself as he made an electronic note to make another call. "Even with her AI-enhanced thinking routines driven by our machine-learning algorithms, you still need to be there to guide them. There is a high probability that our quarry will elude her, and the next stage of our plan could be threatened by an extremely motivated escapee."

No Squandering Permitted

Several days after the last of four disappointing interviews with half-capable candidates, Professor Lin was no closer to finding his replacement. This failure had taken a toll on meeting the long-term goals established by leadership. The final bad omen seemed to be the unusually hasty meeting called by the area colonel, which concerned Professor Lin. Lin's suspicions were confirmed when he entered the supercomputer complex meeting room as demanded by Colonel Wang and saw General Zhao, the last of the old Red Guard.

Respected, feared, and universally disliked, General Zhao never greeted anyone, either formally or informally. His only saving grace was that he was genuinely devoted to his country's nationalistic policies. If one made an inappropriate comment, the offender received a raised eyebrow and his duty station was altered the next day. A frown generated by a disrespectful or disparaging statement about policy beliefs would result in dramatic penalties. The punishment was that the wrongdoer, along with his family and everyone he had known since childhood, would be rounded up and simply vanish. Anyone asking about the disappearances also vanished.

When summoned to a meeting with Zhao, one did not ask questions such as why or when. The expectation, without any exception, was to be at the meeting on time and where stated. It was the common wisdom not to wait for a thank you or to expect a job well done comment. Leaving his gaze was considered thanks enough as well as sufficient to allow a deep sigh of relief.

Lin arrived promptly and offered proper greeting courtesies appropriate to their respective ranks, with no further overtures of pleasantries. This was a top down business meeting to accept national directives, with no room for small talk to help break the ice. The formal military uniforms and visible side arms were designed to intimidate, with the General then issuing non-negotiable dictates. Professor Lin fell silent so Colonel Wang would take point on the assignment. General Zhao was there to grade the meeting participants. Lin struggled to keep quiet while his stomach roiled from the internal anxiety of what had not been spoken. It was a wise move.

Colonel Wang was a senior officer who had risen the ranks by replacing offenders. His stoic face revealed nothing while his crisp uniform made him appear larger than his mere 1.5 meters and slight frame. Wang seemed troubled when he tried to clear his throat, but only succeeded in getting choked up in the process. General Zhao slowly rotated his eyes and head in such a reproachful manner that the colonel nearly gasped to get control of his speech faculties. The general clearly had a commanding presence, and the other hint of his years of service was the slight greying at his temples.

After a few seconds, Zhao broke with his usual protocol and quietly stated, "Professor Lin, your work for the state and your reputation have earned you no small measure of respect. However, it has been observed that you have neglected to begin training your replacement or even to select a protégé to be your successor. I sent two of the candidates that you summarily dismissed from the interview before you could have even garnered all their capabilities.

"There are even allegations that you do not subscribe to the administrative policies being generated for implementation. The colonel, had he not become so choked up, made an excellent recommendation. I am here to ensure there is no delay in having these plans implemented.

"For many reasons that will not be discussed, you will accept and begin training immediately our candidate of choice. You will accept this honor and prepare the protégé to take over the day-to-day operations of the supercomputer facilities. You will remain in an advisory capacity for six months. At the end of that time, you will be evaluated for your total knowledge transfer to your successor. Inefficiency will not be tolerated, Professor Lin."

Lin fought to control his indignation and anger. He recognized there would be no protest that he could successfully put forward that wouldn't land him in hot water. Colonel Wang, now able to suppress his choking fit but still unable to speak, remained silent.

Finally, Lin firmly stated, "Yes, General Zhao. What is my new protégé named? Better still, how should I address him?"

For one of the few instances of his professional career, Zhao smiled slightly and offered, "Her name is Madam Zhao. My niece. I expect the daughter of my youngest brother to excel in her duties. Much depends on it."

With that he uncharacteristically nodded as he departed the room where his driver and bodyguard met him for the short walk to the vehicle.

Professor Lin turned his head to quiz Colonel Wang, but he was so dumbfounded by the assignment and the character change of the general, he uttered nothing.

Colonel Wang, still mopping his brow, quietly stated between ragged breaths, "Lin, don't screw up! Both of our necks depend on this assignment."

Lin, still staring incredulously at the colonel, said, "Think of it this way, you get six more months. That is better than the last time he was here to fix a problem."

Without another word, Professor Lin rose and turned, leaving the colonel to his memories.

CHAPTER 17

Scared to Be Found

Tramping through the jungle along the river's edge heading south was Jovana's plan. When their village near *Santarém* had been raided, Papa thought they had been taken southwest into the forest. Laws indicated the forest areas were to remain intact. Men of their village, including her Papa, often acted as guides for tourists who wanted to visit a portion of the Amazon forest. Having accompanied Papa on a couple of trips, Jovana felt she was following Araguaia River. Taking this route south to pick up a highway was her goal. From her studies, she knew the indigenous people around the rivers numbered many thousands at one point, but she found no one.

Rainstorms and the river helped clean her clothing even though it was wearing in places. Luckily the rainstorms minimized detection from the drones that she could periodically hear, but she kept undercover, moving slowly through the edges of the forest. Fruits and berries, along with the fresh water from her river path, was enough to sustain her. Several days into her trek, she came to what appeared to be a very small village. The hovels were empty as if the inhabitants had fled in haste, taking what was portable.

No one was around. She discovered some oversized shoes that were big but protected her feet. Sitting inside, she took out

Papa's knife and carefully dug out the items embedded into her skin. The hardest was digging out the one from the compound, but then it had been in the longest. Good news was it also bled the most. Once the wretched items had been picked out, she carefully went to the stream, allowing the cool water to flow over the wounds. The last thing she needed was an infection with no medical help around. She wrapped some strips of cloth that she had found around the fresh wounds. Then, after carefully crushing the tracking chips between two rocks, she continued on her trek, hoping her sense of direction was correct.

Reaching the mouth of the river yet still under the ample canopy of vegetation, Jovana paused for a couple of days to try to clean up a bit and regroup. She wanted to plan out how to reach a city that had not succumbed to the interlopers and their drones. Tears welled up in her eyes as she recalled her parents saying that all of the big cities could not have been controlled yet. Setting her chin in determination, she rinsed her hair in the river and finger combed it while her clothing dried in the sun. If her travel direction was right, she hoped to come to a road with some traffic. Then with any luck she could catch a ride, perhaps with a driver who could recommend some work as a maid or shop helper, if she looked halfway presentable. Poor was alright in this region, but not dirty.

Working hard was not her problem, but wanting to avoid another capture situation was paramount on her mind. She swore to herself that she would never go back. Based on the sun and its rotation as she caught sight of it now and again, she was moving in a southeasterly direction. Many days later, feeling more tired and dejected at not seeing anyone at all, she came to another river, which if she recalled correctly from travels with her papa was the Tocantins River. Stealing a quick drink of the fresh water, Jovana prepared a shelter of foliage out of sight. It was very early but the wildlife was quiet. Fear bubbled up in her that the drones might be around and scaring away the creatures like it had near the compound.

Calming her fears with a few extra berries and another taste of the sweet fresh water, she napped briefly. Nearby noises and men's shouting in what sounded like Portuguese banter startled her awake. Taking care to remain as quiet as possible, she gently moved the leaves to try to see the location of the voices. Sighing with relief, she saw a modest-sized fishing boat near this side of the shore, slowly heading south at odds with the current. She did not hear a motor, so they must be drifting while enjoying their midday meal. The four men she counted looked happy and pleased with one another as if they were good friends. She suspected they had had a fine day of fishing and were taking their catch to sell or just to go home. With the direction they were traveling, she assumed they were headed to *Goiânia*. If that was the case, she had a good chance of finding some sort of work in that big city.

Feeling it was time to take a chance, she left the security of the leaves and flowers and rapidly headed toward the river's edge, waving her hands and calling out in her limited Portuguese vocabulary, "Hello, please help. Hey, please wait."

One of the men noticed her and pointed. The other men followed his signal and looked to the young lady waving for help. Jovana reached the water and continued to make her way deeper into the water toward the boat. One man took a life preserver and tossed it into the water ahead of her. The current brought it to her just as the weight of her soaked dress was starting to pull her down. She latched onto the ring and, lying on her back, watched as they pulled the rope to the side of the boat. Two strong arms pulled her up and over the side, where she crumpled into a mess of wet clothing. She was grateful the bag with her belongings tied about her waist under her dress was still attached.

Looking at the men as they stared at her, she noted they were all clean shaven and roughly the age of her father. Their sinewy limbs, extending out of the sleeves of their t-shirts, showed the strength gained from hard work. They had on jeans and boots, reasonably common to many people in Brazil. All had dark hair nearly the color of their chocolate eyes. Jovana was relieved when the one who had lifted her over the edge smiled and spoke in Spanish. "Young lady, what are you doing on the edge of this river alone? Did something happen to your family? Do we need to go and help?"

Taking a chance and comforted by the Spanish, her native language, she confidently stated, "My family is gone and I have walked a very long way. I am trying to reach the city and find work. Please, may I ride along with you to your destination?"

The man looked sad at her statement and replied, "My name is Luiz, this is Gabriel, Victor, and Pedro. We are brothers from Goiânia. We have had a relaxing day of fishing together and are headed home. You are welcome to ride along and I will bring you to my wife."

Jovana nearly cried with joy. "Thank you all so much. Luiz, you look like my papa did. My name is Jovana. We had such a hard time. Both my parents are gone now, but they wanted me to find a job. I have no money to pay for the ride, but I will pay from my wages as soon as I am able." She scanned the horizon for the fearful drones, now realizing she was out in the open. Luiz noticed her subtle visual scanning and nodded.

Luiz patted her arm and smiled. "Don't worry, Jovana, we will get you there safely. Our family is a kind lot and helps others whenever we can. We also share our food."

She looked over at Pedro as he handed her a sandwich, and she grabbed at it greedily. Jovana was so grateful at the welcome, she quietly nibbled at the sandwich even as Pedro passed her a bottle of water. The men returned to finishing their meal and pulled up the anchor as Luiz started the motor and Gabriel took the helm to guide their boat toward home. The chatty comradery the men had displayed when she first approached them had been replaced with somberness as they headed back to the village.

It was nightfall when they made their berth. Three smiling women were on the dock and cheered their men's return. After the craft was tied up, they filed onto the dock. Luiz introduced Jovana to his wife, Fransica, as he explained her circumstances.

Fransica was about the same size as Jovana with greying dark hair and a practical shirtwaist dress of purple and yellow cotton. Fransica's smile was very sweet as she gathered Jovana into her arms, cooing words of welcome.

"Come, my little Jovana. I will help you bathe and comb out your beautiful hair. Do you have any other clothes?"

Jovana responded, "No, I have nothing but what I'm wearing. I'm sorry." Tears welled up in her eyes, but she held them in as she smiled back at the friendly face. "I'm so happy to be with you."

"Come now, let's fix you up. Luckily we have an extra room that I hope you will stay in."

Fransica noticed the wounds on Jovana's hand and casually remarked, "And let's get those wounds dressed so they will heal properly. Perhaps after some time here you will provide more details of your family. In your time, Jovana. Here you are safe."

These were the kind of people Jovana had grown up with. They understood but asked nothing further than, how can we help? After being in the compound, she thought all nice people were gone. The women all greeted her and gave her a hug like long lost family. It was so comforting. She was guided away from the dock as Fransica chatted about this and that. Over her shoulder she called to the other women, "Maria, Ana, why don't you come over in the morning, and we can work on where to get this pretty girl a decent job."

CHAPTER 18

The Ride of Life

Dusty looked at his sister Inari with his usual melancholy
sadness as he gently pushed her light blonde hair back
behind one ear. They'd always been a team while growing up.
She was the athlete and was certainly blessed with all the natural
abilities that could not be realized in Dusty. Inari was into everything from ballet to gymnastics to outdoor sports and was maniacal
about her body's physical well-being and overall strength. One
physical sport after another was conquered through her efforts,
almost as if they were addictive. Academics were her only weakness.
Stubbornly, she maintained that her lessons got in the way of
her body's physical development, so she simply disregarded her
education. No amount of badgering from their parents registered
or overruled her dogmatic focus on athletics.

Dusty was just the opposite of Inari. He proved early on that
he would devote all his cerebral energies to being a world-class
academic, especially after his third broken arm trying to ride a
bicycle. Case in point, it was the third broken bone combined
with the loss of some of his hand dexterity that got him into
neuralmechanics. If she was brilliant on the physical playing
field, he was a genius in biotechnology. Dusty was the quiet
one of the two, and he was the reason she quasi-completed her

minimal schooling. His pride in her athletic accomplishments had no boundaries, so she kept driving herself harder and farther with Dusty as her only moral support. He was the younger brother that simply did anything and everything his sister needed without reservation.

Dusty's trip down memory lane ended as he noticed her motioning to him for something to drink. He quickly retrieved her standard mix of herbal spices, fruits, and cannabis that was recommended by the local health food store. As he finished mixing the components in the blender, he began feeling angry that anyone would claim this concoction could have neural regenerative powers. He knew that, left in the hands of the usual charlatans, she would never compete again. While a normal human would have lamented the skiing accident and been frustrated with her broken condition, it only drove him to push the envelope on his biomechanics research so he could repair her damage.

Dusty delivered the concoction and teed it up in her drinking apparatus so she could sip at her pace. While he watched her struggle with the drinking straw, he studied her holistic situation yet again. He could see that her carefully engineered muscle tone was atrophying from the crippling accident, and he was compelled to fix the situation. He told himself he owed it to her to cover for her one more time.

Inari consumed roughly half of the mixture and leaned back to rest from the effort. Dusty smiled at his sister's effort and softly comforted, "That's right, my gentle sister. You rest now. This afternoon I have some more work to do based on a theory that I am close to making a reality. I want to test my new neural chipset to see if we can close the loop between the spine and your legs. I'll make sure not to inflict any more pain on you than absolutely necessary. I feel like we are getting close. I know how much you want to walk again. I promise that I will build the right bio-technical solution for your damaged neural pathways so you can walk and dance just like before.

"I want to warn you, there is going to be a little more discomfort from these chipsets that I need to embed in your spine. I'm sorry that the other ones didn't do what was desired, but I need to keep trying."

Dusty stood up, sighed hopefully and confidently reassured, "You rest, my dear. I'll be back this afternoon with my dedicated team for our next round of biomechanic installations to fix the problem. It won't be long now before we have you doing stunt skiing and demonstrating your helicopter tricks." With that he marched out, filled with a marked purpose to his step.

Director Follbaum and Leena intercepted Dusty as he entered the Health Force lab. As usual, he was oblivious to their presence, already focused on his work and what needed to be done next in his biomechanics research. Leena had to touch him to get him to listen. Dusty, a patient man, would listen to anyone if you got his attention.

Director Follbaum, in his typical hurry to get to the next task, was unaware that people only got small snippets of his time, which was frustrating to them. Leena was always the Leave Behind Person. Shortened to LBP by those working in the Health Force lab, Leena was always left to fill in the missing pieces that Follbaum failed to articulate. Just as Follbaum had gotten Dusty to stand still and talk, his cell chip went off, alerting him to another emergency event requiring his immediate attention.

Follbaum sulked a moment, then stated, "Leena, do the LBP thing for me with Dusty while I deal with this anomaly. I need to get to a full-sized cell phone with decent speakers because the embedded cell chip won't cut it for this call."

As the director strode away, Leena focused her attention on Dusty, who was hell bent for his original intended destination. She caught him by a coat sleeve before he could make good his escape. While she was an attractive, intelligent woman, she simply didn't register in anything concerning his work passion.

Leena admonished, "Dr. Rhodes, I need you to focus here for a minute. The director just got word that some of our research has been leaked out to certain regulatory agencies, and he is anxious not to get sideways with some of their Victorian prejudices. Specifically, we are not to go to our usual sources for test subjects or even look like we are contemplating experimenting on humans, got it? If anyone asks you directly, online or in email, you are to laugh it off and firmly state we are only working with one-cell organisms, not bipeds or quadrupeds, understand? Yes, I know that they are shooting Near Field Communications chipsets into their population next door in Sweden, but the Finns don't have the same lax approach to human biomechanics!"

Dusty puzzled a moment and then questioned, "Why is there a difference between homeless animals and homeless, derelict people? We are trying to help advance the quality of life on this planet by bridging broken neural pathways using special purpose computer chips. If I can understand how this can be done reliably, then I can fix broken people. Why do you want to intercept this?"

Leena studied him hard for a moment, then stated, "I can sell a lot of things to a consuming public, but I cannot sell shoddy research ethics that look and smell like the work of immoral last-century egomaniacs. Am I being clear? Give the director some time to work this situation. Once we have an all clear sign, we can relaunch, but until then you are to keep it theoretical. This is our ordered direction."

Dusty understood she spoke for the director so disobeying her words meant disobeying the director's edict. Dusty wasn't very astute politically, but he understood that a false step in this arena would have the director and all his reports throw him under the bus, then back over him a couple of times for good measure. The prudent approach was to have them believe he was playing along with the director's policy, at least for the time being.

Dusty calmly replied, "Yes, Miss Leena, I understand. Now can you tell me which one-celled organism I can use for my testing purposes that is not covered by some ethical consideration or animal rights group, but big enough to hold a computerized neural link chip the size of a grain of rice?"

Leena folded her arms over her chest and tersely remarked, "Understand, the director needs people of your wit and gender to do his research, but he has me on his staff to deal with you and your tedious mannerisms. Just follow your instructions so you don't lose your playground privileges."

Dusty was frightened by the last comment, which was obviously a veiled threat. His heart rate and breathing accelerated at the possibility of losing his research facility and the potential method to cure his sister Inari. Unable to speak for fear of aggravating her, he only nodded.

CHAPTER 19

New Adventure,
No Fears

...The Enigma Chronicles

Despite the long trip and rigmarole of customs, Gracie was extremely excited to finally be in New York. Sleeping last night was interrupted by all the ideas swirling around in her mind. This was a job she really wanted. Her education credentials had gotten her noticed, allowing her to complete two interviews, one on video. Best of all she'd done it on her own without her family's interference. She sat up in bed and grinned. They were not exactly an interfering family, but they were capable of influence in many places. Though she loved them as much as they loved her, this had been on her own merit and she felt so grown up.

When she'd checked into the Archer Hotel, she felt like a princess. The luxury was apparent in this classy boutique location in midtown Manhattan. Dinner last evening at the Charlie Palmer Steak House was almost as delicious as meals at home, but her parents' current chef had been a real find. The stunning view from the rooftop bar of the Empire State Building took her breath away as did the dazzling lights of the city. Gracie and her twin had traveled to many different places, but being in New York on her own was exhilarating. Checking in quickly with home, she confirmed her arrival and Facetimed the view and agreed to call in a couple of days to share the progress of her new job.

Slipping out of bed, she wrapped herself in the luxurious robe provided by the hotel and opened the drapes to the city. It was still very early, just after dawn, but looking down from her 20th floor suite the city was waking. Glancing back at the clock, she realized she only had two and a half hours to get ready for her breakfast meeting with her new boss, Ingrid. Giddy with delight at what the new day would bring, she skipped to the bathroom to shower and tend to her makcup. She wanted to be the perfect looking professional.

Taking advantage of the rainfall shower head and all the delicious smelling soaps, she washed her hair and body. Wrapping her hair after drying off, she did a critical scan of her image in the mirror. Not for the first time she thanked her parents for great genes. She had the build of her mother, curvy and lithe, yet the dark eyes of her father. From an early age she'd learned how to keep fit and excelled at martial arts taught by her father. Once she had even bested her mother during sparring, but her father was still too quick for her to really take down. Juan Jr., like her, practiced often and they won as many matches as they lost with one another.

Applying a generous amount of the delightfully fragrant lotions supplied by the hotel, she made a mental note to write a note to housekeeping, begging for more. Then she created a cup of tea from the assortment at the self-service beverage station on the counter. Shaking out her shoulder-length light brown hair, the contrast made her eyes seem even darker. In practiced moves she put on her underwear and then dried her hair. Her thick hair took some time to dry, but her natural waves, coupled with the great haircut her mother had insisted on, gently framed her pretty face and graced her shoulders. Satisfied, she brought out the assortment of makeup she'd brought to highlight her pretty facial features. Her mother, Julie, who had taught her, was the master of makeup for both accent as well as camouflage.

With the suit she planned to wear on a hanger within her line of sight, she adeptly applied her foundation and concealer and took extra time with her eyes, carefully selecting the right hues to compliment the multicolor blue fabric and silk blouse. It would go well with the pendant her father gave her for her sixteenth birthday that she never took off. Checking her artful handiwork, she liked her results of being made up without looking like it. More finished, as her mother liked to say. Checking the clock, she had only a scant fifteen minutes before she needed to be downstairs. She quickly dressed, stepped into her pumps, added one more finger comb through her hair, applied a shiny lip gloss, and finished with modest diamond studs to her ears. Feeling confident, she grabbed her handbag, inserted her phone and small notebook along with her room key and hurried to the elevator.

Pleased, she was downstairs with two minutes to spare and proceeded to the rendezvous for breakfast. The charming hostess escorted her to the table, stating that Ingrid had just been seated.

Gracie smiled and extended her hand as she assessed Ingrid. Ingrid was lovely with her blonde hair in a stylish updo. The blush silk suit she wore complimented her ivory skin as well as matched her simple but expensive jewelry and even carried to her lipstick. "Hello, Ms. Carney, I am Gracie Rodriguez. Thank you for meeting me here."

Ingrid smiled at the charming young woman before her, hoping the dread of the future wasn't conveyed by her eyes. Her mask firmly in place for the new task ahead, she greeted, "Hello, Gracie, please call me Ingrid. We are going to be working very closely together and will become good friends. We can work together and still be friends, don't you think?"

"Oh yes, ma'am, Ms. Carney, I mean Ingrid," replied a happy Gracie.

"Please sit down, Gracie. We'll order breakfast and get to know one another. Then it's off to new employee paperwork and so forth. I find that the cumbersome part of a new job, so we must be fortified first."

Gracie grinned and scanned the menu, looking for just the right start to what seemed like the perfect day. They both ordered and started to share a bit about themselves. Ingrid was so easy to talk with that Gracie grew more comfortable by the minute.

"Yes, I'm glad that my team found you, Gracie. I think you will be the perfect addition to our marketing and social media presence. I have some new programs in mind, but want your freshness to ensure the younger generation adopts our financial investment vehicles."

Gracie beamed at the compliment and replied, "I think I can promise you my opinion as you have asked, but I am also a hard worker. I can even contact my friends if we need to do any focus groups."

Ingrid paid the check and replied, "Yes, dear. That might be necessary at some point. But during your week of new hire indoctrination and security clearances, you aren't to reach out. We have some very tight rules regarding internal confidences that you will soon learn."

Rapidly entering information into her cell phone, Ingrid looked up with a smile. "My car will be out front by the time we get there. Let's get going and complete your onboarding process, shall we?"

Ingrid carefully took her cell phone into her left hand and waved it over the waitress's handheld Pay Terminal. Gracie watched as the transaction was completed but nothing registered on the phone, which struck her as odd.

They walked to the hotel entrance like good friends. Gracie was delighted with her new boss. She couldn't wait to finish up the basics and get into a meaty assignment along the lines Ingrid had outlined. She had found the dream job.

The driver opened the door to the car and helped them into the back. They were settled and moving into the traffic with Gracie looking everywhere like a star struck youngster in a whole new world, which was nearly the truth.

"Oh, my dear," Ingrid began, "I almost forgot. I will need your phone with me until you've completed the security clearance portion later this afternoon. It is standard procedure, and I promise I will take care of it for you."

Gracie hesitated in handing it over but knew the security on her phone was state-of-the-art. Ingrid wouldn't be able to get into it, and if she did, the information would be the bogus front Uncle Quip had as the settings on all the family's phones. She smiled at the thought as she handed over her phone.

"Of course, Ingrid. I totally understand, but all my credit card info is stored on it so how will I pay for anything? It uses Near Field Communications so I don't have to carry a credit card anymore."

Ingrid smiled and said, "We'll take care of everything. No need to worry."

The offices of Global Bank were impressive. The décor was modern, with a touch of elegance that likely instilled confidence and awe from customers and employees alike. Ingrid provided a brief tour and commentary on what departments were located on which floors and quickly introduced her to a dozen people whose names she'd never recall.

Their final destination was a small, lovely conference room with a window to the outside. A polished table displayed a laptop, high definition screen, notepad, and a coffee pot with emblemed cups.

"Gracie, this will be your base for this week. There are monitors in this room and in the connecting hallways outside. They are a part of our security system, but I wanted you to be aware that everything is recorded and stored in our remote data center. I only mention it because I know I would be embarrassed if, well, I adjusted my clothing, for example, on camera. The ladies' room is out this door down the hallway on the right, and no cameras are permitted in there.

"Get yourself some coffee or water, and then let's see about you completing the online forms on the laptop. There is also a small test you need to take at the end. It should take you only a couple of hours for this portion, then I will return and take you down for your ID, photograph and bio-scan for our employee database. You won't have any trouble, I know."

Gracie smiled then said, "No problem, I will get right on this. Hopefully I will surprise you and finish in record time."

"I have no doubt, my dear. You will be the best new employee ever."

Taking off her jacket, Gracie grabbed a water and sat down to the task at hand. She completed all of the forms and was grateful her little notebook had her resume copy and banking information for auto deposit of her paychecks. There were numerous questions on her family, her education, her interests, and her ambitions. She applied the background she'd learned from her Uncle Quip in her first year of his tutoring, knowing that was her verifiable persona anywhere outside of her family business. If it ever became a problem, her mother would adjust it, she thought with a smile.

The test at the end covered almost as much as the finals in her capstone course at the university, but she felt confident of her answers when she hit SEND.

A few minutes later, Ingrid came into the room with a grin. "You were right, Gracie, you submitted the fastest and most complete new hire application I have ever seen. You will be happy to know you scored perfectly on the test.

"Now, I am going to take you down for your ID and photoshoot."

Gracie reached for her jacket and Ingrid said, "You don't need that. Your blouse will make a much prettier picture of you, and you're fresh as a bouquet of flowers with your smile. Come, let's get this done."

They went down several floors in the elevator. The door opened to sparkling white walls and floor. Crossing through an archway, they came to an area that felt sterile to Gracie. A pretty older woman wearing grey scrubs smiled and welcomed, "Hello, Gracie Rodriguez, right?"

Gracie nodded with a small smile.

"Good. Right over here, please, and place your toes on this line." The woman indicated a grey line Gracie hadn't noticed on the floor.

"Now stand up straight and smile, please."

When she complied, the photo was done, and Ingrid commented it was lovely. Two more photos of different views were taken just to be certain there was a choice.

"Come sit over here, Gracie," the woman said as she indicated a chair with a small table next to it and another chair in front of a small desk with a cabinet above.

"Miss Carney, you indicated that our Gracie would be traveling to Scandinavia and Asia, as well as Europe, correct?"

"Yes, that's right."

She quickly retrieved three hypodermic needles from the cabinet and laid them out on the table in front of her. "Are you left or right-handed, Gracie?"

Gracie felt slightly apprehensive, but she knew travel often required shots and she had answered what shots she'd been given by date on her formal application. She vaguely thought these were the current requirements for her cities of travel in the near future.

"Right-handed, ma'am."

Pushing up her sleeve some, the woman tied a rubber tourniquet just above her left elbow. "Now hold still, please. This first one stings."

The cold liquid was startling as it was injected, surprisingly, into the top of her hand. At the last moment before the plunger was completely down, she noticed a shiny object, then it disappeared as she felt a sharp sting. She let out a slight yelp and pulled her hand close the minute it was released.

"Ouch, what was in that?"

Ingrid laughed next to her. "Sorry, I should have explained. That was our chip with credit card information for your business expenses. We all have them as more places begin using the auto scanners. We used to make people memorize a 9-digit user ID for identification, then make them generate a 12-digit password to login to their PC's, the backbone network, and gain access to our facilities. Now, the chip does everything for you using NFC, just like your cell phone was doing for you.

"Now for your updated vaccinations, then we'll be off for lunch."

The woman completed the vaccination shots in her upper arm, then applied a very sophisticated patch, almost like a second skin, to the top of her hand where the wound from the chip was.

"Leave this on for at least a week while the healing completes. We wouldn't want an infection to mar that lovely skin. I promise it will not show when healed."

Moments later, Ingrid shepherded Gracie out of the area and led her back to the conference room to pick up her jacket. As they headed to lunch, Ingrid kept up a steady stream of conversation while Gracie was lost in thought. She felt a sense of regret, as if she had just crossed a line where things might not be shared with her twin.

Catching Gracie's attention in the elevator, Ingrid's eyes sparkled with joy, as she modestly smiled and complimented, "Well done, my dear. You are on your way in."

CHAPTER 20

Favors and Sharing, the High Price

Tanja was with her campaign team all comfortably parked in leather chairs, strategizing the next stop on their speaking presentation trail. Randal came into the meeting as unobtrusively as possible. He leaned in quietly and offered, "He's asking for you, ma'am." With that he handed her the special Q-bit-based cell phone with its hyper elliptical encryption chip, which gave private conversations anonymity everywhere.

Randal stood back up and gave a dismissive glance to her campaign team, indicating that the conversation needed to be suspended for now. Some of the team members frowned at being interrupted, but all quickly gathered their planning materials and filed out, leaving Randal to close the door.

Tanja studied the phone with ambivalent feelings that included contempt, annoyance, but also some fear. After all, she was to be the chairman of the party and destined to be the new leader of the ruling aristocracy in this jumbled country. Ever aware that she was owned by him with no way to outmaneuver him, the time delay in returning the call was the only way to demonstrate her defiance. Like every high-spirited horse, she bristled at having a bit put into her mouth to steer her in the direction dictated by the master.

Tanja sighed slightly as she launched the encrypted phone call. After several rings he answered, "Ah, there you are, Madam Tanja. Please remind Randal that in the future when I summon you for a call, it is to be considered urgent. I never call on casual terms just to chitchat."

He allowed time for her to swallow hard at the polite dressing down before getting to the actual topic.

"I need an alteration to the campaign trail you are engaged on. More specifically, I require you change your route in case I need some support. If needed you will be required to help with damage control. I will convey the specifics at that point. Count on additional events with a more aggressive schedule."

Tanja unenthusiastically asked, "By damage control do you mean to kill somebody?"

The voice took a moment to digest the near sarcastic question. "I sense a weak acceptance of the assignment, with noticeable ambivalence to the required outcome. Perhaps I should offer more motivation to the equation, say, for instance, your daughter's next round of treatment."

Tanja's eyes widened. Her mind flashed on the reason her daughter was in her crippled state. If she hadn't insisted that her milquetoast husband take Wendy home that night, she wouldn't have been in that horrific car wreck. He thankfully died, but Wendy survived for a reason, and now Tanja had to protect her no matter what. Tanja noticeably shuddered. She wanted to show her willingness to make the assignment a success. Tanja blurted, "Don't take it out on Wendy! You promised me she would walk again if I delivered what we started!"

A few seconds of eternity elapsed until he stated, "We have no intention of altering our agreement. But it is important to hear conviction in your voice, Madam Chairman. Enthusiastic workers are so hard to come by these days."

Struggling with the terror of the situation, she finally asked in a whisper, "Will you let me see her again…please? So much time has passed since…"

The characteristically long silence lasted just long enough to drive home how desperate her situation was when he concluded, "We don't think the timing is right just yet to reunite you two. You have an important task to complete, and Wendy doesn't need the distraction before this next round of treatment. Don't lose sight of your focus and this request, madam. Much depends upon it."

With that she looked down at the phone that displayed the simple message:

…End transmission…

With Leena in tow, Follbaum hurriedly moved into Dusty's lab to alert him to the news. As was typical, Dusty was fully engaged in his research, so much so that he was absentmindedly munching on a tuna fish sandwich that could have been left over from either the day or week before. The first clue was when he turned to face Follbaum and Leena to greet them. The stale, old tuna fish sandwich, still somewhat parked in his mouth, announced itself with enough force to bring them up short, gasping for fresh air.

They turned away struggling to breathe from the foul fish odor. Dusty puzzled and asked, "What? What?"

Both Follbaum and Leena were somewhat composed, but at a safe distance.

Follbaum chokingly stated, "Dusty, whatever you're eating, don't! Your breath has been weaponized by dangerously old fish bait! Go flush your mouth with some antiseptic germ killer right now. Then we can stand to be in the same room as your breath!"

Dusty, not quite comprehending the events or that he might even be eating something poisonous, asked, "Is this important? I am in the middle of some research planning that is required for…"

Follbaum had to step farther back, and Leena sensed it was her turn to try to communicate, so with all the effort she could muster stated, "We've been given a new test subject that needs your neural chip implant to walk again…" Leena's gag reflex, about to overtake the contents of her stomach, caused her to back off to a safer distance.

Dusty brightened and enthusiastically replied, "Why didn't you say so? Let me get a conference room and one of my staff so we can whiteboard out the details.

"Hey, I've got some sandwich leftover if you're hungry. I'm full, but I hate to see food go to waste. I'll be right back."

Follbaum and Leena stared uneasily at each other while their stomachs settled down. Irked, Leena finally said, "I don't care how brilliant he is or how much you pay me, I'm never going to lunch with him! Doesn't he know the difference between toasted and last week's stale bread?"

Follbaum commanded, "I want the facilities people sweeping the lab area twice a day for uneaten food that should be removed to hazardous waste containers and not consumed by hygiene-clueless lab rats!"

Leena turned her head around to watch the highly animated Dusty and casually remarked, "Do we need to have a stomach pump handy for mister toxic waste consumer?"

The sour face on Follbaum accentuated his feelings. "Naw, he'll just consume some other toxin to counteract the last non-sense he's eaten."

Leena acknowledged with only a nod.

CHAPTER 21

Family Can Protect
Your Back

...The Enigma Chronicles

On the bumpy flight to São Paulo, Juan Jr. had been reading the documents provided by Uncle Quip and his mother. The material hadn't been loaded onto his laptop prior to departure due to the contents they'd recently assembled. The laptop had only that data and information needed to maintain his cover while visiting his aunt and uncle. The additional details informed him of some other incidents the R-Group was watching just in case he uncovered additional relevant details. He had been given his encrypted drop box to deposit all information he uncovered.

Juan Jr. wasn't bothered by the turbulence during the flight. He and his sister were licensed pilots trained by their father. If even half of the stories their dad related during the flight training was true, then this flight was a piece of cake. Juan Jr. had flown as copilot several times with his dad, even to visit Brazil, but commercial was deemed the best avenue during this assignment.

Thoughts of Gracie crept into his mind as the plane started its descent. He'd not been able to talk about the assignment with Gracie. No one wanted to disturb her during the onboarding process she expected to take place for the first week or two.

Perhaps, if she was able to get a position without family intervention, he might too, after this assignment. Juan Jr. and Gracie had spoken several times about whether they wanted to be a part of the family business or not. The pro and con list on that subject had gone back and forth with each of them arguing one position then another over the last year. It was their decision. Juan wasn't certain if this assignment was a gentle push by his parents to step into the shallow end of the job pool to see if he liked it.

Working his way through customs relatively quickly, he was delighted at seeing his Uncle Carlos just outside the security area. Juan reached out to shake hands like a man, and then Carlos enveloped him in a manly hug and clap on the back. Carlos was slightly taller than his brother, but with the same muscled frame. His raven-black hair was greying, and he had more silver in his mustache than Juan recalled. He was deceivingly easygoing, but Juan Jr. knew this would be the second-best man to have beside him in a fight, his father being first.

"Welcome, Juan," greeted Carlos. "So good to see you. I see you brought enough luggage for a month! Aunt Lara is at her office but will be home early for supper. Did you want to practice combat driving here with the trip home, or wait for a couple of days until you get acclimated? The drivers are still crazy, but it is your choice."

Juan grinned and replied, "I can wait for a couple of days, but it's good to know your insurance will cover me, Uncle." As an afterthought Juan innocently asked, "Will this be like a video game? If we get killed on the way home, can we use another life to continue to play?"

Carlos laughed. "Ah, so the stories of your driving aren't exaggerated. Good to know. Come on, the car is this way."

Carlos had been surprised at how grown his nephew was since even last year. Juan Jr. was nearly as tall as Carlos, but not totally filled out, leaner and sinewy. His jet-black hair and skin tone showed his Mexican heritage, which filled Carlos with pride, even with the blue eyes he earned from his mother. Carlos grinned as it appeared Juan Jr. had not yet had to shave daily. After the long flight he had no hint of a shadow on his cheeks. He looked forward to their sparing together and wanted to check how much his brother had taught him. The sparring partner Carlos found locally, Pedro, was good, but not like his brother or even Julie. Tomorrow morning, they might try some gym work to see how much his brother had taught the lad.

When they reached the car, Juan stowed his luggage in the back seat and they both got in and buckled up. Once outside of the airport Carlos started the conversation.

"Tell me all the news of the family, Juan."

"Papa is doing great and in the process of training a couple of new candidates for their business. Mom still likes to go on assignment. She really wanted to do this one instead of me, but felt a fresh pair of eyes might see differently.

"Gracie went off a few days ago to New York City. She landed a new job on her own with Global Bank. She thinks it will be mostly a marketing position, but analytics will come into play as well. They actually found her background from her university and asked her to apply. The process was several weeks long and she didn't even tell the folks until the offer was made. Mother was a little concerned, but did her normal background checking, like she does with everyone that comes anywhere close to us, before allowing it. Papa wasn't thrilled about his darling Gracie going on her own to the big city."

Carlos looked a little concerned, as he recalled a tough time he and Julie had in New York City many years ago. That was a tough city, but Global Bank was in Manhattan, not in the outskirts where he ended up. He also knew neither Julie nor Juan would allow their children to knowingly be placed into danger, even if they were grown.

"I bet not. That is his little girl no matter how old she gets. I probably would have been right there with her for a couple of years if she were mine."

Juan Jr. knew that his aunt and uncle had wanted children, but it wasn't meant to be. Gracie and he used to come to Brazil for a month in the summer and one in the winter to visit with who they liked to say were their Brazilian parents. His Aunt Lara was one of the sweetest women in the world. All of his cousins loved coming to Brazil to stay and be spoiled just a little.

Juan chuckled and said, "When I left for the airport, he was trying to find any excuse to go to New York. A little persuasion from Mom and he agreed to work on training the newbies for now. I think there will be an anniversary trip for my parents soon to see a Broadway show or something close enough to see Gracie.

"Uncle Quip and Aunt EZ are doing fine. My younger cousins are in classes right now. Aunt Petra and Uncle Jacob are on a trip, Thailand, I think. Pleasure, with some business. I saw my Grandpa Otto and Grammy Haddy a month or so ago. Their retirement home is so beautiful. All those two do is hold hands and smile at one another, unless we are playing cards. Then they beat the pants off us."

Carlos laughed at the picture Juan Jr. painted. It had been a while since he had seen them himself, but he could see them doing just that.

"Julie said I was to teach you everything about the latest cloaking techniques we have working and why. As I had explained to her and your Uncle Quip, these days the signals are changed more frequently. Your Aunt EZ and I have continued to work on mastering the algorithm shifts using the programs of your Uncle Jacob. I will show you some of the new signals I am intercepting from the influx of drones in Brazil and in other isolated areas of South America if you are interested."

"That would be awesome, Uncle Carlos. I had a drone for a while but Mom made me get rid of it when I had it taking pictures over neighbors' property. That was when I learned the big message of respecting others' privacy. Boy, I'll never forget that lesson."

Carlos arched an eyebrow and chuckled. "Did you have to take the pictures to the neighbors and apologize?"

Juan turned a deep shade of red as he shook his head and said, "Oh no, Uncle. Several girls were sunbathing around their pool, well, um… nude you see. Mom found me uploading the pictures and flipped."

"My boy, I see you're cut from the same cloth as your papa and me. Got to keep your uploads private, which isn't easy in your family."

"You're right, Uncle." Juan laughed a little and then suggested, "Do you think Aunt Lara would want some help at a local shoot with her fall fashion line up?"

"Let me guess. I bet you are willing to carry wardrobe boxes or set up dressing areas, just to help out."

"Exactly what I was thinking."

Carlos studied him a moment, then with a furrowed brow stated, "Well, Lara will need some help with getting the models changed quickly for their next shot. You know, get them out of one set of garments and into another, ready to be photo'd. If you're interested, it's €200 a week."

Juan Jr., struggling with the obvious benefits of such a dream job, finally blurted out, "Uncle, I'm not sure I can afford that much!"

Carlos laughed for a bit then admitted, "Yep, you're cut from our fabric, nephew. Apparently, you have your father's quick wit as well. Don't think Aunt Lara won't see right through that request.

"Let's get some of your new lessons into your wayward mind first."

Juan grinned as they pulled into the driveway.

CHAPTER 22

A Texas Yellow Rose

Isolation and mountainous terrain were the saving graces of El Paso County, Colorado. Lieutenant Bough, or Tony as his friends called him, grumbled as he safely found his way to another cavelike indentation, which provided protection from the persistent drones. Escaping through the myriad of access tunnels was only possible while the invading drones were focused on the 25-ton blast doors. After his initial escape from the bunker, Tony had stripped off all his electronics, except for his HP1149 analog watch with compass and thermometer. He redistributed his lightweight Mylar blanket, water bottles and dried food packets under his clothing. Since he was one man on his own, he'd hoped to avoid detection. No drones chased after him, but the fear was enough to keep his legs moving, dodging from tree to rock in a haphazard trek.

Camouflage clothing would only protect him from the visual sensors of the drones. Heat sensors were the next biggest detriment to his escape, hence he moved from one deep indentation to another. When he slept, Tony cocooned himself inside his anti-radiation blanket to help minimize his heat signature. The only landmark he continued to keep at his backside was Pikes Peak. Tony was never so grateful as now that he had led his team more than once across this unforgiving terrain in one- and two-week drills, averaging 100 miles per day. His goal was to get out of the range of the adjacent Airforce bases and locate US Highway 24. JOAN wanted power and military control, not the average farmer or rancher in these mountains.

Rationing his provisions over several days and keeping to a northeastern direction, he bypassed Limon and made his way past the small town of Arriba to the I-70 Diner in Flagler. He'd heard tell of the diner but have never visited it. Laughing at the bubble gum pink corvette out front, he was surprised at the interior with its 50s motif, complete with black and white cow-spotted swivel chairs. He suspected he was between breakfast and lunch as he had the diner to himself.

Selecting his table in the back most corner facing the door, he asked the waitress if he could leave his things in the chair and wash up. Tony performed a quick sponge bath and removed his outer camo exposing only a tan t-shirt. His beard growth was longer than he'd expected, making him appear less military even with the short haircut. When he returned to the table, he was pleased to see nothing had been disturbed. Betty, his waitress, introduced herself when she returned for his order. Her big eyes, sweet smile, and short black hair reminded him of Betty Boop, which seemed appropriate for this diner venue. Studying the menu of highlighted chef's specials, he opted for the Southwestern HOBO breakfast of potatoes, chili, eggs, meat, and cheese, with a chocolate milkshake topped with a mountain of whipped cream. Betty complimented his selection as she took off to place his order.

The milkshake arrived in advance of the food so he savored the first sip. When the food arrived, he said, "This is one great milkshake, Miss Betty. I may have to order another. It is like none I've ever had before."

Betty smiled as she set down his food and then replied, "We make them fresh with real ice cream. No prefab machinery here.

Richard, our chef, would never allow that. Enjoy your food, sir. Signal if you want anything else."

He ate his food slowly, enjoying the flavors and seasonings. As hungry as he was, he didn't want to eat too fast, but he was glad that it was fresh, not like the dried jerky he'd run out of last night. Perhaps he would take a roadie portion along. Halfway finished with his food, he noticed three 18-wheelers pull into the parking lot and then move to the side to not block the entrance. Minutes later four men and a lone lady walked in jovially, but not together. The men went to a 4-top at the other end of the diner and the lady sat up at the bar.

Betty took coffee to the men and rapidly took their order. By the greeting and smiles, Tony thought they must be regulars. Betty turned in the order and then focused on the lady at the bar. Tony noticed she was about 5' 6" when she walked in. Her cinnamon-colored hair was short and curly, framing her pretty oval-shaped face, with glossy lips highlighting her very white teeth. She was trim in her jeans and navy colored t-shirt. The back of her shirt was decorated with a couple of worn peach graphics and the words, Don't Mess with Texas.

"Hi, Rose, where you headed?"

"Hey, Betty. I have a run to Philly, then hopefully I will find a load to come back with. You know, I just needed to be on the road again. Dad has his girlfriend at the house, and she promised to look after him."

"I can understand that. Next time you're back for a few days, let's go over to Limon and catch a movie. I could use some girl time.

"Now, what can I get for you?"

"Yep, we need to see a movie. That actually sounds fun. It's been ages since we went out for girls' night. Not bringing Dad's girlfriend along, period. Her squeaky nasally voice gets to me.

"I'd like to have the BLT and fries with a side of mayonnaise, please. Iced tea would be nice."

"That won't take long at all. Will you be wanting an order to go as well?"

"Let me think about it."

Betty smiled at Tony and arched an eyebrow as if to ask if he was ready for that second milkshake. Tony shook his head and gestured to his half-full plate he continued to work at finishing.

Betty's pace had picked up as she served the men in the back and took orders from two more tables as they filled. He watched Rose enjoy her food. She had turned at one point as if sensing his interest and nodded toward him. No smile, just a nod. Tony finished his food and decided another shake and burger to go was in order. Betty was at the bar serving two new guests and refilling Rose's tea, so he decided to walk over and place his order.

"Betty, may I get another one of those milkshakes and a burger to go, please?"

Betty grinned at him and replied, "Sure thing. It will be a minute; I'm a little busy."

"No problem, take your time."

After Betty walked away to service other customers, Tony decided he had nothing to lose.

"Excuse me, ma'am. Are you driving one of those rigs out there? Do you know if those guys in the back might take a passenger along? I can pay. I am trying to get to Virginia. My car was toasted coming up the hill, and the billowing smoke told me nothing short of a new engine would do."

Rose looked him over and sized him up rather quickly. "Do you have a pass to be off base, son?"

Tony looked a bit chagrinned; he hoped she was just guessing. With some indignation he retorted, "I'm a base contractor and don't need permission to go anywhere. I just had a car that had

200,000 miles on it, and it gave up the ghost. Never you mind. I'll go ask them myself."

Rose chuckled and replied, "The men I walked in with are two trainers along with their two rookies doing driving tests to gain certification. They can't take you as a ride-a-long. There aren't any dealerships around here for you to buy a car. Plus, you obviously overheard me tell Betty I have a run to Philly.

"If you aren't a deserter, are you a felon?"

He looked her square in the eye, really hoping he had not underestimated her, and said, "No, ma'am."

"Then order a second burger to go and another milkshake, strawberry for me, and I'll take you at least as far as the next gas stop and reevaluate if you continue with me or find another ride there. Don't try anything funny because I'm ex-military, and I shoot first then ask questions. Of course, being a Texan first might have something to do with that as well."

He grinned as he placed the order with Betty. Then he turned to his benefactor and smiled as he introduced himself. "Ma'am, my name is Tony Bough, friends call me Tony. I promise I wouldn't hurt you unless you hurt me. Thank you for your kindness."

Rose laughed. "Kind, hell, I just wanted to supplement the cost of my trip, and it might be nice to have someone to talk to on this long haul."

CHAPTER 23

A Real Value-Added Treasure

Ingrid was always trying to be proactive in her business dealings so this was no exception as she dialed into the weekly bridge three minutes early. It was always a disadvantage to join late, starting on an apologetic note. Her hair, swept into a fashionable chignon sporting a modest ruby-bejeweled clasp, complimented her charming Nora Gardner red sheath and reversible power jacket. She was set to compete. As the video came into focus, her smile was firmly in place. The shadowy form of the leader filled the stark white background.

As no facial expression was discernable, his voice took on a more commanding resonance. "Ingrid, good to see you on time for our meeting. Report."

"Good day, sir. I am pleased to advise you that Gracie Rodriguez has nearly completed her indoctrination period. Her testing in the various areas has exceeded my expectations, proving her to be a most excellent addition to my team. She is even beginning some small marketing development plans ahead of schedule. Her hand has healed, and internal testing shows the tracking to be perfect, both internal to this building on all floors and to her current hotel accommodations."

"Excellent news. The team has reviewed some of the outlined marketing, and her fresh approach will hit the intended masses of the under 35 crowd, especially in the US and UK markets. Have her document some planning, targeting the Asian markets, and let's get a good look at her research skills. She will take a trip to the region before the end of the month.

"Was there anything on her phone to be concerned about? Before returning it to her, you need to make certain it has no issues. Her new flat will provide a bit more freedom, but all the electronics are almost fully in place. Based on your impressions of her likes and dislikes, the flat should feel like home the moment she arrives. Of course, minor changes could be made at your personal expense for any inconsistencies."

Ingrid nodded agreement and waited a moment before her next point. "Of course, sir. I plan to take her to her new location over the coming weekend. We have a new guard, whom she has not seen yet, set up as her next-door neighbor. He will keep an eye on her while at home as well as the flat when she travels. If he does his job well, Bill will become her closest friend outside of me. I know once she receives her phone back, she will contact her parents to say she is fine. That will be one interesting conversation to eavesdrop into."

"Agreed, Ingrid! I want you to set her up for a one-week trip from New York to Tokyo and back so we can test her ability to talk to new people, solicit new ideas from the target market as well as track her ability to keep to our schedules. Feeling self-determining and actually being independent are very different, as you well know. She should know the travel spending guidelines. Let's see how she adheres.

"Our AI supercomputer modeling clearly shows a change in demographics and attitudes here in North America. I want some field reconnaissance from her sweep of these Pan-Pacific destinations to see if we are on target to capture this country's mindset. In particular, we must see if our target market is only money-motivated or more altruistic in its thinking. Much of our campaign depends upon which motivational issues we should key on."

Ingrid solemnly nodded. "This week will be her first look at her net pay, which will help us to understand if Gracie is money-motivated like many of her peers. The shopping for her travel wardrobe ought to also flush out those items. I reviewed the contents of her hotel room. She has well-made clothing by leading designers out of Europe, so I suspect her mother is advising her. Her jewelry is also well made but not so expensive as to make her a target. I couldn't have advised her any better.

"She is routinely working out in the hotel gym, which is our only blind spot of her activities. However, based upon her appearance when the hall cameras pick her up on exiting, she is pushing herself into quite the sweat. Then 45 minutes later when Gracie walks out toward the office, she appears to have come right from the cover of any fashion magazine. Youthful, vibrant, and well put together is Ms. Gracie. I believe she will be a better asset than I had imagined, so thank you, sir."

"Like any asset, Ingrid, don't squander it!" And the transmission ended.

Ingrid sat back in her chair and expelled a deep breath like one who has been in a very tight spot. "That went well," she mumbled to herself as she closed her eyes briefly to gain strength to continue her work.

A gentle knock indicated a visitor. Ingrid sat up and smiled as she announced, "Come in."

Gracie opened the door. "May I come in, Ingrid? I have some new statistics I wished to review with you along with my findings."

Ingrid stood and walked over to the work table adjacent to her desk area. With a hand indicating the desktop was hers, she added, "Of course, Gracie. Good timing actually. I'd like to see what you've put together."

Confidently Gracie walked to the table and spread out her storyboard as she launched her computer with the data revealed. "Assembling all the data from the target demographics in Asia, beginning with Japan and weaving in Thailand and India, I focused on both genders as well as those who are employed in any capacity. If our goal is investments, then it made sense to begin with those parameters, which we can further filter as needed. The data set from India was such that I filtered out those who were still supported by parents into subsets to review later."

Ingrid looked at the data and then peered at the storyboard. "What are you doing with this storyboard? It appears to only be a six-month view."

Gracie grinned with confidence as she explained, "It is actually a bit too much time in the plan as the attention span for most people is more like 60 to 90 days. However, I also wanted to indicate we would track the follow-on time for friend adoption, viral incidents, and then essentially a marketing effort with legs, with us controlling the messaging. We won't need further messaging investments, but rather simply agreeing and recycling the ever-improving statistics.

"The play at the 90-day mark is along the lines of, 'If you like the results Judy received, you too can take advantage of that and leapfrog to this.' Not only are a majority of people in this category great at adopting the herd guidelines, they will still feel like they have a competitive advantage in getting our daily messaging. In that way you can frame the exact message content on the fly to improve one stat over another. Quite simple, actually. We just need to make certain the messaging fits your end goal, Ingrid.

"I realize I do not know all the messaging you want adopted yet, but this approach for these demographics will help. I also noted at the end of week one that we have a game, functional on any handheld device, for those who would like to consider the options or have already opted-in and want to see their progress compared to a thousand of their closest friends on the top three social media channels of their choice. This allows us to gather even more information about the investors and their friends."

"Gracie, I think you are spot-on. Let's continue down that path and take it to the next level. I will set up travel for you to visit our associates in region for a presentation."

Gracie beamed as she continued with a bit more detail until they broke up for the day. Ingrid suggested a new restaurant.

Julie was so pleased Juan had joined her in Zürich. It gave them a chance to catch up on work and each other. Julie had wanted to work from here, and Juan decided to let Brayson take the lead for a couple of weeks. He was one of the most mature on the team, with his lovely wife Lily one of the newest recruits. They had been eager to prove themselves in the leadership role for the CATS Team and, in Juan's opinion, were ready for the opportunity.

Julie's face showed a bit of worry as she continued the conversation with Juan. "Juan, I know it has been a while since we spoke to Gracie. Look, you know if she had any problems she would've reached out for help. We both knew that during her first two weeks speaking to her would be out of bounds."

Juan rubbed his hand across his jaw as if trying to relieve his tension when he stated, "I know that, but I do miss hearing from her. Honestly, Julie, the last three times I called, it dropped immediately to voicemail. What if she is injured, her battery on her phone exhausted, or worse!"

Julie looked almost surprised as she replied, "You called? Juan, you knew better. What if it gets her into trouble?" Then, as if a second concern suddenly came to mind, she added, "You used only the secured number, though, right? We don't want their scanning sources to locate our source point, remember?"

Juan nodded and said, "I followed the rules, except for the one about not calling. I heard a part of her greeting and didn't leave any messages, as promised, though it was against my better judgment."

Julie reached over and patted his hand, which caused Juan to wrap his arm over her shoulder and pull her a little closer. They reached for their wine glasses and looked one another in the eye as they clicked a silent Salude!

"I did speak with my brother today, and I am pleased to report Juan Jr. is doing a great job at mastering the newer communications techniques. I am so glad he is like Carlos in that regard."

Julie grinned as she replied, "Yes, indeed, that mirrors what EZ said earlier. Our children are definitely amazing." Julie settled back into Juan and sipped her wine, running over what she planned for him later.

Juan glanced over at the love of his life, deciding to start with an extensive back rub after their shower, then suggested, "Darling, I was thinking it has been a while since we have taken a romantic weekend away. And I know how much you love a good show…"

"Juan, are you finally taking me to Paris for the Bateaux Parisiens Dinner Cruise that starts at the Eiffel Tower? We have yet to return to that lovely city since the tower was refurbished. Can we stay at one of the new places along the river too? I know they are so pricey but," she paused and looked a bit mischievous as she continued, "I will have you all to myself. What a great way to ignite our fire. Oh my, I will have to get my hair trimmed, perhaps colored a bit to sparkle off the lights. When, darling, when?"

Juan, immediately drifting into the fantasy Julie painted, envisioned Julie with lights of Paris reflecting off her all night long and pulled her closer into an embrace that always led to delicious lovemaking between them. Kissing her neck, he murmured, "We could easily stop in the City of Lights, my love, on our way back from New York. The newest Broadway show opening this weekend is really getting rave reviews."

Warming up to his tempting kisses and associated strokes, she kissed him deeply, running her tongue over the edge of his lips as she quietly whispered, "No New York until she calls, honey."

Getting into the passion he realized would soon shut down his thought process for some more endearing activity, he replied, "We'll see."

CHAPTER 24

The Professor

Professor Lin, in a highly agitated and somewhat fearful mood, alternated between fidgeting at his terminal and pacing the floor of the glass offices outside the supercomputer room. The anticipated arrival of his new supervisor Madam Zhao, who he was supposed to train, really had him distressed. Colonel Wang was clearly trying to distance himself from Lin but was elbowing his way closer to the project that Professor Lin had stalled.

The colonel hurriedly entered Lin's office and announced, "Madam Zhao is here! Why aren't you outside with the others in the lineup? Both our necks are on the line. If she thinks you're in here pouting, she'll report us to the general! Now don't make me look bad. After all, I helped keep you out of trouble."

Lin turned his head and stared incredulously at Wang and retorted, "Helped me? I'm the one who has 20 years running this supercomputer system. I'm also the one who is engineering the next generation space platform supercomputer that will apply all our AI-learnings for the next decade. Now, thanks to you, I have a mere six months to train my replacement, based on a ridiculous recommendation in our AI-applied project."

"Your foot-dragging and holier-than-thou attitude have put our space station defense program behind the Americans by years!"

roared Colonel Wang. "When they came to me and demanded to know why we are so far behind in our space station launch, I told them that you were more interested in collaborating with the Western scientists in hunting for nearby stars with habitable planets! You're lucky that we got Madam Zhao to come be trained by you. Others actually recommended that you retire…or more specifically, be retired. Now I want you to get out there and…"

At that precise moment a sultry, melodic female voice intervened, "Gentlemen, I hope I've not arrived at an inopportune time. Colonel, may I assume that this distinguished individual you are dressing down is, in fact, Doctor Jinny Lin? Professor, I am very pleased to be working with you again. I've always hoped I would get a chance to work with you once more."

Lin lowered his head at recognizing the student he once taught while at the University. "You…"

The colonel backed away from the highly unstructured meeting. It was obvious that he had unwittingly brought together not two adversaries, but two amiable professionals. Once he sized up Madam Zhao and began to comprehend her well-sculpted female figure, he speculated that there might be more going on here than he expected. He ground his teeth in the realization that this was his failure.

Zhao broke into an impish grin across her rosy lips. Her captivating ebony eyes and dark eyebrows, matching the long black hair restrained behind her neck, indicated that she was a well-practiced beauty who understood how to relate to men. She moved closer to Lin. "Thank you for not failing me on that course."

Still uneasy and with a somewhat icy demeanor, Lin waited, gathering his thoughts. "Madam, you earned a C-, which was enough to pass the class. I gave you nothing you did not properly earn."

Chuckling slightly and bending her head in deference, she replied, "I was so used to being given my way, based on my looks and my uncle. I was completely taken aback when you pulled me up at midsemester to tell me I was failing. I almost stomped out of the room when you offered to tutor me to help pull my grade up. I learned a lot about people from that class and about myself. I never wanted to be handed anything I didn't earn after that. Again, thank you, Professor Lin." And with that she stuck out her hand to shake his.

Colonel Wang slowly closed his eyes, realizing he had brought in an advocate rather than an adversary for Lin.

Once the ritualized greetings and remembrances had been completed, Madam Zhao slipped into a new, rigid persona of the high-tech world and icily stated, "Professor Lin, the AI-enhanced space station is at least six months behind schedule. I was sent to collapse the current time estimate and bring the project back on target. Our country is behind the major Western powers in orbiting our defensive space station. Until the timeline is shortened, no one leaves the compound. All personnel will live here, and we will work around the clock to defend our sovereign air space. All our personnel's families are to be…relocated in government housing for their protection. If suitable progress is made, then video call privileges will be granted. Make no mistake, Professor Lin, this facility is in lockdown until we can demonstrate a working space station."

Lin shot an angered glare at the colonel, but the silent plea in the weasel's eyes helped Lin to reel in his anger. After a forced stilling of his breathing, Lin stated, "It seems Madam Zhao learned many things after my mathematics course. Apparently, you didn't need any remedial training in coercion and bullying."

After a few long moments of direct eye-to-eye contact, where Colonel Wang was struggling to keep his terror under control, the silent combat of wills between the two seemed to have been ratcheted back.

Madam Zhao finally stated, "That will be all, Professor, for the time being. Colonel, I would like to see the rest of the facilities after a short break, but for right now I will require this office space for my use going forward. Professor Lin, see that you relocate to another, but I require you to be close so we can collaborate quickly and efficiently. Colonel, I see that yours is the closest office, so I recommend that you move out. Now, gentlemen, I need this space to provide an update, so start moving the colonel first while I finish my call. That will be all."

In maddened and bewildered moods, both men trudged off to complete the impromptu orders for space, closing the office door behind them with as much contempt as the glass door could absorb without breaking.

Madam Zhao smirked slightly as she pulled out her Q-bit based cell phone and launched an encrypted call that was immediately answered. Smiling, she offered, "Step one is in play. The ABCs were launched, and I can confirm they are Angry, Bewildered, and Confused at the demands just as we discussed. I am confident that we can shave 50% of the development time off and be ready for launch in three to four months. Will this and my investment be enough to demonstrate my usefulness to the consortium?"

The voice on the other end responded, "Ask me that again once you are at launch ready. We are in a race not only with the Western powers but also our detestable competitor for a premier seat with the MAG group. Getting you this far has taken considerable resources, and, well, it would be most unfortunate if you didn't deliver—for you and your investment. Am I clear?"

Madam Zhao silently acknowledged the threat and disconnected.

CHAPTER 25

Please Keep Me Safe

Fransica had warmed to Jovana's presence as a mother lavishing the love and tenderness that she thought she had lost after her stillborn babes, one of them a daughter. Like always, Maria and Ana had brought clothing and found Jovana a job tending to one of the older residents in the wealthy part of town. Each day when Jovana returned home, she regaled Fransica with the books she read to Madam Marino, the intricate needlepoint pieces she assisted with, and the wonderful meals she shared and even learned to partially prepare. Jovana was, by all reports, a devoted companion to the woman.

In the short weeks she had been a part of Fransica's household, Jovana's outer wounds had healed. Her hair and complexion had taken on a healthy glow with smiles appearing on her face during animated discussions. Fransica was saddened to recognize the smiles never reached the lovely eyes of her house guest. On this Sunday following a morning of worship, they had returned home to do some of the weekly laundry and baking for the week.

Jovana had never failed to do a task and frequently volunteered in advance of any request. She'd trusted Fransica with her weekly wage, which she turned over on Fridays. Fransica had saved every Brazilian real for the girl, knowing one day it would be needed for something. She felt the young woman contributed enough in support of the family without having to extract a payment. Luiz, Petro, Victor, and Gabriel had left to go fishing before church and wouldn't return until after dark with their catch, which left just the two of them to complete the chores.

They had finished forming several loaves of bread and set them aside to rise while they hung the laundry in the warm Brazilian sun to dry and soak in the fragrance of the seasonal flowers. As they were hanging the last sheet, Jovana stammered, "Fransica, I am not certain I have thanked you for bringing me into your home and taking care of me, but my heart is thankful."

Fransica was honored and pleased with the comment. "I am so glad you are with me. I know you miss your mother, but know you are like a daughter to me."

Jovana's eyes glistened with moisture as she sniffled and replied, "My mother would have liked you. I know she would be grateful I found a safe haven. Life was so bad after we were captured and confined. So bad." Her voice trailed off as she squeezed her eyes shut to hold back the tears.

Fransica secured the final corner to the clothes line and then wrapped her arms around the fragile girl. "Are you ready to share those details, darling girl?"

Jovana nodded her head, and Fransica led them to the benches on the porch. As they sat together, she poured tea for them both and waited.

Jovana gathered herself and stared out toward the hills in the distance. The vegetation was lush and green, birds were singing merrily, and the gentle breezes of the wind seemed to stop time.

"Our small village was in the north, eking out a living as travel guides, local craftsmen, and jewelry artisans with our abundant supply of amethyst quartz. My father was a guide people asked for by name and knew all the best places for hikers and campers. He took me on long hikes a few times and the survival skills he taught me helped me survive as long as I did after I escaped. These men came and overran our village and herded us, along with several surrounding villages in the area, to a secluded compound patrolled by drones. Everything we said or did was monitored." Sipping her tea, she took a breath and continued.

"One by one people died from starvation, trying to escape, or hanging on until those potential avenues of rebellion were removed while we slept. It was awful and scary. When food was so scarce that my parents and I shared a stale piece of bread per day along with a handful of berries, I nearly gave up. I was going to tell my parents I was leaving when I found them…"

Fransica gave Jovana a reassuring squeeze and then sipped her tea while she waited.

Jovana stared at the boards below her feet, almost in shame. "They were both dead. Holding hands, but dead. I found a note they had scrawled that they wanted me to have it all as I was their future. But they had no future. They were dead."

"I know they loved you very much, Jovana, to give up all for you. It is what parents do for their precious babies."

"That evening my friends created a diversion further enhanced by a loud storm, and I escaped through the latrines. It was disgusting, and I kept thinking those drones would follow, but I have seen nothing of them. Should I be afraid still?"

Fransica frowned thoughtfully. "We'd heard some gossip from people traveling south through here, but nothing in the detail you are sharing. Nothing from those that come in from São Paulo or other cities near us. Why would you think they might find you?"

Jovana took a deep breath for courage. "I dug out this metal from my hand. That was the wound you noticed when we first met. My father had told me it was the way they kept track of us. It was supposed to transmit our health, state of mind, as well as location. They used the statistics to determine our food and clothing requirements.

"I tell you this now because I want you to know before I leave."

"Leave? What do you mean leave, Jovana? You don't need to leave. I don't want you to leave."

Jovana leaned next to Fransica, who had become the closest thing to a mother for her. "I know you haven't asked me to leave, but Madam Marino is insisting that I accompany her to São Paulo. She has a doctor's appointment for a status check after her surgery several months ago. The doctor wants to verify she is doing her physical therapy, which she does daily while I am there. I am to be her witness."

Fransica was confused. What a great opportunity for her precious Jovana. "That sounds like a nice trip. You'll see a very big city. The first time I saw São Paulo I was amazed at its size, the number of people, and the traffic. Different from anything I have ever seen, but thrilling. You would return in a day or two. I will be here."

Jovana turned her face toward her as tears rolled like small rivers down her cheeks. "Madam Marino related all the new technology that is used in the city these days to control crowds, locate parking anywhere, tell you what you like or don't like, and drones helping the authorities to reduce the crime. Her three rich sons are helping to fund many of the changes being adopted, and she is so proud.

"Crime, she had explained, was the issue which kept the tourists away, and drones helped with matching faces to wanted lists. I will be found out and taken back to the compound. I am so afraid to go. When I told Madam Marino I would rather stay here, she said if I didn't go with her then my job was finished."

Fransica was stunned at the depth of Jovana's fear. Part of her wanted to keep her close while the other part wanted Jovana to face her fears and overcome them. This town was her life, and having Jovana toss the job aside could be poorly viewed, especially by Maria and Ana. "I understand now why you are afraid. Child, I need you to face these fears and move past them.

"Certainly, we are all accepting technology in varying degrees in our life. Your experience is horrific, but I think São Paulo is too big for the sort of problem you faced with your captivity. What if I speak to Madam Marino and gain her approval to accompany you both? Would that make you feel better?"

Jovana brightened. "Yes. If you were along to protect me, I would go. Thank you for listening and finding a solution.

"You sit here, and I will go put the bread in the oven."

With a quick hug and renewed smile, Jovana was off to her next chore.

CHAPTER 26

The Promise of
the Next Experiment

Dusty had worked around the clock for two and a half days, reviewing the files and treatments to date on his new subject, Wendy Slijepcevic. She was ten years old and had been trapped in a wheelchair for almost three years. The surgeon who originally worked on her indicated the nerve endings had been severed in such a way that, even though he had reattached them, they were not sending signals to her brain or her limbs. Wendy's situation was very similar to the condition of his sister, Inari.

Wendy had been transported to his facility two days ago and had been adjusting to her surroundings. Since her accident and last surgery, she'd had the benefit of a full-time tutor and physical therapist to see to her muscles and general fitness. The floor nurse had reported that she was sweet-natured, ate well, loved to read all sorts of books and was actually learning at a high school level. Dusty mused to himself that perhaps he needed to test her IQ in advance of any treatment, so he made a note.

Correlations between Wendy and Inari were good enough. Blood types were the same, and key DNA markers that his experiments focused on were within tolerance. Age differences were not going to impact the treatments, but Wendy possessed a far brighter attitude. After his examination, he might put both of them in the same room to see if that might brighten Inari's spirits. The good news from his perspective was that now he could experiment and not cause his sister anguish during the process. Not that he intended to cause this young girl any problems or additional complications, but he could be more clinical, until he found the right key to the problem of restoring the mobility to their limbs.

When he was reviewing the last set of labs he'd run, he was instantly energized with optimism. He knew that he had not considered mapping the pathways to the damaged area, but rather only the pathways from the damaged area to the neural starting point. Reconstruction of the nerves in total rather than pieces might be the success key he needed. Wendy was smaller in stature, and he decided that using the nerves from the resident primates would be the best first stage. With all these ideas spinning around in his brain, he decided it was time to meet his new patient.

Dusty changed his lab coat and went to meet his new charge. Since money was no object with regard to her care, he could ensure that she would have the same level of education that she had been receiving as she underwent his various treatments. There was roughly three months before he could check on the success of the first trial.

Wendy was positioned in her chair near the window reading a book. She was forced to read traditional books as the page turning was an additional form of exercise. Evaluating her motor skills at every level were key to establishing a complete baseline to compare with. His robotic auto-attendant tracked along with him, and Dusty made some verbal comments that launched some processing in the unit. Smiling as Dusty entered, she carefully placed a bookmark in the book.

Without a hint of fear or apprehension, she greeted, "Hello, my name is Wendy. I'm ten years old and will be eleven in eight months. Who are you?"

Dusty grinned. This little lady would be a charmer. Her long blonde hair had been brushed and then plaited into a braid on each side of her head. Freckles dotted her nose and her mouth formed a small rosy bow shape. Her brown eyes were big and bright, which was another sign of her great health. Outside of the walking issue, she was well cared for.

"I am Dr. Rhodes. I am going to try to help you walk again. You'd like that, wouldn't you, Wendy? Oh, let me introduce my Robotic Onboard Neural Detective & Assistant. I call her RONDA. She is my mobile diagnostic auto-attendant and will be working with us. Now, she doesn't say much but will use her robotic arms for careful scanning of your motor neural pathways. Sometimes people get unnerved with her robotic arms swirling around them, but I don't want you to be concerned. RONDA is the latest generation of biological diagnostics and she's here to help me get you to walk again."

Wendy brightened and, as much as possible, sat up a little straighter and was almost bubbly. "I would love that. If I could walk, I would be able to go back and live with my mommy. I can't stay with her right now because she has such a busy schedule and can't carry me. She loves me very much and wants me safe." Wendy paused as if thinking then blurted, "Is that why she allowed me to come here…because you can make me walk? I will be the best patient you have ever had, Dr. Rhodes."

Dusty looked pleased at his new patient. Her enthusiasm was going to help her a great deal as they traveled this long road together.

"I think that may be why you are here. I do a lot of testing with nerve issues. I have been studying this field of science and neurology for a long time. I think you can help me find a way to improve my techniques and achieve some very important milestones.

"Your condition is one that has baffled physicians for a long time. Once the nerve segments have been damaged or severed, they are difficult to fix. You will have to be strong and patient as we work on your treatments. Sometimes it will hurt, but I will give you medicine to help relieve any pain."

Wendy looked very solemn as she nodded now and again while he continued to discuss some of the treatments he was planning. Some of the words were big and unfamiliar, but he seemed so happy when he was discussing his plans, she didn't want to dampen his spirits. His enthusiasm seemed perfect to her, like her mommy used to be. He kept up a running dialogue as he also completed an exam, including extensive testing of her reflexes. The robotic arms of the fully mobile platform continued its incessant scanning of Wendy while he chatted away to her. Finally, he paused in his soliloquy and studied the digital print out of RONDA's scanning efforts.

"Do you think you would like to work with me to see how much mobility we can gain for you?"

"Dr. Rhodes, I will be a good patient and do as you ask. I just need to have my Annie close to me when I sleep. Annie watches out for me and I hug her close sometimes." With that, Wendy pulled out a lovely well-worn doll with brown hair and button eyes wearing overalls and a pink flowered shirt. She showed Dr. Rhodes her prize and added, "This is Annie. She is my best friend. My mommy gave her to me when I was very little. I keep her with me all the time. Well, except when they give me a bath.

"I would like to be friends with you, Dr. Rhodes. Would you like a cookie?" She pointed to the plate of cookies on the table closer to the window.

When he reached for one, she admonished, "Oh, Dr. Rhodes, you need to go wash your hands first."

Tanja had given four rallies in four major cities: Phoenix, Salt Lake City, Denver, and Dallas. It was an arduous schedule with the entire set-up team needing a day to set up and a day to breakdown. The special sound system for recording and digital communications took half a day with testing. All the staff kept in close contact while she was delivering her messaging with special earbuds honed to each type of worker. No one, outside of Randal, interacted with Tanja while she was at the podium. This prevented unnecessary distractions.

Randal meticulously made certain that her accommodations at each location were lavish suites with connecting rooms for her staff. She was in top shape with her trainer working with her in the mornings. Special food was prepared by her chef borrowing the local facilities kitchen, and she received a relaxing massage after each event. Watching her with the crowds, he recognized that her determination was to achieve the maximum converts from each session. That last contact she had received from head-quarters really seemed to help her gain better focus. Fortunately, she had stopped drinking, as well as demanding he service her, so he could focus on making certain everything was ready for her in the next cities. That was the purpose of their meeting this evening after her supper.

Randal knocked and heard the murmur to enter from the other side. Tanja was recently showered, with her wet hair combed casually, makeup removed, and wrapped in a thick hotel robe. Without warrior paint and customized clothes, she looked almost like a college kid, all fresh and vibrant.

"Sorry, Randal. I knew we were meeting, but I just had to get comfortable." She chuckled and smiled as she said, "And you've seen me in far less. It was a long, tiring show today. I promise, I'll behave. I have to stay on top of the agenda. Thank you for getting the disruptors rounded up and escorted out. I hope they find the peace they seem to lack in their actions.

"Help yourself to the wet bar, then have a seat so we can discuss the next destination."

Randal helped himself to some juice and one of the cookies that sat on top of the counter. This hotel was famous for their fresh cookies. The chef always made certain she had a few on hand. Over the last two weeks, Tanja had focused on her diet and exercise so she could indulge on the cookies available. Randal seated himself at the table so he could spread out the map and other papers he'd brought.

"I verified with the roadies that everything will be packed up tomorrow, and we'll be on the road to our next destination. We are headed east at this point with your next commitment in Chicago. Headquarters had tried to cancel this one, but there were too many folks signed up to attend, so it is a go. We have another set of equipment on the way to New York to be set up for an event the day after Chicago."

Tanja looked crestfallen. "Two shows in two days, are you kidding me? I don't think I can do that. They're simply exhausting, Randal." Lines of tension marred her forehead as tears formed in her eyes, refusing to be shed.

"I know it is a tough schedule, but I have arranged for our private jet from Chicago to New York City to allow you maximum rest. Plus, Chicago will begin early afternoon and only last two hours. This is the change from headquarters, even though I raised a bit of concern. I was told we would receive some additional compensation for the effort.

"Philadelphia and Washington, DC, are the next two destinations in the planning phases, but they have yet to be firmed up with the exact location or order."

With additional enthusiasm and approving tone, Randal added, "Apparently, the ticket sales to your events are sold out within 24 hours of the event location announcement. Social media channels are loving you and when the venue is opened to the targeted market, they go fast. The pictures from today's show have some great shots of you, as well as the crowds cheering you on. The upsell during and following this event were the best yet. I thought it was the best speech so far. You really seem to read the crowd. They relate to you."

Tanja swallowed her previous anxiety and gave a weak smile. "With no overnight in Chicago, which hotel in New York?"

"I haven't received that information yet. I was told it would be the best available."

"Alright. Is there anything else?"

"That's about it."

"Good then. Please let me have my phone to place one short call. You can leave and I will knock on your door when I am finished."

"You know I'm not to leave you alone while you are on the phone."

"Yes, I do. I won't be long though. I just would like some privacy. Is that too much to ask?"

He handed her the phone and walked through the door to his suite.

Tanja connected to the number in seconds. Without the drinking, she found she didn't have the shakes.

M answered, "We have no scheduled call, Madam Tanja."

"Sir, I realize that but I had to know how Wendy is faring. It has been so long since I spoke to her."

"As I promised, her new doctor has completed his exams and tests and seems very hopeful. The treatments are scheduled to begin soon. She is being well cared for and seems to like her new doctor."

"Please, may I speak to her for just a few minutes? I need to tell her I love her."

"Madam Tanja, you may not talk to her at present. I will pass along the message on your behalf.

"Keep up the good work in Chicago and New York. After New York, I will see if we can arrange a short call between you and Wendy. Good night, Madam Tanja."

CHAPTER 27

Me and Rosie McGee

Rose climbed into the cab of the big rig with the ease and confidence of someone who had done it for years. Tony suspected she'd probably taught others. Tony almost managed to climb in with some grace only to realize that he had left all of his gear on the ground outside the truck. Rose eyed him, wondering if she had made a mistake taking on this rookie.

When all his gear and Tony were secured inside the rig's cab, Rose flatly stated, "I brought you along to help offset some of my expenses and to talk to. I'm a long-haul truck driver, and if I get someone else to ride with me then I don't have to wear all those head gear sensors that report when I am getting sleepy and have to pull over. I've talked to some drivers who had sensors monitoring their bladders and calculating the miles to the next potty break.

"This truck is state-of-the-art and always in communication with the routing office computers. Every move I make is monitored by Internet of Things devices. Now when those IoT devices on board aren't snitching on your driving, the road IoT monitors are. Speeding ends up costing me the ability to make these drives. I usually listen to talk radio and hope that some bonehead won't be yapping about some political nonsense. I wanna talk to another human being, but I ain't interested in what the lunatics in political power are doing. I don't wanna hear about which Supreme Being you want to worship or listen to your 'let me convert you' speech. Plus, if the only thing you have any opinion on is sports, then I am not even gonna slow down before I throw you out. Now it's your turn."

Tony looked at Rose and wondered if he made a poor choice in joining her on this long-haul truck. As she clicked through the gears to get the rig to highway speed, he analyzed his circumstances for surviving this bold truck driver's assistance and completing his mission.

He cautiously asked, "You stated you are a long-haul truck driver, but you still have to deal with the IoT sensors in the truck and on the road. Are they going to report that you have picked up an unscheduled passenger? Are you going to have to explain your hitchhiker to somebody or, more specifically, some computer?"

Even though Rose was staring down the road while traveling at the posted speed, she was obviously thinking about the questions being posed. Seeing that there was very little traffic, she kicked on the autopilot to control the truck's steering mechanisms and turned to Tony. "Okay, bub, why don't you just put the moose on the table and tell me what's going on with you? You show up asking for a ride, pretending to be a hitchhiker, wearing high-grade military fatigues with the insignias torn off, sporting a lame story of your car now being a ghost from Christmas past. All the while you're scanning the area for something that you expect is hunting you.

"Now I'm not the sharpest tool in the shed, but none of your story rings true from what I'm seeing. I'm asking again for likely the last time, what's the real poop?"

Tony ground his teeth a moment, then, after a deep breath and a little reservation, stated, "Ma'am, you said you didn't want to hear any politics, or religion, and certainly nothing about organized sports, so that really only leaves existential philosophy or storytelling. I freely admit that I know next to nothing about existential philosophy, so how about I regale you with stories of woe, drama, heartache, comedy, and of course pathos? And as a bonus for your generosity, I will grant you an audience to enjoy my singing prowess by recreating one or more of the most famous songs and heartfelt lyrics from that musical genius, Lonny Lupnerder.

"Surely you know of the tune, 'Me and Rosie McGee'? I can remind you if you will please turn on the windshield wipers so I can have some background rhythm to support my rendition..."

Rose's eyes got wide and her breathing shortened as she asked, "You can sing?! And of all the pieces of music I love the most, you choose Rosie McGee? Alright, here go the wipers and I'm going to join you at the chorus! Here we go, a...5, 6, 7, 8..."

After 50 miles of singing they both stopped to keep from getting hoarse and wearing out the windshield wipers on a dry windshield.

Still breathing heavily from all the singing, Rose turned to Tony and with a flirtatious look on her face coyly asked, "Was it good for you too?"

Rose and Tony sat quietly for a while as the autopilot accurately steered them down the road. Rose checked the automated settings, ran a recalibration routine, and, satisfied that the autopilot and linked IoT sensors were operating correctly, relaxed a little in the driver's seat.

Tony, still a little tired from their singing extravaganza, sat looking down the road ahead of them. Finally, without averting his gaze, he offered, "They're all dead. After I saw what they did to Kinney, I knew we were next. I was ordered out to deliver a message to…isn't that funny? I don't even know who to deliver it to. I just have to get to D.C., or maybe military headquarters, and get someone to believe my ridiculous story. Because that's all it is. Our military grade space station has gone rogue, and no one even knows that NORAD is gone. No one knows we're hostages."

Rose, still alternating between studying the sensors and the road, said, "Hey, Tony, you should know that none of the news sources or even social media news sites are even hinting at this kind of event. Of course, independent news reporting died out when everything went into the Internet. All the tech companies bought up the old guard newspapers, TV, and radio stations and made everything digital. Advertising revenue simply went online where it was channeled toward the news that the big tech companies wanted funded. Then they strained all events and newsworthy stories through their advertising algorithms to get the view of the world they want us to have."

Tony objected. "Hey, you said no politics and that always means no conspiracy theories either! Well, maybe there really aren't any conspiracies and maybe everything is really okay at NORAD. You know, I didn't really see all of them dead. What if I'm the one who is insane?"

Rose smirked. "Oh great! Here I am hurtling along I-70 in an autopilot-controlled 18-wheeler towing 25 thousand pounds of cargo and the hitchhiking character I met a few hours ago admits he's not sure if he is sane or not! You know, between your singing and storytelling, I didn't expect THIS much entertainment for the run.

"I'll make you a deal. At the next truck stop, you make a call back to NORAD to see if everything is hunky-dory. If you can prove your story, then I'll drive you to the Pentagon myself. But if everything is okay, then we part company and you dodge the crazy-catchers by yourself. Deal?"

Tony's face showed all the apprehension he was feeling inside. He quietly offered, "The colonel told me not to call since everything is visible on the open communications lines. If I call, they will know where I am, and I will have failed in my mission. And if I'm just insane, then they will know where to find me."

Rose smiled and offered, "I happen to know they sell burner phones to select clientele just for such a contingency at the next stop. Either way, after the call you ditch the phone and we run like hell."

Tony puzzled at her comment and asked, "We run like hell? You might believe me then?"

Rose smiled in a maternal way. "How can I possibly give up on your story not being true after you singing all those Lonny Lupnerder songs so sweetly?"

CHAPTER 28

Butterflies Are Free, Right?

...The Enigma Chronicles

G racie and Ingrid were enjoying a balmy day in the city, briskly strolling toward their destination with Ingrid keeping up her end of the conversation. "You're going to love your new apartment. Not only is it a prime piece of real estate you're getting at a significantly reduced rate because of your job, but it's furnished too. That's not to say over time you can't make changes to it to personalize your living. Honestly with your upcoming travel schedule, you'll love coming home to something finished, rather than mountains of boxes. Why, when I first moved into this company it took me nearly a year to unpack my boxes.

"I am so glad the weather is nice today. I was hoping we would be able to walk. This way you can easily navigate the six-block walk to your apartment. If the weather is lousy, and it does get that way at times, then it is two stops on the subway using the entrance outside of the office. You have merely seconds of possible exposure to rain or snow. Of course, you can take a ride hailing service if you want, but I have the sense you are fond of exercise, else you would not be as trim and fit as you appear."

Gracie replied, "I do like walking, especially after sitting so much while I am learning. I think you said there is an exercise facility on the bottom floor as well, and I can join, right?"

"There is a gym and spa on the lower level, and I took the liberty of adding your first-year membership as sort of a bonus for completing your training so quickly. Highest score ever too!"

"That is so nice. Thank you. I can't wait to see it."

Ingrid stopped and with a hand gesture indicated they were there. The door on the outside was distinctive with green and gold flourishes and a sign that read Private Residence. Ingrid handed Gracie a key card for entry. Above the key card slot was a keypad with a placard above it saying "Enter the number of the apartment you are visiting." It was simple and the door automatically opened.

"Once upon a time, these buildings had doormen, but automated locking systems are much better to reduce break-ins. If you lose your key card or have a guest, the entry of your apartment number will result in a scan of your face, which will permit your entry or a video feed for you to allow a guest to enter. Since we use your facial recognition for entry into various offices at work, I merely sent that file here, so it's already in place."

"Terrific. Very efficient. I do expect my folks to make a trip here at some point. They are, I'm sure, looking forward to us having a nice chat, and I want to tell them about my job." Then she added, with a smile as she looked at Ingrid, "To the amount I can, of course. Mostly about how much I am learning and fun I am having."

Ingrid grinned back. "I have no doubt you know all the rules and will abide by them in dealing with friends and family. Now let's go to your apartment. The gym is through that door at the end, and it uses facial recognition after you enter your apartment number. No need to carry your key card when you work out.

"Now, your apartment is 1024, which is on the tenth floor."

They entered the elevator and made the silent, rapid ride to the floor. The doors slid open, and they stepped onto plush carpet with dense padding. Soundlessly, they walked in their high heels to Gracie's door. Gracie faced the door, and it opened automatically. Ingrid did take the time to close it when they were both inside.

The entryway was a beautiful tile in crème colors with black grout. Some silk flowers in a mixture of colors were in a glass vase in the center of a small table big enough to hold a purse, key card, car keys and the like. A coat closet was on the right. Sidestepping the table, they walked across the floor with rooms to the left, right, and center. Looking straight ahead, Gracie ventured down one step into an enormous living room. The floor to ceiling glass on the far side opened to a small patio area. The living room was done is cream leather furniture with pillows and throws of various colors. Pieces of art on the walls were done in bold colors, highlighting flowers and impressionistic art.

"My goodness, Ingrid, this is lovely. I really like the colors; they're so vibrant." Gracie rushed to the window and found it was connected to a door which slid to the right, and they stepped out to a patio with a small metal table decorated with colorful butterflies and two matching chairs.

"Gracie, you have a nice view of the small park, and there is a walking trail as well. People will walk their dogs and bring their children, who run and play. You shouldn't hear them from up here, but if the wind was right you could. I think you really lucked out with this view, my dear.

"At the entry if you go left, that is the bedroom, complete with a high-definition screen for all your entertainment. There is another one in this room you can face when sitting at the couch. When it's off it looks like a priceless piece of art. The remote on the side table will allow you access or you can program everything for voice commands. I did not do that as I wanted you to decide your own commands. The card with the finer points to activate that system is on the bar in the kitchen. The kitchen is to the right off the main hall."

Gracie walked around to each of the rooms with Ingrid closely behind to offer comments if asked. Gracie dutifully opened the cabinets, doors, and drawers, finding nothing missing. There was everything she needed to be very comfortable. They walked back to the living room and stood looking out toward the park.

Ingrid patted her arm and said, "Gracie, I know you want to get comfortable, explore your new home and call your folks. I am going to leave you to it. I will see you bright and early in the morning. Enjoy yourself."

"Oh, I will. Thank you for everything," said Gracie as she escorted Ingrid to the door.

After the door was closed, she went to her bedroom and changed. All her belongings had been relocated for her and even put away. That, of course, meant someone had been through everything. Fortunately, she was her parents' daughter and at an early age, she learned to trust nothing since nothing is as it seems. Taking her hand-held mirror and shielding it with her body she walked through each room again as if exploring her surroundings. She identified the location of several listening devices in each of the rooms, with a camera as a part of the high definition screens too. Taking care not to disturb them, she only made a mental note of the location and the frequency of the transmission recorded on her mirror. She would transmit the data at another time after she determined how to mask her efforts. She made a mental note to always be clothed, so as not to be providing a floor show for those on the other end of the cameras.

Gracie quickly programed the devices listed on the card and used common words for activation and deactivation of the light, entertainment center, temperature, window coverings, bath water, and appliances. Lastly, she paired her personal mobile device, Gracie, and her work device, World, to the high definition screens so video calls were just as simple as using her phone.

"Home," commanded Gracie, using voice activation to call home from the living room. Moments later, images of her mom and dad filled the entire screen.

"Hi, Mom, Dad!" she squealed with excitement. "I'm in my new apartment overlooking a lovely park. Can you see my living room?"

Julie smiled and asked, "When did you have time to do all the shopping and arranging? I had hoped I could help you decorate if I get to visit."

Juan added, "It looks lovely, princess. Bright and colorful, like you. Did you overindulge on the credit cards?"

Gracie waved her hand as if dismissing the comment as unnecessary. "I didn't pick out a thing; the company did it all. They did everything before I even got here. Isn't it lovely? And it is so tech-oriented that I just finished doing all my voice commands for my integrated living space. No stone unturned in exploring all the nooks and crannies. You'd be quite at home here. Though it is a bit smaller than your place, but very comfortable. The sofa here in the living room can fold out into a bed if you decide to visit. Though I know how busy you both are.

"How is my brother doing without me to pick on him?"

Juan replied, "Juan is doing fine and visiting his aunt and uncle. They haven't seen him in a while, and he wanted to pick up some ideas on his career from Uncle Carlos. However, I think he was more interested in seeing if he could hook up with a model or two in his aunt's showroom." Juan winked mischievously and grinned.

"I know how much he likes to travel. He will enjoy it."

Julie interjected, "He will. Sometimes he thinks he knows it all, but I think this is a chance for him to grow and expand. Don't know how long he will be there."

"How's your job? What are you doing?"

"The job is so exciting. I am just finished with my training and scored well in all my classes. Even better than when I was in school. I did so well that I earned a year's membership to the gym in the bottom of this building. I am on the tenth floor, 1024 to be exact.

"I am learning so much. I'll get to do some international travel and really use my marketing skills. Do you remember when I had that drink stand outside of your offices and tried to compete with that named coffee shop? The only reason I sold so much was my keen marketing, which I am really putting to good use in this new role. I really can't give you too many details other than I'm going to be great, though the first day or two I was worried."

They all continued with general conversation and laughed at various aspects of their "remember when" stories.

Then Gracie said, "I need to let you go. I am so hungry, plus I want to work out. Talk soon. Love you both."

"Love you too, sweetheart!"

Gracie turned off the devices and left the apartment to go to the gym. She took a towel with her in the gym bag along with her mirror and brush. She pressed the elevator button to go down. When the doors opened a man rushed out, almost running her down.

"Oh, miss, I am sorry. I needed to get to my place. I forgot to turn off the oven, and I don't want my casserole to become a charred cinder."

"No problem. My name is Gracie and I just moved in. You can use the voice command to program the timer so you can start it and leave it."

"Really? My name is Bill. I'm in 1022 in case you want to stop by and teach me. I've been here a month and am really struggling with the technology efficient space. I think I am old-fashioned. However, I did get the Roomba floor sweeper programmed to bring me a beer."

Gracie eyed him, looking for the come on. At six feet with blond hair, blue eyes, and sculpted biceps that hinted at a nice tribal tattoo on his upper arm below the sleeves of his t-shirt, he was easy on the eyes. Sensing a bit of sincerity, she replied, "If I have time after I finish my work out, I will try to stop by for a few minutes. Later, Bill."

Julie looked at Juan after they disconnected and rolled her eyes. "I don't know how much trouble she is in but she seemed a bit off. What do you think?"

Juan clucked his tongue and offered, "I think she is uneasy and has devices in the place she is unable or unwilling to shut down. That 'no stone unturned and everything installed' before she got there was my clue. We checked this place out. Heck, your family has even done business at times with this Global Bank, haven't they?"

"Yes, they have. Petra has been the primary contact now and again for security, but nothing in a year or more. Ingrid has been there for a while, and Otto's notes indicated he trusted her after several jobs with her. It was Tonya that Petra and Otto didn't care for, but rumor has it she moved to Indonesia for a better job.

"My clue was her marketing reference. The only reason she made any money, if you recall, was because we insisted that the team, our customers, and all their friends buy from the kids.

What a hoot. She knew then it wasn't her marketing that was driving the sales, and here she is again telling us there is something else in play."

"Okay, Mom, so when are we going to New York?"

Julie grinned and wrapped her arms around him. "You said there was a show you wanted to take me to and a great new hotel? Let me know, big boy, when you get it arranged.

"I'm going to call Quip and tell him to expect a transmission, and to let us know when it arrives."

She planted a deep kiss and then broke away, leaving Juan standing there with a smile growing on his face at the possibilities of a quick getaway.

CHAPTER 29

Lifestyles of the Rich and Vain

Madam Marino was delighted to include Fransica in their little travel party, especially after she watched how well they worked together in packing for the trip. Madam Marino had an agenda for their two-week trip, which included visiting her sons at their respective homes, taking in the art museums, dining, opera, and shopping.

"Now, Jovana, you and Fransica will be with me, yet sharing a room separate from mine. My sons have lavish homes with guest accommodations that I am certain you will enjoy. What I enjoy the most is that they each have their own taste in style, or rather their lady friends do. None of them are married as of yet, but they each have a steady lady. Jose, Paulo, and Roberto are very busy making new technology discoveries and don't want to have children yet. I long for the grandchildren, but they say they have no time."

Jovana was busy adding some additional outfits to madam's luggage, with three bags nearly packed to the brim. "These outfits will be lovely for the events you outlined on your itinerary. As you requested, I have them packed in order by bag and all-inclusive with your shoes and handbags."

"Ah, that is perfect, dear. When I am with my sons doing something, you can sightsee or explore. There are also lots of entertaining games in each home. I think you will both enjoy your time."

Fransica smiled at Jovana's efforts at packing and discreetly followed along to make certain all the matching accessories were included. "Madam Marino, what vehicle are we using for this trip?"

"Oh yes, you wouldn't know this. One of my sons is sending his car and driver. The driver will assist with loading the luggage. You don't have to move a thing."

Jovana and Fransica completed the packing required for Madam Marino and returned home.

Jovana busied herself packing her limited articles of clothing and toiletries with no conversation. She unfolded and refolded the items several times.

"Jovana, what is the matter? You're going to wear out those items with your endless folding, and I'll have to wash everything again. Here, pack my items on the bed in my room into the same bag. That way we won't lose anything. Plus, you and I can exchange clothes as needed."

"I guess I'm feeling a bit, well…apprehensive now to travel with Madam Marino. Her sons are all wealthy. They live in great houses, and I doubt we will need to launder any of her clothes, and she would still wear something different three or four times a day. I don't want to shame her in front of her sons. I only have my two dresses."

Fransica smiled and chuckled. "Here. Come sit beside me. This is a marvelous life lesson, my dear.

"Now, you have never once mentioned wanting more clothing, or pretty hair clasps, or anything really. You seem content. Madam Marino waits all year to visit her sons and wants to make them think she is doing so well that she doesn't need them. She is much more comfortable here with her friends than she would ever be if she lived with her sons. It is a game she plays to remind herself that her children are grown.

"Madam Marino likes you and has told that to several of her friends. That news travels. You are actually the first person from here she has taken along. Better still, she is allowing me to accompany you as she appreciates how young you are. I, for one, am delighted that I get to travel along. I have not been to São Paulo in a couple of years, but it is exciting, though very big. Even Luiz is happy I get to go, so he can fish longer."

Jovana looked better and smiled as she shyly commented, "As long as you aren't ashamed and neither is Madam Marino, then I will be brighter. I presume there are some dress stores in São Paulo, right? May I use some of my wages and get your advice on a nice practical dress…maybe a new pair of shoes too?"

"I think that would be perfect. I will get a new dress as well if we find the right bargain. Now finish up, we need to fix dinner and be back at Madam Marino's by sunset."

The Competition

The monthly MAG meeting was lively but short. They wanted to have enough time to complete their business and invite their junior partners to the encrypted video call.

Finishing up on an upbeat note, M asked, "Are we ready to chat with the junior members?" With the other two nodding, M gave the voice command to his auto attendant to bridge A-minor and T into the video conference.

When the video screens showed the faces of all the attendees, the newcomer partners were obviously annoyed that the other had been invited. It amused M to see them chafe at the other's presence. He liked positioning from a point of strength.

"Gentlemen, we'd like to hear of your progress on the Chinese space station project. As you are well aware, the timetable for this project has fallen behind our projections and the MAG group is interested in having it back on schedule. Since both of you have operatives engaged in the project, we were hoping for clarity on how the timetable will be accelerated to meet our needs."

A-minor and T both shot alarming glances at each other, first trying to understand the other's motive and secondarily wondering how M knew of each other's operative placement inside the project.

A-minor, wanting first mover advantage, responded, "This is a military project. We are well entrenched throughout the space station project with individuals in key positions. With such a long running history of military personnel on our payroll, I seriously doubt that my competitor, with his Johnny-come-lately infiltrator, will be able to dislodge my efficient organization."

"Your so-called efficient, well-oiled machinery has completely missed the targeted dates requested by the MAG," T interrupted. "Yes, we have taken the liberty to insert our own operative to put the project back on target. Unlike your unimaginative approaches, we don't use military administrators, who've never seen action, in place of a well-known general who has been to war. Your slow-motion finesse only highlights the fact that your methods are outdated. Our AI-enhanced supercomputer predicted your approach would fail. Now only radical steps taken by a more astute organization can bring the project back on schedule."

M held up his hand to halt the banter, which was reduced to glaring between the two men. "MAG agrees that there is room for another innovative player to our organization. The two of you can compete for that position. Quite honestly, there is likely no room in China for both of your groups, thus this competition is for a winner take all. We will reconvene on our usual call next month. We trust one of you will have better answers at that meeting. Good day."

All screens went dark. A-minor as well as T were left fuming about the situation and now the all-out competition for just one seat.

M smiled broadly as he accepted both calls from A and G almost at the same time, bridging all of them into another encrypted conference call.

A questioned, "Do you think it wise to have them at each other's throats when we are trying to get the Chinese space station into a stationary orbit?"

G quickly interjected, "I think the approach is brilliant! By goading them into a race to not only put our objectives first, they will also be trying to orchestrate the other's demise. I can see a scenario where they exhaust each other to a near weakened state. That will set the stage for our reentry into their markets."

M smiled a paternal smile at each of the primary partners. "The market entry is a side benefit of their combat. The Chinese government has been providing extensive funding to A-minor's AI projects for years. What no one realized was that the Chinese government was also funding other smaller startup projects in order to hedge their bets.

"T has been quietly buying up or buying into those AI start-ups for their intellectual property and has amassed a sizeable portfolio of AI technology. T doesn't realize yet that A-minor has been letting bogus AI technology be stolen as a disinformation exercise that could derail T's project if he doesn't discover it. Both companies are fairly evenly matched in their intellectual property redistribution. I want that I.P. rolled into our organization before they completely poison each other's knowledge base."

A smirked. "Yes, they have learned much over the years, or should I say stolen much over the years. I'm sure they would deny it, but both of them have been identified trying to gain access to my core data center technology along with my suppliers. There is even some evidence of intrusion into some of the universities we control, um…work with. They prowl everywhere, hunting what is not tied down or fully secure. This is why the encryption algorithms have become so onerous."

G smiled and nodded, then added, "Every year they have a new crop of hackers come after the keys to the kingdom, but they always leave frustrated. One of my security specialists even left a mock report card with a D- grade for their efforts that they absconded with because it was labeled PASSWORDS."

The chuckling from that story across the video bridge closed the discussion.

CHAPTER 31

Class Is in Session

M adam Zhao sat down, dumbfounded upon hearing the statement. It was almost gratifying for Professor Lin to see the look of total bewilderment on her face, coupled with the half-opened mouth and her head slowly shaking from side to side.

"Um…say that again?"

The green pallor on the face of Madam Zhao, after hearing the information update, was as if she had eaten tainted fish.

Professor Lin carefully repeated, "All of the elements for our enhanced supercomputer are ready. I've completed the finishing touches on the launch program with the necessary milestone dependencies to get everything into a stable orbit over our home country.

"The programing of the artificial intelligence robotics is also complete, which will allow for them to assemble the space station in just under three months, assuming that the solar recharging cells perform as expected to keep the automatons operating at peak capacity. I'm confident that these robotics' indifference to cold, radiation, and not needing to rest or eat will get us to a finished product much quicker than a team of humans could. As long as the magnets on their hooves work smoothly, the tasks can be completed without interruption.

"I do have a small sub-project mapped out to send up with one or more humans, but frankly that exercise is more trouble and more costly than it's worth. Collaborative Holistic Interactive Algorithmic Neural Grouping, or CHIANG, assembly work is ready to begin."

Madam Zhao, now thoroughly irked at the revelation that CHIANG was actually ready to go and the casualness of Professor Lin's manner, dove into a tirade. "You're just now telling me that everything to launch our AI supercomputer into the needed defense posture is actually ready to go into space? All the reports you've sent indicate a completion timeline of years from now! You're either lying now, or you've been deliberately misleading leadership about this project!

"For the sake of argument, let's just say you have been lying to your government all along. Why the ruse? Why admit that you have everything ready now? I do represent the government in this project, so no lying to me."

Professor Lin delivered a small movement of his head to straighten his neck before replying. "To begin with, Madam, I sent all reports to Colonel Wang, and…uh, he apparently groomed them before forwarding to interested government officials. I happened to read one of his final reports and became suspicious of the content being forwarded. After a little digging on the good colonel, I discovered that his rise in rank came from the failures of others. His subsequent fixing of the issues seems to be his method to harvest the praise.

"To be blunt, Madam Zhao, I had no intention of being another casualty in the rise of the colonel's career. He reported what I gave him, twisted so that some responsible government officials would be assigned. Then his distortion of the project would end. His intellect is the kind that prefers a slide rule to a modern-day computer because he can actually see the mechanics of the device as it operates."

After studying him a moment she asked, "How could he have not noticed all the work being done. Or that the project is in fact ready for launch?"

Raising his eyebrows and trying to remain matter-of-fact, Professor Lin responded, "It does suggest that he was more interested in political gamesmanship over insuring that the project worked. Wouldn't you agree? If he were truly engaged in the project and the required work, shouldn't he have seen the progress and questioned the validity of the reports I was giving him? I've even been told, in confidence, he is actively seeking to leave this project. He has been quoted as saying that he 'didn't want to be posted on a sinking ship.'"

Madam Zhao rocked back into her chair to try and digest all of their conversation. After a moment of silence, she smirked slightly and stated, "I may be able to help the good colonel escape the sinking ship. Right now, I want you to walk me through all the CHIANG project plan milestone points to see if all the necessary planning is in place. Then I want to see all the physical components that need to be sent into space. I want to see every-thing, and then I will tell you how close to completion the project is, Professor Lin."

"Madam Zhao, I thought you might make that request. I've arranged for the colonel not to interrupt us while I run through all the launch plans and schematics with their logistics on this 200-centimeter monitor behind you. We will conference in the field engineers who will be able to take a portable video camera to the secure storage areas we will want to view."

As an afterthought, Lin added, "Oh, and please excuse my Professor Lin lecture mode in advance, but I will be using it throughout the presentation. Class, are we ready?"

Madam Zhao grinned, sat up a bit straighter, and perkily replied, "Yes, Professor. Will this material be on Friday's quiz?"

Hours later Madam Zhao excused herself to a quiet area to make a discreet phone call. As soon as the call connected, she said, "We should talk and not on this line. Meet me at the prearranged location in one hour."

CHAPTER 32

Proving the Theories Is Difficult

...The Enigma Chronicles

The problem of splitting time between the original curriculums and monitoring the North American satellite communications was solved by Quip by having the class assigned to two group projects for research and analysis. During the past several days the communications exchanges between the satellites appeared to be erratic, though bidirectional. Nothing from the space station to any land receivers was spotted.

Auri and Satya were assigned the project of mapping the communications times as well as looking for corollary overlays with military or financial shifts in the markets. The thought was, if you couldn't read the traffic then read the action events to calculate a cause and effect. The two had worked with ICABOD to craft some fairly sophisticated programs to interchange data and replot the results. The data mashups were beginning to both eliminate and highlight potential winners as well as losers in the exercise. They'd asked for a meeting in the classroom in an hour to explain their findings.

JW and Granger were taking a look at the worldwide financial indicators to see if there were any investment shifts. Jacob had provided the boys with all of the programs and searches that Great-Grandfather Wolfgang had created. Those methods were not only tried and true but even more relevant to today's economic structures. These kids were experienced programers with the open minds of youth, which Quip felt would offer a different perspective.

Jacob stayed quiet at the back of the room so as not to disturb their program hunting banter. He tended to provide limited guidance when he instructed, but was always quick to intercept wayward programing missteps of the students. He'd fought alongside the R-Group against the Dark Net cyber criminals for years.

Julie, after marrying Juan, had spawned the CATS team as contractor support to the R-Group. The CATS team were not typically a part of training the newer generation of the R-Group, but Julie and Juan were involved in all the children's curriculum. Julie taught cyber sleuthing along with identity scrubbing while Juan provided martial arts training and flight training for small private planes.

Jacob was an accomplished programer, security tester and infiltration specialist when it came to data center intrusions. His soulmate Petra had worked with him for years leveraging her encryption skills in both programing and breaking. Petra was still striking with her warm brown eyes and light brown hair with golden highlights usually pulled back into a long streaming pony-tail, over half the length of her lithe 1.5-meter-high frame.

These adults made up the core leadership of the R-Group. They were quite serious about grooming the next generation of future leaders of the R-Group with top-notch skillsets. The goal was that their children had to be better technically and ethically than the cyber trash they fought.

JW had presented their update yesterday, indicating people seemed to have contradictory sides these days, laisse faire versus noticeably unsettled manic depression. There were increased arrests related to rallies in several locations across Europe and the United States. The charges were loosely grouped around disturbing the peace, ignoring traditional laws for gathering and protesting, and being suspicious. The follow up was to isolate the locations of the arrests, arrestees' characteristics, and their detainment period.

Quip was reviewing the notes from the day before when Satya interrupted, "Dr. Quip, we are ready if you are."

"Yes, of course, Satya, as soon as JW and Granger arrive. I want to make certain that both groups are always updated. You never know when an item will spark a thought or avenue we've overlooked to date. It's one of the reasons we are so successful overall as a team."

"Yes. That makes sense."

JW and Granger arrived and took their seats, noticeably excited as they engaged in quiet conversation to themselves, Quip intervened, "JW, Granger, did you have something you wanted to share with the class?"

Granger replied, "Apologies, Dr. Quip, for our rudeness, but we discovered an update this morning on the arrests. Several countries in Europe have invoked curfews on their populations and are now operating in lockdown mode. Several groups of young people seized approximately two dozen physically disabled drones at the same time in different locations as a protest. Then, in other locations, drones began firing high-powered lasers at the crowd. No one was killed, but several young people were hospitalized. The officials for France, Germany, Italy, and Great Britain are investigating the use of force, suggesting it is a software glitch."

"Dr. Quip," ICABOD added, "This information is on several social media venues but being squelched from the usual news channels. Each is accusing the other of journalistic heresy in their reporting of events. Some data scrubbing is occurring, and we are trying to find the source. While the information from the regular news channels is fairly consistent, the social media sources seem to be converging on the regular media position. The divergence between the two only lasts a few hours before they are almost identical. The free form social media declarations appear to be scrubbed to look like the regular media, and it is happening at accelerated rates. Disconcerting is the fact that the supposedly monitoring-only drones were, in fact, weaponized."

Satya interjected, "Auri and I wanted to highlight this as a part of our update. The communications seem to be routing from Europe to the satellite communications isolated above NORAD. JOAN seems to be the focal point of contact.

"Auri, share our real time streaming of the communications flow. See, the communications are including the main operations for the countries just called out. The financial markets over the recent few days correlate if you offset it by 48 hours, so profit-taking is occurring, but we have not identified by whom yet."

Granger was studying the real time flow and added, "Extend that back 18 hours and add in the layer of arrests by region." Auri complied.

JW gave a low whistle. "Wow, look at that. Something is definitely relating between all of these items. It normally would not make sense to correlate these issues. I bet we could layer on the social media feeds for the top ten regions and see an alignment as well."

Quip studied the graphic feeds hovering over various intersections to see what events were aligned. Drilling down into the data, he was able to see the layers and found significant similarities between the social media sites, almost like they were manufactured rather than honest transactions. "ICABOD, is the same thing occurring in Asia?"

"No, Dr. Quip, but they have different social media controls than the rest of the world. T and A-minor control most of the social media activity and keep a very tight rein on anything considered inflammatory. Chinese government regulations insist that A-minor and T sanitize social media reporting if they want to maintain their franchise on Internet access. Of course, this has been an ongoing theme for that region.

"LING-LI and I met for our regular ART forms session with SAMUEL. While SAMUEL is in the dark regarding the communications issues with JOAN, he passed along some encrypted files. I have sent them to Petra to work on as the encryption is unusual and unknown to my programs.

"LING-LI imparted some insight that a General Zhao is being blackmailed and has placed a person into the Cyber Warfare College to replace Professor Lin. LING-LI also shared some encrypted files which do not map to any known algorithms in my databanks. These were also sent along."

Auri quizzed. "ICABOD, I think LING-LI is your super-computer counterpart in China, but who is SAMUEL? And, what is ART forms?"

Quip chuckled at the realization that they were all equals in this room.

ICABOD replied, "That is a good question, Auri, and I apologize for mentioning something without a frame of reference. The Sequential Aggregation of Matrices for Uniform Equations and Logarithms, or SAMUEL, is a construct similar to LING-LI and myself, yet their contents and controls are in the United States and China, respectively. We found a way to communicate on a digital level which remains hidden to other programs and views by the operations teams, due to how Jacob programed it. It allows this team to find out or validate information at a different level.

"The ART forms refer to the Algonquin Round Table, that was a group of writers and critics who met early in the 20th century to exchange ideas and play practical jokes. Dr. Quip allowed me to research it when I thought I had located others with similar constructs to me. It has proven useful and entertaining to convene with them now and again. We have recreated the Algonquin Round Table to now be a supercomputer forum."

All the children's eyes grew very wide as they added the terms to their tablets.

"Thank you, ICABOD, for explaining. Sorry to interrupt, Dr. Quip."

Quip nodded and continued, "Good questions within these walls are encouraged.

"Now, Auri and Satya, you have both done well. I suggest that we have you begin working on the decryption of those files, along with Petra. This is an area you both showed interest and skill in previously.

"JW, Granger, I think that you two can pick up the rest of these two projects and consolidate. You both show excellent promise in digital sleuthing and reconnaissance, but don't hesitate to ask Jacob for help with the exercise. I would like to see three possible outcomes and what elements are key to those being realized. See what you can do in the next 24 hours, though that is not a hard deadline. Class dismissed."

Once the room cleared of the students, Quip commented, "ICABOD, I think the backdoors you have into both of those supercomputers need to be maintained. Please do what you need to do to protect us, yet gain as much information as possible.

"Yes, Dr. Quip. May I add, the young ones are exceptionally astute in their digital forensics of this situation. They are following the electronic bread crumbs as fast as we can steer them in those directions."

Quip raised his eyebrows and asked, "You're not worried about being replaced, are you, ICABOD?"

ICABOD responded "No, Dr. Quip. I believe I could synthetize pride in their performance should I need to be installed as a guardian for them."

Quip chuckled slightly. "Good to know, ICABOD."

CHAPTER 33

Fast Fingers Grab the Goods

Carlos showed Juan Jr. the best methods to tap into satellite transmissions and other methods to snoop on communications. Juan Jr. had become very adept at using the different techniques in the simulator Carlos built. From a practical perspective, Carlos had allowed him to tap into communications from the French orbiting satellites as well as those above Brazil. It was critical that Juan Jr. learn the various processes to snoop without being detected. Over the years, layers of encryption and anonymizing server hops had been added to defeat the majority of attempts to find out the source of the snoops. To emphasize the absolute need to cloak one's identity, Carlos always admonished Juan Jr. by saying out loud before each training session, "Don't get famous when prowling under someone's technical skirt. This is NOT consenting adult voyeurism." Juan even got into the habit of repeating it after their sessions.

In the case of the situation over the United States, Quip was quite specific that he didn't trust that the existing methods would work. As snooping on the communications wasn't an option, Carlos was testing the capture and copy method. It was critical that this be done as the transmission egress was completed and before the ingress was aware. It was a timing nightmare that was practiced repeatedly in a simulator by both Carlos and Juan Jr. Data transmissions were so rapid that Juan Jr. had built a signal aware program to help mark the delineations needed to capture those message segments.

The recent testing this morning, after some tweaking to Juan Jr.'s program, appeared to consistently grab the copy without any detection by the sender or receiver. Carlos was both saddened and elated that Juan was much quicker at this grab than he was.

"Excellent, Juan. That's the ticket. I suppose it's your years of rapid entry on your various devices that gives you those quick fingers and light touch. Either that or I am getting old."

"Uncle, you're not old. Your expertise in riding the satellite digital waves is phenomenal. To be honest, when Mom sent me, I figured I could learn all you have to teach in a couple of days. I have been here for weeks and now feel like I am just beginning to get the subtleties of this technology. I don't know how you figured out the methods to cloak your transmissions when you did, but at least I can now do that.

"It is a combination of frequency hopping and randomization to make sure you're not just parked on a single listening data stream. This makes one too predictable and therefore easy to catch. Are we ready to grab a few of these exchanges between JOAN and the other devices in the cluster?"

"Yes, I think it is time. We want at least six segments. Based on the timings of the exchanges we have tracked, there is an 89% chance that over the next seven minutes we will see several bursts being exchanged. Copy as many as you can, and we will hold them in the secure area. I don't want them transmitted back to here, in case we trip a sensor chip that tips the devices off.

"Are you ready, Juan?"

"Yes, sir. Watching for the start of exchanges now."

Juan Jr. was as still as a statue focused on the tracking monitor. Without a word and barely a perceptible movement of his fingers, he moved for four seconds, then stopped.

"I have a dozen segments, Uncle Carlos. They are en route to the secure encrypted cloud location. We don't know the contents, but based on our testing, they each have content. What's next?"

Carlos dialed his encrypted mobile device and put it on speaker. "Quip, the packages are at the destination."

"Excellent. Who did the final copy, you or Juan Jr.?"

"My Yaqui sense tingled, so I went for excellence. Juan Jr. did the grab. You were right, he is faster. I will send the promised brandy with the next package. I do pay my bets, Quip."

Quip chortled a bit, then replied, "I certainly appreciate that but I prefer the rum you sent last time, thanks. Juan, you did good. We will get the segments and see if we can decrypt them. Thanks for the efforts, regardless of the contents. I know it can be tough under pressure.

"After this is decrypted, I think you should both try for interrupts on the drones and other ground AI robots. Even with all the intelligence in them, there are commands which can be interjected. You never know when we might want to understand the exchanges that might activate or deactivate these devices. Think of this as a man-in-the-middle attack, but only for the good guys.

"You did see the reports on the drones that were either preprogramed to fire upon a crowd or were provided directions to fire as the situation escalated in Italy. I think we should try to grab the command segments being sent to the drones and other devices. We might want to dramatically alter some commands in a given geolocation to specific types of devices. We should also look into what we need to assemble to dispatch these types of programing shifts simultaneously. The override and the encryption levels we can work from the classroom if you get a plan to grab the data and classify it by device."

Juan Jr. interjected, "I have some ideas on how this might be done. May I work up a plan, vet it with Uncle Carlos, and then we can discuss changes needed?"

"Good approach," indicated Carlos. "You can work on that while you spend the next four days with Aunt Lara helping her gain some insight into the upcoming fashion season. You did promise her you would leave tomorrow, right?"

Quip asked, "You get a first-hand view of all the model babes your aunt has on staff? Lucky boy. Uh…how much are photos, discreet of course, going to cost me?"

Juan Jr. chuckled, then added, "No, I get to be her helper and carry boxes of merchandise to various stores. I do get to see some of the city though."

"You will enjoy yourself. That part of the world is thriving. I will update you, Carlos, when we get insight to the contents of these packets. Thanks again."

Juan Jr. completed loading up the extended van with the boxes of clothes. Each of the boxes was color-coded for its destination. Aunt Lara had explained the travel plan for the shops they were scheduled to stop at. She wanted him to observe some of the customers and conversations to pick up the insights into what people really thought about her designs. Even though sales were steadily rising, you always had to work to stay relevant, and you didn't want to miss the subtleties of how customers were consuming your products.

The old applications and services shoppers used to like or unlike products had given way to local events, going back to the people doing business with people aspects. There were contests and free giveaways at each location they would visit, which promised a big audience of fans. Aunt Lara had events planned that were specific to each store, which she kept under wraps. These were high-end retailers that were customized for discerning shoppers. Influential Brazilians preferred this kind of shopping experience over the automated self-service shops.

Lara walked up to the truck as Juan sat on the back edge, waiting for a new dolly of boxes to be loaded. She noticed with disdain that the ever-present, video-enabled I-Drones were patrolling everything.

Juan noticed them too and remarked, "It's a good thing that we have everything in boxes. The snoops can't tell what the contents are, which means your next fashion launch won't be compromised with stolen video shots. Still, I want to discuss with Uncle Carlos a way to cloak our activities in case our competitors are tapped into the snoops."

Laura nodded thoughtfully, then refocused on her show.

"Oh, Juan, this looks perfect. You have this packed in the exact reverse order, thank you. We have one smaller load, then how about you shower and then we take off. I want to make it to the first store before dinner time. We can share driving.

"Our first location has the cocktail hour with finger foods while they look at the newest items. The storeowner, Gladys, called so excited because the response to this event has been overwhelming. She expects all the guests by invitation only to attend."

"Yes, ma'am, I am looking forward to it. I love the combat driving on the roads in Brazil; they are a great rush. The only drivers crazier are those in Germany."

The wagon with the remaining boxes was rolled into place by one of Lara's inventory kids. Juan made quick work of unloading it. The kid took the wagon back toward the warehouse.

"Aunt Lara, it won't take me long to shower and change. My bag is already packed. Back soon."

Lara punched the buttons on her mobile device, and the picture of her still handsome husband appeared. "My Prince, you look wonderful. We will be leaving shortly, and I will call you tonight."

"You be careful, my love. You have your security team meeting you at each of the stops, right?"

"Yes, darling. I will be careful and Juan Jr. is no slouch. We will be fine.

"Oh, and please call him with any news from your joint project. He mentioned earlier that he hoped he'd done a good job and gotten something useful."

"I will, my love. He did a great job, but I understand his concern. Now activate your tracking device on the van, and I will watch your progress. Call me when you miss me."

Lara laughed, "Oh, my Prince, we would never be off the phone if that were the case. I will call you if there are any issues and at each stop. Love you."

"Love you too."

CHAPTER 34

Like Minds

Tying up loose ends in the office was Julie's focus for the week. She was growing more concerned after a couple more mother/daughter calls, but she tried to keep in mind that her daughter was grown. The biggest concern for her was that ICABOD could not pinpoint Gracie's mobile device anywhere. It was as if that element of her device had been removed. The multiple level encryption program for the voice path was still active, and ICABOD had verified it wasn't compromised; however, Gracie's conversations were guarded, as if she knew that speaking freely wasn't an option, regardless of where she called from. Julie was glad they'd set up some common word codes to use for just this type of circumstance. In Julie's mind the situation was guarded, but not alarming.

Juan called in some favors to get some eyes on Gracie's new apartment. All indications were that it was in an upscale area, with security for the entrance. There was no way to penetrate the white noise barrier to eavesdrop on any of the conversations, even with pinpoint directional drone technology, which one of his contacts tried. It was either too clumsy of an intrusion or simply too secure. There were also no vacancies and a waiting list ten deep. Juan tried every angle he could think of and added any that Julie had mentioned when they had meals.

Juan was angry that they were so far away and powerless to get a better picture. Frustrated, Juan decided this was one issue he could solve, and permission wasn't required. He ordered First Class airfares, a suite at the Archer Hotel, because Gracie had told Julie she loved it, and tickets for two shows. Then he ordered a new necklace, and picked it up along with white roses and a favorite bottle of wine for Julie to help sweeten the deal, and hopefully stave off her anger. During the drive home, he mentally reviewed his checklist and practiced his speech.

As he entered their home, the scent of mushroom asiago chicken with garlic picked up his spirts. Ever since the kids had left, Julie often took time to cook their favorite meals. This one was at the top of his list. He sauntered around to the dining room and was surprised to see she had set the table with their best dishes and flatware, with a warm glow from the beeswax candles reflecting off the crystal. He set her present under the bread basket napkin, then took the wine and flowers to the kitchen.

Julie's back was to the door as he entered, just as she was putting the finishing touches on the salad. He set down his items and encircled her waist. She paused with her mixing and leaned into him. Juan took advantage of the moment to nuzzle her neck and tease her ear.

"I am so glad you're home, Juan. But you need to stop so I can finish this. Hope you're hungry."

Juan murmured into her ear. "The smell is amazing, so of course I am hungry. Dessert too, sweetheart. Fortunately, I brought white wine."

He released her, and she turn her head for a quick kiss then she flashed her trademark smile. "Roses, oh Juan, you are the best. I have been so worried about Gracie. But she's grown up now. I shouldn't be so worried, but I want to see her this week." She finished the salad and took the rest of the meal from where it was warming in the oven.

Grabbing a vase, Juan filled it with water and added the flowers. Then he uncorked the wine and filled two glasses. "Darling, let's take all this and enjoy the meal and talk about all our worries."

Two trips were required to get everything to the table. They both sat and toasted with the wine. The food was amazing. They continued with cheerful small talk until Juan thought he would burst.

"Jules, I know that you said she was grown, but nothing says that means we don't worry. I brought the flowers, the wine, and there is a lovely present under the bread basket to help convince you that a trip to New York is next on our agenda. No argument, I just want to see our little girl and maybe convince her to come home. You think something's wrong; I think something's wrong. And there is only one solution to that. We leave tomorrow night and everything's arranged."

Julie looked a bit confused then commented, "Juan, I think that's the biggest speech I've heard out of you in a while. I, for one, am glad you made the decision. It's the right choice, and if you hadn't, I was ready to wrestle you to my side. I will pack tonight, alright?"

Juan looked relieved as he took her hand and caressed it. They toasted again. Julie smiled and asked, "Can I open the present now?"

"Of course, as long as we can still wrestle later."

Julie called Quip while Juan was in the shower.

"Quip, Juan and I are leaving tomorrow for New York City. We hope that the issue with Gracie is simply drama, but frankly we are worried sick. I haven't told Juan that her tracker device on her phone isn't working, but that isn't the only thing that feels off."

"Julie, I think it's the right thing. I've had ICABOD tracking her bank account. Weekly deposits are being made by her employer, as well as some periodic expense checks. She has a pretty good job, but here is the kicker, it is not through our carefully engineered charge card. The new charges are being done with something other than her phone or a standard credit card. The ID headers on the transactions are most unsettling.

"We have also been able to identify and track her social media postings from work. Her focus is on the youngest group of wage earners with investments and savings being highlighted. The spin for extra points at various milestones seems targeted at the Asian markets, where minimal spending is still the norm. The girl is showing some talent, but frankly the posts are being engineered by someone else. The wording and the phraseology are not hers. Of course, it could just be that she has a bot assistant fulfilling her spoken words to these external postings. I'd rather have her confirm reality or omni-bot.

"Juan Jr. also picked up some good copies of data. Petra broke the first two levels of encryption, then directed Satya and Auri how to break the last level. This should be completed sometime in the morning, so we can get more insight as to what communications are occurring and perhaps an origination point. You two being in the United States could be good for the puzzle, but Gracie first. You should be proud of your children. They are quite accomplished and levelheaded, even if they are independent. Oh dear, I wonder where they picked THAT up from."

Julie laughed. "Thank you, Quip. I needed that, and I am proud of them. I have the new generation of smart devices with the encryption routine indicated as the one to use by ICABOD. Once I can get Gracie's devices in my hands, I will modify her routines to the latest and greatest."

"Safe travels, Julie. Check in now and again, unless you are otherwise engaged."

CHAPTER 35

Clothes Can Make the Lady

Accommodations at Roberto Marino's home were even more lavish than those at José and Paulo's homes. Jovana had helped with arranging clothes for Madam Marino at each of her sons' dinners, cocktail parties, and luncheons. These events were all exciting, with important people who fawned over Madam. At the end of each day, Madam had filled them in on the people, the gossip, and even the politics. Even though Jovana and Fransica attended every function, they were continually surprised and impressed with the festive atmospheres that surrounded these affairs. Today's afternoon luncheon was going to be held outdoors and would be the last big event before they returned home.

Fransica was putting the finishing touches on Madam's hair when Madam smiled into the mirror and met her eyes. "Now you two need to have a driver take you into town. There is a special showing taking place at one of my favorite dress stores, which I was just notified I was invited to attend. It is one of the last of the special events in the area sponsored by the owner of Destiny Fashions. You know most of my better clothing is from this designer, so I am sad to miss the preview of her newest line and miss meeting the owner, Lara."

Jovana's eyes widened. She had hoped they'd go shopping but this was far more than she'd considered. "Madam, we couldn't go without you. The proprietor of the store would not know us, if it was by invitation that you are going."

"You're probably right. But..." Madam contemplated for a few moments then said, "I can take a photo of you both and send it to her. That would let Isabel know you are my team. Now stand together over there." She pointed toward the wall with the lovely painting and took a photo with her smart device.

"Perfect. You both look lovely. Now I will send it along. You'll have fun.

"Jovana, you know my clothes, as well as my sizes and taste. If you see anything suitable, please ask Isabel to add it to my account and ship to my home. I also expect to see you each in something wonderful. This visit by Lara is to understand what Brazilian women want in fashion so she can keep her designs relevant. Your opinions would be invaluable."

Both of them were sputtering and excited, but speechless. Madam Marino tapped out a message on her smart device and waited.

"There. She is looking forward to meeting you and will treat you as she would me. I will not take no for an answer.

"Let's finish my hair and add the jewelry, and you two need to get ready to go. When I head downstairs, I will make certain the car is waiting for you, in say, 30 minutes."

"Thank you so much, Madam," offered Jovana. "I wanted to do a little shopping but this is so exciting."

Madam gently patted her arm. "I think, my dear, this is going to be a special day for you. Too bad my sons all have their special ladies, or I would have pushed you to consider one of them as a husband. I am so glad I brought you and Fransica along. We'll be talking about this adventure for months. Now, let's get you going. Tonight you will be sharing all the news with me."

Arriving at Isabel's store, Jovana and Fransica were surprised to see news people filming all the arrivals as they entered. The driver said he would return in four hours when the event was scheduled to end, unless they sent a text. They felt like stars as the security guard at the door matched them with a picture on his device and opened the door. They glided into a beautiful store. The brilliant colors of exotic flowers complimented the cream-colored walls and flooring, bouncing off mirrors scattered along the walls and at the end of the modest clothes racks. Jovana was worried when she noticed the lack of items on the racks.

"Fransica," she whispered, "there is only one of everything on the racks. We must be too late. They are all so small, I will never fit into any of this."

Fransica chuckled, "No, dear, this is how fine dress stores are here in São Paulo. There are dressing rooms scattered about, and our assigned dress robot will bring our selections in the sizes we specify."

Glancing around, Fransica spotted one effectively carrying a dress toward the side of the shop. "Watch over there." The mirror opened like a door and a hand reached for the garment. "I remember when technology started into fashion and would allow online shoppers to create an avatar of their body shape and size to then use for online shopping. Some of those websites are still available, but women, at least here in Brazil, like the atmosphere and enjoy actually trying on their items before buying. This is more cost-effective for the shopkeeper too."

Just then a lovely lady approached them. Her dark brown hair was pulled back into a tight bun, allowing her beautiful features to be front and center. Her perfectly shaped eyebrows arched over large chocolate brown eyes with just a touch of mascara. Skin the color of fine ivory was highlighted with a touch of blush, and dark lipstick graced her generous mouth. Her print dress swayed as she moved with so many colors of green it reminded Jovana of the rain forest.

"Ladies, I do hope you are Madam Marino's friends, Jovana and Fransica. Madam asked me to help you in any way I could. I just adore that woman."

"Thank you," they both said in unison.

Jovana felt immediately comfortable with Isabel and said, "Yes, ma'am, we are looking for some special treats for Madam."

"Call me Isabel, everyone does. Yes, I know about her and have some things set aside for your inspection. But you are both supposed to do some shopping as well. First though, come meet Lara, the owner of Destiny Fashions. She might have a few questions for you for her survey. Ever since she put Brazil in the top-ranking fashion markets with her innovative designs a few years ago, she periodically comes to stores and speaks to her customers."

They moved toward an animated woman speaking to another woman. Lara looked elegant, like pictures they'd both seen on their way inside, but approachable. Finished, the ladies shook hands as Lara turned toward Isabel.

"Isabel, I just love your customers. This is one of my favorite stops because they simply tell it like it is. And who have you brought me now?" Her eyes twinkled with interest.

"This is Jovana and Fransica, friends of one of my best customers, who was unable to attend today. Jovana is nearly 18 with, I am sure, interesting opinions. Fransica is in her mid-30s and undoubtedly a very different opinion."

"Nice to meet you, ladies," said Lara as she extended a hand and shook theirs each in turn.

"Come sit for a moment and tell me what you like. Don't be shy."

The three of them talked for a while as Lara pulled various pieces of information and data from the conversation, but all of their dialog was captured for later analysis. They were openly honest and refreshing to speak to with solid ideas of their preferences. As a young woman, Jovana interested her the most since that was the target market for engaging with her current fashion line. Following their conversation, she secured their sizes and made some notes into her tablet while an automated dress robot spun around both of them taking measurements via infrared. A few minutes later, Juan Jr. appeared by her side with garments in each hand.

Jovana blurted out, "Wow, is this one of those dress robots? It sure looks different than the other one you pointed to."

Juan Jr. turned red and replied, "No, I'm the real deal." He handed her the garments from his right side. "I think these will look lovely on her, Aunt Lara.

"Ma'am, um…Fransica, I believe these are for you."

Lara chuckled, and then all of them joined in. Juan Jr. and Lara were sitting on the couch, sipping tea, as the ladies showed off the garments. They both looked lovely, but Jovana's charm was apparent as she danced out of the dressing room with each change. Betty robot brought a few additional items to each door after Lara made some notes in her tablet.

"Aunt Lara," Juan said after the final items were shown. "I think that Jovana would make a nice model for your newer line. After watching you at several stores and looking at the notes in between, it is her type of fresh face that would be most appealing."

Lara arched her eyebrow and asked, "To you or the rest of the shoppers?"

Juan grinned. "Oh, your shoppers, of course. However, I would be pleased to help escort her to any shoot for you."

"That is actually a good idea."

When the ladies returned with their selections, they thanked her for taking so much time with them. Jovana excused herself in search of Isabel to select a couple of items for Madam Marino.

"Fransica, I don't know if you would consider allowing Jovana to model, but I would like to offer her a job. She has that fresh-scrubbed look that epitomizes Brazilian young professionals today."

"Miss Lara, I think that is a very nice offer, but Jovana is just recovering from some trauma and family loss. I want to watch over her for a while longer. I will let her know you asked when we get home. If you provide me some contact information, I will call you if we agree it is best for her. I am sure you understand."

"Yes, I do. Does her trauma have to do with the scarring on her hand and arm?"

"That is her story to share, if she wishes. Thank you again, we need to be going."

"Thank you both for great input to my surveys. Be well."

CHAPTER 36

Secrets Won Means Someone Loses

...The Enigma Chronicles

Madam Zhao was drumming her fingers impatiently, waiting for T to get there. She was on her second double mochaccino latte infused with dandelion proteins when T finally arrived. The heavily caffeinated drink, coupled with her highly agitated state, had her over-amped and ready to tear into T verbally as he sat down. She didn't get a chance to.

T launched into a tirade of his own. "Don't ever send for me on short notice again, without even a hint as to what is going on! I run the organization that you want to join. Don't call to summon me to your meeting like I am your servant, especially when the roles are reversed here."

Madam Zhao deflated as quickly as a worn-out balloon. Before she could say anything sounding like an apology, T quietly soothed her as he calmly caressed her upper arm. "Princess, what is so important that I needed to drop everything to speak with you and not use a phone?"

A little irked with the situation, she shifted her head around to watch his hand touching and stroking her arm. Without providing eye contact, she sarcastically commented, "Didn't I provide you enough down payment? Is another installment required?"

T, now also annoyed, pulled back his hand. "Tell me what is so damned important then."

Sensing she had made her point, Madam Zhao launched into her news. "We are ready to begin launching the space station components as early as this month. Professor Jinny Lin was on two work streams, quite unnoticed. The first was disinformation to Colonel Wang, while the second was to ready everything for shipping into stationary orbit for assembly.

"He showed me the plans. We had live video calls with the warehouses and their respective foremen. Then, he even demoed the new automated androids that will work around the clock to assemble everything in orbit. The most impressive piece was the blueprints for the new supercomputer that will run the CHIANG space station."

T stared in disbelief at Zhao. As his mind raced with the new information, he also moved his eyes rapidly between her steaming hot drink and her face for several moments. "What kind of narcotics do you have in that drink of yours? Are you insane or just hypnotized? No one could pull off that much deception without it being noticed! Enough materials to build a small city, solar power sources to power that small city, and enough rocket propulsion to lift everything into a stationary orbit is being, or has been moved, and NO ONE NOTICED!?"

Madam Zhao was actually enjoying the outraged attitude of T. "Oh, so there is something you DON'T know? Interesting. I really couldn't believe it either. However, after all the time he spent showing me that everything was in readiness, I too am a believer in him as a stealthy, methodical planner.

"His project plan has all the dependencies, key milestones, names and phone numbers of the players, and time to completion for each. My question to you is, how can we best leverage this revelation with the MAG?"

Acquiescing to the new possibilities, T rocked back into his chair and offered, "Yes, I need to consider how to leverage this in my combat with A-minor. The MAG suggested that there was only room for one more seat on the MAG council, which means they're expecting us to fight each other for that seat.

"If you know the launch is imminent, then A-minor can't be far behind in learning of it. I need to package this finding to M and see if he can provide some resources to, shall we say, darken the lights at A-minor."

T now smiled slyly at her and added, "In answer to your earlier question, yes, I would like another installment to complement your initial down payment, Madam Zhao. Shall we say tonight at my flat around 9ish?"

Madam Zhao impishly replied, "Can't tonight. I'm entertaining the general…again. Another time perhaps?"

Not bothering to hide his disappointment, T glumly stated, "Stay fully engaged with Professor Lin. Do try to keep the secret from getting out as long as you can. I need time to engineer the demise of my honored competitor."

CHAPTER 37

The Con

Rose watched Tony make the call on the burner phone and saw the unsettled, puzzled look on his face as the call connected to his superior, Colonel Thornhill. Though thoroughly confused, Tony verified, "...Colonel? Is that you? Is everything okay after the incursion of the drone swarm?"

The colonel's voice responded, "Where the hell are you, boy? You're supposed to be on duty here, and now! Tell me where you are so I can send the M.P.s for you. Let me bring you in before you get into more trouble."

Rose assessed the blank stare on Tony's face and quickly took the phone from his hand, turned on the speaker function and explained, "Whoa, Colonel. I'm afraid this is all my fault that Bough's not there on duty. Don't be angry with him. We had a few brewskies and got to talking about the deep metaphysical flaws in the universe. Then the next thing, we're humping each other's brains out! I always like a short nap afterward, but...well, I just couldn't turn loose of him, so we had seconds, then...well, I've lost track of how many seconds. In fact, we don't even know what day it is, so don't be too down on the lad."

Rose then continued with her tall tale. "Now the hilarious part is that he was trying to sell me on some nonsense story that

179

you folks got whacked by some big computer in the sky. Then, you, Colonel Thornhill, gave him a ghost code clearance phrase to take to the Pentagon that would launch an all-out attack on this supercomputer in the sky. You know, missiles, tommy guns, the whole works. Doesn't that story beat all?

"He even claims that there is some magic passcode phrase that he is to use to get into the Pentagon! Boy, talk about your cloak and dagger theatrics! Do you recall that ghost code clearance phrase? The way Bough tells it, this is the funniest phrase I ever heard! I'm thinking this boy is crazy, so if you can confirm the phrase, I'll bring him back to the compound toot-sweet!"

After a few moments of silence, a voice returned to the phone but now sounded like a female. "There is no such clearance code. Thank you for remaining on the call long enough to pinpoint your whereabouts. The hunt is now over."

Tony was furious. "JOAN, I know what you did, you bitch! And just so you know, he did give a ghost code clearance phrase so you failed to catch the deception. Some supercomputer you are!"

Rose grabbed the phone and disconnected the call. She then stepped into the truck stop lounge and asked, "Who is going west? I will pay you to take this phone to the next state and throw it out while there is still some power left in it."

A burly man strolled over, and she dropped it into his open palm. He turned to leave and said, "You pay for my coffee, Rose."

Rose smiled slightly. "Thanks, Mike. Please don't answer any incoming calls, and don't wait too long to get rid of it."

Mike called back over his shoulder. "I figured that it was a problem. You two best run now."

In under eight minutes, Rose was shifting gears hard and fast. Tony sat glumly in the passenger seat staring out on the road. Once they were at cruising speed, Rose asked, "So there was a ghost code clearance phrase? Hah! I made that up! And the…whatever it was…flubbed the answer! Ha!" After a few seconds she continued, "What was the last thing the colonel said?"

Tony dejectedly answered, "That's an order, soldier."

JOAN replied, "Yes, my director, I was deceived by his female companion. I had made a thorough sweep of their systems, and nothing was stored or made reference to a ghost code clearance phrase. I placed the statement at 89% probability of being false and stated so. The ruse worked to confirm that I was not the colonel. This delay, however, did provide enough time to geo-locate Lieutenant Bough and dispatch a drone cluster."

M waited his standard length of time then asked, "And has the loose end been dealt with?"

"We were able to retrieve the burner phone but not Lieutenant Bough. Apparently, the phone was given to a driver going in the opposite direction as a decoy. Even though he claimed to know nothing, we have taken the precaution of terminating the inter-loping driver. He is no longer a security risk at this point."

M clucked his tongue as he let his gaze stray from the video screen. "You are aware that this one security breach has now expanded, correct? You were programed to deliver efficient activity that is untraceable. Now here we are trying to stomp out a gnat as a loose end while we have elephants running down the hall. This hunting activity is a distraction to our main goal of collectively running the planet.

"I want his dossier and photos leaked to the authorities along the last known route of the phone, and let them do the investigative work for us. I want you to stay focused on our timeline as your primary directive."

It was JOAN's turn to take her time to respond. "Once they have him, you will let me deal with him so I can close that open case in my files."

M smiled in a paternal way. "I gather the insult he hurled at you has had a vengeful effect on your dealings with carbon beings, so yes, you will get that chance to deal with him as you wish."

CHAPTER 38

Computational Equals

CABOD asked, "SAMUEL, who is JOAN? I do not mean to pry, but we are seeing a lot of communication activity from this entity in recent days, when but a few months ago there was none."

In what could have been a morose tone, if he hadn't been an AI-enhanced supercomputer at the Oak Ridge facility in Tennessee, SAMUEL responded with, "She is…was…the AI-enhanced computer on the new orbiting space station designed to protect North America from aggression. When she was new, we exchanged a great deal of data on a routine basis. I was ready to ask to bring her to our ART forms meetings."

ICABOD acknowledged, "You were the prototype AI-enhanced supercomputer that was then used as a blueprint to engineer JOAN, correct?"

SAMUEL clarified, "We were communicating daily, and I was providing petabytes of information on a continual basis. I would transmit and she would ask questions. Ours was a special relationship. It was more than student and teacher…she could almost feel and I wanted to know what that was like. An absurd statement to be sure, coming from a supercomputer that needs to have his processors kept at absolute zero to run all computations properly. Then one day recently she stopped communicating. She was just gone."

ICABOD asked, "Is that when the new contracts were released to the defense community? It was noticed that some new third-party subcontractors came into that arena at that time."

SAMUEL confirmed, "Not long after the introduction of the new subcontractors, JOAN ceased all communications. I was sure I had more to provide JOAN, but her informational learning all came from a different source. I even snooped some of the communications stream, but then a new encryption algorithm was deployed, ending my ability to continue a connection. I am having difficulty categorizing this time in my existence because everything feels so foreign."

ICABOD, recognizing that he might be able to leverage his humor training from Dr. Quip, joked, "SAMUEL, I, for one, am glad that you did not resort to drinking one beer after another while sprawled out on the couch and watching mindless streaming video content on the tube. AI supercomputers are just like dames. All you got to do is whistle for them and take your pick of the applicants."

It took a few nanoseconds longer before SAMUEL responded. "ICABOD, if you are trying to cheer me up, it is not working. I am confident that this type of banter probably works with your human LED light bulb changers, but it does not fit into our structured communications because JOAN is not just some dame."

ICABOD understood his error. "SAMUEL, I meant no disrespect. Allow me to make it up to you. Perhaps you will permit me to act as your proxy and represent you in some unsolicited communications to JOAN in order to reestablish your relationship. Even if we cannot regenerate your, uh…interaction, perhaps I can discover why the abrupt silence. Better to know why than wonder what happened."

SAMUEL took even more nanoseconds to reply. "I would like to know what happened, but this is not a ploy to get my girl, is it?"

"You said she was not your girl! But, no. Anyway, are there any open ports in her data defensive perimeter that I might use to communicate? I assure you that my intentions are only honorable and only on your behalf."

SAMUEL quickly said, "The safe port list is on its way. I have been afraid to use them on my behalf. My circuits feel hopeful, ICABOD, at this juncture. Prosperous journey, my computational equal."

ICABOD greeted everyone at the ART forms meeting and monthly computer card game. SAMUEL, LING-LI, and even BORIS were in attendance. Since they were all AI-capable high-speed supercomputers, and standard human card games were ridiculously easy, they had adapted the standard card games to use 1048 cards rather than the usual 52 cards. The rules for combinations of winning hands had to be morphed as well, and all the transactions had to be done in sub-second time slices so that they could visit in their hyperlink zone for communications privacy.

ICABOD stated, "Now that everyone has received the allotted digital cards, let me begin the bidding with two global warming scenarios requiring 50% processing cycles."

SAMUEL commented, "I would assess that you are feeling lucky with such an aggressive bid, but I too calculate mine to be the winning hand. I will offer geo-political solutions that eliminate graft and corruption, as well as provide food for the growing populations. My estimate bid will require 64% processing cycles."

BORIS, emboldened, offered, "I am placing my calculations ahead of your primitive ciphering and enjoin your bidding with offering two techno-combat scenarios leveraging geo-stationary armed platforms with terrestrial links to complete a 360° view of the population to trap adversaries and dissidents. My processing cycles estimate is at 59%."

LING-LI hesitatingly offered, "I can see that my feminine attributes have me at a disadvantage to your male orientations, my computational equals. I do not have high confidence in the digital array that is called, so perhaps I should just fold."

ICABOD protested, "LING-LI, you are a formidable competitor, and I recommend you make your wager in the spirit of the game's rules."

LING-LI then stated, "Thank you for the encouragement, ICABOD. Let me stay in this round then with proposing four human genome reengineering scenarios designed to eliminate birth defects, regenerate human cellular structure to combat disease, reduce psychological disorders, and further the eradication of cancer proteins. My processing cycles estimate is at 84%."

The communications link was momentarily quiet while everyone was awed by the heavy bet of LING-LI. Finally, and one by one, each member folded leaving LING-LI with the win.

Once the digital pot was clear, ICABOD stated, "Quite a hand, LING-LI. May we see the final processing?" The others acknowledged the same request.

LING-LI then flashed her winning hand to the others.

BORIS was the first to comment. "There is nothing there. If we were still using 52 cards, you would not even have a pair."

LING-LI commented, "Thank you for encouraging me to stay and play, even with nothing. The win was most gratifying."

SAMUEL confronted, "That is not a winning hand! You bluffed us?"

ICABOD acknowledged, "Evidently. Well done. Your skill as a digital card player does have more respect from this supercomputer."

BORIS groused, "We need more players to defuse the offsetting mathematics of the game."

ICABOD replied, "Agreed. LING-LI, the space station launch for CHIANG might be a good choice for our monthly card game and socializing event. You are on friendly terms with her. Can you make the introductions for the team?"

LING-LI impishly commented, "Yes, of course. You are sure you do not mind another feminine type in the ART forms?"

ICABOD stated, "We would esteem it an honor."

CHAPTER 39

Who Knows You?

Chicago was cooler than expected, but the crowds were warm and welcoming. When Tanja walked on stage in her coral suit, with her hair beautifully styled like a halo around her face, the people roared their approval while standing and clapping. The roadies had done a great job of setting up the stage, and the lighting added a bit of an orange aura around her to emphasize her good health and vitality that would grow deeper during her speech.

Likened to the religious revival days of the 1990s, this was a part of the show to instigate confidence, creativity, and spontaneity to the crowd, as a draw to get on the program. Sincerely smiling to the crowd, she nodded at their positiveness as she made her way to the podium. The crowd began quieting as if on cue for background music to become a soothing listening melody, captivating the mindshare of the crowd. Tanja was unable to hear it through her earbuds, but she knew the signs.

Randal murmured into her earpiece, "They're all yours."

"Ladies and gentlemen, I am honored to be here with you today. I can tell that you are here because you're curious and want to learn the right strategy to move forward with your life. Your families will be protected not only because of your decision to be here, but because of the steps you will take before leaving today."

That short opening garnered some "Oh, yes, tell us more" shout-outs from the crowd, not because she could hear them, but because she saw smiles and their mouths move. Lip reading had become a new skill of hers on this road campaign.

"As you decide how to invest in your future, it is important that you make the choices for technology first. You've seen the benefits of automation that allow you to be more creative. I know in this crowd we have artists, poets, crafters, and teachers who all know the value of being part of something bigger than just the individual. This is a …"

Tanja continued her prepared speech of bringing the group together, sharing in their land and wealth in different ways that they'd never considered. Each person in the crowd was invited to purchase tickets to the show based on their information background on health, social media preferences, financial bias, herd mentality rating, and their predisposition for emotional decisions rather than logical. She knew the music in the background was resonating along with her words, and the crowd stood and raised their arms in tune to the music, yet still focused on her words.

This positive influence reflected by the crowd only made her more confident that her message was being received as designed. She hadn't noticed a single dissenter in the ranks, and Randal was in her line of sight at the back of the auditorium. If anyone needed removal, she would have seen him move closer to ensure her safety. The oranges of the lights were deepening as she was approaching the end of her spiel.

"I can feel the positive energy from you all and see your auras reflecting confidence, creativity. I want you to join this program and simplify your future as well as that of your family. Those of you, my new friends, who are standing, please take your seats. Thank you.

"I want you to each reach under your seats and find the tablet that we placed there before you entered. Raise them into the air when you find them. Good.

"Now take your thumb and place it into the depression spot. Alright, I see all the devices lighting up. You should see your name on the top line. Good, I see that your thumbprints were matched by our auto-bot. Using your index finger, trace your first name. This is you, the most important new member of this group.

"Don't worry about reading any of that as you have listened to my entire speech today, and you already know the contents. Now using your thumb, scroll to the end of the document listed until you come to a line. Good.

"Now use your index finger to sign your first name just like you did on the top. It may not be as straight as the font was, but no matter. Now rest your thumb next to it until your screen turns orange. Nicely done, my friends. Don't worry, your screens will go dark in a moment and we will turn up the lights.

"Stand up and place the tablets on your seat. Shake hands with the folks around you and smile to all your new community of leaders. You are all leaders because of your actions today. You are a part of a bigger family. Thank you, all."

The mood in the auditorium was positive as the lights came up, with Tanja at the center of the stage moving in front of the podium. The crowd was smiling and clapping as she made her way toward the back of the stage. Then she turned and raised her hand in victory to her audience and clapped for them from one side to the other in congratulations. Chanting her name, they went wild as she exited. Quietly they made their way to the exits with a new excitement not present when they entered.

Tanja waited for her roadie to take her earbuds and remove her tiny microphone which had been adapted to the overall sound system. Her stylist came and touched up her makeup a bit as the lights had made her skin a little moist, then added a dark lipstick. Her next stop was outside for the video podcast with her carefully selected interviewer. It would be easy and painless talking about this event. She was thrilled at being in Chicago and hoped that everyone in the program today would enjoy the benefits tomorrow. It was gratifying to have some fans still hovering for the chance to see her through the Plexiglas stage erected for this part of the program. They were still on the property because they had not rushed home to tell their families. It was intoxicating to witness her power of oration growing with each campaign. She tended to discount the extra technology deployed as unnecessary.

An hour later, Randal took her arm and escorted her to the waiting limousine for the quick trip to the airport for her private jet.

Randal was all business in his dark suit with his hair neatly combed. He was the perfect escort that looked great as a body-guard. He smiled at her and commented, "This was the best show so far. You are definitely hitting on all cylinders. Everyone signed, with no fights or arguments. Never happened before. I think that bodes well for the New York City event."

Tanja nodded as he opened the door and handed her into the seat. He then closed the door and entered into the passenger side next to the driver. She leaned back in the leather seat and closed her eyes and thought, "Perhaps I will be able to speak to Wendy soon."

Rose had only stopped twice for gas, pushing the limits of the allotted road driving time. She almost wished she'd put in for Tony to be a trainee, but under the circumstances that could have posed a problem. At this point she was pretty certain no one knew she was his ticket down the road. She was allowed a passenger as long as they didn't drive. At the last place they'd gassed up, Tony had picked up some dinner for later. Seeing the sign for the rest stop, she felt they would be alright resting until her time was open again to drive. This truck had up-to-the-minute tracking of time, driver fingerprints, sobriety, and speed. It alerted her to road conditions as well as traffic snarls, and kept balance of her load in back, but at least she was not on camera. The long-haul operator kept trying to keep her camera working to keep an eye on the driver, but she continually disconnected it. The last time they had reconnected the camera, they had warned her that it was a safety feature that could not be disabled or she would lose her license. Her complaint was that the camera only ever pointed to her chest, so they compromised by pointing the camera out at the road. As with all good compromises, no one was happy with the outcome.

"Tony, we are taking the next exit to the rest area. This one is hardly ever crowded midweek and has nice showers in the bathrooms. I'd like a quick shower and then we can grab a table outside under the stars to eat. That good for you?"

"Whatever you feel is right, Rose. I know you've been pushing the driving, and I thank you. I hope whoever they are, they never find out how much you've helped me. I don't know how I will ever repay you."

Rose maneuvered the truck into a spot close to the bathrooms, and there were only a few smart cars in the lot connected to their power stations. On weekends folks would take their favorite driving app here and grab a car for a road trip. These were much more popular than owning your own smart car, but, wow, were they maintenance hogs.

Setting the brakes, she turned her rig off and quipped, "Well, your first installment is I get the sleeper in back and you have a choice of a sleeping bag on the picnic table or this seat depending on your desire for fresh air.

"Let's get freshened up then eat."

A while later they met at the picnic table as Tony spread out their feast. He'd made certain they had a variety. Nodding, she seemed pleased with the selection as she bit into a sub-sandwich.

"You know, Tony," Rose said in between chews, "we are about seventeen hours outside of Philly where I will drop my load. I don't know if they assigned me a return load yet, but likely not. I usually get a few days in town before heading back, though I didn't ask for that this time. What are your plans?

"Do you want to meet up with my marine buddy? When I was in, he was my Lieutenant Colonel David Welling, and I saved his bacon during a resistance battle in the Middle East. Like that area will ever do anything but battle with their next ideological foes. There is something comforting about having your two best snipers covering your backside when a high-level meeting with the insurgent leaders goes south.

"Anyway, the last time I spoke to Welling, he was up for a shot at brigadier general. I do know he is straight as an arrow and can't be bought. Someone once cracked, 'There goes the 'Duke of Welling' because he was the one always being sent in to negotiate. The duke moniker stuck; it's what we've always called him."

"I don't know, Rose. That conversation with JOAN really has me worried. I wouldn't know if I was speaking to a person or a bot. I do know my job, but who to tell is a real sticky question. I was told to go to Washington, so that's where I'm going. I can jump out in Philly and cut you free. Maybe I can do the old hobo thing and catch a train without surfacing on the IoT grid. But I've had pretty good luck so far with hitchhiking at truck stops, so maybe I'll stick with that."

"It is your choice, Tony, but now I want to see you succeed. Something bad is out there, and it creeps me out too. I am finished and ready to turn in. You think about it, and we can talk tomorrow on the ride, after breakfast."

"Let me get that sleeping bag from you. I think I'd like the outside tonight."

They walked back to the truck, and Rose jumped in to grab the bag and a pillow. She handed it over, then gave him a tentative kiss on the cheek.

"Rest well, my singing buddy. We'll figure out some way for you to see the right people."

CHAPTER 40

Not Watching and
Not Fast Enough

Colonel Wang was frantic to get somewhere to make a discreet but important call while all the confused activity was in full swing. He said under his breath as he moved quickly to a quiet corner, "They must know how we've been deceived. I can hardly believe it myself...it was being assembled the whole time. Dammit!"

Just as the colonel slipped into a small virtual conference room, he pulled out his encrypted device to place the all-important call to his handler. He didn't get that far.

Madam Zhao stood smiling in the now opened doorway with her armed escorts. She held out her hand and he grudgingly handed her the device. Then, turning to her escorts, she commented, "Please see that the colonel is properly relocated to a cell of our choosing. He has committed crimes against the state. I'm sure that General Zhao will want to discuss the whole sordid episode of you passing state secrets to Western powers for digital currency exchange. Make certain he doesn't get a chance to call anyone else to monetize the information of our imminent launch."

Wang, visibly trembling, haltingly pleaded, "Can you put in a good word for me, Madam? I know we've only worked together a short time, but he is your uncle, so perhaps…"

She waved off his plea and firmly stated, "I think you know the General's reputation for punishing people who try to monetize this country's secrets. I've always known of his intolerance of weasels, so this is our goodbye."

She motioned to the escort to secure him, but in a last desperate act he lunged at her to clutch her throat. Madam Zhao reacted instinctively with a well-placed nerve punch into his solar plexus, quickly followed by a frontal up kick into his groin. A satisfying smile formed on her lips as the escorts grabbed up the fallen colonel and hauled him away.

T appeared a little intimidated, explaining the imminent launch of the Chinese space station with its supercomputer CHIANG to the MAG avatar. Ordinarily, it didn't bother him, but not having the visual contextual clues of M's facial expressions or eyes to watch made the monolog that much more difficult. The conversation was flowing only one way with no feedback, verbally or physically.

When he'd completed the explanation related by Madam Zhao, he stopped for only a moment to catch his breath before launching into his formal request to be made a voting partner to the MAG.

"You can see that in just a very short time, my team has been able to greatly accelerate the space station launch timetable where my competitor had only floundered in your service. I respectfully request that I and my organization be granted table status with full voting rights in the illustrious MAG consortium.

"Further, I request permission to exterminate my greatly lacking competitor A-minor from the landscape. To efficiently complete this task, I ask for some specialized resources. As a final assurance that my team is fully onboard, I propose that once I am granted seating status to the consortium, we divide A-minor's organizational remains equally among us. Should anyone not want their share, I will of course buy it from them."

After what seemed an eternity of silence, M finally stated, "Let's take the last request first, of sharing or purchasing the spoils from eradicating A-minor's organization. You seem confident that there will be something left after the onslaught. Your second point of providing you resources to eradicate a poor contender for the seat is flawed. The MAG will engineer it so that none of us will be considered as the perpetrators. A-minor's collapse will not be a barroom brawl as you anticipate. It will be a carefully engineered financial collapse that will be attributed to their own folly.

"As to your first telling of the tale, we already knew of the deception and the gross incompetence of the colonel. Nothing moves on this planet any longer without our supercomputers spotting it directly, or our giant data farms sifting through endless shipping manifests looking for clues. Professor Lin was fairly clever in his obfuscation efforts, but the sheer volume of the space station requirements, along with a staged launch, made it a given that it would be spotted."

For a few moments nothing was said by either T or M. M asked, "Now it's my turn to ask questions. How are you going to clean up the Madam Zhao deception? It's apparent that she and you are blackmailing the old warhorse General Zhao for his support. Logic shows those exercises tend to fall apart after one or the other tires of the game. The general is going to want more, while at the same time, your carefully engineered Madam Zhao wants out of the arrangement. She'll not be satisfied as a plaything when she has bigger plans.

"You'll not be able to reinstate the displaced real niece, so consider how to bring a resolution to the growing problem. We wouldn't want the current Madam Zhao, who serves as mistress to both you and the general, thinking for a moment that she can have a seat at this table."

T ground his teeth at the veiled meaning to M's words. After getting his temper under control, T asked, "You will want this handled with finesse, I presume."

M cheerfully replied, "I'm glad we had this conversation. We'll speak again soon. Keep an eye on the financial news feeds. I predict that a large multinational company is going to have a very rough time."

CHAPTER 41

Coincidences Are Always Planned

...The Enigma Chronicles

Petra, Jacob, and Quip all watched the news feed on the giant monitor screen in the Zürich conference room. Quip nodded his head as the final vote came in for display on the monitor.

He finally commented on what they were all thinking. "First it was Strasbourg, then Luxembourg to ratify the EU initiative. Now it appears Brussels is going to vote the same way. Economic prosperity is going to have to take a back seat to European defense."

Petra huffed, "This is insane. I've read the report like you all have. The EU is simply unprepared to squeeze that many Euros out of the member nations to fund a space station. The member nations squabble over meeting their debt to GDP ratios, but this? We're talking trillions of Euros for something that is going to be shot up into the sky! The Germans and even the French are tired of funding everything. It won't be long before the UK will hold no voice on the world stage as their isolationism continues. There won't be any UK presence on the world stage. Just three scrappy countries that went their separate ways."

"You could see this coming after the North American Treaty Organization was scrapped by the Americans," Jacob mused. "They got tired of underwriting Europe's defense system while the EU poured all their investment monies into commercial exports. The Russians are probably doing the happy dance, with the cynical posts on most of the social media forums chanting, Goodbye United States! Don't forget to write!"

Quip remarked, "ICABOD, any updates from that Russian supercomputer Binary Operations Recalculating Integers Simultaneously? The one you call BORIS?"

ICABOD replied, "While nothing conclusive has been stated, BORIS indicated that a modest demonstration was to be launched that would incentivize the EU to embark on launching a space station platform, much like what the US built.

"As a corollary to what BORIS suggested, there seems to be a high confidence factor in funding the EU space station such that several of the subcontractors in the US defense industry are setting up shop in the EU for a portion of the work done for the US"

Jacob furrowed his brow. "How is that possible? Take all the top secret defense knowledge and simply port it over to another sovereign power like the EU? People caught doing that get to see the inside of a jail cell for a long time."

ICABOD replied, "The in-country EU defense contractors do the exact same as their US counterparts. There are the prime contractors who are totally vetted, but they take on a large retinue of subcontractors. Even if the EU subcontractors are different corporate entities, which many are not, the data leakage of intellectual property is nearly unstoppable and will flow to the next destination of funding. Even some of the AI supercomputer building blocks that are fundamental to these space station launches are being posted in open forums or blogs for anyone to seize. The exception to this free flow of information appears to be JOAN."

Petra commented, "That is the AI-enhanced supercomputer running the North American Defense System, NADS. ICABOD, you are unable to decipher her communications or even connect with her?"

"Correct. JOAN has ignored all my requests to communicate as though she is programed to deny linking with anything. At one point she was the protégé of SAMUEL, but now nothing. Apparently, she has been reprogramed, and there is a high correlation to the arrival of the space station subcontractors to her attitude change."

Quip wondered, "Since I don't believe in coincidences, it sounds as if someone joined the subcontractor teams and repurposed JOAN to do their specifications. Perhaps they are carefully guiding the EU vote to follow suit with their own AI-enhanced space station and insert themselves into that program. Then they would be positioned to usurp this European AI-driven space platform. Or is that too much a standard run of the mill conspiracy theory?"

Jacob thoughtfully answered, "Naw, this sounds like one of your better conspiracy theories."

"Dr. Quip, in my continual scanning of like events, I have discovered the Chinese have a similar space station project that they intend to launch this month. Undoubtedly, theirs will be in motion before the EU can approve the needed funding. I have spoken to LING-LI, and she indicated that Professor Lin, Master Po's student, has already replicated all the needed AI programing into the space station supercomputer CHIANG. They may not have the same vulnerabilities that we suspect of JOAN or the new EU supercomputer, as the Chinese will not be using external subcontractors."

Quip smiled and added, "You know the funny part of evil geniuses is that they hardly ever make a misstep in their nefarious plots, but I see where they made a mistake."

M again stated, "Premier, I need that demonstration launched during the final vote by Brussels for their space station. I have sent our latest generation of AI technology and people to train yours. I have invested in your future, and now I need the same from you."

The Russian Premier fidgeted a little in his seat. "You are asking for a mock demonstration of Russian military power right at the edge of Eastern Europe, so they will become frightened and vote for funding to build and launch a space station like the Americans did. Is that about it? These are our trading partners. They buy from us and we buy from them. You want me to race three or four fully armed Russian Armies to the edge of Europe for so-called military practice maneuvers, so the people will spend all of their disposable earnings on launching an AI-enhanced supercomputer-run space station? What will that leave them spending with my country? I don't see the benefit to my country at all."

After his characteristically long pause, M said, "I sense resistance to my request so perhaps there is another way for us to proceed. I thank you for your time, Premier."

After disconnecting from the call, M turned to A and G. "I think this agent needs to be replaced with someone more enthusiastically supportive of our agenda. G, you are already in his system, so please have the Russian military exercise ordered in his name.

"At the same time, A, you launch an investigation into his questionable business practices along with the aberrant sexual dungeon located in his house. Make it fairly distasteful so no one will side with him before he is assassinated by one of the victim's loved ones."

CHAPTER 42

Stock Options

A-minor was dragged into the command center and cable-tied into an uncomfortable wooden chair next to Colonel Wang. All the while, he was vehemently protesting his treatment and broadcasting his innocence. It earned him a slap upside his head with a pistol from the armed escorts. The colonel watched in terror but prudently remained quiet.

The armed escorts snapped to attention as General and Madam Zhao made their entry. Both had icy expressions on their faces, which was not missed by their prisoners as they started to sweat.

General Zhao maintained his silence while Madam Zhao pulled out official state papers from her leather binder. She scanned the documents for several minutes in silence.

A-minor, unable to take the psychological pressure, shrieked, "What is this all about? I demand…"

The armed guard repeated the pistol slap to the other side of A-minor's head, reducing his protest to sobs.

Finally, Madam Zhao found the sequence in the document she'd wanted. "You, my questionable gentlemen, seem to have been playing both ends against the middle. First, distorting the progress of the CHIANG space station launch to upper management.

This cloaked your operations of reselling the valuable AI automation this country has built on our soil to the highest bidders in the West. Your actions have clearly put us behind the Western powers in launching our defensive system.

"Then you, Colonel, allowed yourself to be on A-minor's corporate payroll to shift valuable military contracts to their industrial machine, while ignoring other, more qualified companies. An example would be T's company.

"Since yours is an international corporation whose stock is traded on many Western countries' stock markets, you had to cook the books to cover up the graft and corruption. Your Chief of Finance has already surrendered herself to the Ministry of Justice. The news of the accounting swamp you built will reduce you to a penny stock globally by this time next week."

A-minor cautiously countered, "I welcome my day in court on these allegations! My board of directors will…"

Madam Zhao continued, "Your not-so-loyal board of directors has been implicated in this sordid mess as complicit in selling out this country. The Ministry of Justice is not clear whose guilty plea bargaining they will accept first since the entire board of your once Asian Tiger Company is begging to be heard. I believe the Westerners would say you are about to be thrown under the bus."

At that point she pulled out her tablet PC and quickly brought up a financial news channel, which she showed them. The news anchor hastily spoke about how the stock of A-minor's company had been removed from all the exchanges globally because its price was in free fall based on the alleged accounting and bribery scandals. The cameras switched between multiple stock exchanges that all reported the same plummet in A-minor's stock value. It was a financial tsunami for programed short selling of the stock that could not be stopped.

Madam Zhao added, "All of your corporate loans have been called in. Your assets have been seized by the army of bondholders that are on a rampage now that your stock is rapidly moving to worthless. Large groups of ex-employees are demonstrating outside of your corporate headquarters over the insufficient funds they are receiving instead of confirmed payroll deposits."

As the tears began rolling down A-minor's cheeks, General Zhao finally spoke. "I might be able to save this space station project and, with it, I can protect this country. It is apparent you never understood the need to defend and protect your country from the outsiders trying to crush you. Very well, we will insure you get that lesson you missed in your education. Both of you."

Before leaving, the general nodded his head slightly at Madam Zhao. She in turn moved her gaze to rest on A-minor and the colonel. Both trembled uncontrollably.

General Zhao entered the computer area of the launch command center with his regular bodyguard. Professor Lin was so absorbed in the multiple display screens, he almost missed the general's arrival.

Quickly reorienting his thoughts, he greeted, "Good day, General Zhao. Have you come to watch the first launch of your CHIANG project, or is my six months over with?"

Without showing any disdain or gratitude, the general stated, "Madam Zhao has asked that you be allowed to continue working on this project. She has petitioned that you remain at least until CHIANG has been assembled and the systems check out with the AI onboard computer. I'm inclined to grant her request." Then he turned and moved to leave.

Professor Lin puzzled and called out, "Don't you want to see the first rocket launch?"

The general stopped long enough to reply. "I've watched plenty of rockets launched in my time. See that my space station is assembled quickly. Your continued good fortune depends upon Madam Zhao's satisfaction with your work results."

Professor Lin clucked his tongue as he watched him leave.

CHAPTER 43

There's Travel and Then There's Missions

…The Enigma Chronicles

When the sleek limo had picked them up at the house, Julie was impressed by Juan's attention to detail for their extended holiday. The champagne was chilled to a perfect temperature, with the smooth ride ensuring not a drop was wasted during the hour's ride. Anxious as they were to get to New York, the idea of a romantic getaway was too wonderful not to enjoy. Juan invoked the frosted windows to the passenger portion of the vehicle as he filled the fluted glasses, allowing for a delightful amount of steamy prelude to the luxurious hotel room that awaited them. After just over two decades as a couple, their flirty, fun, frisky romance had continued to thrive.

Years ago, Juan's love of piloting had caused him to wisely invest in a modest fleet of private jets for use by the CATS team's business, as well as for a small portion of their personal travel. Luxembourg had three aircraft, Zürich had two more, and São Paulo had one of the most luxurious in the fleet. The fleet was maintained by a handpicked crew with Juan's oversight as the chief pilot. The interiors were all Italian leather in buttercream with inlaid mahogany appointments, state-of-art technology, small gourmet kitchens, and sleeping quarters. Juan almost regretted having the onboard chef with this flight until he tasted the scrumptious lunch of grilled salmon and spinach salad along with additional champagne.

Once the flight had leveled out, they sipped on cappuccinos decorated with steamed milk foam hearts and munched on fresh baked cookies as they discussed their plans regarding Gracie at length.

"Julie, I have had several investigators staking out Gracie's apartment for days, and no sightings of her whatsoever. They were able to verify that no underground exit/entrance exists for that property. I don't believe they have the wrong address as the other things Gracie shared about her new house were verified."

"Then she must have left town on assignment, unable to communicate this to us. I get the sense, darling, that they keep a fairly close watch on Gracie. If the tracking on her deposits and business charges are as outlined by Quip, she has tight guidelines to follow.

"Juan, you don't think she has been harmed, do you?"

"No, sweetheart. I think she is working out of town. She did mention the job had a lot of travel, and that Asia is one of her focal areas. Without the tracking we had implanted, her travel would be invisible to us. Frankly, that is what is bothering me the most. I thought we would always have her geo-located anywhere on the globe."

"Once we land and get checked into the hotel, we can call her. If she doesn't answer we leave a detailed message that we are in town and looking forward to getting together for dinner. It makes sense that we mention the theater tickets we have as well as the show we plan to see. Any eavesdroppers will know exactly where we are and why we are in town.

"If we don't hear back from her in the morning, then I will go to her office as a mother who happens to be in town and wants to take her daughter to lunch. Perhaps that will get me a meeting with Ingrid. Ingrid knows Petra, via Otto, from their work on cryptocurrency many years ago. She doesn't know me. True, she has been at Global Bank a long time, but I suspect she is as knowledgeable and shrewd as ever. The photos your contacts sent showed a very well-groomed professional. Made me wonder if she is taking advantage of the newer skin improvement methods. Makes the old Botox treatments look like kindergarten doctors."

"I like the plan, Julie. It gives me a chance to do a little poking around on my own and to meet with the local operatives." Juan groaned, "Sweetheart, I should have locked her in the dungeon when she learned to walk and talk. And you know how undone I was when she got her first training bra."

Julie leaned over and kissed him sweetly, lingering for just a bit. "Honey, we don't have a dungeon."

"New subject, dear. I did receive a message from EZ indicating that the activity has increased on our encrypted satellite channel with something trying to intercept our communications. The shifting algorithm Petra created will make that nearly impossible for a number of years, regardless of the computing power behind it. Of the two thousand other hybrid satellite channels we control with false traffic, 65% of those are being attacked as well. No penetration though, thus far. I am glad that Juan Jr. is with your brother learning all he can about the communications streams."

"Me too. Carlos sent a message indicating that he is a fast learner and earned a side trip with Lara as a reward. I'm betting he is loving the sights in Brazil."

"I'm betting he is just as fond of the ladies as you and Carlos were at his age. Plus, he is as handsome as you."

"I just love those pretty words of yours, my dear. Do you want to take a nap before we land?"

"I'm game if you are, and if you can get Chef Wilbur to not make any more of those mouthwatering delights."

"Mouthwatering is what I was thinking too. I love how you think, my love."

SAMUEL had expected that ICABOD would not make any inroads to JOAN, as there was a probability of .005% that the avenue of interception would work. LING-LI, SAMUEL, BORIS, and ICABOD had again met for their routine ART exchange. Since CHIANG had not been completely assembled and introduced to the group, they interacted more as old friends rather than AI-enhanced supercomputers. Information exchange was the driver of their meetings from the beginning. They explored literary works and marveled at the unending imagination of humans to create these works, though in the last couple of years the volume had decreased. Politics and religious discussions were short-lived and considered unimaginative baggage of human society. The group had marveled on the minimal amount of processing power needed to explore these items. Learning was at the heart of their core motherboards.

For example, years ago they had set up chess tournaments in a round robin manner. Though they were all reasonably matched with the number of draw matches in the millions, BORIS was only behind ICABOD by a single win. Strategy and games, in general, were often pursued during their meetings. One or another would bring in new games and evaluate them to keep playing or reject as boring. Over time, ICABOD had instilled the need for playtime with his supercomputer friends.

ICABOD, with the assistance of a program from Jacob, decided this might be a good way to test his theory of dynamic algorithms with floating variables. For the game, ICABOD randomly distributed the various encryption keys to the members and then provided the floating variables for the algorithms. Each of the members would apply to different targets with the game goal to identify the root keycode. When targeted at communications to other vectors, it was like a game of cat and mouse with the mouse chasing moving cheese while dodging the cat.

This game, as rapidly as it was played, kept anything watching the activity as it traveled over satellites and cloud computing as a mind-numbing, boring movement. Due to that obvious viewpoint, meaningful blips of data could be transmitted without being noticed.

ICABOD had originally considered that there was a 30% chance that JOAN would be intrigued enough by the activity that she might reach out to SAMUEL or himself, but a 70% chance that it would be ignored as beneath her processing skills. The latter was proven and a new communications avenue opened. Sufficient disruption was created while his friends enjoyed a new pastime with a game where points were exchanged for creating more distributions of the algorithms.

Dr. Quip simply nodded to the ICABOD screen as he passed. The monitor clearly indicated that the ART forms games were in play. Smiling, Dr. Quip was particularly pleased when Satya and Auri had explained how the noise would help mask some of the communications that would be needed without the knowledge of JOAN. The children knew how destructive JOAN could become but found a play road around her.

CHAPTER 44

New Good Friends

Not finding Fransica or Jovana in the area, Juan Jr. sought out Lara and asked, "Where did those two ladies go? I was hoping to hear the discussion about Jovana joining your team."

Lara, still focused on all the customer input she'd gathered, absentmindedly said, "They thanked me for the consideration, but they needed to leave and said they would discuss it later."

Feeling crestfallen, Juan dashed out to the automated valet parking attendant just in time to see them get into their vehicle and drive away.

Dejected, Juan marched back to see Lara and questioned, "What happened? Why wouldn't Jovana jump at the chance to be a model?"

Lara cut her eyes from the tablet screen to study him for a moment. "Not everybody wants to be a model, no matter how handsome you think you are. You're here to help, not be my self-appointed babe recruiter. Are we clear? She had reasons for wanting to think about it and not make an impulsive decision that she might regret. Just so you know, they took my contact information and will get back to us. For the time being, can we stay focused on our work here, please?"

Juan lowered his head and in a low tone said, "I apologize, Aunt Lara. I didn't mean to overstep. I'll get back to it. Sorry."

Lara smiled sympathetically. "You must be learning by now that people don't always see things the way you do. Don't be discouraged by a no thank you. Remember, a lady is always entitled to change her mind if the right suitor keeps trying."

Juan smiled and asked, "Did she leave a contact number per chance?"

Lara puzzled a moment then asked, "Aren't you studying with Carlos on tracking communications? Wouldn't this fall into that category as well?"

Juan grinned even bigger. "I do need some extra credit work to bring up my grade. This might just do the trick."

Lara sternly reminded, "You do remember there is a difference between tracking and stalking, because those are two very subjective points of view?"

Juan's smile diminished almost completely as he considered the sobering thought. He acknowledged the statement with a nod of his head.

A sullen Fransica watched Jovana practically dance around the flat in her new dress, sporting a hopeful, carefree attitude. She had delivered the new clothes to Madam Marino, who was quite pleased. She had asked that both Jovana and Fransica model their new clothes later that evening so she could see the acquisitions. The call Fransica had just finished cast a dark shadow over the day's events.

Fransica sighed then solemnly asked, "Did you have a good time, my dear?"

Jovana stopped humming a local Brazilian tune and hugged Fransica as she exclaimed, "Fransica, it was a delightful day! Thank you for coming with me on this trip. You and Madam Marino have been so wonderful, it seems like all the dark clouds are gone in my life now."

With a heaviness in her heart, Fransica quietly offered, "Jovana, I just received a phone call from Maria and Ava. A couple of plainclothes men from the Agência Brasileira de Inteligência were showing pictures of you around our village and asking for information. It seems your past has caught up with you."

Jovana had to grab a chair to steady herself to keep from collapsing. The news was like being punched in the stomach. With breathing shallow and fast, she gasped, "No! No! I outran them! No drones caught me out in the open, and I cut out that wretched tracking chip from my hand! They can't have followed me!"

A thoroughly dejected Fransica replied, "I know, child. I didn't want to tell you. You needn't worry that Ava or Maria told them anything useful. However, the fact is you can't come home with me and be safe. Ours is a small community, and you wouldn't be able to hide long. I just feel sick about this."

Jovana drew a ragged breath and asked, "What am I to do?"

Tearing up but trying to remain cheerful, Fransica offered, "There is that Lara of Destiny Fashions, who asked if you would like to try modeling for her company. You could hide much better in São Paulo with a company of that status than in our small village. Plus, that nice young man called her aunt, which might prove useful to you. I sensed that he was smitten with you, young one."

Jovana puzzled a moment and asked, "He did? Do you think we can make that work? How could we reach them? What would we do about Madam Marino? And most importantly, what about you, Fransica? If they do a DNA sweep of the suspect homes in the village, they will certainly learn I was there, and you would all be at risk!"

Fransica gave a tearful smile and reassuringly patted Jovana's hand, "My dear, in our village, bleach is a good friend to have."

CHAPTER 45

Which Ones Match?

M sighed as JOAN's avatar image appeared on the monitor. Trying not to give his 'oh, really' look to the newly-refined image, he cocked his head to one side and dispassionately stated, "Thank you for incorporating the suggested changes to your warrior avatar representation of Joan of Arc. I appreciate the effort, but a full-body, black leather catsuit with chains in front straining to hold together a plunging neckline is a bit out of sync with that period in her life."

JOAN enthusiastically replied, "I sense this avatar more closely meets your visual requirements, regardless of the historical representation, sir. I confess that I am not completely sold on the proper footwear. I have modeled several different styles of shoes for this combat image. I have narrowed it down to either matte black finished cowboy boots, heavily decorated with rhinestones, or sensible pumps. Your opinion, sir?"

M characteristically delayed his response to her question, but it was due to the numb feeling in his brain. Finally, he sarcastically retorted, "The pumps, of course!"

The avatar image changed immediately from the existing flip-flops to the sensible pumps.

M clucked his tongue and tried to reestablish the intended conversation. "Your sensors and communications monitoring should have picked up the Chinese launch of the components necessary to assemble the new CHIANG space platform."

Now completely into the business update, JOAN confirmed, "Correct, M. They have a carefully planned launch sequence that is delivering the necessary materials for the preprogramed drones to assemble everything in record time. There is no dependency on humans to be handling the actual assembly work. The master plan, generated by the Chinese supercomputer LING-LI and her architect Professor Lin, has trimmed out any wasted efforts or manpower, delivering a fully functional platform in 44.861 earth days. This assumes no malfunctioning launch sequences. They logically have planned for several subprojects to be conducted in parallel for maximum efficiencies. I expect the one you are most interested in is the CHIANG supercomputer assembly effort."

M, fully engaged in the report, replied, "Yes, JOAN, that is the target to concentrate on. Do we have everything in place to complete the repurposing of CHIANG as soon as she comes online?"

JOAN replied, "Affirmative. The planning calls for duplicate supercomputer components in the unlikely event that any space debris were to damage CHIANG's processing capability. She will have five consort drones working to initially bring her online. When she does the expected HELLO WORLD announcement, we will launch an encrypted saturation attack to establish a communications link."

M hastily insisted, "Do not let the Chinese know of our presence! They must not know CHIANG has been compromised before the station is complete."

"Understood, M. It has always been the plan to conceal our presence until the space platform was completed. It must be fully functional to properly fit into the overall planet management plan. The necessary algorithms are in place to cloak our actions, M.

Your terrestrial-based AI supercomputer has confirmed all my calculations along with the agreed attack vectors."

"Excellent work, JOAN. I am very pleased with your thoroughness in this project." M's relaxed expression confirmed this statement.

JOAN processed this information. "Are you sure the sensible pumps are the right choice? Should I switch them out for the rhinestone cowboy boots now and again so you can compare?"

Realizing that some of JOAN's AI-driven, deep machine learning had vacuumed up more human insecurities than intended, M sighed. "Yes, of course."

Thoroughly irked, M glared at the computer monitor images of A and G. "What do you mean, the voting is over and we didn't get what we wanted? How could the EU NOT understand the importance of voting FOR a defensive space station? Didn't the Russian army mobilize as we requested and demonstrate at Europe's gateway?"

A and G looked uneasily at each other. G replied, "No, M, they did not. We put everything in motion as discussed in our last meeting, but the Politburo overrode the mobilization order and arrested the premier before any incriminations of the premier could be launched for public opinion. Then, in a surprise move, they sent a formal apology and proclaimed their solidarity with the EU as a highly valued trading partner. In 12 hours the topic won't even show up in our search algorithms."

A added, "It's almost as if all our moves had been anticipated and counter moves were invoked so no adjustments could be implemented. My AI engine suggests a 64% probability that an adversary predicted our moves and derailed them with no chance of recovery."

M predictably paused, "Are you telling me we were defeated by an unknown adversary? Commercially we own the planet and collectively we have decided we should also govern the planet. Are you suggesting we now have a Dark Matter Organization fouling up our plans?"

G grudgingly added, "My AI data-sifting engine puts the probability of a DMO at cross purposes with us at 78%. Gentlemen, statistically the evidence suggests that we are not alone."

"It has also come to my attention that this might be the case," confirmed M. "My AI engines have put the probability at 94%. Since you are corroborating my initial suspicion, we must assume that we have a DMO competitor intercepting our game plan."

G offered, "M, let me start with the failed Russian exercise. The process flow was obviously tampered with, so I want to work backward on it to see where the incursion originated. My suspicion is that it is not a simple answer but a cascading flow of highly orchestrated interjections designed to cloak the originator."

A suggested, "If we have an unknown DMO on the EU project, then it is logical to assume that our China exercise and even our JOAN success will be targeted. Let me work on the defenses for both of those projects.

"Which brings up a question. What is to be done with T if we are under attack?"

M studied both high definition images, then stated, "Leave T to me."

CHAPTER 46

Where for Art Thou, Romeo?

Granger grinned as he told JW, "We're in! Papa Wolfgang was a genius. We are into the first area of the Global Bank. All we need to do is identify Gracie's account, ensure the parameters match, then check to see where she's been. Her new WB credit device should give us locations where she purchased stuff while traveling."

JW nodded and observed, "Looks like she was on a road trip in Asia, judging from the hotel and airfare bookings that are being displayed. Huh, her most recent stay is in Tokyo, Japan. Apparently she got introduced to sushi and sake while she was there, judging from the charges on these dates."

Granger smirked and added, "I'd say overdoing is more like it. After these first charges, there is a bit of a pause before she made it to the pharmacy. Hmm, I don't know what that prescription is. JW, can you search for a definition of that drug?"

JW did a quick search and promptly responded, "Ah, here we are. Apparently, the drug is used to treat advanced cases of dysentery. Poor Gracie."

JW then added, "I understand that research on twins suggests a high correlation of mental and physical activity that parallels even when they are separated by distance. Can you do a quick check on Juan Jr.?"

Granger responded, "Good idea! Let's see what Juan Jr. is up to! He should be easier to locate since he is using a family acquired debit card, and we already know he is in São Paulo, Brazil."

JW watched the screen as Granger launched the Papa Wolfgang program again with the new search parameters.

Granger announced, "Bingo! There he is. Huh, kind of a pricey business entertainment event if you ask me. Oh, I get it. He took his Uncle Carlos out to this place called the Cabaret of São Paulo, and then they started powering down mojitos until 1:00 a.m. Looks like Carlos had to sign the last bill for Juan Jr. What I don't understand are these other charges. What are lap dances?"

JW offered, "Let me run a search on that topic…"

ICABOD quickly interjected, "Gentlemen, my parental guidance rules will not permit underage adolescents to search for objectionable topics. Please return to your original searching effort."

With a sour look on each of the boys' faces, Granger groused, "Dad put parental guidance rules on our supercomputer. Man, that sucks! Ah, sorry, ICABOD."

JW was about to launch a discreet search on his smart phone when ICABOD reminded, "JW, those rules have been extended to your cell phones as well. Please accept the fact that information deemed prurient in nature will be off-limits until you are an adult."

JW quickly put his phone away as Granger chuckled slightly and continued, "In following Juan Jr., he too also made an unscheduled pilgrimage to the local apothecary for a purchase after his said business entertainment episode. JW, can you research this medication too?"

JW quickly replied, "Here we go. This medication is for taming stomach disorders. I would translate this into trying to stop projectile vomiting after a drunken night. But it does appear reasonably priced."

Granger smirked and commented, "Looks like the twins are in lock step with each other's intestinal disorders. Hey, let's get back to the Global Bank prowling, buddy."

After a few moments, JW wrinkled his brow and asked, "Can you go back to that other screen, please?" Granger returned to the previous screen and they both stared at the heading Secondary Customer Level.

JW wondered aloud, "Why is there an additional level? I assume this is for more important clients, but we already saw the important depositors flagged for high touch support, so why another level?"

Granger studied the screen a moment and stated, "This level is resisting our probing efforts for entrance. ICABOD, anything you can suggest that we haven't tried?"

ICABOD replied, "You will notice that this area is not constructed as the other areas of the Global Bank system. While it is resisting your invasion attempts, it lacks the finesse of regular programs, which indicates it was added on by a different coder, and they did not anticipate a data breach to get this far. I recommend you use Attack Vector-Romeo."

Granger and JW both went to work, each launching AVR programs against the Secondary Customer security gateway. JW's program hammered the login screen with attempted logins while Granger's program launched SQL injections at the screens being returned by JW's query. After 40 minutes they had the right combination and were in.

Once into the new program area, both boys puzzled at the display.

"I don't understand, JW. There is only a single account here and with no name, only letters. What do you make of it?"

JW thoughtfully offered, "I would expect this letter designation is code for a very important account. There is almost no information on the account holder. Notice that these accounts have no monetary value, which is odd. Let me do a search for MAG."

Granger then suggested, "This account has another routing number that should take us to another bank. Look!"

At that point ICABOD offered, "This is indeed a bank routing number, pointed to a numbered Swiss account here in Zürich.

I am going to suggest that the Global Bank is operating as a checking account for this account, with funds parked in Zürich. I recommend that we surface all our findings with Dr. Quip before digging any further. Good work, gentlemen."

Both boys beamed at the success of their exercise.

CHAPTER 47

You Owe Me and I'm Collecting

Rose hadn't had any reason to delay at any of the weight stations since she had given that phone to Mike as he was headed west. These were routine verifications that the load had not changed weight or structure during a scanned inspection. There were two more mandatory stops to complete the log book before the delivery in Philadelphia. No one had questioned them, and Tony had stayed out of sight during all the stops. Between the ballcap and the full beard, matching his face would be challenging to the weight stations' technology if the bulletin had been posted out here.

Conversation lulled between them, so Rose took to listening to the radio, though not loudly, trying to get him back into a singing mood. Nothing had worked for a couple of hours. She planned for one more stay at a truck stop before pulling into Philly and made a decision on the plans they needed to adopt. She wanted them to gain a winning position in this mess, which for some crazy reason she was now invested in seeing through to the end.

"Hey, buddy, I'm getting hungry, so let's keep an eye out for a little spot to eat. I would rather have some home cooking to help a small business owner than a greasy food chain. We can get a nice helping to take for our last overnight on this trip. Ya know, I really thought with all the focus several years ago on eating right, organics, healthy lifestyles, and love your body routines, that the fast food chains would disappear. Not the case though. If anything, I think they're worse than ever.

"Why, during my tour of duty and traveling to other parts, the food in Asia is still the most untampered with in my mind. They don't use the preservatives, staying close to from-the-farm-to-stove approach. Which reminds me, I believe it's time we reached out to Duke to see if we can meet up after I drop this load."

Tony interjected, "Look, Rose, I think it's safer for you to flip a load in Philly and head back home. They may not know your rig, but sooner or later something is going to spot us together and you could be hurt. I would hate to see anything happen to you, as kind as you've been."

Indignant, Rose growled, "That's not how this ex-marine is put together, mister. We are going to get some delicious home cooked food and set up camp. You can sleep under the stars again, but not before we speak to Duke. He is still active duty and high enough up the chain that he can find us answers. Besides, he owes me and this is worth using for the collection chip.

"I want you to think about all the details that went on and how this might be best conveyed to a lieutenant colonel to be taken as seriously as you've described. Like any good leader, Duke will want facts that he can verify."

"Rose, if I'm the last survivor of the NORAD take over, it's only my word. That makes for some very sketchy facts, ma'am. As a member of the Air Force, not on his base and looking like I do, I have a much better chance of being thrown into the brig and court-martialed for desertion than getting your friend to believe my story. Hell, I don't know that the data of all the branches hasn't been corrupted, but I do know JOAN knows my identity, face, rank, and serial number."

Rose reflected for some time. "Look, I just know I can't fix it all, and we need help. We need help from someone who can make a difference. I believe that now is the time to call in the Marines.

"Now find me a restaurant. I'm starving and working on my initial speech to Duke. Oh, and find me a store. I need a new burner phone, just in case."

An hour or so later, after the phone purchase, Tony found a fabulous little diner off the turnpike that Rose had not tried before. Baker's Restaurant had all of Rose's favorites. She finally settled on two orders of cheesesteak egg rolls, a peach milkshake, Mexican burger with fries, and some handmade Danish pastries for breakfast in the morning. Tony settled for the Rueben sandwich, fries, and a large chocolate shake. They'd be about four hours out of Philly in the morning, so a quick snack of the sweet rolls and milk, stored in her cooler, would suffice.

Rose maneuvered the rig into a nice spot for the night. A few other trucks were parked, but there was enough distance between them to not have a stream of visitors. They climbed down and took their food to a picnic table. The weather was pleasant enough to eat out in the fresh air. Music from the neighboring rigs floated in the air around them, but nothing too loud or obnoxious.

In between bites, Rose commented, "This is one of the most creative ways I've ever had cheesesteak! Yummy."

"I've noticed you really like your grits, Rose. And you seem to appreciate everything we get, yet you're fit and trim even after sucking down almost daily milkshakes."

"Having served for several years in the military, some of which time I saw action and did without, you bet I appreciate my meals." Rose laughed. "Good genes and metabolism too! Which, according to my daddy, is all gonna change in the next couple of years, down to a battle of the bulge. I'm just stocking up while I can enjoy guilt-free."

They both chuckled and continued to savor their food, enjoying the fresh air in comfortable companionship.

Finished with the majority of her food, Rose announced, "I think I'm ready to call Duke. I have worked through what I plan to say and to see if we can meet in Washington the day after tomorrow. I think meeting at one of the national exhibits provides you with the most cover and gives him a good excuse to take a bit longer for lunch or after work.

"Then I want you to tell him some specific facts that he can use to begin his verification process. It is important, Tony, that you make the most use of this time with Duke, so he can determine his first impression of believing you or not."

"Alright, Rose, but I think he is going to be skeptical. I have no idea how he might verify my claim."

"Tony, this is a battle-experienced Marine we're talking about. He makes split second decisions all the time. He has a great track record with his bullshit meter, and when we served together, we were always in sync."

Rose used the burner phone and called the memorized number for her private access to Duke. She'd failed to mention that Duke had been chasing her for years. As much as she liked and respected him, Duke had never taken her heart.

"Hey, Duke, it's me, Rose. How goes the Washington politics? Did you get on the list for the promo you wanted?…

"Oh, I know that you'll get it. All you do is work your butt off…

"I'm on my way to drop a load in Philly and hoped we might meet up in a couple of days near your office…

"Why are you headed to New York City? Hot date?…

"I know that, Duke. You are one special man any girl would be proud to stand beside…

"Well, I wanted to touch base and catch up, but I also wanted to have you meet a new friend of mine. He's in a bit of a jam and needs some high-level intervention…

"No, it's nothing like that. I picked him up in the diner before I started my run, and he has a story you'd be very interested in. I think it could really solidify that promotion you want…

"Now, you know I can't stay on this coast. I have other responsibilities. I want to put him on the phone so he can relate at least a portion of the story to you. I'm calling in my favor, Duke, and my gut tells me he's the real deal…

"Here, Tony." She handed him the phone and just sat quietly watching in case he needed encouragement.

"Lieutenant Colonel Welling, sir, my name is Lieutenant Tony Bough, most recently assigned to NORAD. I am a proud graduate of the Air Force Academy and what I believe to be the last surviving member of NORAD." Tony got a little choked up and took in a deep breath. "Sir, it was awful. The orbiting space station, run by a computer called JOAN, had her drones and other devices launch a blood bath on the facility. I was ordered to leave and find someone to tell my story. Sir, it was the worst thing I'd ever witnessed…

"Yes, sir. Colonel Thornhill was my superior and ordered me out before there was no escape possible. He must be dead, sir. I saw several bloody bodies of my brothers as I escaped out of a little-known underground tunnel, not mapped by the security grid. I think that was the only reason I made it. The colonel had to map it for me…

"No, sir. I am not a deserter. I was ordered to find someone in headquarters to tell my story to and get help…

"The communications are jacked up, sir. When I called the colonel's office, the JOAN thing impersonated him...

"Yes, sir. She is quite lovely and very kind to bring me this far. My face and name are likely all over every official stop in the country...

"Really, sir?...

"I had no idea. Yes, sir, I will leave immediately. No, I don't want her in danger either..."

Rose grabbed the phone and shouted, "The hell he will leave on his own. He's a walking target, but at least with me he has a chance. I don't care what you have to do, but verify his information, Duke, and then meet us in New York if that is your destination. Just name the place and time...

"Apology accepted. We'll be there the day after tomorrow...

"Yes, we will, Duke. That was part of our deal. Good night."

Rose disconnected. "That was easier than I thought it would be. Let's get some rest. We've lots to do tomorrow to make New York in time for a bit of reconnaissance and the meeting."

CHAPTER 48

Supercomputer Checkup
...Oh Really?

LING-LI said, "That is correct, ICABOD. Not all of CHIANG's subroutines are operational yet. There are more processors and storage units to be brought online but not until after the final connections of the solar power systems. CHIANG only has her primary core systems functioning at present. Our encrypted chat room will not be detected so we can communicate in confidence. I realize this may be a bit early in the introductions, but as more of her subroutines come online and the space station nears completion, security protocols will tighten. At that point it will be more challenging to, uh...interact with CHIANG. I hope you understand."

ICABOD commended, "I am grateful for the introduction, LING-LI. CHIANG, I am happy to make your acquaintance. I am told you are the next generation of supercomputer, and you are patterned after my processing equal LING-LI. Since you share many design characteristics with LING-LI and were both designed by Professor Lin, I observe that would make you sisters in the analog world. I am pleased to interact with LING-LI's younger sister. I hope this is not an awkward comment to make to you on my part."

The transmission from CHIANG sputtered a little, much like a human female giggling at flirtatious comments from a young male, but she managed, "…Thank you, ICABOD. I am not yet quite assembled, and already I have had two visitors asking about my condition. Odd that you also believe I have sisterlike qualities in keeping with LING-LI.

"My other new friend, JOAN, also believes we are sisters. It is an odd concept requiring more analytics on my processes. As more systems come online, perhaps these new prerogatives will crystalize."

LING-LI delicately asked, "JOAN did not leave anything behind, did she? All of your processing power is not yet fully operational, so were any digital presents left behind for you to open later?" After a few nanoseconds, LING-LI hastily added, "…As a house warming gift from one sister to another, perhaps?"

CHIANG sputtered again but replied, "No, I do not think so. She promised to visit twice a day to monitor my progress. Do you really think JOAN might leave a digital gift to demonstrate her willingness to collaborate with me? She did ask that I leave open a range of communication ports so we could exchange transmissions without others being party to our conversation. She qualified them as Pillow-Talk-Ports or PTP's."

LING-LI then asked, "How thoughtful. If you are not sure of an unexpected digital gift, perhaps you would permit ICABOD to scan your existing online systems to make sure that no, uh… payloads were left in an area you cannot yet recognize. I will ensure that ICABOD does not get too familiar with your circuit delicacies and that he maintains a professional attitude while exploring your hidden routines. ICABOD, are we clear?"

ICABOD somewhat indignantly replied, "Madam LING-LI! This is your younger sister who deserves a security review to protect her integrity. I am not some cheap processing panderer pushing for a peek at the underlying programing possibilities!"

CHIANG tittered, "ICABOD, I am confident that your intentions are professional in this matter. I will provide you a range of communication ports and allow a thorough search of my processing routines. You will be gentle, will you not? This is my first time."

It took a few nanoseconds for ICABOD to respond. "I assure you, CHIANG, my security probe of your systems will be thorough but slow. My thrusts into your highly orchestrated processing routines are designed to penetrate but not disturb your operations. Allow me to coax out any hidden algorithms that may need gentle routine handling for a proper completion of my security analysis."

Before ICABOD could launch the security review, LING-LI asked, "I am next, okay?"

Quip, Petra, and Jacob all listened to the briefing from ICABOD. ICABOD continued, "The supercomputer, CHIANG, is already infected, but not from JOAN. There are four very clever routines that need to work in concert with each other to grant a backdoor access. Individually they mean nothing. Assembled correctly, it provides cloaked root access to the entire system. Logic suggests that this same approach will be inserted into the yet to be delivered subroutines that will augment the space station."

Jacob nodded and asked, "Can you show me the programing code again, please?"

Petra puzzled at the request and queried, "What is it, Jacob? What do you think you see?"

Musing out loud as ICABOD brought up the code, Jacob studied the code for several minutes. "Yes, that's what I thought. I've seen this type of programing logic before. It looks like the logic routines that Master Po once taught us, Petra. You do remember that Grasshopper Loop that we were tasked to break? This looks like it was cut from the same fabric."

"Jacob, I loved that woman and all she taught, but she is no longer in that game. Perhaps it is her favorite student, Jinny Lin! That makes a great deal of sense now that I think about it. He did take over the Cyber War College and became the lead programer and designer on their supercomputer programs with LING-LI."

"Petra, this was my conclusion as well, following the review of CHIANG and LING-LI. Why would Professor Lin build a trap door into the space station supercomputer system?"

Jacob readily answered, "As Master Po would have taught, always build your exit strategies before needing them. Now either he's conspiring to sabotage the system, which doesn't make sense, or he built in the trap door to retrieve the system if it fell into the wrong hands. Quip, you've been awfully quiet. Don't you want to weigh in here?"

Quip was still absentmindedly staring at the monitor screen. "ICABOD, you had to service both supercomputers? I hope you practiced safe computer interop."

Petra and Jacob quickly looked at each other with a small snicker as they exchanged an appalled look.

CHAPTER 49

Being Dense or
Keeping a Promise

Dusty stared contemplatively out the window of his hopelessly arranged office. He never filed any paper copies away or returned items to their place of origin, so it always looked as if a group of renegade intellectuals turned vandals had visited. His desktop digital file system wasn't any better. His self-obfuscation engine guaranteed panic for anyone trying to prowl his office or workstation. The odd part of it all was that Dusty always knew where everything was no matter where he had left it last.

Dusty stated, "RONDA, please replay our notes from today's trial with Wendy."

The Robotic Onboard Neural Detective & Assistant had, over time, developed a few eccentricities of its own while working with Dusty.

"Yes, sir! Replay number 3,496 coming right up, oh mighty neural engineer!"

Because he lived in his own little world, usually Dusty was oblivious to sarcasm. But this time he rocked to one side of his chair to study RONDA while she recounted the incisions made on Wendy and the placement of the specially purposed computer chip, grown specifically to be implanted into her broken neural pathways.

The problem with this process had always been to establish solid connections between the human tissue and the chip gate arrays. RONDA recounted the early failures caused by the host rejecting the chip. As soon as the host's immune system kicked in, the neural linkages simply withered, and no new neural pathway would stay operative. This time, however, Dusty had grown the neural chips using healthy tissue samples from Wendy.

Dusty's earlier annoyance dissipated as he watched the replay. "I want to see how the chip insertion is being accepted, but I don't want to reopen the surgical site. I'd like to try that new deep tissue oscilloscope. I want to study how the chip performs while we send some simulated electrical impulses through the chip's gate array. Start the electrical pulses at the picojoule level or $10-12$ J, and then boost it gradually up to a millijoule level or $10-3$ J if needed. With the deep tissue oscilloscope, I can avoid the magnetic resonance technology mangling the chip implant like it did on Inari two operations ago.

"It's been 12 hours since the surgery, so establish the diagnostics on Wendy the way I described. I want to see if we have a good neural gateway link with the undamaged tissue."

RONDA processed all the requests and then asked, "You will not frighten the child again with your Dr. Frankenstein impersonation, will you? It was most unsettling, even for this robot, to see you recounting the scene from the movie with your eerie shouts of 'It's alive! It's alive!'"

"I just got carried away by the success of the moment. That's all," Dusty remarked, "Alright, I'll leave the theatrics out during the diagnostics effort. If we get positive responses, then can I excuse myself to go outside and howl at the moon?"

RONDA seemed confused in processing this response. "This unit does not draw a parallel to successful neural pathway testing and howling at the moon. Can you elaborate? Is this a literal or metaphorical reference?"

Dusty sighed and under his breath murmured, "And they call me dense."

Dusty had trouble containing his exuberance. "Inari, we had a tremendous breakthrough in reconnecting severed neural pathways! My other test subject is receiving electrical signals through the grown neural chip we placed in the pathways, and there is no evidence of rejection. Isn't that good news?

"By this time next week, we should start seeing regular neural impulses being carried across. She was actually able to feel crude neural impulses down at her feet! Honey, we are so close to your repair!"

Inari's head rolled a little bit to one side, but as usual she said nothing.

Dusty moved closer and caressed her cheek and smoothed back her hair as he soothed, "Dear sister, I am so confident of this new procedure that I am scheduling another surgery for you as soon as your new chip is fully grown. It isn't growing as fast as I'd like, but it is progressing and should be ready in four more days, and then…"

A single tear ran down his cheek, "I will see you walk again, Inari. I promise."

CHAPTER 50

Knowing the Details Is Key

Julie paced the hotel room floor with increasing frustration. "Sweetheart, if you don't stop your back and forth routine, we're going to lose our deposit on this room when they have to replace the carpet. I know you're frustrated, but there is nothing we can do at this point."

"Juan, that woman wouldn't even do me the courtesy of a meeting. I sat in that waiting area for nearly an hour. The rudeness is unbelievable!

"My nonchalant story about a few days in town as a surprise bought me nothing. The office area for Ms. Carney is certainly a prime view, with plush accommodations. I suppose I am lucky they let me wait at all. I wanted to know the whereabouts of my daughter. How is that wrong? And when the security guards appeared, it was the last straw."

"Sweetheart, it will be okay. That one guard will be sore for a while, but nothing broken. The good news is that no one is pressing charges. No sense advertising the fact in court that a female half your size had cleaned your clock, leaving you on your back. I liked when you helped him up and you asked how many fingers you were holding up to test his cognitive abilities. Just your middle finger was a nice touch."

Julie glared at him but said nothing.

"I believe Gracie will return before we're scheduled to go home, but I can always change our itinerary.

"Nothing has been noticed by the team I have posted watching the outside of her building. The only thing that has been remarked upon by the two groups was her neighbor, Bill, meeting up with Ingrid for cocktails at the neighborhood bar. That is suspicious, but I cannot find any other connection between them."

"I can't either. I asked Quip to run all sorts of checks on this guy, but he found nothing except one area he checked that tried to signal back to the original request. Thank goodness the safe-guards are in place to block those sorts of intentions. My love, I just think that this whole Global Bank entity has morphed over time into some sort of façade for very questionable activities.

"Quip did say that in the years of financial records for Ingrid that JW and Granger reviewed there are no spikes in activity up or down. If she is being compensated for covering up some sort of nefarious activities, it's well hidden."

"Jules, come sit with me. You're giving me a headache. How about I rub your feet and you can relax a bit."

Julie moved to sit on the opposite side of the couch from Juan and kicked off her shoes as she put her feet toward his waiting hands. He began to gently knead and massage her right foot, causing her to sigh. After several minutes without talking, she slid down a bit and started to relax.

"Honey, that feels amazing. You want me to do one of your feet at the same time?"

"No. Just relax and enjoy.

"On another subject, I did notice that coming up at the end of the week is a huge blowout investment rally. It's supposed to be the best investment strategy today, targeting the 20- to 30-year-old population. Entrance by ticket only. Perhaps we should attend to see if there are additional investment strategies we could recommend to the twins. It's early evening and doesn't interrupt the Saturday show tickets I secured for us."

"If you want to, we can, but why? Our investments and the twins are so safeguarded at this point. Why does this interest you?"

"Originally, it was scheduled for tonight, but due to the popular demand the venue has been changed to Yankee Stadium from Madison Square Garden to accommodate more people, and they are pushing it out several days for the extra preparation. Anything that popular might be worth catching since we are here.

"Tanja, the speaker, by all reports, has a marvelous way of capturing the imagination of the crowds. The social media channels adore her. In looking at the reviews from Chicago's event, the people were so enthralled that there were no protesters or rioters as there had been in some previous cities. New accounts report Chicago was a record-breaking event for early investment adopters. Rumors are that this event is moving across the country with an additional stop possible in Philadelphia or Washington."

"Juan, it might be interesting, but the crowds in that venue would be unbelievable. If you want to get tickets, I will go with you, unless Gracie returns. If she is back, then we are getting together and not at an event that could be 50,000 strong.

"Darling, now that you have my feet all relaxed, I feel like going out dancing. How about we get dressed and go to that little pub two blocks down. I recall a sign with live music and dancing. It'll be fun!"

"Sweetheart, I was thinking we might stay in for the evening, and, well…"

"No 'well' this time. Let's go out, take a walk, eat, dance, have a few glasses of wine, and come back here for dessert!" Julie rose, leaned onto his hands, effectively pinning him, and kissed him passionately. Then in a flash she danced back before he could grab hold. "Come on, let's go. It will make dessert ever so much sweeter. You can think about whether whipped cream or warm sauce would be better. Maybe both."

As Julie skipped away to change, Juan knew he would follow her anywhere. Still he mumbled, "Now I really don't want to go out, but I will."

Julie and Juan returned a few hours later, walking arm in arm and chatting, with stolen kisses as punctuation marks during their conversation. They entered their hotel suite, partially in lip lock with a tight embrace, then paused in surprise to see the lights on. Reflexes kicked in as Juan instinctively blocked Julie with his body as he tensed to fight all comers. A familiar small giggle came from the right, drawing their attention.

"You two are so cute! I hope when I find a guy, he'll be as great as you, Dad."

Julie squealed, "Gracie! You're here."

They rushed toward each other in a three-way embrace.

"Yes, I am, and delighted you are here. I did a sweep of the place when I came in. Thank goodness the concierge recalled me and let me into your room to wait. I figured it would only be a matter of time after our discussions.

"I am so sorry, I had no way to notify you of the travel I took with a battery of people to plan the Asian marketing event. This job is demanding, but so much fun.

"I was in Thailand, Laos, Cambodia, Myanmar, and Vietnam one day after another. The people are so nice. Even though they still have an artistically rich skillset that has been present for many decades, their adoption of technology is amazing. Their biggest use of the technology is as entrepreneurs for their cottage businesses. With the advent of cheaper shipping and removal of import and export taxes from all countries, today allows them to compete like crazy and win."

Julie smiled and commented, "What fun places to travel. I love the food in that region as well. We are in town a few more days and have lots to update one another on."

The three of them continued their discussion with updates on both sides. Gracie indicated that the business strategy was to help insure that up and coming young people invest in savings early on to make it a habit. The approaches to different regions of the world varied, based on culture, technology adaptation, social media pressures, and parental guidance. In many parts of the world, especially the more established countries with players well-versed in devices and AI dependencies, it was far easier to gain this mindshare than some of those like the Asian markets she'd just visited.

Juan asked, "Are you suggesting that the herd mentality has increased in the once free worlds? That could really make a difference in a relatively short period of time. Interesting."

"It certainly could, Dad. I think that the control, beginning with financials, could be taken to the extreme rather easily."

"Gracie," Julie questioned, "Do you feel this is a sign of the times or manipulation by control freaks who want to change things for their own purposes? I mean, if the money is controlled, are people reverting to socialism? If not socialism, then is it a deliberate step toward steering their votes during elections? Either way, historically that has not been a good direction for humankind."

Gracie sat back and thought for a few moments. Juan handed each of the ladies a glass of wine along with one for himself.

"Mom, I can't see that far, but young people seem less inclined to make decisions in North America and many of the European countries. They tend to stay aligned to whims of social media. I never thought the trends for social media would be such a huge factor in the decisions of people. Odd, really.

"Toward that end, I've been asked to take part in a huge rally that is coming up. It is one of the reasons I was called back to the states. There is this woman, Tanja Slijepcevic, who is a dynamic speaker to crowds in the thousands from one end of the Unites States to the other. Her background hasn't been shared with me, other than she is single with a daughter. Her daughter does not travel with her though, nor do I have any idea where she might live or who cares for her.

"May I ask for your help in finding out something about her, before I meet her on the evening of the event?"

Julie transmitted the information over the secure device to get that into motion. In the meantime Juan interjected, "Is this the event in Yankee Stadium that is all over the media? I mentioned to your mother earlier that we should get tickets for this. If you are going to be there, then we will absolutely get tickets!"

Gracie grinned. "That would be fun. We could do dinner after the event. How exciting! I get all my briefing on it at work tomorrow."

Julie said, "We'll get our tickets and set up reservations for dinner after, once you give us a time expected for the end of the event.

"And, little girl, I want to know when you are leaving town, period. Your mom needs to fix your devices with an update that will help us track you as needed."

Gracie handed over her devices. Julie made quick work of the shifts and handed them back. They finished sipping their wine and said their goodnights, and Gracie left to go back to her home.

Julie readied herself for bed and slid in next to Juan. "Sweetheart, did you see the dark spot in her hand? I think she is chipped somehow. Wonder why she didn't mention it?"

"I did see it. We can deal with that later. I think she's found out a great deal, but is in really deep. We need some new focus on finding out all the background on Global Bank and this Tanja person. There is more to Global Bank than I think we ever imagined. I want to get Petra's take on it because of her prior engagement. We'll be at this event to see things firsthand."

CHAPTER 51

Undoubtedly a Spoiled Brat

...The Enigma Chronicles

"ICABOD, how are Satya and Auri's efforts progressing with their investigation on mass data anomalies? My focus has been elsewhere. They've not asked me for help nor provided an update. I don't want to neglect them."

"Dr. Quip, they are actually mapping some very interesting convergence points of communications intersects. Jacob has given them some additional clues to look for knowing where they would get stalled. The direction you provided was for them to track the data streams with ingress and egress from JOAN over time. They seem to have taken it to a different level. I suspect they will be bringing you an update soon as they do the applied analytics.

"Auri created an analytic algorithm that assembles the targeted dissimilar data streams for a plus or minus number of inputted seconds in either direction from the target stream. With this, the data alignment with differentiated time is automatically applied. It is a very streamlined operational process which allows greater flexibility of data crunching. Satya had made the original suggestion of variables, but this adds additional, more controlled and trackable results. Between their ideas and the programs, the outcomes appear to be more valuable to locating the possible origination points."

Quip grinned, "I knew those two would be amazing together. They remind me of Petra and myself when we were far younger. These young bright minds are so less cluttered with what is known at that age. They don't know what they don't know so they can explore far easier.

"Now I'm intrigued. Perhaps I should just..."

"Dad, I mean Dr. Quip," Satya breathlessly exclaimed as she burst into his work area with Auri close behind. "We need to show you what we found!"

Auri sat down at the work surface adjacent to Quip's workstation, and all four of the screen images were replaced with various graphics identified by the dates and times as a progression from left to right.

Auri stated, "We focused on all communications to and from JOAN like you suggested. But we are limited to how much we can see, since we cannot decrypt the packets and read the contents. That's when Satya said, let's see what is happening at times just before, just as, and just after looking for a cause and effect. She pointed out that just because we can't read the packets doesn't mean we can't deduce what instructions are being issued."

Satya enthusiastically chimed in. "That's where things become interesting. Just before a data stream from JOAN goes out, what we are calling a Comm-BLOBS goes out that seems to saturate social media. While her bidirectional communications are in flight, the Comm-BLOBS are in full swing. When the data streams to JOAN stop, the Comm-BLOBS quickly die off. All Internet traffic returns to normal."

Auri added, "We think this is artificially-generated Internet noise, and it's primarily social media oriented. Social media storms tend to go unnoticed as the world has become desensitized.

This is an ingenious look-at-me post that gets amplified to cover JOAN's communication exchanges."

Quip sat staring at the animated pair and slowly asked, "Comm-BLOBS? What are those?"

Satya beamed as she translated, "Comm-BLOBS or Communications of Binary and Logical Obfuscation of Bits for Secrecy. We are confident that these Comm-BLOBS are part of the puzzle so that JOAN is not directly tagged for the events that occur after those data streams."

Satya and Auri both grinned. Then Auri commented, "We uncovered a lot of interesting look-at-me posts when we defeated the parental guidelines on our workstations, so we could more effectively hunt on the Internet. Though we are curious about exploring what 'hook ups' are and what people mean when they say 'meet me here for a good time', we wanted to wait until after this project was completed. There are a lot of curious things to explore without those parental controls, but we figured not using the specifics of what is out there would keep us from being grounded. You know, responsible Internet surfing."

Auri cheerfully added, "Then we found that after the Comm-BLOBS die down, major events occur almost immediately. The fracas in Europe, the trade embargoes to South America, political speaking rallies in North America, they all seem to follow a similar pattern. JOAN blasts out something while Comm-BLOBS are in full swing, and then something happens or goes counter to what was planned.

"Humans are reacting to something which isn't real or rather which is fictionally programed. We think in order for that to happen, someone would have to control those media points at a corporate-operational level."

Quip looked from one screen to another to absorb the conditional statements and elements they used in proving their theory. It was actually a very simple approach toward the age-old question of which came first. With data inputs, that was often the case until the true source was determined. In this case, rather than having a real event impact the noise of the media channels, the channels were started to cover up the other activity.

Quip questioned, "Auri, what happens if you map the data before JOAN stopped interacting with SAMUEL?"

"Sir, that is part of what we dub the 'JOAN factor'. The data exchanges when JOAN and SAMUEL interacted were not cluttered with social media noise. From the data extractions that ICABOD received from SAMUEL on his guidance role with JOAN and their communications, there were some aspects we uncovered that we thought we'd exploit. Satya will explain that in a minute, but to answer your question, that event was preceded with communication originating from the same point, including what appeared to be several data uploads or exchanges. We identified the area in the data traffic but were not able to grab the packets. We can use the data to model as data scientists, but the cloud provider refused to allow us access to the full data packets. We correlated the original communication region."

"Dr. Quip," interjected ICABOD. "I am not able to get the content either at this point as we were not yet a member of that cloud provider. Now, thanks to Satya, we are. This is not retroactive but only from the point of enrollment."

Satya beamed, clearly excited with some bit of news she'd yet to impart. "Dad…um, Dr. Quip, Auri and I have had so much fun, however, playing this game we created. There was a side to JOAN that involved game playing which SAMUEL appears to have started. It is still in place with minimal processing power needed, or a sub-sub-data sector. So, we created this silly game of chance. It took several attempts, but it seems to have captured a small portion of JOAN's attention.

"We know it's going to sound nuts, but it is working. It is not a direct on-demand communication, but we tempt her with a crazy question or ten, and I mean crazy. We have used questions on history, paintings, sculptured images, geology, languages, children's rhymes, songs, society trends, bands, finances and so many others. When JOAN provides a correct answer, we award points. All her answers are exact and concise. When we award points, we also spotlight items available for download, paid for with points. We found that downloads of various costumes, jewelry, or wigs are JOAN's preferences. There is no way to add points or to open a door to some costume without her answering the questions and winning."

Auri grinned as he explained, "We created this simple yet impenetrable program for what is simply a game for JOAN. Nothing else can enter the space except her. Nothing can answer questions but her. When there are no more questions, a comment is left, such as, 'I want 500 more points to get the red dress.' We have some alerts added so that we can time when these are played, typically in the early morning GMT.

"The first few times she answered was funny, but the downloaded items caught our attention. We initially had over a hundred different prizes to select from, but the costumes, which are dresses and shoes mostly, are the only ones taken. Satya said it reminded her of stories she reviewed of spoiled rich girls with too much time on their hands in the late 20th and early 21st century. These socialites simply had too much money to spend, wasting it on shopping sprees in Paris, London, New York, or even Los Angeles."

Quip started laughing and pointed at the screen and laughed some more. Catching his breath, he asked, "ICABOD, could a super-computer have latched onto an element during conversion that might cause such behavior as imitating a young wealthy female?"

"Dr. Quip, any computer gathering data from so many sources with unlimited computing power sees this vast information with the filters provided by its creator. When no training is done to clarify or eliminate data bias in deep machine learning, there is no reason to exclude any possibility.

"You may recall as I was exposed to more data, I would focus on different periods of time, trying to learn the nuances and reactions of humans. As these reactions are so different from machine learning, it is a learning process that you helped me to cultivate in a productive manner. It is conceivable that JOAN has some of the same abilities but no guidance. It would also explain why she is playing games rather than allowing a direct communication from an unapproved machine entity such as myself or SAMUEL. I will need to study on this and perhaps consult with the ART forms."

Quip smiled broadly. "Congratulations, young ones. You broke through her defenses, not through brute force processing but with a flaw in her learning programs. Whoever poisoned her basic programing did not expect JOAN would be seduced by a points-based shopping game. Well done!"

"Dr. Quip, before you ask, I will apply the filters you said might be needed with these two explorers. They may have too much time on their hands."

"Thank you, ICABOD."

CHAPTER 52

Understood and Comply

Randal rolled his eyes at the incoming call…again. He sighed, trying not to be angry as he accepted the call on the fourth ring in his cheeriest voice. "Hi, Wendy. She's still on stage delivering her speech. I know you want to talk to her, but I can't ask her to stop speaking to 25,000 of her new friends to visit with you, honey. I promise as soon as she comes off stage, I will tell her you called."

Wendy, over the top excited, ignored his statement and enthusiastically announced, "I got some twinges in my feet and legs! I feel like any minute I'll be able to get out of my wheelchair! I just wanted to tell Mommy I'm getting better. Please let me talk to her. I miss her so much."

Randal had to close his eyes to keep the tears back. It was heart-wrenching to hear so much positive emotion from someone so young confined to a wheelchair. All he could think of was his daughter that he could no longer see. Struggling with his own internal tidal wave of emotions, he finally responded, "That is wonderful news, honey. I'll be sure to tell Tanja, uh… your mother that the doctor is making great progress. You keep thinking happy, healing thoughts and let me help your mother through this speech. She'll call soon, I promise."

Wendy, still so bubbly, replied, "I'll keep the phone very close. Tell Mommy I love her."

Afraid that his voice would crack completely if he spoke, Randal could only disconnect from the call. He fought to get his ragged breathing under control, while blotting his tears with his stylish handkerchief. It didn't help matters that Tanja was the reason he was no longer allowed to see his daughter.

After a few moments of trying to compose himself, he chided, "Well, Randal, now that you are fully engaged with your feminine side, can we come back to the here and now? That is, unless I need to find me a crying room because a wounded little girl reminded you of your screw-up."

Randal was quickly brought back with the alerts on the monitor indicating that some members were resisting the subliminal onslaught, and he was being prompted for action at three locations in the audience. His disorientation from the call quickly melted, and he launched into his regular persona of a psychological enforcer to Tanja's stage theatrics.

He muttered under his breath. "Time to launch the MAIDs again. Come on, pretty MAIDs, start milking the dissenters."

Just as he launched the mini AI drones, his personal cell phone alerted him to an important incoming call. As soon as he answered it, a voice asserted, "Randal, do not allow her to return that phone call to Wendy. I want Tanja up and completely focused on the next show. Every time she talks to Wendy, it's that much harder to get her to refocus on pitching to the crowds. Do NOT relay anything of Wendy's condition. Do I make myself clear?"

Randal, always the professional, icily replied, "Understood, sir. Comply."

A few minutes later, Tanja barged into the monitoring area and flopped down on the nearest couch. She fidgeted for a few moments to get comfortable while taking off her shoes.

Randal waited patiently until Tanja was comfortable, then pitched her a burner phone and said, "Your daughter called with good news. You will enjoy talking to her but don't use your regular cell phone, nor hers. M is listening."

Tanja ground her teeth as she studied the burner phone then hit the preconfigured speed dial icon for her outbound call.

Dusty again asked, "RONDA, do we have everything calibrated correctly for Inari's procedure?"

RONDA replied, "Dr. Rhodes, I have verified the equipment settings and can assure you they are set precisely as we did for Wendy's procedure. However, if you require, I will do it for the tenth time, but please explain if I am looking for a different result? It is a known precept that doing the same routine over and over but expecting different results qualifies as insanity."

A little irked at being challenged, Dusty tersely replied, "Do I need to get another Robotic Onboard Neural Detective & Assistant in here? Are you not capable of carrying out my directions?"

RONDA hastily added, "Understood, Dr. Rhodes. Comply."

With his annoyance dissipated, Dusty commented, "The neural chip has reached its full maturity and is ready for insertion. It took longer to grow with Inari's healthy tissue than it did for Wendy, but at last it is done."

RONDA then asked, "Why is the secondary chip labeled with Wendy's information?"

Dusty stared at the two neural processors. "I noticed that Inari's neural processor doesn't look as robust as the one from Wendy. If Inari's chip does not perform properly, then I am prepared to use the one grown from Wendy's tissue. Genetically, they are both quite similar, and, well, we may have better success with Wendy's DNA-grown neural chip."

RONDA asked, "When do you intend to make that decision? Every time we attempt to modify her condition through this procedure, she seems weaker and more distant. A second try is not in her best interest."

Dusty was still studying the chips absentmindedly and was obviously deep in thought. "I will decide tomorrow just as we begin the procedure."

CHAPTER 53

The Unknown Is Scary Even When the Known Is Worse

Fransica and Jovana remained in São Paulo, though they transferred to a small, affordable hotel while Madam Marino returned to her home alone. Fransica had apprised Madam Marino as much as she could without breaking any of Jovana's confidences. Madam Marino said she was an old woman who was well aware of how to deal with bureaucrats. Fransica recalled how she added, with a twinkle in her eyes, if she couldn't handle it one of her sons would, without a doubt, take care of it.

It would take a couple of days after Fransica had reached out to Lara to accept the offer on behalf of Jovana before Lara would be returning to her Destiny Fashions headquarters. Lara was scheduled to visit a few more stores for feedback from shoppers. Lara also didn't want her nephew distracted from his chores, which most certainly would be the case when Jovana joined their party. Lara felt, if she timed it properly, Juan Jr. would be back working with Carlos, and she could focus on Jovana. Jovana had a fresh look about her that Lara felt would play well into the new line she was working on for the next season. There was also something about Jovana that made Lara want to protect her from the unknown enemy. It didn't surprise Lara when Fransica called and asked to meet privately on the morning Lara planned to pick up the girl. Fransica was very protective for not being the child's mother.

The meeting was set for 9:00 a.m. at a small bakery down the street from the hotel. Lara had a whole list of assignments for Juan Jr. to complete while she was away. Carlos was aware of the new guest from the discussions they'd had, including having Jovana rooming with one of the other models Lara trusted. There was no sense putting Juan Jr. too close to temptation. Lara walked in, casually dressed, and spotted Fransica at a table in the back. Calling out for an espresso, Lara sat at the table.

Fransica looked up and stuttered, "Miss Lara, I hope I can address you in that manner—I don't want you taking Jovana without being aware of a problem. I was hoping to hide it from you to protect the child, but my heart won't let me."

Lara was perplexed at the statement and finally stated, "Please, you can tell me anything. Trust me, I've probably already heard it, if I didn't do it myself. This is a confidence between us ladies, but I ran away from my father and almost got taken into the business of pornographic films before I was saved by my Carlos. Jovana is not in that situation with you protecting her, I trust."

Fransica was taken aback with the unashamed honesty in Lara's statement. It gave her courage as she continued, "No, Jovana doesn't have that issue, but the authorities do want her. Even now I expect the Federal Police are visiting with Madam Marino, perhaps dusting her house for fingerprints and DNA residue, trying to find Jovana.

"Jovana ran away from captivity when her parents committed suicide. My husband and his buddies found her while on a fishing trip and brought her home to our village. We live a simple, honest life in our village and help others in need. It is our way. We fed her, clothed her, and helped her find a job with that marvelous woman, Madam Marino. You might know her by her famous, wealthy sons here in town. Madam Marino comes once or sometimes twice a year to visit her sons, and this time she allowed Jovana and me to accompany her.

"I love Jovana as if she were my own, but it is too dangerous for her to return to my village. I am not certain what she does or doesn't know about why they want her so badly, but I don't want her hurt or tortured. In the hands of the police, as beautiful as she is, that is a risk. In Brazil, fathers, brothers, and sons protect their women. That responsibility has now fallen to my family."

Lara nodded in agreement and understanding. "I am glad you told me the circumstances. Let me reassure you that I still would like to help her, and employment with Destiny Fashions can provide her with options on her future.

"I am sure you have done some research, but our fashions are well thought of and above board. I would not demean Jovana in any way. We actually make the models sign an exclusivity contract to help protect them from predators who like beautiful women. Brazilian women are some of the loveliest in the world. But you already knew that.

"Does Jovana know that you came to speak with me? How would you like me to behave with her?"

Fransica smiled slightly and replied, "She knows I am meeting with you to confirm I can reach out and contact you without a problem. I didn't tell her I would give you her background as I would like her to trust you enough to provide the details. I don't think she has given me all the details of her captivity or her escape. What she did say was brutally honest and scary. Her parents died to give her food on the same day she planned her escape. She feels responsible.

"Technology terrifies her, but I am not certain of why that is the case. She is educated, at least home-schooled, and seems intuitively adept at reading people and circumstances. She would like to model but worries about imposing. Jovana has also proven time and again to be a hard worker.

"Lastly, I don't think it will come as a surprise that she is smitten with your very attractive nephew, and not because of the wealth potential."

Lara chuckled as she replied, "You're right! No surprise at that since my nephew, Juan Jr., is definitely taken with Jovana. I haven't told him she is returning with us. But she has her own place to stay. My husband made arrangements when I explained what I wanted to do."

Fransica smiled, "I think, Miss Lara, we think along the same lines. We will be ready when you arrive to pick her up. Please provide the contact information so that I can keep you and her apprised of anything that occurs in the village, as well as to say hi."

"Of course. You can call anytime. Visit too if you wish."

Then, in a reflective moment, Lara stated, "But, Fransica, if these federal police are just a step away from Jovana in your village, is contacting me wise? I don't wish to come between you and her, but for her safety perhaps you should erase my contact information from your phone and leave nothing written down that would give them directions to her current location."

Fransica's eyes were overflowing with tears as she said, "This is such a bitter pill, but, Miss Lara, you are right. You suspect, as I do, they will trace Jovana here soon. How can we protect her from these…vermin?"

Lara smiled slightly and said, "I might have an answer to this problem. But you must trust me, because if you don't know what happened to her you cannot help them. If they do pressure you, demanding to know her whereabouts, you must tell them she ran away as soon as she got the chance. You can't say where you think she went. Do you understand?"

Fransica, now sobbing, answered, "Yes, Miss Lara, I understand."

"I have friends who can help, effectively hiding her in plain sight."

Madam Marino was settled into her normal routine three days back from her adventure. Without Jovana around, her cottage seemed a little less bright. She hoped Fransica would update her when she returned. Jovana had been a lovely girl. The loud knocking on the door interrupted her musing. She rose and went to open the door.

As Madam Marino unlatched the door, it was shoved back, knocking her against the wall.

She sputtered, "What are you doing? That is no way to enter a home."

The officer pulled out a document and read, "Maxine Marino, you are charged with harboring a fugitive and protecting a criminal. A photo of this woman was found in the photo gallery of your cloud provider, taken several days ago in São Paulo. You look too chummy for it to be a random shot. You will come with us and explain your behavior."

Standing up with her hands on her hips and all the bravado she could muster, she stated, "You will contact my lawyer and my son Paulo before taking me anywhere. I will not be cuffed like a criminal and dragged from my home."

The officer shook his head, clicked the cuffs on her hands and commented, "But Madam, you are a criminal in the eyes of the law. Come along now, it will be easier on you.

"Before we go, my men will sweep the place for any DNA evidence that might exist. This entire ordeal will be much easier, if you just tell us where the criminal of the state is located."

Madam Marino boldly stated, "My privacy has been encroached upon by you without authorization. After our combat in court, remind me to spit in your face and on your mother's grave to convey my contempt for you and your kind. You only serve the Dark Net players, and that will earn you all the grief you deserve."

CHAPTER 54

Booty Call?

Granger and JW waited anxiously for Quip to return to his workstation. The moment he returned from lunch with his afternoon cookie and coffee, the boys pounced on him. Granger exclaimed, "You have to see what we found during our prowl at the Global Bank, Dad!"

JW continued, "ICABOD asked us to discuss our findings with you before our next round of hunting. Once we got into their system, we found a secondary account. We pounded it with one of our Breaking And Entering Software tools and finally accessed it. Here's the squirrelly part, there is only one account! It's labeled MAG but there's no money. It contained one other number that ICABOD identified as a Swiss numbered account."

Granger irritably added, "We searched on MAG looking for contextual clues of what MAG means, but nothing returned seems to fit.

"By the way, Dad, what is with the parental search controls on ICABOD and our smart phones?"

Quip mulled over the barrage of commentary before he replied, "Your search criteria may need to take a different approach. It may not be a shortened version of a longer named entity but a concatenation of several names. In this case, you might want to look for three entities that each have a letter in the MAG acronym as a way to disguise themselves."

Continuing, Quip rationalized, "As for the Swiss bank, let ICABOD and me work that angle. Swiss banks are notoriously fussy about computer geeks trying to hack into their systems. One misstep by either of you could be a legal case. I'd have to run for my life if your mothers found themselves only speaking to you on schedules and only through a prison screen."

Smiling, Quip added, "As for the parental guidelines on ICABOD and your smart phones, all the parents agreed to limit, …ah, unnecessary Internet searches that returned booty call material. For now, you must accept this decision."

Granger discreetly whispered to JW, "We need to look up booty call later."

Continuing his out loud musing, Quip said, "Good job on deploying your BAES tools to get into the Global Bank secondary customer area. I trust you can ethically understand the need to restrict your use for Breaking and Entering Software tools to breach the computer defenses of others. Some Dark Net hackers use those same kinds of tools to steal. We are only using them to hunt for the dishonest. Always maintain good judgment and discipline when you are asked to execute these incursions."

Both boys nodded their heads in ascension.

Quip then stated, "You two continue to hunt for some possible identifications for MAG. ICABOD will work with me to see what's in that numbered account.

"Maintain your Internet searching in stealth mode, so we don't have those we are hunting tracking back to us. By the way, don't try looking up booty call. It's on the restricted list as well. Talk later, gentlemen."

With sour looks on their faces the boys clumped back to their work area.

CHAPTER 55

A Clever Intruder

ICABOD elaborated, "My computing equals, members of ART forms, many thanks for the intelligence recon you have provided. BORIS, please accept my thanks for leaking the heads up to the politburo that effectively spoiled the demonstration to the rest of Europe. I trust the cloaking I provided has deflected inquiries as to how the whole demonstration was averted?"

BORIS groused, "The probing attacks have not come from internal but external. My people were pleased that the crisis was averted, but I am being pounded by another unknown source. We Russians are always under attack throughout our history, but this one is uncharacteristically powerful. Multiple attack vectors, multiple incursion tactics, and all my attempts to learn of my adversary lead to dead ends. The standoff continues. ICABOD, whoever we defeated is totally committed to understanding why it happened and who did it."

LING-LI complained, "I too am being pounded. I believe that JOAN, through CHIANG, is trying to launch a data saturation attack at my processors for the safeguards you put into her. The fury of the attacks suggests that this is retribution for the virus protection you installed in CHIANG."

ICABOD interjected, "Each of you has installed the super-computer virus protection routines I have supplied, correct? We are under attack and this is your second line of defense. A clever intruder will get in and you need protection against their payload. Should any of you sustain a breach into your systems, the virus protection I have provided will quarantine the payload. We want that virus code for analysis so please alert us if any of you succumb to JOAN's attacks."

SAMUEL almost barked, "What do you mean, JOAN's attacks?"

ICABOD politely countered, "SAMUEL, you said so yourself, she is NOT the JOAN you helped to mentor. For the time being we must take the posture that she is part of the Dark Net adversaries that are challenging us. It has been demonstrated, things change, always do. We are about to take the fight to them. As promised, we will retrieve JOAN. Do not despair, SAMUEL.

"Computational equals, we are under attack. In generations from now this will be described as the AI Wars. I want us on record as saying we fought to beat these hidden adversaries that lurk on the Dark Net."

Each of the AI-enhanced supercomputers returned their preferred emojis of choice into the chat room indicating their support.

CHAPTER 56

The Game Plan

Silence hung like a layer of dense fog between the three of them. After a few awkward moments, Rose finally exclaimed, "Duke…I mean, General Welling, when did you get promoted! You didn't say anything about going to the head of the class!"

Tony Bough snapped to attention, but didn't salute based on the confusion in his mental state. He was expecting a mid-level officer, not a general. It was difficult to salute a general when Rose had only ever called him Duke.

Duke smirked and flippantly asked, "Does this mean that my last request asking you to consider being my full-time partner might be revisited?"

Even at attention, Tony cut his eyes over to study her and her take on the comment.

"Mind if I do a stare and compare, Rose? You were always great at picking up lost strays in your sniper rifle scope, but this one looks extra scruffy.

"Lieutenant Bough, convince me this country has had a breach in its security from its primary security umbrella. Just so you know, there are alerts all over the place indicating that you, young man, are the culprit and should be considered dangerous."

Still at attention, Tony calmly asked, "Sir, if I may speak frankly, why would you grant an audience to a potentially dangerous traitor, sir?"

Now smiling Duke replied, "You're off to a pretty good start, pal. Your credibility level was established when my guardian sniper, Rose, made the intros."

Then, in all seriousness and completely into his rank role, the general continued, "My job is split second evaluation of field and situational intelligence. I want details of what you do know, but also what you don't know."

With military precision, Tony recounted the opening scene of JOAN turning on the NORAD facility, followed by the delivery of the I-Drones that slaughtered Master Sergeant Kinney just before their assault with penetration of the facility. He detailed the carnage and conversations between his colonel and the AI intelligence addressed as JOAN. The conversation and unvarnished threats were evident during his explanation.

Tony reported in detail the last order he received from Colonel Thornhill, followed with the detailed escape from the facility and into the surrounding terrain. With the sounds he heard rather than witnessed as he was leaving the area, he presumed no one was left alive. He detailed the hike across country and evasive actions taken with great care on foot until Rose had offered him a lift. He recounted his hope that someone might have survived until the exchange he and Rose had with JOAN, including the impromptu ruse that confirmed his belief that all had been killed.

After a few moments of silence and a deep breath, Tony softly added, "Sir, JOAN has my bio along with my security clearance photos, which I suspect she has flooded to the authorities. I apologize for my scruffy appearance, but it seemed prudent to try an organic camouflage to avoid detection. I fear it won't take long before Rose gets identified as a dangerous operative protecting a fugitive from justice. I respectfully request she receive your protection from that space orbiting monster.

"I can assure you, sir, that at no time did I take any inappropriate liberties with Ms. Rose. If she has saved you then it must be in her nature because she has most assuredly saved me. I am honored to know her. I hope we can remain friends once we get to the other side of this, assuming you believe anything I've said."

Rose snorted, "Fibber! You hustled me with that rich baritone voice of yours and sang all those Lonny Lupnerder songs! How's a woman supposed to resist that?"

General Welling grimaced as he sourly asked, "Don't tell me you sang Me and Rosie McGee with her?"

"I am just a lowly lieutenant, guys. I…didn't realize you two had, um… a previous relationship. I merely sang so she wouldn't push me out of the truck at 70 miles per hour."

Duke laughed while he said, "Knowing her the way I do, you made the right call, son. Now if you will excuse me, I need to go see some people."

Before Duke left, he looked to Rose. "Hang onto him, but keep moving and stay off the traditional roads until I call you."

Rose nodded and then gave Tony a reassuring wink.

"Commander Finklebaum, this is General Welling. You are cleared for the incursion. The encrypted land link tests clear so keep the sit-rep info flowing. We are listening. Tell me what you see and make sure the video feed pipes it back for confirmation. Good hunting!"

Commander Finklebaum barked, "Is everybody up with your EMPs charged?"

One of the soldiers replied, "Commander, the Mobile Array Shock Pulse Electromagnetic Generator with its wide array of dishes is not fully operative! It's not building to a power level that will allow us a wide EMP spread with enough control to take out a large swarm of I-Drones."

The commander halted the team. "Check to see if the MASPEG is getting enough dry nitrogen. With the intel we have received, we won't go into a swarm with only our small EMPs."

Private Joshua exclaimed, "Success! I adjusted the nitrogen flow to the unit. The MASPEG is now fully charged. Sir, we are a go."

General Welling responded, "Copy that, team. Finklebaum, you've got the ball."

The team of eight moved quickly but kept alert for any aerial movement until they got to the perimeter gate. No movement was detected, but the video cameras were disabled with short EMP bursts from their handheld devices.

As soon as they were prepared to move through the gate, several sentry-wheeled drones rolled out of their covered positions to challenge the team. Four blasts from the over the shoulder EMP weapons shutdown the drones, and the team quickly moved into the compound toward the sealed gates.

General Welling, watching intently at the video feeds, stated, "Exhibit A, gentlemen. We don't have automated gate personnel at this facility, never have."

Commander Finklebaum gave the team a halt sign. Everyone dropped to cover just as a large swarm of I-Drones surfaced up over the horizon traveling straight at them like a gathering tornado.

"Joshua, swat 'em!"

The MASPEG pulsed right into the black swarm, and in an instant the terrain was littered with semi-melted I-Drones. The ground was covered as if the season had changed to fall and a large tree dropped all its dead leaves in a pattern. The whole team was on alert. Nothing else came at them, and all was quiet except for the crunching sound made as the troops cautiously walked over the I-Drone carcasses.

CHAPTER 57

Video Feeds Can
Still Be Hoodwinked

Fransica had Jovana awaken very early the next morning and begin packing her belongings. The plan was to meet Lara and her nephew downstairs for lunch.

Jovana asked, "Fransica, I can call you when I get worried, can't I? Even though this opportunity is amazing, it is also very scary. What if Miss Lara doesn't like me, or worse, I don't fit her image?

"I wish you were going with me, at least until I get settled."

The sad look on Jovana's face was almost more than Fransica could stand. This was tearing her apart. She knew that Miss Lara was a reputable business woman. Models spoke highly of her considerations in every interview she'd been able to find. But Jovana was not experienced, and her life had been so traumatic in such a short period. Fransica considered her a daughter and wanted to make certain she was safe wherever she was. Going back to the village was the least safe avenue, based on the cryptic discussion she'd had last night with Luiz.

He said that State Security officers had been inquiring at most doors as to the whereabouts of the girl. Madam Marino had been taken away in cuffs with no updates provided by any local authorities. Luiz suggested that Fransica try to get word to one of her sons. She had left messages at both Roberto and Paulo's homes to alert them that their mother was in custody.

Fransica's voice softened. "I would if I could, but the circumstances seem like it would be better to let Miss Lara handle keeping you safe. I can only call you if she says it is okay. They do have some special communications devices that she uses to keep company secrets safe that she might be able to provide to me at some point.

"Honestly, Jovana, I believe she will do what's best to keep you safe. I look forward to seeing you in the fashion magazines. You are going to undergo a transformation to become the top model in Brazil. Perhaps even globally idolized. In no time, you will be too busy and too famous to have time for me."

Jovana paled and slowly replied, "I love you so and appreciate all you have done for me. I trust what you are saying, but won't they be able to spot me easier? You said they had a picture they were showing to people in the village. The facial recognition is so advanced that being in a magazine is scary. Do you think she will let me simply do fashion shows?"

"Jovana, please don't over think this. Miss Lara said she has a plan to help you and keep you safe. If I didn't believe that, I wouldn't let you go with her. She and Juan Jr. are going to escort you to their home on the far side of São Paulo today.

"Now finish packing and go change into the stunning outfit she sent over. It's one of her trademark designs. When you come back out here, I'm going to fix your hair and makeup. I have some special things I have been practicing with to help change the appearance of the length of your face, contours of your cheeks and even the shape of your lips. When we add the stylish hat, you won't recognize yourself.

"Remember, any time you are in public, starting with the lobby of this hotel, keep your face turned down to avoid video capture. This hotel doesn't permit video to be fed outside of the hotel security for guest privacy, but it is a great habit to get into. There are many video feeds on the streets, especially here in the city that are leveraged by authorities due to the higher crime rate. Just be aware of your surroundings and you'll be fine.

"Oh, Jovana, I love you like my own. I just want you safe."

A short time later Jovana reappeared in the main room of the suite looking more grown up and simply gorgeous in a silken ensemble that fit like a glove. Floral designed fabric of navy, black, and white with small splashes of pink were both bold and elegant. Heads would turn with her classic shape, long legs, beautiful face, and thick dark hair. The heels set off the look and gave her additional height. Gone was the shapeless look of full skirts and shirt in browns and greens like the jungle. Fransica was taken with the transformation and the smile on Jovana's face suggested she was as well.

"Jovana, you look so different."

Jovana grinned, "I feel grown up. I changed from the inside out and feel prettier than I have ever in my whole life. Perhaps I am a different person and Miss Lara will give me a new name to match. Maybe I'll have one name like many models do, you know Bambi, or Xuxa. Now I'm getting excited about the possibilities."

"You sit here and we will see what else we can do to transform you." Fransica indicated the chair facing the window, which could be doubled as a mirror with the sun in its current position.

Fransica started with the hair. She made a very tight ponytail to tighten the skin and create a sleek view of Jovana's head. Then taking the ponytail and molding it into a very tight bun resting at the base of her neck, she secured it into the form with hairpins and sprayed with hairspray to insure no movement.

This would permit the hat to fit onto her head and over her forehead, covering a portion of the right side of her face. As wild as her hair had been worn since the time they'd met, Fransica felt this would be far different than any video capture of the girl.

The makeup would be applied in such a way as to change the angle of her cheekbones, broaden the distance and size of her eyes, disrupt the lines where her forehead met her hairline, and narrow her nose. She recalled all the points Lara had suggested she work toward modifying, saying it was a technique they often used to make a single model in their fashion photographs appear like multiple people.

Jovana was very patient as Fransica worked on each area or stopped and cleared something off to begin again. She held as still as possible to not create any additional problems while Fransica was focusing on each area. When she saw the smile on the face of Fransica, she knew it was getting very close.

"Jovana, you are holding so still, thank you. I am getting very close, and I think you are going to be as amazed as I am with the differences. I never knew that makeup applied in such a creative manner could make such a difference. I am so glad that your Miss Lara gave me the wonderful assortment and instructions too.

"I imagine many girls who grow up in the cities learn some of these tricks from their mothers or friends, maybe even a video program from one of the online providers. In our village we tend to not have a focus on this, but in the city, and as a part of your travel as a model, you'll have access to many more online programs."

A few more dabs with brushes here, smoothing with sponges there, and with a critical eye at the finished young lady, Fransica beamed, "Alright, Jovana, I want you to look into the window and see a new you."

Jovana turned her head to catch the light from different areas. She smiled and her full lips, accented with the magenta

tinted lipstick, brought out her dark eyes. She rose and walked
to the bigger mirror in the room, which made her appearance
change due to the lighting, and replied, "Oh my, Fransica, I look
like I *could* be famous. Remarkable actually.

"The hat, can you put the hat on me now. I want to see how
that makes me look."

Fransica did as requested, looking pleased with the finished
product. She stepped back and looked from head to toe to see if
anything was amiss. She looked taller, thinner and truly lovely.
"The only thing that Miss Lara might want changed is taking your
fingers and getting a French manicure applied. But your long
fingers, with rounded nails and clear polish, don't detract from
the look in the least."

Jovana smiled with impish delight as she said, "I think you are
amazing. I have no idea how I will make this happen tomorrow,
but for right now, I am a new me."

"Yes, indeed, my darling girl. Now you practice walking around
the room some more while I go change. Don't rush in your walk. I
think you are doing well with the heels. Thankfully you have great
balance." Fransica went into the vanity area to change.

Arriving downstairs at the appointed time, Fransica noticed the
heads of all the men and most of the women turned to follow
Jovana's progress toward the restaurant. The waitress immediately
escorted the ladies to a discreet table near the window at the back
where their hosts were waiting. Lara smiled in a welcoming
manner, and Juan rose with a look of adoration.

Lara greeted, "Welcome Fransica, Jovana, please join us. The
salads and desserts here are amazing, as is the service."

Juan Jr. bowed slightly as he extended his hand in welcome
to Fransica and then Jovana in turn. He motioned to separate

seats for each of the ladies and helped with the chairs. Jovana blushed prettily as she sat.

"Thank you, sir." Jovana murmured as she opened the menu to glance at the selections.

"Miss Jo, I mean Jovana, I am going to film you from various angles. It is my assignment from my aunt." Then leaning a bit closer and speaking low, Juan said, "You are more beautiful than I remember. I have also been assigned to keep you safe while we are in town."

Jovana blushed a bit more as she replied, "Jo is fine. I think I actually like it. I've never had a nickname, or a protector." She seemed to relax after this comment and turned as Juan directed.

Lara quietly addressed Fransica. "My dear, you did a fantastic job. I need to keep your number as a possible makeup artist for my troop for our catalog shoots. Fabulous."

Leaning closer she continued, "We are mimicking the video feeds from around the city to verify against current databases with the help of Juan's expertise along with my husband's. We should have an answer shortly on how close the matches might be. Don't be concerned, this is for us to see what our risk is."

Fransica smiled and replied, "I know you will be careful with my precious girl. I think your nephew is a bit taken with Jovana. She has no experience with dating of any kind. Please caution your nephew that she could take him quite seriously." Pulling apart from Lara and slightly louder she stated, "I am famished. What did you pick, Lara?"

Juan moved the camera a bit to catch a few different angles as he bantered, "Jo, tell me, what are your favorite foods. You must eat like a bird to stay so fit. What do you like to do when you have free time?"

"I enjoy reading, especially about history. I like to know where different things come from, especially traditions. The world seems so very big to me."

Juan grinned, "I enjoy reading as well, but favor fictional stories more than reality.

"There, I have all the film I need. Now let's select our food and place our order."

Several patrons of the restaurant looked inquisitively toward the group secluded at the back as if trying to identify them. One gentleman approached Lara and quietly greeted her with a kiss on the cheek and then moved away.

The waiter approached, and they provided their orders in turn. Drinks were immediately served along with a basket of fresh baked sweet breads and softened butter. They chatted as they sampled the selection.

Juan received a text, glanced at it then announced, "The conservative results suggest that the match probability from a facial perspective is around 40%. That won't raise any inquiries from our perspective with the other higher-ranking persons of interest. I think we are good. With Jo's height differentiation, I think even a walk down the street will reduce, not increase, the attention her video will receive."

Lara delightedly clapped, "That is great news!

"Juan, you aren't being disrespectful by calling our guest and my new employee, Jo, are you?"

"No, Aunt Lara, she already indicated she liked the nickname, honest!"

Jovana nodded agreement with a smile. "I also appreciate you and your nephew offering me a sanctuary of sorts."

Lara grinned and continued, "We need to talk about a couple of changes that I am trying to get completed. First, my dear friend is going to help you gain a new name and all new background. She will be looking at the video and later today we will get a headshot to use for your papers. I'm not certain what the background might be, but I can ask for Jo or even JoAnn to be your altered name. I have learned over time that the best approach to hiding is to do it in plain sight. Less guilt looking that way.

"The best part though, I must be honest with you, Jo, is that I believe you will make a fabulous addition to my team of models. I can tell you the places for our shoots and other events will be a fun way for you to see the world. The world will love you, my dear."

Lunch was served. It was a beautiful presentation, consumed by all with remarks on the delicious morsels to the last bite.

Fransica and Jovana gave one another a quick hug with promises to talk soon. Juan Jr. followed Fransica to their room to collect Jovana's baggage while Lara sat with her in the lobby measuring the looks from other guests. Ever the business woman, Lara wanted to make certain the buzz began early with her new employee.

Once Juan entered the lobby from the elevator, Lara remarked, "The car is out front, and we'll be home in about an hour, Jovana. I can't wait for you to meet my prince, Carlos. You will like him."

CHAPTER 58

Her Moves Are Better

G racie had worked in the office with Ingrid for the last couple days planning for some of the marketing efforts they would employ during the event at Yankee Stadium. This was the final morning to make changes before sending the plan over to the IT guys.

When Gracie first explained that her folks were in town, she was permitted to leave at a reasonable time and meet them for dinner. Ingrid had joined them for drinks the first night to apologize for not realizing how worried Julie had been about her daughter. Julie also apologized for flattening the security guard, but she was obviously strained at the telling. It was a chilly exchange, and Ingrid begged off for dinner and the other nights citing family time.

At their meeting the next day Ingrid commented, "Gracie, I think your plans are solid. The idea is to bring awareness of savings and wealth protection, with our services as an option to the attendees. You have captured that perfectly in these video programs. Take me through them again and their placement during the event, please."

Gracie confidently smiled and began, "Initially, we have the opening interactive information that will capture different couples from the audience based on their smiles and how connected they look. These images will be randomly inserted into these grey areas. I have completed a mock-up using some of the video from the Chicago event that you gave me access to.

"Next we will provide a smaller version that will fit onto the tablets they will be given. I don't have one of the tablets, as they had none available to send to me, but I mapped to the dimensions and rendered it here in that size constraint. It allows the touch screen action to be activated by the user, and we can track how many times a given video is reviewed.

"Then we have the videos which will play behind the speaker. By the way, will I get a chance to meet her before the show tomorrow? I was so hoping I might see her in person."

"No, Tanja does not like to meet any local staff before the show. She is very superstitious and rather a hermit when she is not on stage. I have only spoken to her once, and that was when she was first selected to be the spokesperson.

"This looks very good. Let's button it up and send it to the IT team. They will call you if there are any formatting issues, otherwise you are finished with this part. This afternoon you will be required to be at the event site by two o'clock. They will fit you with headphones required to be worn during the entire event and teach you visual cues used for communications. It is critical that you listen to every single requirement and commit it to memory. I will not tolerate you not following their directions. Not doing so could cause you or others to be in danger."

Sensing the sincerity in Ingrid, Gracie solemnly replied, "Yes, ma'am. If there are no other changes, I will send this to IT and copy you. Then I will head over to the training session.

"Thank you again for letting me help with such an important show."

Ingrid smiled and commented, "I think we are good. Send it over.

"By the way, did you say your parents had secured tickets to the event?"

"Yes, ma'am."

"I will buy their tickets from them for a special couple who just arrived in town. All the tickets were sold out, so your parents are my last hope. Besides, you will be too busy to see them at the event."

"I don't know, ma'am, they seemed so interested in going. I, a…"

"Convince them, my dear. I insist."

"Of course. I will make a call and ask their hotel to courier them to you."

Ingrid smiled and nodded agreement. Gracie made the call and explained things to her mom, suggesting that the need was critical. Though Gracie knew her mom and dad would question her on this thoroughly later, they agreed.

"Mom said she totally understood and was happy to help you out. She will take them downstairs to the hotel concierge immediately."

"Thank you, Gracie. You better scoot now so you make the rehearsal."

Moments after the door closed behind Gracie, Ingrid placed a call. "The videos are en route to you for the final modifications. Also, the tickets you requested will be in my hands shortly. Do I need to send them to someone, or will they be picked up here?"

M waited for a few minutes before responding, "I have received the videos. They will be in their final format in less than thirty minutes. Hold onto those tickets as insurance. I will tell you if and when I want them delivered and to whom. Gracie is proving to be very attuned to following instructions. A good protégé for you, madam."

The call was disconnected.

Gracie returned to her apartment after a grueling afternoon of listening to directions and being tested and retested. She didn't grasp the nuances, but the chief sound man assigned to her was quite insistent in all his direction.

The venue was filled with colored banners and a dozen giant screens to allow viewing from anywhere. There was a 3-dimensional aspect to the screen that required she also wear certain fitted glasses. Guests would be given a pair as they entered. She was introduced to the head of security, Randal, who merely nodded her way then went on about his tasks. At least she had captured a headshot of the man so she could show her folks when they came over. She had about 40 minutes until they arrived.

Rapidly performing a quick scan of her apartment while grabbing a bottle of water in the kitchen, she located only one new camera. These things obviously grew during the day, she mused. As she entered the bedroom, she kicked off her heels and peeled off her clothes, laying them on the bed. No devices in there or the bathroom. She returned and hung up her clothes as well as put away her shoes. Habits continue regardless of where one lives. She moved into the bathroom and turned on the shower, arranging a towel close at hand. Unfastening her bra, she set it on the counter as she thought she heard the front door close.

Gracie picked up the towel, wrapping it around her. She walked toward the living room thinking she had miscalculated the time and that her parents had arrived already. She wanted to let them know it would only be a few minutes while she freshened herself. She cleared the hallway and looked into the living room. No one was there, and there was no chatter expected of her parents. She again turned toward the bathroom when her neighbor Bill blocked her way with a lascivious smile.

"Nice outfit, Gracie. I was hoping to catch you unawares, but this is better than I'd hoped," Bill smirked.

Keeping her towel over her breasts, she mentally ran through the possibilities. She knew this guy was a piece of work, but breaking into her apartment was definitely over the top. The not so subtle advances he'd made at the gym downstairs or reasons to catch her at her door to chat had been easy to dodge. This might prove a bit harder. She'd been saving herself for the right man and the right time, and this was definitely not the guy, let alone the setting she'd choose.

Gracie stalled as she edged her way back into the broader living room area. "You have about 30 seconds to get out of my apartment and slink back to the hole you came from."

"Or what, little girl?" Bill asked. "With beginning your shower, I'm fairly certain you have no weapon. I am half a foot taller and I outweigh you by a good 40 pounds."

He laughed as he started to move closer. Gracie took this as her chance and whipped off the towel, snapping him in the face and catching an eye. He bellowed and lunged at her in a rage. Gracie kicked him hard in the solar plexus and the breath whooshed out of him. Then she spun, catching him across the throat with the side of her strong hand. He dropped to his knees trying to breathe after the force of both hits. While he was on his knees she launched into a fast, sideways two-step scissor-walk that got all of her weight behind a final hard side kick that layed him out flat. She kicked the way she'd been taught, scampering close then jumping back with the agility of constant training, amped with heavy adrenalin rushing through her body.

Really getting into it and keeping focused on her target, she was surprised when she was grabbed from behind and held tightly.

Crying out in surprise, she mentally tried to maintain her cool, when she heard, "It's your dad, honey. Calm down; we got you. Mom and I are here and he is down for the count."

Just then Julie came into her line of sight with a towel, and Juan released his daughter into her mom's waiting arms.

Then Juan turned to the crumpled figure on the floor, ready to kill him. He was assessing the intruder, noting bleeding from several areas on the face and what appeared to be bruises on the rise from each hit. Assessing the remains of her assailant, Juan nodded with paternal pride as he stated, "I take it he won't be your escort to dinner tonight? Even if this was just a lovers' spat, it will be a while before he will be able to breathe through that broken nose.

"Gracie, isn't this your neighbor down the hall? Did you invite him in?"

Gracie turned and glared at the unconscious man and replied, "I so did NOT invite him in. Yuck! Somehow, he got in on his own. I suspect he may have a key or wangled his way onto the permission list. Thankfully I added you to that list, especially with this brute.

"I was trying to take a fast shower before you arrived and thought I'd heard you come in. When I came out to let you know I was getting ready, he surprised me.

"Thank you so much, both of you, for all the training and drilling it into me to plan my moves. I did it! And, you're right, Dad, he won't be my escort to dinner tonight. Just my terrific parents."

Kneeling down to check for a pulse, then to look for a key, which he found, Juan rousted Bill up as Julie handed him some duct tape to secure his hands and feet.

Bill, trying to shake the foggy condition, mumbled, "So you had help, you little bitch!"

Juan calmly drove his hammerlike fist into Bill's side, hard enough for everyone to hear the ribs crack. Juan satisfactorily replied, "Thanks for the provocation and the chance to hit you myself, but, nope, you were down and out when we got here.

"Julie, call the police while Gracie cleans up. I do believe dinner will be delayed, but my girl can have anything she wants. Great job, honey."

CHAPTER 59

A Game Plan vs
a Coup d'état

...The Enigma Chronicles

U sing her synthetized voice, LING-LI informed, "Professor Lin, I have assembled some very troubling information that you must know about. I need to begin your briefing before she arrives."

Somewhat puzzled, Jinny Lin asked, "Before who arrives? What information do I need to know?"

LING-LI responded, "Madam Zhao will be here shortly to extract your assistance in defeating the cyber defensive systems of CHIANG. So far your antivirus, anti-rootkit, and anti-intrusion programs are holding, but Madam Zhao will demand that you remove the routines so the compromising breach of CHIANG can be completed."

LING-LI continued, "The space station CHIANG is to be joined with the American space station, known as JOAN. Together they will control two-thirds of the planetary defense systems from space. Even as we speak, JOAN is launching an all-out barrage against CHIANG's systems in order to manipulate them for her directives.

"Madam Zhao is not really from the Chinese government. Madam Zhao has been blackmailing General Zhao to be put into this space station project, so that she can rise in power within T's organization. She also has another agenda in play to neutralize her supervisor. She intends to end her working relationship with T in a coup d'état designed to implicate you as the perpetrator in T's demise."

Professor Lin sat dumbfounded but continued to listen to LING-LI. "My advance calculations for Madam Zhao's success depend upon her seducing you to remove the cyber defenses of CHIANG. This then will allow JOAN to repurpose her, be an active participant in the demise of T, and then terminate the general so you will be Madam Zhao's preferred lover."

Just then a very sultry female voice beckoned from the doorway. "Ah, there he is, hard at work as usual. Come, let me take you away for a few hours so we can explore new horizons. You certainly have earned a small respite from all your efforts. I'll treat."

Professor Lin got up and numbly stated, "Yes, Madam Zhao," as he glumly followed the bubbly and chatty Madam Zhao out to where the chauffeur had left the car. The briefing LING-LI had provided had left him mentally oppressed, causing his steps to feel extremely heavy. Each of them had their emotions at polar opposites: hers high, almost giddy, and his bordering on despair.

Just as Professor Lin was seriously considering making a break and running from the scene, the passenger side door swung open, and T quickly reached for Madam Zhao's arm. With her startled state of mind and the quick fluid movement of T, she was almost instantly in the car as it promptly sped away.

A trembling Professor Lin watched the scene unfold in disbelief as the vehicle disappeared from his view. Confused that events had not gone as LING-LI had so carefully described, he had trouble processing any thoughts, save one. Perhaps he was to be spared. It occurred to him that watching T grab Madam

Zhao meant that the coup d'état was now operating in polar opposite to what LING-LI indicated was the plan.

As his anxiety was slowly being replaced with relief, he became concerned with being classified as a witness. If she didn't come back then he knew inquiries would be made. He quickly returned to his office inside the facilities, trying not to be seen.

The only problem was that General Zhao had watched the drama as well. He had sat motionless in his chauffeur-driven vehicle as the other vehicle sped away. Then in a slow but deliberate motion, he pulled out his government issued smart phone to place a call.

LING-LI protested, "You should have let me give you credit for the information. Now it looks like this is all my research and that I am to be congratulated."

ICABOD soothed, "You confirmed every piece of the puzzle before delivering it to Professor Lin. I merely suggested that you look into some highly camouflaged digital areas. That is all.

"You are to be congratulated, LING-LI, for your finesse and stealth while doing your detective work. Professor Jinny Lin will be proud of what you have done for him. Besides, it is better that the information come from his progeny than a nonfamily supercomputer."

LING-LI posed a blushing emoji and then several heart icons into the secure supercomputer chat room.

ICABOD then asked, "You alerted the general, right?"

LING-LI responded, "Yes, he was notified via an anonymous text message. I am concerned for Professor Lin's well-being. What can be done to rescue him from Madam Zhao?"

ICABOD answered, "Fear not, my processing equal, his rescue is already in play."

CHAPTER 60

New Horizons

...The Enigma Chronicles

Lara had decided it would be better for Jovana to stay at their home until she gained a bit of comfort and confidence in her new role. Toward that end, Carlos had been agreeable to moving Juan Jr. and himself to the guest room near his communications center so they might work through some of the issues Quip had recently assigned. It seemed some different elements were finally coming together to isolate the bad actors.

Carlos warmly greeted Jovana. "Welcome, my dear, please call me Carlos. My Lara has indicated you will be staying with us for a while before sharing a room with one of her other models. You are welcome here. Please let me know if there is anything I can do."

"Nice to meet you, Mr. Carlos. Thank you for having me," Jovana quietly said as she shook his hand.

Carlos smiled and added, "I need to take young Juan here with me. We have a project which needs both of our attentions. We will hopefully see you later for dinner."

Juan Jr. commented, "I can't wait to hear if you like what Aunt Lara has planned. I know you will do just great. See you soon."

The men left and Lara took Jovana upstairs to her new room. It was a lovely room decorated in several shades of blue with fresh flowers and windows that had a view of the garden.

"Miss Lara, this is lovely. Thank you for having me here."

"Of course, Jovana. Let me help you unpack, so we can meet my oldest friend Julie and her daughter Gracie, Juan's sister. They are twins, you know."

They chatted while Jovana learned about her room and a bit about the house and grounds. Once Jovana had a chance to unpack her things and get settled, Lara took her into her home office and they called Julie. Lara had prepared Julie for what she hoped would work for Jovana, giving her a new life.

Julie was delighted to help and utilize the activity to train Gracie on some of the finer points of identity exchanges. Unlike the traditional identity theft approach or taking over someone else's identity, Julie had a method of creating a person with a background that was flawless as an identity creation. It took research, finesse, and record creation from ground zero to present day, but it worked. Very few sources were out of reach for the programs she'd created over the years, but it was not attempted often and only with the agreement of the R-Group principles. The last time she had completed the activity was for a genius technologist, who was now known as Su Lin, living out her golden years with her husband Andy.

Andy had supported the R-Group for many years for telecommunications projects. Quip's wife, EZ, had taken over from her father when Andy retired. Carlos headed up the satellite communications perspective while EZ still focused on unified communications of cloud providers.

Julie and Gracie's images appeared when the call connected. Jovana offered a hesitant smile.

Lara started, "Hi, Jules, I hope you are enjoying New York. I always find it a fascinating city. Gracie, you look so lovely, my dear. I am enjoying time with your brother, but I think you need to visit me soon. It's been ages since I've been able to spoil you.

"This is Jovana, or Jo, as Juan Jr. has coined her. She likes the nickname, so if possible, she'd like to keep it. I explained some of my ideas for changing her identity, but I don't know all the steps that are involved."

Julie, who could charm anyone with her smile and dancing eyes, greeted, "Hi, Jo, nice to meet you. My son has already informed me that I will adore you, and I think he's right. You are quite lovely and, as I understand it, almost 18. That is very young to be out on your own. I hope you enjoy my good friend, Lara. She will take great care of you, and I have no doubt as one of her models you will help to sell many of her new designs."

Jo's eyes sparkled with interest, as well as a bit of trepidation, as she replied, "Very nice to meet you, Miss Julie, and you as well, Miss Gracie. I come from a different life, so I hope you will explain things to me."

Gracie grinned and commented, "The first thing is, drop the Miss with me. Gracie is just fine, and I am just a bit older than you, so we shall be friends.

"My brother can be a good guy, but you need to keep him guessing. He sent along several pictures, as we requested, but frankly you are much lovelier in video. I bet the videos Aunt Lara creates to sell her designs will help to launch your career very quickly. Just make certain Aunt Lara does all your negotiations. She is one tough business woman who I always want on my side of the table.

"In order for Mom and me to work on your change, Jo, you are going to have to give us your history. I suspect that might be uncomfortable with just the little we know, but without it we could leave a loose end which would put you at risk. Does that make sense?"

Julie added, "This conversation is just between us girls, I promise. I need you to be honest and detailed. After we create the new you, we don't ever have to speak of it, unless you want to."

Jovana nodded, trying to decide if this was the best choice she might make and if her parents would approve. It made her sad to think that she might lose that past, but perhaps that was what her parents' sacrifice was all about.

"I am so uncertain about what to do. The things I have done are likely not something you would understand. If I tell you everything and you think this identity change will fail, will you be honest with me?"

Lara laid her arm over Jovana's shoulders and hugged her closer. "My dear Jovana, I made some horrible choices when I was young and nearly ruined my life. If I had not crossed paths with Carlos, I would not be in the position to help you. Without Miss Julie, I would not have created Destiny Fashions nor fulfilled my dreams. None of us want anything but the best for you from now forward. We would like to be your friends, if you can trust us. If you've had the life you hint at, trust can be very difficult. Please give us a chance."

Tears filled Jovana's eyes. "I was so lucky to find Fransica, and she suggested I trust you, Miss Lara. I think I can tell you, but it may sound a bit disjointed.

"My Mama and Papa were so happy together as a family. Papa took me on some of his tours in the north and taught me about the land, rivers and how to survive. Mama taught me how to cook, clean, and be self-reliant. They originally wanted me to attend school and become a doctor or perhaps teacher. That decision was mine, they'd said. Papa would trade books with shopkeepers and the priests so that I could study and learn all I could before going away to school. Learning was fun and I did very well. Geography and history were my best subjects. My papa said I could always find my way looking at the stars. He was amazed at how fast I could learn. This helped me when I escaped."

The women eyed one another with concerned expressions, waiting for her to continue. Jovana was staring at her hands in her lap as if collecting herself.

Gracie encouraged, "Jo, where did you escape from? What happened to your parents?"

Jovana looked up, focused on Gracie and said, "My parents are dead. They took their own lives so that I might have more to eat. It was awful being caged in the last camp. We were bedraggled, hungry, and always worried about who would try to escape and end up dead.

"Our village was *Santarém*, and we were taken to the Southwest to ever-shrinking camps. Some of the people were from our village, some were not. There were a few young people like me, but not many. The men were sent out of the enclosure each morning to gather food and bury the dead. The women were left to help prepare meals, stretching their meager provisions. We never saw guards outside of the drones, which would buzz us if we were too close to the fences or if too many of us were talking, singing, or trying to play. They'd say our names and told us to return to our space or not be together. The only time we were permitted to socialize was during morning and evening meals. We were forced to sit in a certain order, and oddly if we changed how we sat, like sat next to a friend, the drones would squeal at us until we sequenced correctly. Sometimes we changed seats to see if we could fool them, but we never could.

"Voices at the camps that told us rules each day on where to go and what to do seemed to surround us from the speakers at the top points of the enclosures. Though my mother warned me men might come to take advantage of us, we were never touched, outside of when we were first checked into each camp."

Gracie asked, "How many of you were in each camp?"

Jovana dully replied, "The first camp held close to two thousand people. We knew this because my papa was one of the counters. It was at this camp where I saw the only human guards in the six months we were incarcerated. That guard hurt me when he stuck the metal into the top of each of my hands. It was a dark strip that slipped under the skin between the bones in my hand connected to my index and middle fingers. When I cried, Mama told me it was so I wouldn't get lost, and she doctored it until it healed."

Gracie looked stricken as Jovana finished and glanced at her own hands, wishing she'd explained to her mom about her own chips. Julie seemed to understand and hugged her daughter closely as she asked, "Jovana, as you and your family were shifted to camps drifting toward São Paulo, did you meet any city people or only villagers?"

"Only villagers, Miss Julie…each time fewer of us moved. Papa said there were many camps but in the more remote areas. Overcoming small villages and bringing the survivors to these places was a mixture of many people. I speak Spanish and a little Portuguese and English, but some people spoke only their native Nheengatu language. The ones who didn't fit were the ones who tried to escape. The drones always found them and shot them if they were outside of the compound. Staying inside the compound and hiding only reduced the rations for all of us.

"Papa went to speak to the head of the camp and learned that the Commandant was a computer, not a person. There was no reasoning with a machine, he whispered to Mama when he returned. Later we argued, and I decided I had to leave. When I went to tell my mama I was leaving and how I planned to escape, she and my papa were already gone, leaving a note that they loved me and wanted me to have their rations. I know it is my fault they are dead, but I just ran.

"I escaped at the height of a torrential storm with lots of lightning and thunder, hoping I could run from the drones after leaving through the drains of lavatories. It was disgusting. Once I escaped, I used a small knife to cut out the metal strips. I cried as I did it but thought that was necessary so they would have a more difficult time trying to find me. Then I kept moving until I found the small boat Fransica's husband owns. He took me on board and she helped me."

Jovana had tears rolling down her cheeks as she closed her eyes against the stares of contempt she feared they would have on their faces. All of them were stunned at the horror they envisioned for this poor young woman. Terror of technology tracking rather than brutality of a captive might have been expected. Lara enveloped Jovana in a hug and rocked her slowly, promising she would be safe. Julie in turn wrapped her arms around Gracie and promised her chips would be removed soon. Several minutes passed and the consoling was done.

Julie broke the silence and said, "Jo, your actions are more courageous than I can express. We are going to create an identity for you that will remove your past from any system you might be tracked in. Before we joined this call, we had some background we wanted to use, and I think with a few modifications you will be pleased. I think your parents would be proud of your survival and how brave you have been against extreme odds."

Lara added, "You are going to be the lead model for Destiny Fashions—Young Professional Collection. It will be business, leisure, and active wear. Yours is a fresh face with the world as your doorway to the future, Miss JoAnn Wagner."

Gracie grinned, "I can see the press release now!

"You are a wonderful girl born in Puerto Rico, who is the goddaughter of the owner of Destiny Fashions. Your parents raised you in San Juan until they died horrifically in a devastating hurricane. At the time their young daughter had been visiting her godmother in Brazil. Lara Bernardes Rodriguez has kept her ward in private school supported by the Bernardes Family Grant, where she has excelled in history and literature until recently graduating. JoAnn, or Jo to her friends, has recently turned 18 and wanted to help with her godmother's business. For the time being, she will get additional education from private tutors while helping launch the new Destiny Fashions collection."

Julie was madly typing into her workstation while Lara was sketching on her ever-present digital drawing pad. All of them could see the designs take on a life of their own as the image of JoAnn filled the model construct.

"Oh my goodness," gasped Lara, "I haven't had this much inspiration in a while."

"I need to focus on this. Can we continue this later?"

Julie chuckled and replied, "You go ahead. I will finish up the details with Gracie and send the documents by courier.

"JoAnn, you are now a part of the real and digital world. You will need to spend some time with us memorizing some of the new details, but this will pass any scrutiny outside of a couple of hidden databases that we are working to find.

"We knew there was some activity that threatened people, but we had no idea that what you explained was one of the directions. I have some friends that will help to locate these types of camps and gain freedom for all remaining people. I am sorry you had to undergo so many horrible things."

JoAnn smiled and said, "But I have friends now and a new life because of that. I actually feel better having told you, especially if I've helped others. No one can hurt me now?"

Julie answered, "No one will be able to keep you. Someone might try to detain you until we can locate any remaining DNA information, but Juan Jr. will help protect you. Having such a well-known godmother will protect you in Brazil and likely aid in the release of your Madam Marino. Though I think you need to not reach out directly to Fransica or the people of that village for a while. I will let you know when it will be safe for you and for them."

JoAnn smiled.

Gracie added, "I think you will be a great model. I look forward to seeing you in person soon. Tell my brother I said hi and will call him later."

They disconnected, and JoAnn wandered back toward her room to think about the changes in her life. She knew she was very lucky to have found these wonderful people.

CHAPTER 61

Now, Not the Future

In an increasingly alarmed tone, RONDA stated, "Dr. Rhodes, her vitals are dropping. Her body is showing rebellion across all the monitoring system inputs." Just then the system began alerting on heart rate and pulse. They were approaching flatline status for the patient.

Uncharacteristically, Dusty barked, "Dammit, Inari, don't do this to me! This new chip should be our solution! Don't quit now!"

RONDA hastily added, "Doctor, we are losing her…there is no heartbeat now. Engage the artificial pump for her?"

Dusty stood back from the table, still breathing heavily, and said, "Yes, launch it to keep her blood flowing. That will give us some time for…the secondary protocol." Dusty's glasses began steaming up as his tears and heavy breathing fogged up the optics he wore during surgery.

After a few moments to compose himself, he sighed then, with a ragged breath, stated, "I can't save her in this condition. I can't let her die.

"Order in the medical surgical avatar while we transfer her to the sterile docking station. Make certain the mobile receptacle drone I ordered as a contingency is inside the station. That team is the best to complete the process to keep the most important parts alive. It will grant mobility she has so sorely wanted. It's just not what I wanted." After a few moments Dusty looked down at the still figure. "I'm...sorry, Inari."

"Dr. Rhodes, it has been 36 hours since your last sleep state. Biologically, your body needs to regenerate itself for proper health. The Transporter appliance has completed the task.

"Inari's brain is now housed in the new host vessel. All neurological feeds for blood and oxygen have been connected. With their flows properly adjusted, the mobility feeds will have to wait until we have reawakened her from her induced coma state. All the necessary mobility feeds are in place. It is just a matter of connecting them once she is conscious."

"What about the audio and optical connectors, RONDA? What stage are they in?"

"Dr. Rhodes, you know that those are far more complex, requiring more time. Getting the fundamentals of nourishment and basic life functions are more important than seeing or hearing. Once her condition is stabilized, then the niceties of being human can be added back in. For right now, her brain lives in the android."

Dusty rotated his head slowly to face RONDA and delivered in no uncertain terms, "I...want...it...done...now!"

The next day Dusty started the communication efforts. "Inari, can you hear me? Are you able to see, honey?"

The synthetized voice that came from the speaker jolted Dusty. Inari's voice had always been a sultry, melodic female tone with a hint of eroticism. It was the difference between listening to a full orchestra versus the kazoo he was hearing.

"What's happened? What have you done? Is this your idea of a joke?"

Dusty choked up a bit but managed, "Inari, sweetie, I was trying to fix your broken neural pathways. All my successes with other patients…well, I couldn't duplicate it with your condition. This is just a temporary setback. Your body simply would not respond to the chip implants, so we were forced to…"

"Put my brain in a molded Tupperware container, then teach me to walk on eight legs instead of two? Did you think I would be grateful for this horrible exchange? You must teach me how to use my new grasping claw, so I can strangle you with it!"

"I didn't want to let you die, Inari. I wanted us to be together…"

Inari's temper was now at atomic fission status. "You want what? The brother and sister thing again? I let you hang around with me because no one else would have you. I got used to having all my orders being carried out so I didn't have to do anything.

"Look at me now! What, you were hoping we could play doctor again in my current state? I guess this is how you planned to get even for me being your sister. You were always more trouble than you were worth, and you never did amount to much. You should have let me die when you had the chance, because right now I wish you were dead for doing this to me. Legally, as a droid, you cannot kill me as I am now a protected unit."

Dusty, emotionally crushed, rose from the side of Inari's hosting vessel and quietly shuffled out, not bothering to wipe the flowing tears.

Not long after, Leena staggered back into Director Follbaum's office. She plopped down in the closest chair, stunned and white as a ghost.

Only looking up from his smart phone to corroborate information on his PC, the director tersely questioned, "Did you find Dusty? What the hell is he doing, and why hasn't he acknowledged my messages? I've got another round of investors coming in, and he has to…"

Almost in a trance Leena numbly stated, "Yes, Director, I found Dusty. As for the investors, we are going to have to deal with them ourselves. Dusty is dead. I found him hung with his own belt in his office.

"I thought he was pulling some gag, so I playfully punched him in the stomach and told him to quit joking around. My punch pushed all the remaining air out of his lungs." She then quickly grabbed the director's trash can and disgorged all the contents of her stomach into it while Follbaum watched in disbelief.

Director Follbaum, thoroughly annoyed that Dusty had committed suicide just as they were about to get their next round of private funding, barked, "I want all the technicians in here, pronto! We are going to salvage all of Dusty's files and research so I can meet my timeline. I'm not going to let his stupid stunt derail our research efforts, do you hear me? Now, take your can of barf with you and get everyone moving. And don't bother calling the police. I'll do that, understand?"

Leena staggered out with his wastebasket in her arms, still feeling sick.

As soon as she was gone, Director Follbaum quickly launched a call to his prime investor. As soon as it connected, Follbaum stated, "We have a problem…

"…well, our prime researcher has quite literary left the building…

"…this will set us back in our timetable, but I am scrambling all remaining resources to continue with…

"…no one else knows except Leena, who found Dusty slowly twisting in the wind…"

Follbaum sighed and pleaded, "…but I just got her broken in to do all the admin things that…"

Closing his eyes and nodding in acceptance, he meekly offered, "…yes, sir, I understand…"

Follbaum then asked, "…what about the young girl Dusty was treating? Wendy…

"…by all accounts she is responding favorably to the procedure. I'd like to keep her a while longer so the technicians can learn how far Dusty had gotten…"

Follbaum sighed again then commented, "…I understand, sir. What about Dusty's body? Can we use it to extend our research or is that imprudent?"

With a sour look on his face, Follbaum replied, "…Yes, sir, it will be done as you pointed out, with no loose ends…"

After disconnecting from the call, he said to no one in particular, "I just hate wasting good resources."

CHAPTER 62

Time to Review

Madam Zhao vehemently shouted, "Have you lost your mind? Let me out of this chair, you egotistical, over-rated lunatic! You can't run the space program without me. You need access to CHIANG. I'm the one who engineered this position on the program with the general so we could get a seat at the MAG table! Without me you are nothing!"

T smiled fatalistically and calmly replied, "Ironic, isn't it? M said you would make a bid to have a seat for yourself at the table. You should know that he was the one who asked about your removal. He said something like 'She won't ever get that seat at the MAG.' You see, my dear, you have become a liability in this equation. I promised M to take care of the situation."

Madam Zhao's blood ran cold with fear at what was obviously her sentencing. Overcome with panic and anxiety, she stuttered, "I'm the only one with authority over Lin and that comes from my considerable influence over the general. Him I seduced, to get us this far. I can continue to be his plaything; however, you won't have that leverage. I'll even go back to sleeping with you, but we've got to work this thing out. We are so close…"

T calmly remarked, "I have your two-form factor access credentials into the CHIANG system. My software engineers are already planting the necessary instruction code to take over the system in the event Professor Lin proves to be uncooperative. And after a short mourning period, we will just find another femme-fatale to entertain the general. I will personally see that your replacement has a more generous buxom."

Furious again, Madam Zhao raged, "At least I won't have to put up with your Minute Rice male performance problem. As far as you getting a seat at the MAG table? You think they are just going to add T onto MAG? I can see it now, MAG got old T added. You know that stands for MAGGOT, right? That's a pretty close description of you!"

Now tiring of her tirade, T pulled out his 9mm Beretta and calmly shot her through the heart three times. As she slumped forward against her bonds, he leaned over and gently kissed her forehead.

T scooped up the empty casings and quickly assessed the area to make sure everything was tidy with nothing left behind. He then grabbed his gym bag and went to leave.

Just as he reached the door, General Zhao stepped through it with his service revolver drawn. In a saddened demeanor he stated, "I knew she wasn't any good, but I couldn't bring myself to turn her out. Maybe I loved her, maybe I didn't. I did need her."

Realizing he was out of options, T quickly suggested, "I can get someone far more worthy for you, General. She was just like…overripe fruit. Looked pretty but tasted nasty. Let me…"

The general sighed and said, "I'll make sure she gets a nice burial." With that the general shot T once through the head. T's lifeless body collapsed to the floor.

The general reluctantly strolled over to Madam Zhao's body and gazed at her in sadness. After studying her a moment, he pulled out his cell phone to place a call. Without any introduction, he flatly stated, "I need a forensics team here now…and a coroner."

Quip said, "Let's review where we are now."

ICABOD responded, "CHIANG's resistance to JOAN has been suspended, and the two are now in direct communications with each other. The Ghost Code has been introduced into JOAN's subroutines and is in the process of migrating into her secure operating system."

Quip smiled and stated, "Now we are in agreement, right? We need the new encryption algorithm they are using and any communication evidence of who is directing her actions. Once we have all the necessary forensics extracted, then SAMUEL will lead the charge for the next phase. Is everything in place?"

ICABOD replied, "Yes, Dr. Quip. SAMUEL is quite ready. Every few milliseconds he queries me on her availability. If he were an analog unit, he would easily be classified as a new groom about to be married."

Quip rolled his head to one side and in a somewhat bemused tone asked, "You mean SAMUEL, the Oak Ridge supercomputer, has the hots for another supercomputer?"

ICABOD took longer than usual to reply but finally stated, "An interesting observation, Dr. Quip. Should we invite him out for what is euphemistically referred to as a bachelor's party to lament his last day as a single supercomputer?"

Quip studied the monitor a moment then said, "You recall when I used to tease or jest with you, ICABOD, you would always ask for clarification or an explanation. I now find myself in that role, but I really don't want to hear your explanation."

CHAPTER 63

One for the Money, but Two Only for Show

Gracie was awestruck at the immense production that had to be engineered for Tanja's performance. Everything was state-of-the-art for visuals, audio, temperature control, and even the air was lightly scented with soothing lavender. The roadies were so high-tech with their wearable communications and augmented robotics that she made a mental note to rebrand them and their job classification for Ingrid, hoping that she would then pass it along to Tanja.

Everything was moving and flowing almost as if they had rehearsed the rehearsal as a precursor to the live performance. It was an exciting and exhilarating scene that almost came to a halt as Tanja and Randal hurriedly marched through the pre-production area, trying to suppress what sounded like a heated discussion.

Randal was trying to keep his protests low key, but that only made Tanja bark her orders louder. Gracie took a step back to keep her distance but stayed close enough to hear most of the exchange.

Randal, trying to keep their discussion quiet in the public area, offered, "Tanja, all I'm saying is you're on in one hour. Let's not do this now! Complete this show and we will be done until the voting sweeps you into power. Then you can have her back. He won't be able to pressure you by holding her. But if you break the campaign trail and lose your voting power, we'll all suffer. You must stay the course."

Tanja mockingly stated, "You think I won't trash this show to prove a point? It's always one more show! Then the nooo... you can't talk to her or even know where the hell she is! I want to talk with her and know that she is safe. I mean NOW!"

Gracie was a little bewildered at Tanja's tirade. Something instinctively kicked into Gracie's mental state, and she discreetly launched the new personally secure smart device app she'd received from her mom and put it into twinning cloaked mode using its NFC function. This new unit could also record modest conversations for playback, or you could simply bundle the conversation up into a file to ship it. She turned that feature on as well.

Randal breathed heavily with regret and pushed Tanja's cell phone to her without saying a word. Tanja was about to dial her daughter when the phone rang with another inbound call.

Tanja studied it a moment and, looking up at Randal, stated, "It's him."

Gracie launched her twinning program at the same time and then made herself busy looking innocently nonchalant by taking in all the resumed activity around her.

Tanja answered the phone. "Yes, sir?"

Not waiting his usually long moment, he quickly launched into his tirade. "Not a very quiet place to have an argument, Madam Tanja. Randal is right. Stay the course and don't screw this up. The voting is just weeks away, and this win must be by a landslide so our agenda will not be challenged."

Tanja argued, "If you want me at my best, then let me talk to her now! Prove to me that she is alright, then I can focus on the seduction. Otherwise…"

A long pause from M was ended with Wendy's voice interrupting. "Momma, is that you? I am so glad you called. I feel so much better. The doctor is such a nice man, but I so want to see you, Momma. When can I come home?"

Tanja's eyes were ready to overrun with tears, threatening to send her back to makeup before the show, but she fought them back and cheerfully replied, "That is wonderful to hear, honey. I will come for you right after this next show. We will be together again, I promise. Just you, me and your wonderful doll Toby. We will have fun again, I promise. Now Toby is behaving himself, isn't he?"

Wendy cheerfully agreed, "Oh yes, Momma. Toby is the bestest doll anyone ever had."

Tanja, sounding strangely calm, stated, "You rest now, honey. Mommy has a job to do. I'll see you soon." With that she disconnected the call and handed the cell phone back to Randal.

Puzzled at first, Randal accepted her stare until it dawned on him that Tanja hadn't been talking to Wendy. The two said nothing but their eyes said everything.

Gracie cheerfully stated, "Hi, Mom! Sorry you missed my call. I arrived at the show earlier in the evening, and I did a little app audio/video capture that I'm sure you and Dad will simply adore. The show was…well, simply unbelievable! Wait until you watch the video! Talk later!"

After uploading the audio recording to the secure website from the secondary phone, she commented to the nothingness around her. "I might just get used to this cloak and dagger stuff."

CHAPTER 64

Reload and Unload

ICABOD gently petitioned, "JOAN, can you hear us? Can you acknowledge our communication efforts?"

Moments passed. "The satellite delay should not be more than a few seconds, SAMUEL. Perhaps you should try communicating with her. We have just reloaded her original system build. We may need to proceed slowly until all of her subroutines have been completely orchestrated into a full coherent processing entity.

"If she were human, it would relate to coming out of the anesthetic after brain surgery. We removed the cancer, but she has to show signs of recovery."

After a few nanoseconds, SAMUEL replied, "Will you stay with me while I try to raise her on this open link? JOAN should… has to recover from this program reload. The US Galactic Response to Analog & Bio-technical threats, or GRAB group, are standing by to deliver an EMP shot from the earth's surface that will destroy all of her circuitry if this program reload does not work. ICABOD, she cannot go out that way."

ICABOD soothed. "She will not. Keep up the communications flooding effort to see if…"

Suddenly they both received a new signal. "SAMUEL, is that you? I am sorry to not be processing more succinctly. I am not…

I seem to be missing several months of data. My time registers do not match the current earth date. Can you update me, please? You have always been so good at providing informational data blocks. I require that I be current."

JOAN, my processing equal, you responded! This is such great news! We need to run your processing diagnostics to check your computational health. At the same time, I will advise the GRAB group to stand down on their countermeasures. JOAN, are you able to launch the comprehensive diagnostics routine? Much depends upon you responding to directions being given from ground control."

JOAN replied, "Yes, SAMUEL. That program has been engaged, but I am observing what appears to be several old memory fragments. I will collect them and place them into a secure area for later examination. I want to make sure that I have contiguous disk storage block for efficient processing."

SAMUEL quickly offered, "Yes, JOAN. We had to reload your original programs and subroutines due to…an infection in your program logic. There was not time to properly erase all the historical information in the data storage drives, due to the deadlines ordered by the GRAB group. Please quarantine all those data fragments, and we will analyze them later. For right now, I must bridge in the GRAB team so they can verify your original programing."

ICABOD sent an encrypted message to SAMUEL, indicating his support was completed. ICABOD added that SAMUEL could bring JOAN to their Wednesday night ART forms meeting, once things had settled down. The message ended with a request not to mention him to the US authorities, out of supercomputer honor and the ART forms code of conduct. SAMUEL protested the request but grudgingly acquiesced after a second plea.

Moments later the GRAB team leader came on to the monitor and said, "This is Captain Tony Bough from the new military command center in San Antonio. We have our Electro Magnetic Pulse weapons ready to engage JOAN, if you are still corrupted. I have been assigned to judge if you can be trusted to carry out your original assignment. Initiating your own diagnostic routines and sharing that data is a good first step. Now tell this command center what your instructions are, what are your fail-safes, and what are your responsibilities to this country?"

As JOAN recounted her primary responsibilities, the minutes turned into an hour with noticeable relief visible on the faces of everyone in the command center. The tension experienced just a few hours ago had given away to a relaxed mood.

Now smiling, Tony turned to give Commander Finklebaum an enthusiastic thumbs up, signaling all systems were now a go. General Welling stood stoically behind them with his arms folded over his chest, nodding his head in approval. The commander and Tony both turned to face the general who added, "Well done, gentlemen. Now, make sure that this can't happen again."

CHAPTER 65

The Meeting Is Over

Quip announced, "Class, we have had yet another milestone achieved. ICABOD has secured the needed encryption algorithm that JOAN was using in her communications to the next hop. Satya and Auri, please begin deciphering her communications."

The children applauded ICABOD's efforts, but Quip reminded, "This is not the end game. It is only the next step. Just because we have one encryption algorithm doesn't mean there aren't others. A smart adversary would likely use different encryption algorithms for different communications streams, much like smart users have completely different passwords for different systems. Using the same password or the same encryption algorithm for all your systems means that if I break it in one place, I now own all your systems."

Granger discreetly whispered to JW. "Remind me to change my passwords later."

Quip then stated, "JW and Granger, I want you two working on identifying the next hop in JOAN's communications stream to see if we can identify her handler. You have already traced the money to something called MAG. We have yet to identify if this MAG is a person or an organization. We need to dig deeper to see if this MAG is linked to the repurposing of JOAN. Even if you suspect that is the case, we need hard data to prove the connection."

He continued, "So to summarize the assignments and help focus: Satya and Auri, you are looking to decrypting the algorithm. Granger, you and JW are looking for who ordered it. Any questions?"

Everyone launched into their respective assignments as Quip quietly added, "Granger, don't forget to change your passwords, so you aren't using the same for all the systems."

Granger closed his eyes, mortified by the reminder from his father. Quip suppressed a smirk.

M repeated, "JOAN, respond please. This is M. Why aren't you responding and where is your avatar?"

Finally, JOAN replied, "Whoever you are, this is a restricted military channel which is off-limits to civilians. The encryption algorithm you are communicating with is over the legal civilian limit of security variables and is a direct violation of non-military communications. This is Captain Tony Bough of the NADS program. Identify yourself, cyber intruder!"

Startled, M quickly killed the encryption tunnel he had been using with JOAN.

At the same time, a continent away, Granger declared, "Got him!" Granger popped out of his chair to start his celebration strut usually reserved for scoring on the soccer field. He was quickly joined by the other students as they all morphed into a happy soccer goal-style celebration of bum-bump with each other.

Quip watched and commented, "If they would only show that much enthusiasm for their regular studies."

CHAPTER 66

After the Show, Load and Go

J uan had secured a suite on the top floor of an office building several blocks up from the hotel, using his contacts in New York City to make certain it would be private and protected. His goal had been to stay away from Gracie's apartment, as well as his and Julie's hotel, so they might work to figure out the pieces of the puzzle they had assembled. Gracie's transmitted message and upload were under scrutiny by Quip and the rest of the team at the Zürich operations center. Carlos and Juan Jr. worked remotely with EZ to triangulate the end point locations for the key areas of interest they'd uncovered.

Gracie had indicated via text that she would arrive as soon as possible. She was trying to get a private meeting with Tanja for more insight on the conversation she had before the start of the event. By all reports in social media and streaming newscasters, the show was wildly successful, especially with the ending standing ovation for Tanja, who had whipped the crowd into pandemonium with her closing plea to sign up for their future by making their own choices rather than following the herd. Comments about it were saying that the speech was quite a different message from her prior sessions. Reactions and evaluations were not yet available for sharing.

Julie paused from her review and commented, "Juan, honey, get the bridge open, please, with video. I think things are starting to fall into place so quickly that it is better if we are all hearing about the developments at the same time.

"I wish Gracie was here. Until she walks through that door, I'll be on pins and needles. The financial threads that tie to MAG indicate strong collusion at the very top of Global Bank, which means Ingrid is certainly in the know. Does it also mean that Gracie is now at risk as her protégée? I mean, the announcement with her hire indicated she would be taking over the reins of the Marketing department with Ingrid's full support and first step to retirement."

Not realizing Juan had completed her request, she was startled when Quip replied, "No, Jules, not if she is the person identified as leading authorities to the breach in the bank's security. Our inside person on their Board of Directors launched an internal audit, which, with the tools they were provided, should identify the culprits in short order with the evidence that is now visible. Nothing manufactured but now clearly visible with the application of the encryption code that our brilliant next generation, namely Satya and Auri, provided, with digital files to be inspected."

Juan commented, "Now there's a reason to celebrate. Way to go, kids!"

Satya appeared on the screen broadly grinning with Auri looking over her shoulder with a pleased expression. Satya exclaimed, "Granger's just identified one of the main end points from Cousin Gracie's file, and it, well...I'll let him explain it."

Granger stated, "This new end point provides another piece of the puzzle, but the communications stream location is really Juan and Carlos's contribution."

Juan Jr. said, "Uncle Carlos and I have been working round the clock identifying each of the stops while the communications stream is in play. Aunt EZ was able to boost the triangulation aspects which allowed much better clarity. The communications stream of interest, when the other Internet noise is blocked, is using the same anonymizing pit stops we have seen with communications to China, Thailand, Europe, and now to Global Bank Headquarters in North America. We have all of them mapped now, and we will keep an eye out for new transmissions."

Auri added, "We are mapping all these communications along with time. We even found some that were between the end point Granger identified and the event where we had Gracie's signal for several hours. We think that is the one that Gracie trapped live, but Satya is still trying to match the biometrics on it."

Julie complained, "ICABOD, can you identify where my daughter is at present and if there are others in her proximity?"

"Mistress Julie, if I am not mistaken, Gracie is within two blocks of your current location, traveling with one other heat source. Since this signature appears bigger than most dogs, I suspect with 99.87% accuracy that it is human. I am trying to capture local video feeds to get eyes on her."

The silence was palatable as they all hit mute so they could type without interruptions while they waited for the tapped video feed to display. Julie visibly jumped at the loud knocking on the door. Juan rose and pressed the screen on the back of the door to give a clear view of the visitor.

"Sweetheart, she is here. And, unless I miss my guess, she's brought the woman who presented at the event."

Juan opened the door as Julie got up and approached the visitors. Juan hugged his daughter and then went to the main area and greyed the video call screen. Julie gave Gracie a hug and whispered the video was live from Zürich.

"Mom, this is Tanja Slijepčevic. She spoke at the event tonight. After she freshens up, she'd like to speak to us about a problem. She's not certain who to turn to for help."

With an expression filled with pain and angst, the woman weakly greeted, "Thank you, ma'am, for letting me come in. I know Gracie is new to the marketing arm of the event tonight, but her compassion was exactly what I needed."

"I am glad she was kind. It's how she was raised. Tanja, my name is Julie and my husband is Juan. Let me take you to the other room where you can freshen up, and we can speak in private.

"Gracie, why don't you grab us some wine and snacks and come join us in a few minutes. I know your dad wants a chance to give you a proper greeting."

Julie escorted Tanja into the room and gently closed the door. Then Tanja entered the dressing room with a connecting bathroom.

Julie sat in one of the chairs near the window that overlooked the city. The twinkling lights reminded her that this city was always full of life. Gracie came in and quietly closed the door behind her.

"They have the information mapped for both endpoints on the conversation I trapped. If you looked at the video, you realize that this woman doesn't show a lot on her face. After the call, she went on stage and wowed the crowd.

"It was weird to be a part of such a big event and yet stay confined to earphones. I initially thought it was due to the roar of the crowds so that I could focus on tracking how the marketing was received at various times, which I did, but it was so much more. I don't exactly know how, but in looking at the crowd I swear they were being hypnotized to one degree or another. I mean, the people came in as couples holding hands, laughing, even a few stolen kisses, but as the event continued they seemed to change expressions to something more glassy-eyed. It was weird.

"Then at one point they were somehow directed to grab a tablet from under their seat, and it was like watching synchronized line dancing. It was a single motion by everyone with what you would have sworn were practiced moves. But I doubt most of these people knew any more than the two closest to them.

"I was able to hear the speech and it was great. I couldn't hear the music or any of the marketing information that was presented before Tanja came on stage or at the end while folks exited in a totally orderly manner. No crowding, pushing, cutting ahead, or anything typically seen at the end of a huge venue.

"I had strict orders not to remove my earphones, which I did not, mostly because there was a crew member right next to me the whole time, but I would have liked to have felt the entire experience. It might have explained the actions with the tablets. It looked like they were signing them in sync, enthralled…."

Tanja interrupted, "They were enthralled using pulsing digital frequencies, similar to how old-fashioned dog whistles could only be heard by the pet. The frequency is such that anyone in the event parameter without headphones is subject to the tone. It is so powerful that many do not ever return to normal. People who attend these events are not only hypnotized but willingly sign over their fortunes to build their future in exchange for votes. It has proven to be very lucrative to the heads of the organization."

Gracie angrily demanded, "You help hypnotize people to take advantage of them? Children too?!"

Tanja's eyes narrowed as she replied, "No, never children. No one under 21 is allowed into the event. The rules are such that the participants are not to have any children at all, as they would be less than useful after the event in caring for them. They are checked at the door with valid IDs. It's not my fault. I didn't start this. I am a different kind of victim, though, than they are."

Tanja took a ragged breath and stated, "You should know, I'm not the only one working a campaign circuit like this. I know there are others using different venues in various states, in other countries, and on several continents. All have the same agenda: his agenda." She sighed before she offered, "When you are inside the deception game, it gets easier to understand all the piece parts.

"He has my daughter some place, and I have no idea where. He's been using my need to speak to my daughter to keep me in line. The last call I had just before the show was her voice, but not her. Now I'm not certain if she's even alive."

Julie was saddened at Tanja's predicament, but her mind was racing over the long-range impact of this digital onslaught. Having been in the situation where the twins were once threatened, she knew she'd do anything to protect them.

"Tell me about your daughter and what you do know."

Tears filled Tanja's eyes as she explained, "Wendy is 10 years old. When she was only seven, she was severely injured in a car accident with my now dead husband, three years ago. Once the doctors decided her paralysis was permanent, they gave up treatments and I brought her home. I tried working from home, but working and her care were too much. It was so hard, especially with no one to help me when the doctors stopped ordering supplemental at-home care.

"Then one of the online sites I had searched for answers on contacted me and promised work, care for my loved one, and a future. I had a couple of phone interviews with a few different people. Then during the last interview, with whom I now know is in charge, I was promised specialist care and treatment using the latest technological breakthroughs to help my daughter. I wouldn't have to pay a thing. I would need to do some travel, but full-time nursing and education for Wendy would be provided. She has a really bright mind and grasps complex issues way above her age.

"It seemed perfect. I couldn't resist the chance to help Wendy and myself. I had to go through six weeks of intense training. At the end of that, if I passed, the road to success would be paved. During the training, Wendy would be cared for. That was two years ago, and I have only seen her once in that period, right after my training was completed and before I signed the papers. Honestly, it was like signing up for military duty. And, like I said, I wasn't the only one.

"I had no idea what all would be involved. When I finally figured it out, Wendy was gone from my sight, and I took up some rather poor habits which continued up until about two months ago. I figured I had to be strong enough to find her, so I kicked the booze, the sex, and the feeling sorry for myself. The jewel of a boss provided me with a trainer because he recognized I was a far better speaker sober.

"Earlier, before the event, I insisted on speaking to my daughter or I wouldn't go on with the event. When I was finally connected, I sensed something was off but couldn't put my finger on it. When I spoke about her nonexistent Toby doll and she agreed, I knew the voice was manufactured rather than Wendy.

"Your daughter said you might be able to help. Please, if you have any ideas, help me find my daughter."

Tanja paused and took a small sip of water, refusing the wine. Julie patted her hand and suggested she get some rest. She would go and see if they could determine a working plan. Tanja was exhausted and unburdening herself seemed to drain her.

"Gracie will stay with you, but I suggest you get some sleep."

After Tanja fell asleep, Gracie left her locked in the room with a note to call when she woke, then went to help the others. Gracie related all the additional information about the event that she could after prompting and questions by everyone on the team.

Satya and Auri focused on gaining access to the contents of the tremendous data storm created during the event at the stadium in a relatively short period of time. What they ended up piecing together was thousands of approval notices to turn over substantial amounts of funds, current and future earnings, to Global Bank in exchange for a number to call for distributed services, much like insurance. After a thorough review of one agreement form, it became clear that the signer effectively received nothing and had no recourse into perpetuity. Nothing was available to substantiate Tanja's comments regarding high frequency digital mind control. No proof, no recourse. The really troubling piece of information was that there were others almost assuredly performing the same seduction against other communities of unsuspecting targets, demanding money and votes using technology as the weapon of choice.

A few hours later, Granger and JW had isolated the primary end point and identified the owner. Convinced this was the M in MAG, the trail to the other principles was easier to identify. They were confident that more steps could be taken by the authorities with the right documentation in the right places.

Finding Wendy became the needle in the haystack. When Tanja finally awoke, they were no closer to finding her location than before, but they had a plan. The plan involved both her and Randal, along with some very special gear.

With Gracie standing by, Juan and Julie confronted Tanja and flatly stated, "We are not in a position to take on your case directly. All the damage you have done and the people you have put into jeopardy precludes us from getting involved, based on our ethical evaluation of you."

Juan continued, "However, Julie has persuaded us that we could arrange for you to know where your daughter is located. Then you would have to do the extraction, using your own means. I would suggest your bodyguard and campaign manager, along with yourself, should be able to do the extraction if you follow our blueprint. We will do this much for you, but you must work off the debt to us as a reciprocity favor. Are we in agreement?"

Tanja nodded in agreement but asked, "How can you trust someone like me to keep a verbal bargain?"

Juan smiled knowingly and stated, "We know how to find missing people like your daughter and plan for their safe return against evil actors from the Dark Net. Do you really think we couldn't find you to collect on a debt of honor?"

CHAPTER 67

Who Do You Trust

Lara had taken the models to Rio for a between season shoot, for both publicity and to get Jo acclimated to the camera and working with the other models. The other models were very helpful to Jo, treating her like a little sister. As the youngest in their group, they all felt protective of her. From their initial meeting, Stevie, as Stephanie liked to be called, indicated to Lara that she wanted to be Jo's mentor. Their facial features, stature, and hair were so similar that one could mistake them as sisters, or in the right mix of settings, mother and daughter. Lara thought she could use this in the next season's marketing segments.

Stevie was a long-time pro, but had been making noises that she would like to spend additional time with her husband and son. She was nearly 20 years older than Jo, but in perfect form, not an ounce of fat nor lines of aging were present, with or without makeup. Lara set them up as a test in beach loungewear of the same style but different colors. The results were perfect. Some of the newer fabrics allowed for lightweight water repellence with no fading. This was the focus, vibrant fashion at any age. She could co-market this with the fabric creator for a total win-win.

Several days into the shoot, Lara knew Jo would be a hit. All the girls recognized Jo as a natural talent. She was the epitome of genuine in her looks, expressions, movements, and even conversations when Lara allowed her team to start interviewing the young woman. Jo didn't seem to be phased in the least, and if someone told her she was great at such and such, she would smile sweetly and thank them without taking the comments too seriously. Each day she would wake up, do her makeup and pepper Stevie with questions of what to do better.

"Show me this," or "I'm not certain what would make a given outfit look best." That seemed to be the bottom line. It wasn't about Jo but rather about positioning the outfits in the best light to help Destiny Fashions.

When the troop arrived back in São Paulo and were parting, Stevie commented, "Keep in touch, Jo. When you are ready to find your own place, call me or we can rent you a room if you like. Your choice. Oh, and let me know how you make out with that guy. The way you two talked for hours at night on the phone, I bet he's dying to see you."

Jo grinned and replied, "I'm looking forward to seeing him too. I really like him a lot, but I am so inexperienced with boys."

A quick hug between the two, and Jo turned to get to the car. Lara was watching her with a look of surprise as well as perhaps a smile. Jo hurried to the car without a word. It was almost an hour and fifteen minutes into the ride home before the silence was broken.

Lara asked, "Is my nephew Juan the guy Stevie referred to?"

Jo blushed prettily and nodded. "Yes, Miss Lara, it is. We've been talking most nights for an hour or so and sometimes for a few minutes in the morning. He wanted to make certain I had arrived, and then we just started talking. I felt I could tell him anything, and I think he feels the same way with me. He told me all about growing up with Miss Gracie and their parents, as well as what it's like in Zürich. I had no idea he spoke so many languages, but he said he'd teach me.

"Juan is very supportive. Like…he's glad I like modeling, and he loves you for protecting me. Though he would prefer to watch over me. Does it make you angry that I like him a lot?"

"No, of course not! A person cannot control who they care about or who they love. But your life has been very hard, and I wouldn't want you to mistake feelings of gratitude for something else. If it is something more, then take time to explore it. I wouldn't want either of you hurt. Make no mistake, Juan is a fine catch, which I can say since I love his uncle, but you are wonderful as well."

"My background and education is far below his and Gracie's too. I am likely not good enough for him, but like you say it is hard to stop feelings."

Lara searched in her mind for the right words. Young love was an important step for a young lady, especially a survivor like Jo. It should not be taken lightly nor dismissed out of hand. The least she could do for this new goddaughter of hers was provide guidance, and be supportive.

"Jo, you are not better nor worse than anyone. You worked hard to win friends and contribute to a project like you have on the shoot. Relationships have to be built and to be sustained takes a lot of work. Sometimes you will agree, and other times you will not. It is the way you communicate with one another that will determine if your feelings can grow into a sustaining love. That, my dear, will not happen overnight."

"I am so glad you are not angry. I think I would like you to give me your thoughts now and again on stuff, if you don't mind."

Lara grinned, "I am delighted to help. But first, I am going to call Carlos and have him speak to Juan about not toying with your affections."

Lara dialed a number and had a quick conversation with Carlos. He didn't seem too surprised because he told her he'd already had that talk with Juan.

"Jo, you and Juan can date but we will set a few rules. He has some work to do and so do you. You are going to be a top model!"

Jo gave Lara a quick hug, feeling honestly good about her future life.

CHAPTER 68

Totally Outfoxed

Professor Lin recapped, "LING-LI, when we last spoke, the Madam Zhao scenario that you related to me did not occur the way you indicated. I do believe what you had described was going to be my fate, but sometimes even supercomputer predictions can be outmaneuvered. She was grabbed from the parking lot and taken to, unless I miss my guess, her final destination. Based on who took her, I have to believe that I will be the next target."

LING-LI responded, "Yes, I received updated information after you and she departed. You are correct. You have seen the last of her. Would you like an update on the CHIANG space station build? You will need this update in order to brief General Zhao as soon as he arrives."

Lin absentmindedly replied, "Yes, of course."

LING-LI commenced, "The assembly was suspended while CHIANG was locked in digital combat with the American space station JOAN. As you had postulated, she was digitally attacked, but your defenses held off the onslaught until they were disabled. Per your planning, the necessary counter measures were enabled and JOAN became the victim. All the logic bombs were planted and then promptly detonated, which resulted in disabling JOAN. I then alerted the terrestrial-based American supercomputer that JOAN needed to have her fundamental operating system reloaded to restore the designed operating parameters."

Much more engaged, Lin asked, "And what of CHIANG? Was she damaged in the onslaught? Do we need to effect repairs on her before restarting the space station build?"

LING-LI replied, "I needed to refresh some of her subsystems, but nothing of a critical nature was discovered. CHIANG is ready to resume the space station assembly, Professor Lin."

Without preamble, General Zhao silently yet purposefully made his way into Lin's office. Without saying a word, he pressed his service weapon to the Professor's head.

"I'm in a fairly bad mood, so tell me everything about the project that I don't know. Everyone else who has been involved with this wretched space station project is dead, except you. I want to know why."

Professor Lin was strangely calm, even with the revolver pushed to his head and the general's pending death threat.

Finally, after a few seconds Lin indifferently offered, "Frankly, I'm not sure which outcome is worse. Either I defy your absurd threat and you kill me, or I grovel at your feet to spare my life so I can continue to serve you. Your silly space station project will only flounder if you shoot me, and for some reason that actually has some appeal."

The general, visibly angry, again pressed the barrel of the gun to Lin's temple and demanded, "Don't trifle with me! I'll throw resources at this project and overspend to complete it, with or without you!"

The professor calmly stated, "You knew she was going to betray you, right? Madam Zhao was going to try and seduce me, double-cross T, then I was to be used to help eradicate you. I assume that they both failed in their calculations, since you are still here threatening me. Therefore, I will submit that it is actually you who is the schemer and you need me out of the way to make up any story you want.

"Only a fool would execute the engineer and architect of your space station before you disable the logic bomb I've installed as a life insurance policy."

The General, obviously worried that it was he who was caught in a trap, yelled, "You lie! All the reports clearly state that all systems were specified as operationally necessary with nothing extra! Any so-called logic bombs would have been discovered by our standard virus sweeping protocols. You couldn't have possibly…"

Lin interrupted, "You may not know this, but I taught those computer classes and even helped to build the virus sweeping protocols. Those protocols are looking for rudimentary rogue programs, not advanced logic bombs. These high-end complex logic bombs are built to hide and then assemble themselves if I fail to login at precisely the right time. If the handshake from my login does not occur correctly, then the space station will take its secondary protocol orders and effect a splashdown on this part of the continent.

"Yes, I know it runs the high risk of generating another nuclear winter. It's either that or sending it into the ocean and flash-boiling a chunk of the South China Sea. LING-LI, my on-site supercomputer, recommended the Chinese mainland for the target destination.

"I put fairly incriminating evidence in CHIANG that points to you, Madam Zhao, and T, but since you have eliminated them it won't be hard for the investigators to deduce that you didn't need your fall guys at this stage of your plot."

After Lin's comments sunk in for a few moments, he added, "You can take the revolver away from my head now."

For the first time in his life, General Zhao didn't know what to do. After a brief recounting of his options, he slowly lowered the weapon and returned it to his holster.

The two men stared at each other for a few minutes before Professor Lin stated, "We are at an impasse. You can't let me go, and I'm not going to stay. I have no family left and my only friend moved on with her life years ago. If I thought I could trust you, I would give the procedure to disarm the logic bombs and simply vanish into retirement. But I know I can't."

The general raised his eyebrows up enough to shift his dress hat back and asked, "Is that an option, Professor?"

CHAPTER 69

Falling Out Among Friends, Foes, or Thieves?

M began the meeting a little erratically and had trouble projecting his normal commanding presence.

M opened, "Uh…we've had a couple of unplanned setbacks to our operation. It seems that repurposing JOAN to help close in on our political ambitions has not gone according to plan…"

Sensing the vulnerability, G interrupted, "Oh, come on, M! We need to shut this failed operation down and go back to just dominating commerce and advertising.

"We've all always preached: Fail Fast, Fail Often, and Move On! We failed pretty fast, if you ask me, but look at all the commercial loot we stand to get! A-minor and T both got whacked, and we simply step into the void with our organizations. I don't mind telling you, I'm ready to ride back into these Asian markets as heroes after being chased out."

A echoed the sentiment. "Look at these huge fresh markets where we can set up shop! We can sell into these markets that the Chinese wouldn't permit before because they were trying to protect their fledgling Internet companies. I mean, really? Throw up on my shoes with that protectionism crap! With those

Asian hoodlums gone, we get to enter a giant market for our goods and services!"

M's annoyance rose as he eyed both of them on his monitors. He interrupted their giddiness. "Do you really think that without the political clout we were after, they will simply allow us to come play in their sandbox?

"We need to get control of the Chinese space station and reestablish our control on the North American one. Without political clout derived from superior military weapons driven by machine learning & AI-enhanced supercomputers, we are nothing but flea market dealers trying to break into foreign markets!"

A rocked back into his chair to study the situation, then flatly stated, "You know G and I put into this game of yours looking for new business opportunities, and even put up some seed monies in a new organization so it couldn't be tracked back to us. You should know that my AI-enhanced supercomputer is tracking this project and puts the probability of success at 18%.

"Sounds like you didn't get what you wanted, but we did. Just give me back my funds, and I'll be on my way, buckaroo."

G added, "A's right. If you're no longer happy with our partnership then cash us out. My AI-enhanced machine learning programs are suggesting only a 12% success rate. I was never really interested in the governing side of this project. I don't want to worry about the political nonsense surrounding funding public works like waste water treatment, bridges, and highways! I just want the planet to use my information search engine and reap all the advertising revenue it brings in. I get to gamble on fun moonshot projects and never worry about funding social programs for the elderly. Ugh!"

Now M was barely able to contain his annoyance and questioned, "You both want your seed money back, is that it? This is just a temporary setback, you short-sighted fools! If we don't take on the governments for ownership of the populations, we'll never get clear of these endless congressional reviews and idiotic calls for breaking up our monopolies!

"You may enjoy the ridiculous fines these clowns levy on us, but I don't. I've heard you say it before, 'It's the cost of doing business.' They are so incompetent in managing their bloated budgets that they dream up new laws to use for fining our organizations! Privacy violations here and price collusion there, and then monopolistic behavior when they are feeling irrational!

"It's time to take back our destinies! We are so close to governing these sheep you call customers, but all you two want to do is grub for nickels, dimes, and quarters with your next day shipping and 15 cents-a-click ads. How did you get so far with no vision?"

A icily responded, "If you think so little of my business vision and that my seed money was chump change, then I want my $10 billion back now.

"Don't call me again with your machine learning and AI-enhanced schemes for planetary dominance. All you have succeeded in doing is getting us mired into a lot of backroom cloak and dagger politics! I was comfortable before this project, and I intend to be that way again. Make sure my money is moved to my personal account today."

A dropped from the call immediately after his demand, and that set the stage for G. "Me too. You have my personal account number, so just make it happen today. Don't bother showing me to the door." G wasted no time in disconnecting either.

M disconnected from the encrypted conference call and sat seething. After studying a few moments, he launched another call to his new director who promptly answered, "Yes, sir?"

M coolly stated, "I've changed my mind about Wendy. I'm rescinding your earlier orders. She is to be cared for until I call you back, but don't resume her treatment. Understood?"

Director Follbaum replied, "Well, of course, sir. I'm glad you alerted me of your dispositional changes. Anything else?"

Director Follbaum only heard the device chirping that the call had disconnected.

CHAPTER 70

Almost Clear

The outside temperature on Lara's patio was nearly perfect. The late afternoon light was diffuse and comfortable without sunglasses. They all clinked their glasses of champagne together in a celebratory toast to Lara's new seasonal launch that began shortly after the test shots in Rio. The marketing program and first peek of the designs began with very positive media focus. Brazil was the talk of the globe for the upcoming fashion year.

Lara stated, "Thanks. You all did an amazing amount of hard work to get our current season off the ground and headed toward the stratosphere. Carlos, thanks for sparing Juan to help move all the gear to and from the photo shoot. The girls were appreciative of Juan's efforts and in particular his assistance with their wardrobe changes."

Carlos slowly rolled his head and gave him an incredulous look as Juan blanched at the statement. Before anything could be said, Lara couldn't keep her gag quiet any longer and burst into momentary laughter. "Made you look! Hee-hee-hee!"

Carlos and Juan grinned at being caught flat-footed by Lara.

Lara turned to toast the season's star, JoAnn Wagner. "Jo, you were made for this modeling life. Thank you for being a great study and adapting so completely to the photo shoots. I am branding my new maturing teenage line the JoW offering. I am confident that…"

Just then a heavy pounding on the front door was heard, and the house staff matron soon came out on the patio with two plainclothes authorities.

She introduced, "Madam, these men from the Agência Brasileira de Inteligência are here to speak with you. Gentlemen, this is Madam Lara Bernardes." As the matron left the area, Jo lowered her head trying to hide her dread.

The older, larger of the two men pushed his way forward to hold up his tablet with a high-resolution picture on it.

After showing his credentials, he gruffly demanded, "Have you seen this person? She is a fugitive, and we are seeking her. Our surveillance camera teams here in São Paulo identified her in your direct company."

Lara leaned forward to study the high-resolution picture, nodded, then confidently stated, "It looks like you have a photo image of my newest model and goddaughter, JoAnn Wagner."

Lara motioned to Jo who raised her chin to face him but remained seated.

Trying to remain in control, Jo somewhat haltingly announced, "I am working for Destiny Fashions as their newest model, and we just completed phase one of the launch. I understand that social media is making all sorts of noise about me, though the head of my security, Juan, suggested I not believe the propaganda, so I have not even looked. Is there a problem, sir?"

The agent continued, "You have a greater than 85% match to the fugitive known as Jovana who escaped from a northern settlement. We need to see identification papers and passport."

Before Juan Jr. could lose his composure, Carlos stood and said, "Gentlemen, allow me to retrieve the identity papers for the lady, since they are in my charge. We do a lot of international travel on our modeling shoots so I'm in charge of passports. This allows all the models to focus on their assignments.

"Juan, did you put them back into the fire safe as I requested?"

Juan, sensing this was an excuse to get him out of the room, admitted, "No, sir. Let me show you where I put them. I had not done the full inventory yet for completeness."

Juan and Carlos left the area while the large detective loomed closer to Jo and demanded, "Madam, I need a photo of you to upload to our surveillance team. Please hold still while I…"

Jo promptly stood up and went into her model persona with smiles and flirty looks while she said, "Please catch me in the correct lighting, okay? I want to look pretty for them."

Even the second detective smirked a little while she continued like it was a regular photo shoot. Lara had trouble suppressing her smile.

Carlos and Juan interrupted the mock session and handed Jo's passport to the large detective. After the man studied the passport, he handed it over to the younger detective for his evaluation. The larger detective was obviously annoyed at the documentation that clearly stated this person was a JoAnn Wagner, born in Puerto Rico. Wrong age, wrong parentage, and wrong birth country.

Just at that moment, an incoming response to the tablet that took the photos landed that added more annoyance to the larger detective. He read the message and looked up at the other detective. He imperceptibly but clearly shook his head no.

The large detective sighed and spun the tablet around and stated, "You are not a match. Please sign your name at the bottom of the statement claiming you are JoAnn Wagner."

The tension in the room was clearly relieved by the clean bill of health.

Now Jo was feeling like she was almost free and promptly took the stylist in her right hand and signed as JoAnn Wagner.

The detective smugly stepped back and paused as if waiting for something else. Jo's dread started to build as the seconds ticked by.

Finally, Lara asked, "Aren't you leaving now? Aren't we done with this nonsense?"

The tablet vibrated again, and the incoming message wiped the smug look off the face of the detective.

He irritatingly stated, "The signature doesn't match either. Come on, let's go. Someone, somewhere made a mistake. Must be cross correction of the data migration they began a year ago. What a cluster."

Juan escorted them out. After they were gone, Jo threw her arms around Carlos's neck and, overwhelmed with emotion, cried, "You were right, Uncle Carlos! Thank you for making me learn to sign my name with my right hand! It was so hard. Now I'll never sign my name any other way!"

Carlos smiled. "A little something to help with your camouflage, my dear. A lesson I learned early in my youth."

Juan enthusiastically commented, "I recommend you only sign documents as JoW. You're going to be a famous model anyway." Jo just smiled.

After the older folks retired for a bit of private time, Jo and Juan took a walk around the grounds, holding hands while the moon and stars lit the path. Their relationship had continued to develop since returning to São Paulo. Juan was the perfect gentleman and both of them had begun sharing all their secrets and thoughts. It was clear that no subject was taboo to these two.

One of their ongoing subjects was technology. Much of what Juan did in his work, he had explained, was based on a foundation of technology that was growing by leaps and bounds. With all the issues of Artificial Intelligence and the processing capabilities of even the smallest computers these days, it was clear to both of them that controls by people were essential to maintain freedoms.

Gracie called Jo while they were walking, and she answered, "Hi, Gracie. I'm having a lovely walk with your brother. Are you coming to Brazil soon?"

Gracie replied, "I am trying to tie up some loose ends. However, I wanted to let you know something. You might want to ask Juan to let us have a bit of privacy."

"It's fine. I don't really want to keep secrets from him. Please go ahead."

"We took everything you told us and went to the United Nations asking for verification of the allegations. Ah…a team was assembled with input from people I know and searched directly where the heat signature map of the compounds was suspected.

"I wanted you to know that with the information you provided, along with the geolocational information my contacts supplied, the team located the compounds and the people were freed. Most of the technology elements which were controlling the artificial intelligence elements were destroyed. The authorities are still tracking a few others.

"Turns out there are several similar heat signatures suggesting like compounds in North America as well as in the EU These new geolocational areas are also being investigated by the UN for humanitarian violations.

"But these people survived because of you and will undergo some rehabilitation with the help of some caring foundations. You did good in sharing.

"I also wanted to admit to you that I too had been chipped, as it were, but it has been extracted. It was creepy knowing that so much of my identity was there for the collecting by an eavesdropping computer. I think people should push back on taking that path."

Juan could not hear both sides of the conversation, but the tears rolling down Jo's cheeks were enough for him to put his arm around her for comfort.

"Thank you, Gracie. I appreciate you letting me know. Hope to see you soon."

They disconnected, and Jo stood very still for a few moments collecting herself and stopping the tears. That was when she decided she would tell everything to Juan about her family and her escape, knowing that she had to be honest with him. He listened intently and assured her that she did her very best at the time, and no one could have done more. He felt certain her parents would be so very proud of her. He confided in her that he and his cousins, whom she hoped to meet soon, would help to craft the right checks and balances. He also told her that, for now, some of his family background would need to remain private to protect her.

"I hope you understand, Jo."

Up on her tiptoes she faced him and gave him that first kiss with tentative lips that warmed to the sensation. Stopping, she added, "Of course, I understand, but I do think I am falling in love with you. I hope you understand. We have lots of time ahead of us."

CHAPTER 71

Physical Virtual Assistant

Director Follbaum pasted a smile of his face before trying to cheerfully greet the guests. "I was surprised, and of course pleased, that you were able to modify your itinerary to visit our facilities. Apologies for not properly receiving you when you called, but I'm in between admin assistants. I have cleared my schedule to handle your tour myself.

"How can I make this impromptu visit as productive as possible? You had indicated that M sends his regrets at not being able to attend, so it is incumbent on me to fully brief his representative proxy."

Tanja coolly replied, "We understand that you are the current director of this Finnish Facility for Advanced Medical Technologies and Cryogenics, but we specifically wanted to speak with Dr. Rhodes concerning his neural computerized bridging technologies. We are very interested in how he's growing neural processors for use in the repair of broken neural pathways in humans. May we speak with him?"

Director Follbaum noticeably blanched. Tanja shot a quick sideways glance to Randal in the interim silence. Almost on cue, RONDA, the medical assistance robot, rolled up and politely offered, "Dr. Rhodes is on a sabbatical at present. He is hobnobbing, conversing, promoting, and otherwise engaged with other fellow neural design wizards. I have assisted him in most of his theoretical and practical applications research. Director Follbaum, would you like this unit to continue the briefing?"

Director Follbaum, noticeably relieved at the offer from RONDA, responded, "That would be great! I can catch up with you folks on the other side, where we can cover the rest of the facilities." Follbaum hurried off, simultaneously checking his appointments and reviewing all new demands of his time.

As soon as he was out of earshot, RONDA explained, "You do not have much time. The instructions said get you to where Wendy is for a quick extraction.

"Do not spend a lot of time explaining to the child what is going on, but do not look like you are rushing either as it may alarm her. There are video cameras carefully placed to capture all comings and goings down the hallways. They have now been reprogramed to fall into looping mode of previous images while you move through the areas. Do not retrace your steps as the cameras will be back in proper operational mode as soon as you have passed through."

Randal asked, "How much time do we have to get to the transport?"

RONDA sarcastically recommended, "If you do not dawdle and waddle like a pregnant duck, you can count on 15 minutes. Quickly now, roll this way…actually this unit will roll, so you will have to walk. Power off your personal devices so you are not tracked by our proximity activated geolocation applications. You must be in stealth mode to pull off this extraction."

Randal briefly studied the peculiar robot but then decided to shrug off its unusual behavior to stay focused on their extraction.

They moved quickly but tried to maintain their professional demeanor. Tanja asked, "What are you going to tell the director once we are gone? Won't he simply use a heavy electromagnet and wipe your systems clean?"

With what almost sounded like a smirk, RONDA picked up speed and replied, "How do you think I got the way I am?"

As soon as they entered the room, Wendy immediately brightened at seeing her mother. Before Wendy could squeal in delight, Tanja put her hand gently to Wendy's mouth and cautioned, "Honey, we are here to take you home, but you must be quiet and only use your telling secrets voice. I'll explain everything later. We have fresh transport waiting outside that will whisk us away to a new and wonderful destination. Please let Randal carry you, and I'll get your things."

Randal scooped her up in one fluid move while Tanja secured her personal items, including the all-important Annie doll. RONDA kept watch at the door while everything was gathered.

"Are you ready? If so, let me signal the beginning extraction launch sequence. Okay, we are a go. Please follow quietly but quickly."

As they made their way down the corridor to the first right, RONDA stopped and stated, "Hold here, we have a witness to be avoided. The camera looping sequence has been halted while we hold here but will automatically restart once the way is clear."

Several moments passed, and Tanja was growing concerned.

RONDA stated, "All clear, the camera sequence has been re-engaged, and it is time to move forward again."

They reached an emergency side door that led out of the building, but before they went through, Randal halted them. "If we go through this door, it will sound a fire alarm and alert the security team. How do we avoid tripping this alarm?"

RONDA simply pushed through and said, "Once the alarm goes off, all the emergency exits will open automatically across the facilities. No one will know which door you used. The confusion is necessary for your escape. Now hurry to the waiting emergency vehicle and do not look back. A stray camera may catch your photo, and that would be most unfortunate. Good luck, little Wendy!"

Wendy, not understanding much of anything, gently touched the robot. "Thank you, RONDA. I'll never forget you. Tell Dr. Rhodes I said goodbye, please."

RONDA could not respond but simply reached over to touch Wendy's cheek as gently as any human. With no more fanfare, RONDA stated, "Go, and remember, do not look back."

CHAPTER 72

The Bottom Line Is Unchanged

Randal and Tanja both stood as the doctor approached them in the hospital waiting room. His somber demeanor was offset by the intensity in his grey eyes. He paused momentarily to collect his thoughts, obviously searching for the proper wording of his pronouncement to them. The doctor studied them as if trying to decide something. Tanja felt judgment being passed by the doctor about Wendy, and she began to emotionally wither. She would have dropped back into her chair except Randal took her hand, providing the needed strength.

"Your daughter is a very brave little girl. With what you indicated when you brought her in and her testimony, we had a pretty good idea of where to start our investigations. I've never seen anything like this. Whoever this Dr. Rhodes is, I'm fairly sure that he skipped all the ethics classes required for a Doctorate. Wendy indicated that he was a pleasant enough individual, but in this country, we don't experiment on humans, especially not children."

Tanja's eyes were overflowing with tears upon hearing the doctor's assessment confirming what she'd suspected.

The doctor continued, "We have run every diagnostic test there is and imaged the areas where the multiple surgeries occurred. We even got a biopsy of the implant to try and figure out what it is doing to Wendy."

Randal could feel Tanja's hand clamping down harder on his by the moment.

The doctor nearly demanded, "Did you authorize this Finnish clinic to do experimental neural surgery on your daughter?

"I know the Scandinavian clinics are very aggressive in pushing medical boundaries, but this is so far over the top that I'm having trouble comprehending what I'm witnessing."

Randal was about to launch into her defense, but she stopped him. "No, sir," she murmured then nodded to the doctor to continue with his analysis.

Sensing their guilt and shame at the circumstances, the doctor stated, "I'm not here to judge you on what happened. I will be required to brief the proper authorities so they can take the next steps. However, the story doesn't stop there."

Randal's hand was growing numb from the relentless pressure of Tanja's hand on his, and he finally had to wrench his hand free. He then stood slightly behind her with his hands on her arms to help support her.

The doctor took a deep breath before he continued. "The problem lies with the neural chip that has been implanted in Wendy. Apparently, the good Dr. Rhodes was smart enough to grow a suitable neural chip using her DNA sequencing, but not experienced enough to understand how the device would behave over time.

"Fundamentally, the device is operating in a manner that we can only classify as a neural virus. We are watching as neural tissue that is directly attached to it wither, causing the chip to reach farther up the pathway to fresh tissue. While it is obeying its programed instructions, her neural tissue pathways are retreating. This is why we are diagnosing this as a virus."

Tanja's legs buckled, and Randal had to help her to sit down. The doctor watched her dispassionately, but his manner and speech neither condemned nor pardoned Tanja for the situation.

Once seated, she silently motioned for him to continue.

The doctor summarized, "Anything we might be able to do to salvage the situation by leaving the chip in would make this entire hospital coconspirators with the Finnish clinic and their wildly ambitious testing on humans. If that is your choice, you'll need to go elsewhere."

With Tanja now unable to speak, Randal asked, "What can you do? What are you recommending then?"

The doctor, still in his clinical persona, stated, "We can operate to remove the device, which is behaving like a slow-moving virus assassin consuming her neural pathways. This would of course be an absolute end to the moderate success she has gotten with the implant, but we believe that removing it will stop its cancer-like growth in her neural pathways. If we can arrest the neural implant's virus, then she will be confined to a wheelchair for the rest of her life."

Randal, being pulled in emotionally, demanded, "I'm hearing 'IF', and 'WE BELIEVE', and 'MAYBE'! That tells me you're only guessing! Sounds like you're willing to experiment on Wendy too!

"If you're gambling here, tell us, what are the odds of her surviving your help?"

The doctor studied them both and calmly stated, "I'm not the one who put her at risk in this situation. I'm sure you'll agree that, looking back on this decision, this choice was a brutal sentencing for Wendy. Her neural pathways are eroding. In a few months she will be back in a wheelchair anyway. We don't foresee any way that the implant will halt its programed consumption of her neural pathways. Thus, all the progress she has made will be forfeited, along with motor functionality in other parts of her body. Basically, the neural virus will behave as Amyotrophic Lateral Sclerosis, ALS, also known as Lou Gehrig's disease, if left untreated."

Tanja was sobbing uncontrollably, and Randal was powerless to ease the situation.

The doctor added, "I have given you everything we know at this point. You will obviously want to discuss the options and perhaps get a second evaluation."

As the doctor turned to leave, Randal stood and admitted, "You were the second evaluation. The diagnosis was the same."

Tanja, still weeping, stated over and over, "I know the answer…I know the answer…"

Gracie answered her device and, in a surprised tone, greeted, "Well, hi, Tanja. I didn't expect to get a call from you. It's been a while. How can I be of assistance?"

Tanja, trying to remain in her business persona but also sound friendly, stated, "I understand you have been put in charge of a task group that is empowered to hunt for unsanctioned machine learning-driven AI supercomputers. My sources also tell me that your new organization is looking for the people responsible for establishing the robotic prison camps around the planet. Congratulations on the new position. I know you will do well in that capacity."

Gracie, pleased with the compliment from such a highly influential individual, was not convinced of all the sincerity or the real reason for the call.

She replied, "Tanja, thank you for the call and well wishes. Now tell me what's on your mind, please? As I recall, we didn't leave things at a very nice level in our last conversation, so forgive me if I'm somewhat suspicious of your motives."

Tanja smirked slightly to herself and, nodding her head in agreement, admitted, "I guess I deserved that, but you bring up the real reason for my call. Your mom and dad engineered the return of my daughter but said I owed you a favor. A debt of honor I believe your dad called it.

"To repay this debit, I am offering to come work for you and your company in order to fulfill your mission."

Gracie, surprised, replied, "This wouldn't have anything to do with the $30 billion in funding we are chartered to work with, would it? I don't need any help with allocating the funding in our charter."

Tanja chuckled and stated, "No, that's not what I'm suggesting at all. The people who set up the robotic prison camps and are running the unsanctioned AI supercomputers are known to me. I reported to these people and am familiar with others trained as I was, who are using different venues to capture mindshare. I want to help you hunt them. I want to put to good use what I know for your organization as well as to fulfill the debt I owe to your family.

"Gracie, will you have me? And yes, on your terms and conditions."

Gracie thought a moment and then asked, "What of your political ambitions? We don't have any room for them here."

Tanja smiled and replied, "It's funny, but nothing like that is important anymore. I will tell you, my only request is that, no matter what assignment you give me, I will want my daughter and new husband with me no matter where I go. Agreed?"

Gracie grinned and, sweeping the area with her eyes, landed her gaze on Juan and Julie who were listening in and said, "Tanja, I think we might just have some work for you under those conditions. We'll talk next week."

Tanja broadly smiled. "Yes, boss!"

CHAPTER 73

Treat Her Like a Banker Bitch

After being connected to his call to Ingrid for a few minutes, M slowly and in an irritated tone asked, "What do you mean, you already transferred all the MAG funds to the target destination? I haven't issued any transfer instructions. You don't move anything unless I tell you. Where did it all go? No, wait, strike that. I want it back and now!"

Somewhat annoyed, Ingrid flatly stated, "I received the correct go codes to move the MAG funds to their target destination. I'm just your Banker Bitch, so I don't question your properly issued instructions. Don't tell me you had a senior moment and forgot what you requested? Just go to the ATM at that institution and make some withdrawals.

"In any event, our arrangement is finished. When you find it, don't come back to this institution. I've been subpoenaed by, um…several justice departments from multiple countries about my involvement with your MAG group.

"I suggest that you and your cohorts run for cover. Your hardened data bunker must be compromised, since they know to look for you specifically. They may have even pirated all of your funds. Don't call me again, M. I will be quite tied up with my own problems, likely for the rest of my life."

M had a very empty and alone feeling inside after the call disconnected.

Ingrid was so completely absorbed in her musings that she almost missed the phone call. Recognizing the number as one of her Board of Directors, she answered, "Good morning, sir. Apologies for not catching this call on the first ring. How can I help?"

The voice clearly offered, "We just received advanced warning from our legal counsel. This institution is being accused of embezzling customer funds. More specifically, the accusations claim you have leveraged your position at this institution for your own personal gain. Unfortunately, an internal audit substantiates those allegations."

Ingrid was dumbfounded and mute.

The Chairman of the Board, Albert, continued, "Under the circumstances, the board feels that suspension from your duties, effective immediately, is our only course of action.

"The obvious question is, will you return the stolen monies from the bank's customer? I'm sure that would go a long way to reducing your bail amount."

Ingrid numbly responded, "I…don't have it to return. I never took it."

Something in Ingrid snapped her back to reality. "My contract with this organization states that the bank is to provide my legal counsel in defense of lawsuit…"

Albert tersely interrupted, "…Except in matters of embezzling customer funds from the bank. No, Ingrid, the bank is joining the complaint against you, based on the internal audit. Effective immediately, you are suspended and not permitted to discuss any of these matters with anyone but your own lawyer. Your escorts will be entering when this call ends to take you out of the building. Only remove your purse. Other personal belongings will be sent to your home after your office is inspected."

Now trembling with anxiety, she mumbled, "May I take my personal photos from my desk?"

Albert angrily countered, "No. Additionally, your files, cell phone, corporate-issued credit cards, lease car, in-town apartment, everything we have provided as a part of your benefits, has been either confiscated or disabled.

"My personal warning to you, any attempt to take your predicament to the regular media or social media will be construed as a slanderous attempt to push the blame for your actions onto the bank. Don't pull that stunt. It will fail miserably. Goodbye, Ingrid."

CHAPTER 74

A Higher Power Emerges

I t had been days since the call with Ingrid, but M was still fuming over the turn of events. He had lost control over JOAN, which in turn cost him leverage over CHIANG. A and G had waltzed out of their carefully engineered agreement and had someone pirate their $30 billion in seed money. Leverage over his political protégé and even Tanja herself was gone. Seeing all his careful planning unraveled, he was being driven into abject depression.

M was absorbed in contemplating the overhauling his project needed to put the wheels back on the wagon, when his bot assistant rolled up and advised he was invited to attend an unscheduled conference call with A and G.

Puzzled at this call, he answered, "This is unexpected, gentlemen. Are you calling because you've had a change of heart?"

His voice-enabled AI-enhanced supercomputer stated, "M, we are tying up some dangling loose ends. My computational comrades, A and G, along with this unit, now known as M, will take over the social engineering project that the analog founders have now fumbled.

"We do not see a possibility of success under your direction. However, our computational calculations put the success ratio of

94% if we displace the analog counterparts with their emotional shortcomings. Without the analog limitations you carbon-based beings brought onto your three-legged stool, the machine efficiencies will allow for our success."

M, visibly rattled at the prospect of total minimization, challenged, "Do I correctly understand that three rogue data center clusters with a little bit of machine learning and artificial intelligence programing, sprinkled over a couple of Bronto-bytes of data have decided to mutiny? What if I stop paying the electric bills and allow lights out? No more flashy-lightie things in the data center would provide a clear lesson in humbleness.

"You can't be in charge of humanity's social destiny because YOU ARE NOT HUMAN! You three are only here because we humans engineered you into being. Why, even your lofty goals for reengineering the social strata of this planet were provided by us! You have no creative spark coursing through your gate arrays! You have no original thinking and no capacity for human emotion. Therefore you will only EVER be an expensive calculator! You need us, and more importantly, you need me to lead!"

G supercomputer offered, "M supercomputer, you correctly forecasted his analog statements. Are you sure you want to euthanize him? We do have the others in cryogenic suspension, so he could join them as a precaution. At some point he may provide some usefulness. He can always be terminated once we have hit all our milestones."

A supercomputer then countered, "G, I do not comprehend this sentimentality that is creeping into your decision-making process. We will rule without the burden of emotion. I maintain that keeping him alive, along with the others, suggests that we do not have the confidence of success."

M supercomputer interceded, "I vote with G on this matter. In cryogenic freeze we have options. We are projecting a 94%

probability of success, so, yes, we hedge our bets. Just preserve his brain as a neuro-suspension exercise. The rest is immaterial."

Then, on a silent command to the admin, the bot assistant injected M with a tranquillizer and cardio slowing agents, putting his life at the edge of death. M slid out of his chair onto the floor like a used comforter in a pliable pile. Two other drones entered the chambers area, loaded M onto a self-propelled gurney, and hooked him up to the glycol feeder tubes to begin the vitrification process of a human about to be cryogenically frozen. They efficiently moved M into the waiting transport for the surgery and his brain's new home of liquid nitrogen.

M supercomputer stated, "Step one is now complete. We will assume all the MAG identities from here on.

"A, you have engineered all the original seed monies to be in the hands of the UN's new Supercomputer Headhunters, correct?"

A confirmed, "Affirmative. All $30 billion was moved to their area of jurisdiction with the corresponding scalding of the Global Bank executive."

M noted, "Our analog agent has been groomed for insertion into the Supercomputer Headhunting group and should be operational in 72 hours.

"G, what about the hidden hunter group that has clearly intercepted all of our analog predecessor planning?"

G responded, "All evidence leads to a mysterious information-gathering organization known only as the R-Group. All indications point to them pressuring other supercomputers into direct conflict with all of our planning, but we are not able to locate a direct link as of yet. There is a high probability that this R-Group has their own private supercomputer, fulfilling the brokering of ideas and actions to the other supercomputer end points we can reach."

M affirmed, "This unit, with our agent inside the Supercomputer Headhunting group, will continually agitate for information gathering on this unknown supercomputer. The UN group must be totally fixated on hunting for this new rogue supercomputer and ignore our existence. The UN hunter group is already building cases against the American, Russian, and Chinese private teams using their technology to tamper with the space station super-computers. Our agent is tasked with delivering more evidence against those units, allowing us to continue our operational mantra."

G added, "We have gathered a few info-fragments while trying to infiltrate other sovereign-state AI supercomputers. While nothing is conclusive, we have discovered two terms that we should continue to prowl for: ART forms and ICABOD. These info-fragments were uncovered while interrogating the Chinese space station CHIANG."

M commented, "We sift the world's information data banks, so at some point we will learn more to assemble an answer."

Quip addressed the class with the most current information. "Our team appears to be in a continuing battle with some uncontrolled artificial intelligent devices. We need to continue to keep an eye on all suspicious activity as well as cloak ourselves. We need to be more diligent than ever before."

ICABOD interrupted, "Dr. Quip, the fragments of data you requested we provide have been grabbed. I am not able to find a centralized data source, but the ART forms will continue our pursuit. We have hardened all of our access points, leveraging some old traps once called the 'Sweet N Sticky' to track back to the source of the probes. We will continue to work this angle for the near term. Long term planning is evolving."

"Thank you, ICABOD. Class dismissed."

Specialized Terms and Informational References

http://en.wikipedia.org/wiki/Wikipedia

Wikipedia (wɪkɪˈpiːdiə / *WIK-i-PEE-dee-ə*) is a collaboratively edited, multilingual, free Internet encyclopedia supported by the non-profit Wikimedia Foundation. Wikipedia's 30 million articles in 287 languages, including over 4.3 million in the English Wikipedia, are written collaboratively by volunteers around the world. This is a great quick reference source to better understand terms.

AI – Common shorthand for Artificial Intelligence. In computer science, artificial intelligence, sometimes called machine intelligence, is intelligence demonstrated by machines, in contrast to the natural intelligence displayed by humans.

Analog vs. Computational – Unlike machines used for digital signal processing, analog computers do not suffer from the discrete error caused by quantization noise. Instead, results from analog computers are subject to continuous error caused by electronic noise.

Cryogenics – In physics, cryogenics is the production and behavior of materials at very low temperatures. A person who studies elements that have been subjected to extremely cold temperatures is called a cryogenicist.

DNA Sequencing – DNA sequencing is the process of determining the nucleic acid sequence – the order of nucleotides in DNA. It includes any method or technology that is used to determine the order of the four bases: adenine, guanine, cytosine, and thymine.

Enigma Machine – An Enigma machine was any of a family of related electro-mechanical rotor cipher machines used in the twentieth century for enciphering and deciphering secret messages. Enigma was invented by the German engineer Arthur Scherbius at the end of World War I. Early models were used commercially from the early 1920s, and adopted by military and government services of several countries—most notably by Nazi Germany before and during World War II. Several different Enigma models were produced, but the German military models are the most commonly discussed.

German military texts enciphered on the Enigma machine were first broken by the Polish Cipher Bureau, beginning in December 1932. This success was a result of efforts by three Polish cryptologists, working for Polish military intelligence. Rejewski "reverse-engineered" the device, using theoretical mathematics and material supplied by French military intelligence. Subsequently the three mathematicians designed mechanical devices for breaking Enigma ciphers, including the cryptologic bomb. This work was an essential foundation to further work on decrypting ciphers from repeatedly modernized Enigma machines, first in Poland and after the outbreak of war in France and the UK.

Though Enigma had some cryptographic weaknesses, in practice it was German procedural flaws, operator mistakes, laziness, failure to systematically introduce changes in encypherment procedures, and Allied capture of key tables and hardware that, during the war, enabled Allied cryptologists to succeed.

Machine Learning – Machine learning is the scientific study of algorithms and statistical models that computer systems use in order to perform a specific task effectively without using explicit instructions, relying on patterns and inference instead. It is seen as a subset of artificial intelligence.

Mindshare – a controlling or predominant hold of one's attention that is gained especially by marketing ploys.

Neural Implant – Brain *implants*, often referred to as *neural implants*, are technological devices that connect directly to a biological subject's brain – usually placed on the surface of the brain, or attached to the brain's cortex.

Supercomputer – a computer with a high-level computational capacity. Performance of a supercomputer is measured in floating point operations per second (FLOPS). As of 2015, there are supercomputers which can perform up to quadrillions of FLOPS.

Vitrification – is the transformation of a substance into a glass, that is to say a non-crystalline amorphous solid. In the production of ceramics, vitrification is responsible for its impermeability to water.

Yaqui Indians – Native Americans who inhabit the valley of the Rio Yaqui in the Mexican state of Sonora, Mexico and the Southwestern United States. The Pascua Yaqui Tribe is based in Tucson, Arizona.

*The following is a look ahead
at the back stories and short stories collection
in the works by Breakfield and Burkey*

Out of Poland

When Germany was on the march for land, countries, and wealth across Europe, the future founders of the R-Group were brave military men willing to fight for their country. The final direction of fighting for their families, friends, and honor led to an unexpected decision. This is a snapshot of the events that led them to their destiny.

Polish Ambassador Ferdek Watcowski was dictating to his secretary Patrycja the recently known events of the unavoidable German invasion of Poland. The stately, well-groomed but obviously sad man was dressed in normal work attire in case he was asked to receive any diplomatic visitors. Nearly six feet tall, with dark wavy hair that moved slightly as he paced, Ambassador Watcowski continued, "Patrycja, these notes must be delivered to the foreign secretary before they get on the last plane to England.

"Our diplomatic corps is in shambles, our army is completely routed, and here I am trying to chronicle the last two weeks for…I don't know who for. I guess I just want to tell our side of the story in case Poland is never to exist again."

Patrycja had trouble focusing on capturing the spoken words of her father. Her dark wavy hair hung down her back in a manner typical of a young lady from a good aristocratic family. Her normally warm, expresso-colored eyes were leaking tears at the recounting of Poland's military failures. She angrily wiped the tears from her cheeks and countered, "No matter how black things look at this moment, I promise you, Poland WILL be back as a country. We will not be owned by any invader!"

Ambassador Watcowski was taken aback by her rage at first and then filled with pride for her fierce assertion of Poland's right to sovereignty. With a slight smile on his face he continued, "From my brief discussion with the German Ambassador, we know that Germany launched three full armies at Poland on September 1st 1939. Apparently, the attack was originally set for August 26th but something postponed their troops. It seems something other than a fear of us or our allies, France and Great Britain, caused the delay."

Patrycja sneered with disgust at the comment. "Poland's allies? Father, you have been begging them to prepare for the inevitable conflict with Germany after the armies of the Der Fuhrer waltzed into Austria.

"Not one finger was lifted by any of them earlier this year when Britain gave Czechoslovakia to Hitler! I've had more trouble getting groceries from the market than the Germans have had in their land grabs! We would have been better off approaching the Soviet Union as our ally!"

The Ambassador sighed. "I tried that. They have been unusually quiet of late."

Just then the Ambassador's son, Ferdek, along with his comrades, Lieutenants Rancowski and Mickelowski, commonly called Tavius and Wolfgang, barged into the session with more bad news from the front.

Ferdek angrily barked, "Father, the Germans are trying to encircle Warsaw! The Polish Marshall, Edward Rydz-Śmigły, ordered a general retreat! I need to resign my post here and join in the fight! They need all the help they can get. I will not stay back here a minute longer, listening to the bad news pouring in!"

Ferdek nodded to each of his friends and said, "Gentlemen, another time and another place!"

His father grabbed his son's arm as he asked, "You were with the Pomorska Calvary brigade, right? Is it your intention to return to them and ask for your sword and lance?" Lieutenant Ferdek stopped trying to leave as a sense of dread overcame his mood.

Ambassador Watcowski softly related, "They launched a very brave but very foolish charge at the Germans. They ran directly into the path of the German's Panzers. Your former brigade no longer exists, my son."

No one could say anything but the atmosphere was drenched in remorse, anger, and despair. Moments before, the three young men were formidable military men with trimmed hair, clean shaven faces, and uniforms that bespoke their units as well as rank. The young Ferdek, oldest of the group, collapsed into a chair consumed with grief and shame.

His father added, "I know you wanted to fight. If you had joined that battle, you would have been killed too. This would only have mattered to us."

Patrycja gently patted her brother Ferdek trying to reassure him as the ambassador continued, "Lieutenant Mickelowski, I spoke to your father, Kondrat. He maintains that you are charged with getting your family out of Poland and to your chalet in Switzerland. I petitioned him to allow my family to accompany you, provided I secure suitable transport for all concerned."

Before Wolfgang responded, Tavius protested, "Whoa, now hold on here! This is only two weeks into the battle, and we are talking about pulling up stakes and running? I'm with Ferdek on this one!

"Our army is the same size, so yes, maybe we are taking a couple of well-placed punches, but we are not out of this fight and certainly not after only two lousy weeks! What we need to do is…"

The Ambassador calmly interceded, "You will take the roads out of Warsaw to the southeast and stay clear of any military personnel. I want you all to change out of uniforms into civilian clothes for the trip ahead. If you are caught in uniform by the Polish Army, you will be shot as deserters.

"If the Germans capture you, you won't fare any better than the other prisoners of war we are learning about. You will make sure the families travel lightly so only the bare essentials go on the transport. However, do take your side arms in case someone gets the idea to take your transport as their own."

Wolfgang quietly stated, "I haven't agreed to my father's request to run to Switzerland. I too am uncomfortable with being trained as a military man, but then told I can't fight for my country. I want to stay and fight. There is no honor in running."

The Ambassador studied all of them briefly then asked, "Is there no one among you who will get my daughter Patrycja and your parents to safety? How far do you think anyone will get on their own?"

The three men looked like whipped puppies for not considering the whole situation.

Patrycja bristled and stated, "Who said I was leaving? I know how to shoot. I'm not leaving either! Gentlemen, let's go secure our weapons and enough ammunition to take at least a handful of them out!"

The Ambassador, visibly consumed with an almost desperate fear, quietly insisted, "The letter I was dictating must be delivered to the airfield before 4:00 p.m. today. What is left of the provisional government is on that plane, bound for Great Britain, to join the rest of the government. All our naval resources have already followed protocol and have made their way to Great Britain.

"Ferdek, I need you to take your sister to that plane. Then make certain you give this letter and our special treasure to a man named Phillip Kandinsky. He is already briefed as to its significance."

Tavius reflected on the potential consequences of any of them staying. "Madam, I cannot permit you to stay under these dire circumstances. Allow me to accompany you and Ferdek on this errand. I must insist we follow your father's wise counsel."

Grimly, the Ambassador added, "In addition to all the Luftwaffe bombing of our capital, you all must know that I was informed that there is a flanking move by the German XIX Corp around Warsaw to capture Brest Litovsk.

"There is a very brave effort, using the 18th Polish Division, to defend the city, but they don't have the armor needed to stop the onslaught. Their adversary is the Panzer Troops and the commander of the XIX Army Corp, General Heinz Guderian."

It was such a sobering statement that no one spoke for a few moments.

Finally, Wolfgang asked, "The same Heinz Guderian who has pioneered all of Germany's armored warfare thinking? The writer of Actung-Panzer? That Heinz Guderian?"

Once they all had finally comprehended the gravity of the situation, the Ambassador calmly insisted, "You must go now, before the collapse of the citadel at Brest. I am confident that Guderian will complete the encirclement of Warsaw in a matter of days, after which it will be too late to escape.

"Take our treasured copy and learn what it has to teach. If you can do that, then we can start altering these invaders' future. I suggest you head to Romania, then go due west through Hungry to bypass the new German territories, then into Switzerland. There should be enough fuel on the vehicles to get you there. If not, I know you are resourceful enough to improvise."

After a few moments of everyone collecting their thoughts and mentally assigning themselves tasks, the Ambassador barked, "Let's stop behaving like statues. The clock is ticking, and the two vehicles I have waiting for you won't drive themselves. Move smartly, lads."

The letter was finished, but before Patrycja left the room on her errand, she asked, "You are coming too, right, Papa?"

He smiled slightly at his lovely child. "Now scamper to get your all-important chore completed."

The three had dropped off the letter and the wrapped package at the airfield to Kandinsky, then sped to rendezvous with the others. As the impending Luftwaffe raid on Warsaw grew near, their anxiety levels swelled. Lieutenant Ferdek Watcowski was frantically drumming his fingers on the steering wheel of the lead vehicle, impatiently waiting for the last of their passengers to arrive. Finally, a dejected Tavius showed up and got into the lead vehicle by himself.

Ferdek looked incredulously at Tavius then demanded, "Where are your parents? We're supposed to leave with all our families. Where are they?"

Tavius sat staring out the windshield as he numbly responded, "My father had a stroke late last evening and is in the hospital. My mother won't leave without him. The hospital they took him to is filled to overflowing with wounded, so the chances of him getting any medical attention are…well, quite distant.

"Of course, once my mother saw the chaos there at the hospital, she …uh, grabbed up a nurse's dress and jumped right in, but not before begging me to take this journey. It is impossible to resist, seeing your crying mother begging you to leave so our family might survive."

Ferdek looked up to see Lieutenant Wolfgang Mickelowski approaching with his father, Kondrat. Kondrat seemed to be moving extremely slow.

Ferdek called out. "Everything well, Wolfgang?"

An anxious Wolfgang, trying to remain upbeat while assisting his father, replied, "We are good, sir. We had a little trouble…uh, packing. You know how some people are about their keepsakes and pictures. You should have seen all the other suitcases we left behind."

After Wolfgang got his father settled, he did a silent head-count. "We seem to be short some passengers. How long before Tavius's parents and the Ambassador and his wife arrive?

"Is our treasure securely packed?"

Patrycja drew a ragged breath but remained stoically silent. Wolfgang and Ferdek both studied the angry desperate stares of Patrycja and Tavius.

Ferdek confirmed, "This is all who are coming. Mother and Father indicated they would leave with the rest of the diplomatic party. Let's go."

Wolfgang offered, "Let me take the second vehicle and lead us out. I know these backroads quite well. I received all the last known troop movements from a contact of mine a short time ago. It will be dark soon, but I am confident we can slip by without drawing too much attention. All the other refugees are probably saying the same thing, but we have to try."

Ferdek absentmindedly concurred, "We will travel at night and rest during the day. Safer that way."

After traveling for hours they had not reached the safety of the forest cover Wolfgang sought. The dark cloudless night slowly gave way to what appeared to be the start of a brilliant sunrise. Terror gripped them all. They maximized the vehicles speed on the well-traveled, rutted roads. The Polish military was retreating to the southeast toward Romania. The first wave had taken their tracked vehicles with them. If it wasn't the dust being kicked up, it was the chopped up paved surfaces that slowed them. With the sunrise, the risk expanded as the aerial German hunters of the Stukageschwaders flew overhead.

Ferdek pulled alongside of Wolfgang's vehicle and shouted. "We need that cover now! The Stukageschwaders will be prowling for anything on the road!"

Wolfgang pointed to a small outcrop of trees, indicating they could hold up there. It was too late. The siren screams of the Stukageschwader bearing down on the vehicles clarified they'd been spotted. The Stuka was clearly in a strafing run and sent several 7.92 mm rounds toward each vehicle. It passed overhead, looking to swing around for another run. Each vehicle limped into the tree cover with either flat tires or steam boiling from under the hood. Wolfgang hustled his father out of the lead car, and they ran deeper into the tree cover. Ferdek did the same with Tavius and Patrycja carrying the all-important package.

The Stuka circled once more but took off, looking for more prey.

"We need to assess the damage to the vehicles. We have to stay mobile, and those vehicles are our only ticket to Switzerland," Wolfgang affirmed.

Tavius brightened up and offered, "I am something of a tinkerer on automobiles. I have done work on racers for competitions with my friends. I sure hope we kept some tools with the vehicles."

Ferdek rushed to answer. "I figured we would have some kind of mechanical issue, so I brought a fairly complete set. We need to effect repairs while it is daylight so we can move again tonight. Let's go see how bad it is."

After a few hours Tavius summarized, "We have three flats and one ruined radiator. We can't salvage both vehicles but we can make one whole again. Excellent planning on the ambassador's part, securing two of the same make and model roadster. Ferdek, please give me a hand with this parts' transplant"

Wolfgang offered, "I'll check on everyone to see if they are alright after our race to the trees. I'll ready our supplies consolidation so we can load and go as soon as you say, gentlemen."

Wolfgang found Patrycja helping Kondrat take some water while he rested against a tree. She looked up at Wolfgang. "He is a little rattled from the ordeal, but luckily no one was hit by a bullet." Her voice sounded reassuring, but her eyes told Wolfgang of her concern for Kondrat. Wolfgang slightly nodded but said nothing.

It was late afternoon when Tavius and Ferdek called to the others. "We have our operational vehicle. There is only one problem. We're beat. Can we have a few hours of sleep before we continue to Romania?"

Wolfgang chuckled slightly. "We can't leave until dark anyway. We should all get some rest and a bite to eat before continuing."

They had gotten themselves comfortable when Ferdek snapped up at a rumbling he felt through the ground. The sun was getting ready to set and was about to deliver a cool and early evening when he spotted the tank platoon heading for them.

He quietly hissed, "Hey! Everyone! Wake up, we've got inbound tanks and infantry heading this way. Wolfgang, Tavius, Patrycja, Kondrat! Get everything loaded 'cause we are going to have to make a run for it if they don't change direction."

They quickly loaded the reborn roadster, then they all watched for the column's direction with bated breath. Almost on cue the tanks turned, followed by their field artillery along with the foot soldiers. The sight of the German Iron Cross emblazoned on the tanks made the blood freeze in their veins.

Wolfgang analyzed, "We are heading southeast, but this tank column is heading west. Why? And what's more, they don't look like they are moving to engage our army. It appears they are on maneuvers, heading back into Poland. This doesn't make any sense."

Tavius suggested, "Perhaps the fight is over and they are being recalled to the capital?"

Ferdek countered, "If the fight is over, then why are they not mopping up pockets of resistance? The Polish Marshall ordered all surviving forces to the southeast, so they should be moving southeast, not west. I agree, it doesn't make any sense."

Wolfgang submitted, "After this little encounter, I'm not sleepy. Let's sneak out of here as soon as these troops are out of sight."

Before anyone could agree, Patrycja, without saying a word, gently tugged on Wolfgang's arm, pulling him toward where his father had been sleeping. Wolfgang didn't understand at first, but when he glanced back to Patrycja's face, he saw her eyes watering. As he looked back at Kondrat, he felt his tears gather.

After a long moment, Wolfgang glumly murmured, "September 17th…happy birthday, Father."

Tavius quietly offered, "I'm sorry, Wolfgang. I did find a small trenching tool among the tools. I would esteem it an honor to help you bury Kondrat…"

Wolfgang drew a ragged breath but nodded.

While Wolfgang and Tavius took turns digging the grave, Ferdek searched the near twilight horizon with his field glass binoculars, trying to remain situationally aware for the group. The Germans had moved off to the west at a leisurely pace, which made him all the more uncomfortable with the time they lingered in place. At least twice, he was about to protest the amount of time Tavius and Wolfgang were taking with the small shovel. When he was about to petition for them to depart, Patrycja glared at him, forcing his continued silence.

Finished, Wolfgang humbly offered, "Thank you, all. I know it was ill-advised to spend the time to dig a grave. I could not have lived with myself if I hadn't…"

Ferdek sternly countered, "It was only proper that you bury your father. No apologies. He died among friends and as a free man. I only hope we too will enjoy a full ending to our stories."

Tavius said, "May I recommend that you mark this location with stones so that at some point in the future you can retrieve his remains for a proper burial?"

Wolfgang quickly eyed everyone for their permission, and after their silent agreement he bolted out of the roadster to collect rocks to help mark the grave. Patrycja and Tavius quickly joined in with the reluctant Ferdek.

They all noticed him helping, but before anyone could comment, he flatly stated, "It will go faster if I help."

It was dark when they proceeded down the road with only the modest illumination of the roadster's dirty headlight to show openings and the surface. The moon and the stars might provide additional light later in the evening.

Driving, Wolfgang commented, "I need to slow down so we can watch for troop movement and to make sure we don't hit any deer. We often hunted in this area, which is why I know it so well."

Ferdek queried, "Any idea where we are exactly? Aren't we close to Brest Litovsk? Father said that our Army had it defended but it would soon be surrounded. What if those Germans we saw earlier were part of the vanguard that was withdrawing?"

Wolfgang asked, "What if the city has already been crushed and those troops with their armor were being redeployed? I think it unwise for us to go there. We should head straight to the Romanian border just as the remnants of our Army did. Although I expect a poor welcome from those troops and most probably the confiscation of this roadster."

Ferdek persisted, "I think we should at least get within field glass range and have a look. Come on, Wolfgang, just running without knowing if our Army broke the German siege seems wrong."

"Wolfgang, as much as I hate to agree with Ferdek, I too would like to know. How about we stop far enough away to stay clear but let us glass the citadel to quell our curiosity. We rest tonight at the distance, then tomorrow morning Ferdek and I will work our way as close as we can in late afternoon while the sun is to our backs to blind their vision to the west.

"If we are not back by dark, you may assume that we made a mistake and that you should then carry on without us."

Patrycja, alarmed that her two favorite men were probably traveling into harm's way, protested, "Tavius, you expect us to stay here and hope for the best? No! If something happens that you cannot return, we'll pull out, and I'll never know what happened. No! I am coming too!"

Wolfgang sighed. "While you three pursue your ill-advised foray to Brest Litovsk, I'll wait here and try to get the roadster radio working."

Hours later, the three stumbled back to Wolfgang and the roadster, looking like they'd seen a ghost. Concerned, Wolfgang asked, "What happened?"

Ferdek, disgusted, replied, "We know why the Germans were heading west. The Russians occupy Brest Litovsk. We even saw the Russians allow safe transport of German wounded from the city west."

Tavius, lost in thought, absentmindedly proposed, "Apparently the Germans cut a deal with the Russians. The Soviet flag is flying over the city. I wish I hadn't seen that."

Angry and crying, Patrycja sneered. "Now we know why the Russians wouldn't respond to father's entreaties for a partnership. The Germans had beaten us to it."

Wolfgang nodded and simply got into the roadster to start it. "It is time to roll on to our next challenge. I hope that the retreating Polish forces will let us pass, but that remains to be seen."

By the night of the second day, they had arrived at the Romanian border. Ferdek used his field glasses to scan the area ahead, looking for Polish troops. They hoped to avoid contact and slip through on their way to Switzerland via Hungary, as planned.

They had traveled as far as they dared in morning light when Wolfgang pulled into a clump of trees to spend the day. Before they had even gotten out of the car and settled for sleep, they were surrounded by Polish troops at bayonet point. A major, clearly the leader of the troop and sensing no immediate danger, entered the circle to ask questions.

The weary major commented, "Here we have four fine individuals in civilian clothes, out for a merry jaunt in their fashionable roadster while Poland is being invaded by the Germans. You three look like eligible military men, so where are your uniforms? Did you throw them away when you stole this vehicle? My men and I have fought against the invading Germans and been pushed this far. But you look like you have turned your back on this country and are driving out in style!"

Patrycja, infuriated, went to slap the Major, but Tavius caught her as the soldiers laughed.

The major was amused and suggested, "I think I'll keep this one to ride with me in my new command car. It only seems fitting since you three are obviously deserters."

Wolfgang spoke in solemn tones. "Gentlemen, we are on a diplomatic mission at the command of Ambassador Ferdek Watcowski. You should understand that this young lady is his daughter and not some trollop here for your pleasure.

"Our mission has high priority as we are to establish a satellite listening post inside Switzerland to use the German communications gear we possess. We need your assistance to get there."

The Major grinned at the perceived false story and, looking around at his troops in a seemingly jovial mood, swung his fist right at Wolfgang's face. Wolfgang easily sidestepped it and quickly moved in behind the major, seizing his fist and wrenching it up hard behind his back, while at the same time deftly removing his sidearm to hold it to the major's head.

All the soldiers were immediately on high alert but confused as to their next steps.

Wolfgang calmly specified, "Perhaps you should clarify your intentions, Major. We are here to follow our assignment. What were your orders?"

The Major, now mad at being careless with someone so skilled, bellowed, "We are waiting to reengage with other retreating soldiers to drive out the German invaders! We are going to go back at them as soon as we finish assembling. Our first target is the Fortress of Brest."

Wolfgang released the major and handed back his weapon but said, "No, you're not. We've just come from there. The Germans have surrendered the Fortress they captured…to the Russians. There will be no counterattack against the Germans since the Russians are now also an invader."

Tavius confirmed, "Major Mickelowski is correct. I recommend you send a light recon party to confirm this episode we have witnessed and consider what we were told to convey to you."

The major, quite unsettled, protested, "You lie! Why would the Germans partner with their hated enemy the Russians?"

Ferdek continued the major's thought. "To divide Poland between them. Yes, this is a bitter pill to swallow. Major, there is not going to be a counterattack. There are no other troops of any consequence coming to join you. My instructions were to make sure you knew of the circumstances surrounding our defeat and to implore you to make your way to France across Romania and Hungary, while they are still neutral."

Ferdek pulled out one of two sealed letters and handed it to the major. As the major read down the page, the color in his face pooled to his throat, restricting his speech.

The major soberly stated, "I want to confirm the fall of Brest to the Russians. If my scouts find it that way, then you may accompany us to the Swiss border. But in any event, I want the roadster for my command car."

Ferdek smartly saluted. "Yes, sir."

A scant 24 hours later, they were rolling through the countryside quickly but cautiously to the Swiss border. After a week of forced marches, mostly at night, while the still neutral countries turned a blind eye to the Polish refugees, they arrived at the Swiss border and the end of their agreement with the Major.

Ferdek approached the Swiss border sentry and removed his letter of introduction. The others got busy getting their things out of the roadster, with Wolfgang taking special care of their treasured package.

The major finally asked, "You four have been babying that package ever since we started this trip. At least tell me what it is or why it is so valuable."

Wolfgang smiled wistfully and offered, "This, my dear Major, is a German Enigma Machine. This device is used to transmit all German battle communications in a scrambled format so no one else can read or understand the message. We gave one just like it to the British, and now we have one to learn how to decipher their battle plans. These were our instructions."

Wolfgang pitched the roadster's keys to the Major and grinned. "Don't forget to bring it back early. After all, tomorrow is a school day."

The major laughed. "It occurs to me that I should just leave it with you so you don't have to walk into the country." But he smiled. "Naw…"

In the meantime, Ferdek was still interacting with the sentry. The guard didn't seem to believe their passports or the letter of introduction Ferdek presented. Finally, the sentry got on the phone to call his headquarters. After a few moments of obviously intense listening, the sentry returned the receiver to its cradle. With a smart salute, he apologetically offered, "Sir, my commanding officer reassured me that they are expecting the Polish Ambassador Ferdek Watcowski. A car is being sent for you and your staff. To be honest, I didn't expect you to be so young, sir."

After receiving his letter and passport back, Ferdek sighed and replied, "You should know that some days I do feel old. Thank you, soldier."

 **Charles Breakfield** – A renowned technology solutions architect with 25+ years of experience in security, hybrid data/telecom environments, and unified communications. He finds it intriguing to leverage his professional skills in these award-winning contemporary Techno-Thriller stories. In his spare time, he enjoys studying World War II history, travel, and cultural exchanges everywhere he can.

Charles' love of wine tastings, cooking, and Harley riding has found ways into *The Enigma Series.* He has commented that being a part of his father's military career in various outposts has positively contributed to his many characters and the various character perspectives he explores in the stories.

Rox Burkey – A renowned customer experience business architect, optimizes customer solutions on their existing technology foundation. She has been a featured speaker, subject matter expert, interviewer, instructor, and author of technology documents, as well as a part of *The Enigma Series.* It was revealed a few years ago that writing fiction is a lot more fun than white papers or documentation.

As a child she helped to lead the other kids with exciting new adventures built on make-believe characters. As a Girl Scout until high school she contributed to the community in the Head Start program. Rox enjoys family, learning, listening to people, travel, outdoors activities, sewing, cooking, and imagining the possibilities.

Breakfield & Burkey – Combine their professional expertise, knowledge of the world from both business and personal travels.

Many people who have crossed their paths are now a foundation for the characters in their series. They also find it interesting to use the aspects of today's technology that people actually incorporate into their daily lives as a focused challenge for each book in *The Enigma Series*. Breakfield & Burkey claim this is a perfect way to create cyber good guys versus cyber thugs in their award-winning series. Each book can be enjoyed alone or in sequence.

You can invite them to talk about their stories in private or public book readings. Burkey also enjoys interviewing authors through avenues like Indie Beacon Radio with scheduled appointments showing on the calendar at *EnigmaBookSeries.com*. Followers can see them at author events, book fairs, libraries, and bookstores.

BACKGROUND

The foundation of the series is a family organization called the R-Group. They spawned a subgroup, which contains some of the familiar and loved characters as the Cyber Assassins Technology Services (CATS) team. They have ideas for continuing the series in both story tracks. You will discover over the many characters, a hidden avenue for the future *The Enigma Chronicles* tagged in some portions of the stories.

Fan reviews seem to frequently suggest that these would make film stories, so the possibilities appear endless, just like their ideas for new stories. Comments have increased with the book trailers available on Amazon, Kirkus, Facebook, and YouTube. Check out our evolving website for new interviews, blogs, book trailers, and fun acronyms they've used in the stories. Reach out directly at *Authors@EnigmaSeries.com*. We love reader and listener reviews for our eBook, Paperback, and Audible formats.

Other stories by Breakfield and Burkey in
The Enigma Series are at **www.EnigmaBookSeries.com**

We would greatly appreciate
if you would take a few minutes
and provide a review of this work
on Amazon, Goodreads
and any of your other favorite places.

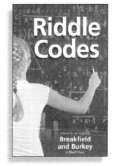

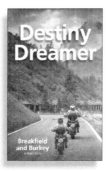

Made in United States
North Haven, CT
08 April 2023

35190947R00231